THE UNFINISHED WORK
OF ELIZABETH D.

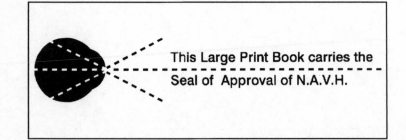

This Large Print Book carries the
Seal of Approval of N.A.V.H.

THE UNFINISHED WORK
OF ELIZABETH D.

NICHOLE BERNIER

WHEELER PUBLISHING
A part of Gale, Cengage Learning

Detroit • New York • San Francisco • New Haven, Conn • Waterville, Maine • London

LIBRARY OF CONGRESS CATALOGING-IN-PUBLICATION DATA

Bernier, Nichole.
    The unfinished work of Elizabeth D. / by Nichole Bernier.
      pages ; cm.
    ISBN 978-1-4104-5363-1 (hardcover) — ISBN 1-4104-5363-4 (hardcover) 1.
Female friendship—Fiction. 2. Diaries—Fiction. 3. Large type books. I. Title.
PS3602.E7623U54 2012b
813'.6—dc23   2012032036

Published in 2012 by arrangement with Crown Publishers, a division of
Random House, Inc.

Printed in the United States of America
1 2 3 4 5 6 7 16 15 14 13 12

To Tom,
so generous with works in progress,
and to all unfinished women,
gone too soon

Somehow I should have been able to say how strong and resilient you were, what a patient and abiding and bonding force, the softness that proved in the long run stronger than what it seemed to yield to. . . . You are at once a lasting presence and an unhealed wound.

— *Wallace Stegner, "Letter, Much Too Late"*

ONE

June 2002

The George Washington Bridge had never been anything but strong and beautiful, its arches monumental, cables thin and high. Kate watched them spindling like ribs past the car window as her husband drove eastbound across the span. It was a testimony to optimism, a suspension bridge, each far-fetched plate, truss, and girder an act of faith against gravity and good sense.

The sun was strong, glinting off the bridge and hitting the river like shattered glass. Drivers traveling in both directions were shielding their eyes, staring as she was down the length of Manhattan. She didn't know what any of them expected to see. Mushroom clouds? Skywriting in Arabic? She wished for some visible sign of drama where the towers had once stood. Then she looked toward Queens, even though it was impossible to see the site from this distance. Few people were even looking anymore, though she always would.

The car reached the end of the bridge and she exhaled. Chris glanced over and she faced the window with what she hoped looked like ordinary interest, damp-palmed hands loose in her lap.

He angled the rearview mirror to check the backseat. The children were still asleep.

"Has Dave gone back to work yet?" His voice was grave, in the way someone speaks about a bad diagnosis.

She put her foot up on the dash. "A few months ago. His company let him take as much time as he needed."

Chris nodded, satisfied. It was the right thing for the company to do, and he liked when the right thing was done with a minimum of drama. "What's he doing with the kids? Did she have family close by?"

"No. There's no one." A trickle of cool air from the vent brought gooseflesh to her leg. "He found a nanny through an agency."

"It's strange to think of Elizabeth's kids with a nanny."

That was the first thing she had thought too, like Julia Child farming out the cooking to a housekeeper. "People do it all the time, Chris. Not everyone stays home with their kids."

10

He looked over, gauging her. "You know that's not what I meant, Kate."

She turned back to the window and wiped the corner of her eye as if she were ridding it of an irritation. A *nanny* in Elizabeth Martin's house. The obvious things weren't what affected her most — the obituary, the service, even visiting the crash site, a charred hole in Queens that seemed inhospitable to anything ever being grown or built there again. The smaller details were the potent ones. Seeing the open can of infant formula on the Martins' kitchen counter the first time she'd visited to help. Hearing that Jonah had lost his first tooth a few weeks ago, but Dave had forgotten to tell the tooth fairy. These were the things that gave certain days a dull ache she could not explain, or shake.

A sign ahead marked the turn toward Connecticut. If the parkway was less choked than the others there would be only an hour more. In the two years since they'd moved down to Washington, D.C., they had not found a good time of day or night to travel. Traffic on the Northeast Corridor was unrelenting. Tonight, they'd find some hotel around the Massachusetts border, and in the morning they would be on the first ferry to the island, seven weeks this summer

11

instead of their usual two. If Chris had agreed because he knew how much Kate needed it, he hadn't let on, and she wasn't saying.

Dave had asked if they could stop for the trunk on the way through. She could not imagine having it on vacation with them, but Dave Martin now had that effect on people; they jumped, they put things on hold, they accommodated.

This would be the first time they would be getting together with the children but without Elizabeth. Kate and Chris hadn't brought James and Piper when they came up for the funeral, a maudlin affair made worse by the baby in the front row drooling and pinwheeling her arms at the photo of her mother on an easel. Now the kids would be playing together like old times, but for the adults, all the roles would be unfamiliar. Dave would be host and hostess, Kate just a polite guest in the kitchen. He might jiggle the baby on one hip as he composed plates and poured small cups of milk, and Kate would offer help, trying not to sound as if she questioned his competence. She would have to be social glue for the men, who had only ever come together because of their wives, and someone would have to take the lead with the kids. *We don't throw sand at*

12

our friends, and *It's time to take turns with the backhoe.* That had been Elizabeth's job.

It had all been Elizabeth's job.

As Chris turned the car from the interstate to the parkway, Kate pulled out the note the lawyer had forwarded to her in lieu of any other instructions. Its even script evoked the to-do lists always strewn across Elizabeth's counter, the ticker tape of tasks to be done and groceries to be bought, looping in perfect penmanship. A small antique key was taped to the notecard. *There's something I'd like to add to the specific bequests section of the will. Please amend it so that Katherine Spenser gets my trunk of journals. In whatever legal language is appropriate, please indicate that I'm leaving them to her because she's fair and sensitive and would know what should be done with them, and ask that she start at the beginning. I'll come soon to drop off a letter for her that should go with it.*

The roadside clutter thinned near the Connecticut line, old tires and abandoned appliances giving way to birches, azaleas, roadkill. Trees lined the median like suburban sentries. The sun hadn't let up and Kate's sunglasses weren't doing much to cut the glare, reviving the headache she'd had on and off all day, and yesterday too. A two-day headache. Brain tumor, she thought. Ocular cancer. Aneurysm.

She lowered the window a few inches. A warm wind cleared the recirculated air and the smell of old peanut butter sandwiches.

Several things struck her each time she read Elizabeth's note, one thing more than the rest. It wasn't that Elizabeth had kept journals, though there was that, or the wonderment of what such an uncomplicated person could have written. *Today I got Jonah and Anna to agree to turkey sandwiches in their lunchboxes.* Or the realization that Elizabeth had been so phobic about flying; Kate knew she'd been a bit of a nervous flier, but enough to make a summer addendum to her will before she traveled? And it wasn't the contradiction that she had been meticulous enough to name a trustee for her journals, but had never followed through with the letter expressing her intentions. What struck Kate most was a single word choice — *sensitive.* Not a word people used often to describe her. Even with Elizabeth, her most frequent contact in the dailiness of mothering, sensitivity wasn't something Kate wore on her sleeve. But Elizabeth had seen it. Each time Kate thought of it, she felt the loss of something she hadn't known she'd had, an unscratched lottery ticket

14

found years too late, a winner.

When Kate first heard about Elizabeth's trip out west, it was last July. The Spensers stopped for an overnight in Connecticut on their way to the previous summer's vacation, and the two women had gone walking on the beach, as they did when Kate came back to visit. Elizabeth mentioned her birthday gift from Dave, a long weekend away for a painting workshop. There was an opportunity with a Mexican painter famous for abstract landscapes, she'd said, a workshop guru who almost never left Oaxaca. She spoke in a gush with agitated movements, working a chain of dried seaweed between her fingers like rosary beads.

It had been strange, such fidgeting from a person usually calm as tranquilizers. Elizabeth called the trip a fortieth birthday present two years early, one she'd requested herself from Dave. She'd found a cheap flight from JFK to Los Angeles on August 9; Joshua Tree was about 120 miles east, and she was even looking forward to the drive alone. A getaway to recharge her batteries, she'd said, as the seaweed strand snapped in her hands.

At the time Kate had been surprised. Elizabeth hardly ever traveled, rarely expressed an interest in it. Kate knew Elizabeth used to paint before she and Dave were married and still dabbled here and there, but nothing Kate would have thought worth taking a trip across the country without a baby so young.

That was the last time she'd seen Elizabeth. Her plane never made it past Queens. Officials called it a freak accident, a confluence of bad things — bad wind, bad rudder, a bad call by the pilot. Any deeper consideration of the flight, or the arbitrariness of Elizabeth's having been on it, was quickly overshadowed by all that came in September.

Two

June, and the Martins' front door was still decorated with sun-bleached Valentine paper hearts drained to gray. Dave pulled it open as Kate walked up the steps, followed by Chris and the kids.

"My darlin', if you aren't more gorgeous every time I see you. Washington must be doing something right by you. Come here and give me a hug."

The sweep of his arms was wide and athletic, more like a quarterback than a middling golfer who had dropped off the tour. He had never quite made the northern parts of the leaderboard, and his standard line had always been that to be a great golfer you had to really be in your head, the last place on himself that he wanted to spend time. Each time he said it she could hear the triple beat of a comedian's backup drum.

Kate pulled out of his hug, touching his

back to convey support without having to say the clichéd things. He gave a small nod of appreciation. Her eyes fell to Jonah.

"Look at how tall you are! This is what finishing kindergarten does to you?" She stood aside to allow Chris and the children to join her on the step. "Kids, you guys remember Jonah, right? We gave him your goldfish when we moved?"

They stared. It had been a year since their last visit and nearly two since they'd moved, an eternity for six- and four-year-old memories.

"Hey man," said Chris, reaching out to give Jonah a high five. When his hand remained stranded in the air, he dropped it and ruffled the boy's hair instead. "We haven't seen you guys in a long time. How's it going?"

"Good." Jonah squinted up at him in the late-afternoon light. The emptiness where his front teeth had been bore the serrated edges of new growth. "Did you know my mom is dead?"

Chris's hand went still on the boy's head, and Dave looked down at the floor. Kate waited for Dave to say something soothing to his son, or something to them to indicate that this was not uncommon, just part of the process. He continued to study the wooden threshold, curling his bare toes on the floorboards.

Chris bent until he was eye level with the boy and squatted with his forearms on his thighs. "I know, buddy. I'm really sorry about that. My mom's dead too. It's hard, isn't it?"

"Yeah," Jonah said. "She's in heaven now, taking care of Dad's dog. And I wish —"

In the kitchen there was an electronic noise, an instrument or a video game, and he looked back, sizing up which of his sisters might be playing with which of his toys. "Um, I just wish . . ."

Kate and Chris waited with tight smiles. There were a number of things he might wish, none of them easily addressed. The boy pulled his arm in and out of the sleeve of his shirt, and either lost his train of thought or let it drift away. "Dad said we're going to Disney for my birthday. Right, Dad?"

Dave lifted his head like someone waking. "Sure, bud. We surely are." He put his hand on his son's shoulder and gave a strained smile. "Come on now, let's get our friends inside and offer them something to eat instead of talking their ears off in the doorway."

■ ■ ■ ■

In the summertime, the Martins' house had been the address for late-afternoon play-dates and margaritas overlooking the sand-box. Their backyard was ideal, children contained and safe, but so subtly fenced they didn't feel restricted. The simple swing-set was not so extravagant that parents had to be vigilant, but was so well designed that kids believed they were pushing the envelope on their own safety, emboldened to small acts of rebellion. Parents never turned down an invitation to a Martin picnic because it was one of the rare places where grown-ups talked and children played in coexistent peaceful worlds. They even seemed to have fewer mosquitoes than the neighbors. It was a charmed setting and had added to the sense that God smiled on the Martins.

Chris stood quietly at the grill scraping burger residue with a steel-bristled brush, his back radiating to Kate that after a few hours of small talk, this was hers to wrap up. Dave sat with his feet up on a deck chair, beer in hand, calling directions to the children playing hide-and-seek. When a child came close — a Martin or a Spenser, it didn't matter which — he'd reel the runner in by an arm or a leg. If his tickling was a bit more exuberant than necessary, the children were either unaware or did not mind. Kate sat quietly on the deck amid the noise. The sense of the missing member of the party was a fog low over the patio, changing the look and feel of everything.

She surveyed the familiar yard. The patch of weeds where tomatoes used to grow. The rose trellis against the house, indifferent to its missing gardener. The wrought-iron bench — chipping, from its first season left out through the winter — where they'd been sitting when Elizabeth told her she was expecting again. Kate had felt a surge of happiness as if she herself were gaining a life. Now thirteen months old, Emily was no longer quite a baby but not yet a toddler. Kate held her on her lap, the small sturdy body warm and close, hair soft against Kate's cheek.

It was fascinating the way children grew, features morphing in and out of their parents' likenesses in genetic peekaboo. The girl had her father's full mouth like her four-year-old sister, Anna, but her eyes were all Elizabeth, an arresting blue halfway between cornflower and sapphire. All three children had inherited Dave's thick dark hair, and their mother had been loath to cut it on any of them, even Jonah. So far Dave had left it alone, and the boy with collar-length curls looked more like a soulful Giovanni than a Connecticut WASP. Elizabeth had loved comparing their features, exhibiting the fascination of an only child when it came to the similarities and differences among her own children. Giving them siblings, she'd said, had been the best thing she could ever do for them. Kate lowered her nose to Emily's head and breathed in Johnson's baby shampoo, a hormonal cocktail that among women who have children not long out of diapers drew the Pavlovian, *Another.*

Emily reached fat fingers toward the pastries on Kate's plate, a slice of fruit tart and colorful petit fours. Kate had stopped to buy dessert at her favorite bakery in town though she knew the teasing it would bring from Dave. It was an endless source of amusement, the pastry chef who barely cooked.

"Kate, I swear," he'd said in his accent of peaches and bourbon as she'd placed the cardboard box on the counter. "You are the only one of us with a professional skill worth a damn and you're the one who uses it the least."

"You mean, the one who has the skill *you'd* most like to enjoy," she replied, nudging him with her elbow.

It was true that she cooked less ambitiously since having children. Cooking took time, even with skills that had become second nature since culinary school. (*Such a good career fit*, her parents and older sister always said — the subtext being, *for someone who's not the academic type*.) Soufflé and flambé weren't exactly in high demand in a family of young children, and these days she channeled her efforts into more practical recipes. Chicken pot pies for dinner and sugar cookies with the children, using her elaborate collection of shaped cutters. Crepes on weekends, flipped from the pan with more bravado than she'd ever dare among colleagues, for the entertainment of the kids. Every so often she'd get a call to cover for a pastry chef who'd quit or been fired, and they'd always request that crème brûlée that got her nominated for the James Beard Award. From time to time there'd be a promising job offer, like the one currently on the table. Each time the call came she'd pause before saying *No thanks, not yet*. But with this latest one, she hadn't yet made the call to decline.

Dave knew what she was capable of creating when she took the time. For Elizabeth's thirty-sixth birthday, she'd made a three-tiered work of chocolate excess that had taken her all day. That night after the third bottle of wine the two couples had broken out Scrabble, but Kate and Elizabeth sabotaged the game with giddiness, stealing letters and rearranging words into obscenities. They'd picked at that chocolate cake until they had felt ill, and vowed to do the same thing each year.

But Kate thought it best not to remind Dave. Last week, Elizabeth would have turned thirty-nine.

Dusk came on with the chirping of crickets. Dave drained his second beer and got up to take the empty plates inside. Kate followed with bowls of picked-over salad and salsa. The kitchen looked much as it always had, only more cluttered. The counters were scattered with Tupperware, the shelves piled with kid art and old catalogs. The same two paintings hung on the wall: a portrait of a young girl eating ice cream, and an exterior view of two city brownstones. In one bright window a mother combed out a girl's long wet hair, and in a window a few feet away, people attended a party in a dimly lit room, a woman's head thrown back in decadent laughter. Kate had never been fond of it. The juxtaposition of scenes was unnerving;

even the oils seemed thick and angry.

On the refrigerator, the same Martin family photos were held to the door with alphabet magnets. Shots from last summer's vacation in the Hamptons, Elizabeth's shoulder-length hair gone platinum in the sun. Photos of Anna's birthday two years ago, and Christmas with Dave's parents sometime before that. In the center was a photograph from Emily's birth; Elizabeth cradled the puffy-eyed newborn against the breast of her hospital gown with a Mona Lisa smile, captured in the peak of a motherhood that would never go gray.

Kate's throat clenched with the effort to swallow emotion. The photo blurred, fading Elizabeth and her pale gown into the bland sheetscape of maternity ward bed. Kate blinked and exhaled, keeping her breath smooth. She opened the refrigerator and put away the milk, then slowly dumped the nachos and salsa in the garbage can, chip by chip, buying herself a moment to swipe at her eyes.

Dave hadn't seen. He stood with his back to her, scraping the plates at the sink and loading the dishwasher. Then he mumbled something over his shoulder, words half lost in the running water. She caught *workshop*.

"Sorry?"

"There's something you should know about her painting workshop." His voice was nonchalant, but the set of his shoulders was high and tight. He shut off the water and turned to face her, wiping his hands on a towel. "She was meeting some guy in L.A. You might as well know it right off."

She looked at him, trying to recall any previous thread of conversation, but there was none. She had to assume he was talking about Elizabeth. "What do you mean?"

"She wrote in her journal just before she left about traveling with some guy named Michael. The workshop painter guy wasn't named Michael." He turned and began wiping dishes from the drying rack.

His words and bearing were too casual. Kate did not know what to say — denial or sympathy seemed called for, but he seemed closed to either one. Instead, she fell back on the most mundane thing he'd said.

"So you read them?"

She knew it was wrong even as she said it. He looked up at her, his broad face inscrutable, none of his usual amiability there.

"Not really. Just a little. It's always been a given, you don't touch the journals." The way he drew out the word — *jyouuu-nuls*, with weight on the first syllable — gave it an emphasis that was quaint, even sarcastic.

26

Sarcasm, from Dave Martin.

He turned to the coffeemaker even though Chris and Kate had declined his offer and began to load scoop after scoop, far too much for one pot.

"These past months it's been there sitting in the nightstand drawer, this last one, plus a whole trunk of them locked in the closet. She was different last summer, wiped out from the baby, probably. But I just wanted to know whether she left the house feeling a little sad that she'd miss us, or if she was too damned glad to be getting away to care. I expected it was probably a little of both." He closed the filter hatch on the coffee-maker and pressed the red button. "On the last page I saw something about her looking forward to seeing this Michael guy, and more about him a few pages before that. I just thought I'd mention it in case you opened the notebook and got all worked up."

Kate looked out the window. The sound of squabbling filtered through, kids who had reached the height of goodwill and were headed down the other side. The pot groaned as water struggled through impossibly dense grounds to make coffee no one wanted.

"Dave," she said. "This is *Elizabeth*." The

emphasis on her name conveyed the absurdity of anything inappropriate.

He turned away from her to rinse out the pasta bowl. Huge amounts of leftovers went down the disposal, days of potential lunches. Then the rest of the green salad. From the counter, a freshly cut quarter of tomato, a wedge of red pepper. Elizabeth would have folded each into a neat ziplock bag, saving it for the next meal.

"The little bit I read didn't sound much like Elizabeth. Not that it was ever intended for my eyes, anyway." He shoved a length of cucumber down the drain. The unsaid thing hung in the air: *Or she would have left them to me.*

When Dave had called Kate to tell her about the addendum to the will, he had not offered her any direction as to what she was supposed to do with the journals. *It's not exactly something Elizabeth and I discussed,* he'd said, voice flat. Then he'd fallen silent waiting for her to say something insightful, something that would show her to be this deserving of his wife's trust. She could not imagine what might be in the journals, but very likely he could. Or, perhaps, the problem was that he could not.

Dave ran the disposal for a long minute, its whine rising through the produce and letting Kate off the hook even if she'd known what to say.

Chris walked into the kitchen holding two pairs of pajamas. "I'm going to get the kids changed before we go. It'll be easier once we get to the motel if they fall asleep on the drive." He looked from Kate to Dave, taking in their proximity and silence.

Kate put a hand through her hair and willed him not to ask. "If they're changing upstairs, tell them to say hi to their old goldfish."

"Goldfish?"

She rubbed her eyes, weary. "Remember? We left them here with the kids instead of trying to move them to D.C." Chris raised his eyebrows but she didn't say more, and he left to change the children.

She looked to the wall, to the girl with ice cream, the tense discordant brownstones. Dave broke the silence.

"It's funny, Elizabeth couldn't stand goldfish. They gave her the creeps. But she took care of yours like it was her mission, and Jonah's kept it up pretty well."

The night before the Spensers had moved to Washington, D.C., Kate had shuttled between the broom-swept emptiness of her own house and the Martins', pawning off things that wouldn't travel well: some houseplants and a propane tank, food from the freezer, the goldfish. After the last load, Elizabeth stood under the porch light holding a desiccated jade. The plant's fat teardrop leaves were molting and the aquarium smelled like sewage, but Elizabeth had taken them with the gravity of precious offerings.

There were finally small signs of normalcy for the Martins. The older two kids were sleeping through the night again, Dave said. People had finally stopped bringing lasagna. Now this, the journals and whatever they contained, agitating the healing. Kate tried to muster some argument, some bolstering thought, but came up with nothing.

"You know, I never heard her say the slightest thing about being unhappy. God, she loved you guys more than anything." It was the best she could do under the circumstances.

He wiped his hands on the dish towel and looked at her with an odd smile, pained with the effort not to be wry. He was too polite for that.

"Come on now," he said. "Let's get your car loaded up with that beautiful family of yours."

Kate stood in the driveway looking into the tightly packed car through the open rear hatch door. On top of the suitcases, linens, and beach toys, there had been just enough room for the small antique trunk. Dave was inside corralling his kids to say good-bye. She pulled out the key from the lawyer and slipped it into the brass lock. The aged hardware turned with the solid tumble of fine luggage, and she lifted the lid to find three stacks of thick books, maybe a dozen or more. The spiral-bound notebooks had decorated covers, painted, some of them, or laminated with photos. As she reached in to touch one textured with thick paint, Dave appeared beside her. He glanced inside and then away, as if from something uncouth. She closed the lid, regretting her impatience. To free the key she had to relock the trunk, an excluding click that felt a further insult to him. Then she placed the key in the zippered compartment of her wallet.

He held a manila notebook with an undecorated cover, and handed it to her without meeting her eye. "Here. It was the one in the nightstand." She took the plain book and rushed it into her tote like pornography.

As the car backed out of the driveway, Kate gave one last wave to the four Martins in a row, looking much the same as they had in so many vacation pictures with Elizabeth behind the camera. Dave was still holding the piece of paper she'd given him with their telephone number at the rental house. *In case you need anything, or can come out for a visit,* she'd said. *My cell never works well out there.* He'd made an agreeable sound, but she knew she wouldn't hear from him. After he'd handed her the last journal, his farewell had had the brisk tone of a person glad to have finished a task and brushing off his hands afterward.

Chris turned left, up the ramp and onto the interstate. "What was that all about? There in the kitchen."

Kate glanced at the children in the rearview mirror. The kids stared back at her reflected eyes, curious. "I'll tell you after they fall asleep."

He clicked the radio on to his favorite news station, and an announcer's voice filled the car with words — *terrorists, threat levels* — that she did not want the children to hear. She turned off the rear speakers wishing she could turn it off altogether. All her life she'd been a news junkie, but now the flood of information was unwelcome. She fingered the metal spirals of the journal on her lap, then looked back in the mirror to the trunk wedged on top of the air mattress. It was a miniature steamer with a bowed lid, solid and heavily shellacked and who knew how old, perhaps a hundred years or more. The kind of trunk that would outlive all of them. It had already begun to.

Chris drove north on I-95 parallel to the ocean, past a small inlet of the Long Island Sound rimmed with sea grass. The water at dusk looked solid as blacktop, the homes around it a dark cul-de-sac. She flipped through the pages of the notebook. Only the first few had writing. The cover was fresh and undecorated.

No matter how Kate had tried over the past month to imagine what Elizabeth might have expected of her in leaving her the books, she came up with the same few options. She could put the journals in a safe-deposit box for the kids. She could designate them for the children's children, people for whom the uncertainty of a painting workshop would hold interest only as a footnote to family history. She could give them to Dave, even though Elizabeth had not done so herself. Or there could be the mother of all memorial bonfires.

None of these choices must have been certain to Elizabeth, or she would have written them into her will. Perhaps she hadn't known what she wanted; maybe all she'd known was that she wanted her books in the hands of someone with a bit of objectivity, distance. Maybe she'd planned to decide later, only there had never been a later.

The July sun had been shining on the beach that last time they went walking. The chain of seaweed twisted between Elizabeth's tense fingers. *The chance to do a program with him in the U.S. is rare*, she'd said. Kate remembered the conversation well. The instructor was famous for nature paintings. He was Mexican. And his name hadn't been Michael. It was Jesús.

Kate looked down at the notebook in her lap. Memories of her time in Southbrook had been shelved, simple years with a circle of earnest new moms behaving in predictable ways. Reading these books, she suspected, would not contribute to the peace and stability she was hoping to gain from the summer.

THREE

In Kate's midnight mind, the crash went like this. The plane dipping severely after takeoff. Mild gasps of surprise. An unnatural twist and an overkill correction, views of the borough rising at surreal angles. Overhead bins falling open like startled mouths as the plane swung from side to side, then the scream of machinery failing somewhere below. In the middle of the cries and terror, the laptops and purses streaking down the aisle, there had been a pale, still Elizabeth, frozen in her seat with the realization she would not see her children again.

If she'd had long enough, she would have seen a parade of nevers: all the birthdays, graduations, weddings. The way her children's faces would look as adults at ages when they would barely remember hers, no longer certain of what was a memory and what was a photograph posing as one.

If there had been only a few seconds of

awareness, it went more like this: Elizabeth grasping the armrest, perhaps the hand of the person beside her. Fragments of prayer, a desperate reflex. Calling out her children's names and calling for Dave, but in the end calling last for her own mother, as we're all said to do. Sudden pain, or more likely, suddenly none.

These thoughts always led to the same place: Kate's vision of her own children alone with Chris after something had happened to her. Disease, collision — it didn't matter how it would have come about. Loss would hang on James and Piper like poorly fitting clothes as they moved through town, people touching their hair and saying hello more attentively than they ever had, some even offering small gifts, which would cause the children to confuse death with a holiday. The kids would walk to school with their father, his vacant eyes an open door to a corridor of endless tomorrows. As they moved down the hall the crowd would subtly part. Preschool staff and parents would greet them a little too warmly, and if the children remained affectless, the adults would move on, taking consolation in the fact that they had tried. The Spensers would move in a bubble of grief and everyone they passed would be briefly enveloped, but it would stay with the Spensers wherever they went. She knew this because she'd seen it with the Martins. The public grief, the children so ill at ease and still confused by the never-coming-back part. Kate shook her head in a reflexive shudder to rid the image.

She rolled onto her back and wiped her face with the motel sheet. Then she creased it double across her chest and laid her hands over the top, a position of tranquillity that sometimes worked. The window was outlined in light around poorly fitting shades, and a wide band glowed under the door. The smoke detector was an unblinking eye on the ceiling. Chris's exhale of coffee through toothpaste was too close at her ear, damp and rancid.

She eased out of bed, one leg at a time from the cheap sheets, and crossed the room. The small table lamp beside the armchair would not wake Chris.

Two newsweekly magazines lay on the bureau beside the car keys and his wallet. One featured a story about anthrax, and the other, al-Qaeda. Kate cringed at Chris's idea of beach reading. A hollow-eyed bin Laden glared from the cover. A T-shirt lay at her feet and she threw it over the magazines, then sat on the edge of the armchair.

Passing trucks on the highway were loud through inadequately soundproofed windows. The table lamp gave off the buzz of electronic white noise. In the bathroom, a faucet dripped.

Next to the bureau, metal spirals gleamed between the twill handles of her tote bag.

She reached in and pulled out the manila-covered notebook with only a few entries, Elizabeth's last.

July 9, 2001

Saw Michael again in the city today. We met in Central Park and sat cross-legged on the ratty old blanket I use at Tiny Tot Soccer. We talked for a long time, probably more than he had to spare, and I felt even more comfortable. He held both my hands and told me he felt my pain, which was somehow not hokey. I think he's incapable of irony.

He asked me to come to Joshua Tree, told me all about the house and land, the horses, the miles of trails, the desert at night. When he touches my arm, it's electric. The sun radiates from his smooth head instead of just shining on it. The way he looks in my eyes makes me feel thoroughly known for once in my life and yes, makes me want to follow him anywhere.

Kate came this weekend with her family, passing through, heading out on vacation. Went walking on the beach, a beautiful morning but I felt ready to explode, so on edge and exhausted. I can't believe it's possible to walk around feeling this way and no one can see.

We talked about art and college, and man, more than anyone in this place, she gets me. But I didn't give in to the temptation to tell her all about the trip, just gave the party line. Confiding in people rarely makes you feel any better; just feeds them information that they don't know how to respond to and changes the way they see you. But mostly I don't want it out there, don't want any chance of this affecting the kids. It's worked so far and warped as this sounds, it's one of my proudest accomplishments.

Kate raised shaking fingers to her brow. She didn't know if she was ready for this. Not just the possibility that Elizabeth was having an affair, but seeing what her friend had really thought of her, the small impressions

39

and judgments we all hold privately.

August 6, 2001

Printed out directions to Joshua Tree, reservations reconfirmed, and took out the last of the money I'll need from the ATM. I can't help thinking Dave noticed the withdrawals this month, and sometimes I worry that I should lock away this book too.

Three days until I leave. Never anticipated anything so much or expected this much.

August 9, 2001, 6 a.m.

The sun is up but the children aren't, not quite yet. The baby fell back asleep after her feeding and I have a few minutes before showering. I can't wait but can't stand it, leaving her so little.

Now I have to get myself together and say good-bye to the kids and remember to make a fuss over packing the painting supplies they bought, jam them in somehow with all that awful writing. Even in the middle of this my mind sticks on the little things: Will Dave hear Emily when she cries in the middle of the night and get Jonah to the bus stop on time and remember that Anna gags on apple skin? All that could go wrong if I leave, vs. all that could go right. So selfish.

Depends on how you define selfish, Michael says.

I can't think about it or I will be unable to get down the driveway when they're blowing kisses and singing See ya later alligator, in a while, crocodile.

Kate closed the cover and rested her head against the stiff motel armchair that stank of some past guest's cigarettes. She scratched at worn fibers of seat cushion, ripped bits of brown and green in a hybrid of linen and plastic. Chris's breathing snagged on each inhale.

She saw Elizabeth at an ATM kiosk making withdrawals she hoped would go unnoticed, telling the older two children to hold the sides of the stroller. Pulling bills from the metal slot, a furtive look over her shoulder through loose strands of hair, the only gesture suggesting the cash would not go for gas and groceries. Kate tried to imagine her cross-legged on a blanket with a man who was not Dave, imagine sun and an electric touch, but could not. She tried to imagine feeling really known.

Chris was snoring heavily now, and in the

adjacent kids' room there was silence. She pulled the car keys from beneath the T-shirt on the bureau, uncovering the photo of bin Laden and those eyes that followed her like a painting possessed, and clicked off the lamp. At the door she paused, remembering the motel key-card and the antique key to Elizabeth's trunk.

The light from the outdoor walkway flooded the room, but no one stirred. She closed the door behind her softly and headed to the parking lot, barely lit and surrounded by trees. Cars passed regularly on the highway just beyond.

Kate unlocked the car's rear door and then the trunk, putting the plain notebook back on the top of the stack and digging for the one that would have come before it. She flipped open the covers, saw dates through the 1980s and 1990s, and then finally, one bearing dates from 2000 and 2001. The notebook was covered in a photograph of Elizabeth with Jonah and Anna, all three laughing in the sun. Elizabeth's smile and posture were free and unrestrained in a way they had not been often. It was a stunning image, bittersweet in the way an occasion can be nostalgic for its loss even as it unfolds.

Kate opened the book. She meant to bring

it inside but couldn't resist skimming by the dim light of the car's interior dome, eager and miserable to learn how this Michael came to be holding hands with the world's most earnest woman — a mother who had embraced each day as parenting magazines advised because the children would be grown before you knew it.

She felt as if someone were nearby, watching. Gooseflesh rose on her arms. She turned fast but saw no one in the lot, empty but for a few other cars. Only a thin fringe of trees separated the motel from the highway, and the asphalt under her feet vibrated when a semi rumbled past. She turned back to the car and the notebook, but the sensation of eyes on her remained, eyes halfway from cornflower to sapphire. *Ask that she start at the beginning.*

Slowly, as if for someone else's benefit, she replaced the photo-covered journal in the trunk — on top, where she could always come back to it — and reached for the book at the bottom of the far left stack. She looked at the dates from several until she found a black-and-white composition-style notebook. The cover was brightened with stickers, the sort found in greeting-card aisles: tulips, smiley faces, kittens. The date on the first page was 1976, which by Kate's reckoning put Elizabeth, who'd been a year older than she, at about twelve. She pulled it out and held it briefly — *see, I am beginning here.* Then she opened it and began to read.

April 12, 1976

Dear Diary,

Dr. Trinker says I should start keeping a diary to write my thoughts, and do it like I'm writing letters to my best friend or to myself, and that it will help me "process" and "move on." For the record I think this is a stupid idea, writing to make yourself feel better. But when I rode my bike today past the sub sandwich place where I took Anna for her birthday in February, I couldn't breathe and actually had to get off and put my head between my knees like an asthma attack. So I will give it a try. She was so proud of turning eight and really psyched to be biking into town, and I thought she'd explode when we went to the pet store and I told her I was getting her a fish for her present. She made me get one too so it would have a friend in the tank to keep it company. Hers died last week. Figures.

When you write a letter to your diary are

you supposed to sign it?

Yours truly,
Lizzie Drogan

Kate stopped reading at a sound, a rustling in the trees behind the car. The wooded fringe was a wall of shadows. She held her breath but there was only stillness, then the trembling ground of a truck beyond the trees. Her car's rear hatch was still raised, and she realized she was fully backlit and visible to anyone coming off the interstate, anyone roaming at 2 a.m. near the rear entry of a motel.

Kate closed the car door, then pressed the lock button on her keychain, and the alarm chirped. Something darted from under the car by her feet. She gasped and jumped back, dropping the notebook. Low and dark, a small animal loped away toward the Dumpsters, its striped tail bobbing like the flag on a girl's bike.

The motel room was dark and quiet when Kate let herself back in. She settled into the armchair and switched the table lamp back on, then sat considering the sticker-covered notebook in her hands. Kate had never seen a photograph of Elizabeth as a child, and the disaffected tone of the journal entry did little to evoke her spirit. Kate tried to imagine her biking into town at twelve, April spattering the back of her pants. Walking through the aisles of a stationery store, muttering *Stupid* under her breath, then riding home with her selection and later pressing kittens onto the cover in a small spasm of preteen cheer. In this way, under duress, she'd begun the journal-writing habit that would last her entire life.

April 15, 1976

Dear Diary,
Another day of no one talking to me on the bus. I stared out the window and tried to think of something else when we passed Taylor Street and the little cross on the side of the road. I've never felt lonelier in my whole life. Everyone is so freaked out around me that for the last month it's been like I'm poison. It's like having a sister get killed is contagious and I'm glowing with it. I wish I could move away.

Yours truly,
Lizzie D

A sister. Kate felt the chair sink and the floor become unsteady under her feet. How was it possible Elizabeth could have had a sister and not told Kate? Not about the loss, or ever having had one at all. She'd mentioned being an only child, but had spoken so little about it that Kate assumed it had come about in the usual way: parents ambivalent about the demands of children found that one was quite enough, or perhaps were unable to have another, creating an emptiness that had fueled Elizabeth's decision to have three of her own. *Maybe more*, she used to say.

Kate exhaled. She thought of how Piper curled into James as they slept in the car, head to head, their high symmetrical eyebrows like two parenthetical statements to Kate's fulfillment as a professional, and then a wife. She thought of her own sister, Rachel. A sister was a companion and competitor, the person who best understood the crucible in which you were formed. One of the few capable of completing you, and if lost, of cleaving you cleanly in half.

But in the wash of sympathy, there was a sting that she hadn't been told.

April 27, 1976

Dear Diary,
I told Mom I was going to Sherry's house after school. I've never been in a grave-

47

yard alone before. I passed a grave where people put stuffed animals and little toy cars by the headstone, and when I read the dates I saw that a really little kid had been buried there. I was afraid I'd have another breathing fit but when I got to Anna's I stopped crying. The grass hasn't grown and there's no stone yet. So I sat and looked at dirt.

I don't know what people do when they go to graveyards and I was probably supposed to pray or something, but I couldn't stop thinking that she was right down there under the ground. Her actual body wearing her green school picture day dress like at the wake. But it didn't look anything like her except for the charm bracelet and the hair, and even that was weird, all stiff like a doll's. There was not a single thing that's the way she really was, nothing about her goofy face and the way she always followed me that was so annoying but I couldn't yell Quit it. Because what kind of person would be mean to a kid who only wants to be with you all the time?

That's when I knew that she's with God, because there was no Anna in that box at all. I didn't feel it as much at the funeral, which is when I guess you're supposed to. But when you look at a body and there's not a bit of life in it that was anything like what the person really was, not even like someone sleeping and more frozen than a statue, then you just have to know there's a God. Because something has to make that body more than a body, not just blood going around.

April 29, 1976

The school guidance counselor set me up with Mother's Helper work. She thought it would be good for me even though I don't like babysitting and little kids kind of bug me. The mom smiled a lot and was always touching the little girl's hair and giving her little hugs and squeezes, and I wondered if Mom was ever like that with me when I was little, before she started calling me Sourpuss and Grumplestiltskin. The mom was asking me questions about how I like school and about my family, so I guess the counselor didn't tell her about Anna. Which was weird because even though she lives the next town over I think every other single person in the county knows, or at least it seems that way at the grocery store. When she asked if I had any brothers or sisters I didn't know what to say. What am I supposed to say now?

I asked Mom this while she was doing the dishes and she was quiet for a long time, and then she looked out the window behind the sink, and I couldn't tell if she was going to get mad or cry. But she didn't do either. She told me that it's better to say that I don't have any brothers or sisters because to explain to other people that I had a sister who just died would make them really uncomfortable, and people don't like to be uncomfortable. There are things you say, and things that are better not to. And anyway, it's the truth.

I wish Mom and Dad had more than just two kids. It doesn't seem like a very smart thing to do if you're a parent, when the good one can get killed and then you're left with only one, the grumpy one.

May 12, 1976

I went back to the graveyard today and brought Anna's palomino pony. I had to sneak into her room to get it because Mom doesn't like it when I go in. Everything's the same, even her dirty clothes are still on the floor and the bed isn't made.

I told Dr. Trinker about how I got in big trouble last week when Mom caught me sleeping in Anna's bed. Dr. Trinker said she'd talk to her, but a few days later Mom said I wouldn't be going to Dr. Trinker again. She said I didn't need to go talk to a doctor anymore and that we were all doing just fine.

June 15, 1976

Happy birthday to me. 13! I'm a teenager now. I guess I'm supposed to do things like talk on the phone and hang out downtown. Sherry is still my friend, that's about it. I think no one knew what to say at first and neither did I, and then they kept on not saying anything until it became too weird and now no one says Hey Lizzy D anymore. I'm just The Girl Whose Sister Died.

But here's the big news: We're moving to Connecticut. Mom said it's okay if I cut my hair and get my ears pierced, and I'm going to call myself Elizabeth, not Lizzie. And in Connecticut the only thing that will make me different is that I'm from Vermont. People we meet there won't even know I had a sister. Mom says it will be good to get a fresh start and private things are best kept private, and we don't want people constantly being weird about it like they are here. She also tells me I have to smile more if I want to make friends.

I went to the graveyard to tell Anna about Connecticut. I feel bad that we're leaving her here. It seems wrong that she'll be alone without anyone to visit and bring flowers. I planted some of Mom's tulip bulbs even though the sign says you're not supposed to plant anything. I hope I did it right. I can't stand the thought of tulips growing with the pretty part facing down where no one can see it. And I said I'm sorry, as well as I could choking that way, I'm really really sorry.

Kate came up out of sleep aware of two things: a child to her left, and a kink in her neck that kept her from turning that way.

"Mom, why are you sleeping there?" Tinker Bell was at eye level, silk-screened on a polyester nightgown. "Are you sick? Can we still go to the ferry?"

Kate stretched her arms over her head and felt the tug of knots in her neck and shoulders. She should not have slept in the chair.

"Nope, not sick. We're definitely going to the ferry today. Is James up?"

"He's reading in bed," Piper said.

James had started reading young. In the beginning he'd read aloud to her, but stopped once he'd realized that grown-ups read silently. Now he would read anything — older chapter books, newspapers and magazines, even Kate's e-mail if her computer was left open. She didn't know how much he understood, but she'd begun to feel she should edit the media left around the house. Current events these days were no Dick and Jane.

Kate rubbed her daughter's back as she stood. "Okay, let's get dressed so we can make it on time."

Chris still lay in bed, one leg thrown out sideways from beneath the sheet. She walked to the bed, stretching her neck side to side. "It's seven forty-five. We should get going if we're going to make the nine."

He mumbled, but there was no movement under the sheet.

"I'm getting in the shower. Make sure the kids get dressed, okay?"

She walked into the motel bathroom, pulled off her yoga pants and tank top, and twisted the water dial as hot as it would go. Let other women have their baths; a solid driving shower relaxed her more than a massage, woke her better than coffee. She stepped under the spray with her head bowed, letting the heat drum on her tight neck and shoulders. Many of her best ideas came to her in the shower. Years ago when she worked in Manhattan restaurants, she would step out of her apartment's tiny stall with new dessert concepts, sometimes literal — lavender soap, lavender-scented Bundt cake — and sometimes abstract, ice cream tiled with pale diamonds of caramelized sugar, patterned after the geometry of her bathroom wall.

Water pulsed through the motel's old showerhead and echoed in the small tiled room. She thought of the things that needed to be done after they arrived at the rental house. They'd promised the owners they would fill the propane tank, clean the outdoor furniture, check the basement for rodents and the perimeter of the patio for rabbits. And she should book the restaurant soon for their anniversary dinner; it had become so popular. But amid the practical tasks her thoughts kept hitching on young Elizabeth. A small serious face pressed to the window at Taylor Street, a girl called Sourpuss trying to figure out whether she met the definition of an only child. Twenty-five years later, Sourpuss had sat cross-legged on a blanket holding hands with a man who was not her husband. And had taken steps to ensure that when she died, her husband would not be the one to receive her journals.

Kate usually resisted making assumptions, passing judgment; it was impossible to know what was happening in someone else's world, what possessed a person to do the things he or she did. It was the closest thing she had to a governing principle. *Fair and sensitive*, Elizabeth called it.

Their closeness had not been automatic five years before. In the beginning, playgroup was just playgroup. Kate's long-standing friends, the ones from culinary school, were now scattered around the country and cooking throughout the world. When she got together with them, everything was fast and ironic — even the humor felt hungry — and she felt at home in a way she hadn't when she was younger in the quiet, cerebral confines of her parents' house. Among her peers, she finally felt measured by what she could say and do rather than by what she could not. The one conscious omission was family life; few of the women with whom she'd graduated now had children, and the men who did rarely mentioned them. Kate made a concerted effort not to drift into mommy terrain when she was with them, though she sometimes slipped and saw their eyes glaze over, like her older sister's would.

Elizabeth was the opposite of fast and

ironic. She didn't say anything she didn't mean, and she didn't forget anything you said. She remembered birthdays and old stories, called to check in after your wisdom teeth were removed. It was true that with her you couldn't go to that place of unsentimental candor, giving air to the ugly pissed-off things, like how you could love your family but hate your life sometimes. But over time, that seemed less important. You could vent your frustration over a child — the dinners not eaten and the tantrums thrown, omitting the part that you had to step outside gasping like a beached fish so you wouldn't say or do something you'd regret — and she would listen and pretend not to see the tears you pushed away, knowing you didn't want them seen. It was easy for Elizabeth to become the person you saw more than anyone else, the comfortable T-shirt you reached for mornings when there was no need to impress anyone. Even after Kate moved away, Elizabeth was always there, checking in with a phone call at regular intervals, reliable as the tide. And then, one day, she wasn't.

Kate turned off the shower, and the squeak of the dial reverberated in the tiled room. She squeezed the excess water from her hair and toweled the ends dry, remembering, with a catch in her throat, how Elizabeth would do that to all the playgroup children after they'd run through the sprinkler. Walk among them like she owned a little piece of them all, rubbing the small heads of the world a little drier.

At first, Elizabeth's death had been a terrible shock, and with it, so much grim activity: endless lists of people Kate needed to call, and details she'd volunteered to arrange. But it hadn't felt like something that nearly a year later would continue to knock the air from her lungs like a swift jab of grief to the solar plexus. Their close friendship had not been a typical one. They didn't have the shared history of work and old boyfriends. Elizabeth had never taken the bait to talk about marital chafe or admit there might be a thing or two you wished you were doing in addition to, or even instead of, diapers. She wasn't even a neighbor any longer, someone with whom you could pass a slow afternoon at the playground.

But that's the funny thing about people who don't fit into a box. They grow to infiltrate everything, and when they suddenly go missing, they are missing everywhere.

FOUR

Cars idled behind a rusty chain on the road leading to the ferry terminal. Shortly before 9 a.m., vehicles drove up the ramp one by one and into the potbellied lot of the largest ferry that served Great Rock Island. Cargo trucks eased in, scraping through the doorway and inching forward until they stood bumper to bumper, swaying with the ship's movement like zoo animals sedated for transport.

The number of cargo vehicles on the ferries seemed to increase every year. When Kate first started coming to the island twenty years earlier — as a high-school babysitter accompanying a family on its annual monthlong vacation — there had been only two ferries a day, and no trucks. Back then, very little could be gotten on-island that wasn't grown there. Sweet corn came from one of several nameless farm stands, and everyone bought pies from the front-yard gazebo of a woman who didn't keep a menu or a schedule of hours. Lines formed daily for seafood on the southwestern docks, fresh fish, lobster, and clams nearly every afternoon.

The history of the docks was the dominant history of Great Rock, though for years that was forgotten, until it became profitable to remember. Whaling had been the community's livelihood in the nineteenth century, when most of the residents were either involved in the chase for oil from sperm whales or consumed with the well-being of others who were. In many ways, the harborfront village still felt like a whaling town. Sea captains' mansions claimed the prime harborfront real estate, and the old whaling church was still the centerpiece of the village, its narrow bell tower peaking in most postcards and paintings.

In the second half of the twentieth century, after large fishing conglomerates had run smaller boats out of the water, the fishing history of the island slipped into irrelevance. The mansions sat empty and crumbling, many subdivided into condominiums and sublet. Petty crime grew, and shops that remained shuttered in the winter were visited by vandals or squatters. Even the whaling church fell victim to weather, graffiti, and neglect, and by 1980 it was used less for prayers for the fishermen than for various support groups for year-round residents, groups like Alcoholics Anonymous, Narcotics Anonymous, and the Off-Season Artists' Association, which derived most of its membership from the other two.

It had been decades since local fishermen were able to make a decent living. But as Great Rock's popularity grew as a tourist destination, a reverence for whaling returned. Nostalgia became marketable, and local businesses doted on the whaling memory like grandchildren of a wealthy ailing matriarch. Shops and restaurants were named with every possible pun. There was the clock shop named Whale of a Time, the hair accessories store, Thar She Bows, and the tavern, Blubbering Idiots. Each year Kate visited, it felt more as if the care and feeding of tourists had become the prime industry. Visitors were now the bread and butter of the island, and the island worked hard to satisfy their appetites.

But the appetites had become voracious, and the change in town was palpable. Where once there had been a needlepoint shop run by the crafts guild stood a boutique with artfully displayed $400 shoes. The village diner served Coke in Simon Pearce goblets.

The harborfront captains' homes had been renovated back to single-family mansions, popular as rentals among studio executives. The whaling church had been restored and was in demand for weddings ever since its gleaming banisters had been photographed for the *New York Times*' wedding pages. All of it kept the preservationists very busy, forever backward-looking and perpetually defensive against the new.

Which was not to say the island had been ruined. If you kept to the north shore, the sleepy agricultural side, and ventured into town just for ice cream and the occasional dinner, it was still possible to have a time-less island vacation. Which was more or less what Kate and Chris did. Before they married, they had discovered an unadvertised waterfront rental, simple and spare with a sliver of beach. They had been quiet about their find. Each September, they sent the homeowners three things: a thank-you card with pictures of the children playing in the yard, a box of Kate's homemade madeleines, and a deposit check for the same two weeks the following summer. This year the owners were experiencing some sort of hardship and had consented to seven, cheaply, in exchange for caretaking. Chris had negotiated with his firm and would be working from there.

When the ferry was well away from shore, the children asked to go inside the cafeteria to play cards. Kate slid into a booth while Chris walked them through the line for orange juice and bagels. Large windows overlooked the Atlantic on three sides. The color of the sky matched the water, today more oyster than leaden. It had been overcast on almost every one of the ferry trips she'd ever taken, and she'd come to associate gray with vacationing as people do navy with sailing or pink with baby girls. Gray was the shingled house they rented and the darkly opaque waves outside its windows. It was the sweatshirts the kids threw on over their bathing suits, and the steamers she ate several times a week dipped in dun-colored broth. Gray represented freedom from ordinary time, and gray was the uniform of the cavalry riding in, the child-care cavalry, since Chris was with them most of the time.

Kate and Chris had met in New York ten years before, when she was twenty-eight and he was thirty-two. She was a pastry chef at a boutique hotel on the Upper East Side, and he was part of a small team of hotel developers finalizing plans for a new location. Talks were held over dinner in the small private nook in the back of the kitchen itself. This was the hotel's most exclusive location for special events, a table for eight set in the corner beneath a collection of vintage copper pots. It bloomed with a stratospheric centerpiece by Marcel, the renowned florist who did the arrangements for the couture wedding shop across the street, and was laid with the hotel's best signature china. Never mind that it wasn't out of grease-splattering range, a finer point that once went to litigation over a ruined Hermès suit. The table drew some of the biggest heads of commerce, and was known simply as The Kitchen Table in a pretentious attempt to be unpretentious.

But the real selling point of The Kitchen Table was the interaction with the chefs. Just a few feet from the guests, the chef de cuisine elevated meal preparation to performance art along with line cooks that included Kate. It was an exalted position for someone her age, and confirmed for Kate's parents and older sister that everyone just needed to *find their thing.*

The early nineties marked the beginning of the dinner-as-theater trend, when chefs were achieving the status of minor celebrities, and The Kitchen Table staff would demonstrate techniques and answer questions if guests were truly interested, which they rarely were. But Chris had been, as well as drop-the-whisk handsome. When Kate stood at the range stirring butter and flour and saw him watching her, she had nearly ruined a pâte à choux. His rusty blond hair was long for investment circles, and the creases around his eyes — age, sun, or smile lines, she couldn't tell which — looked as if they belonged on someone older. For his part, he would later say that her face — pale against a black bob, with dramatic straight-cut bangs, framed in the opening between the stainless-steel stovetop and the ventilation hood — made him think of 1940s Parisian cabaret.

She'd noticed him throughout dinner, or more accurately noticed him for what he was not: pompous, loud, or demanding, which was the norm among the egos that came into the kitchen. He thanked the staff when they brought each course. He didn't treat the waitresses as if they worked at a gentlemen's club. He did not laugh at the crude jokes made by a red-faced colleague. And he was the only one who hadn't lit up a cigar in violation of kitchen rules — ironic, since she later learned that he was a smoker, and when she pressed him to quit before they got married, it was not easily done.

So when he offered Kate his business card and asked if he might call for cooking tips (he was having a dinner party that weekend, and what was a choux anyway), she'd consented. It was a transparent excuse, particularly flimsy given that in all the years she'd known him, the closest he'd come to cooking was stirring onion soup mix into sour cream. But that hadn't mattered to Kate, drawn to a kindred directness and a suspicion that he followed his own lead.

Marrying Chris was easier than Kate ever thought a life-altering decision could be. Certainly there was attraction and romance, as there had been with others. But never before had someone listened so intently with no expectation of what she could give him — a laugh, an entwining of limbs at the end of the night — except her own strongest self. They lived in Manhattan for three years before James was born. As Chris rose in the ranks of the hotel investment firm, they traveled to places where his group had brokered deals on small independent properties: Belize, Siena, Phuket, Goa. She left the hotel restaurant and became a partner in a bakery-café in the West Village, and hosted a small cooking show on local cable television. Her shtick was tough-love remedial cooking for homemakers who thought they were too busy to bother.

"You show me three small holes in your schedule, I'll show you a great meal by the end of the day," had been her trademark challenge. "If you want it enough, you can make it happen."

A few viewers had taken issue with her message. *How about showing me three minutes of peace and quiet and an easy three-ingredient meal*, someone had written in. And another, *Give her a few toddlers underfoot and see if she can "make it happen" then. Not everything is as simple as it seems.* She usually threw away her mail after reading it. But this second note she brought home and tucked in her top drawer like a report card. The show enjoyed high ratings and ran for three years, reinforcing her belief that most things could be made possible through the sheer force of will.

Next week would be their ninth anniversary. She could still say in all honesty that Chris was her best friend, and she was certain he'd say the same of her. On business trips he always packed his favorite photograph of her, charmingly, a still shot from the cooking show at the moment she'd dropped a soufflé on-air. He said her hilarity at her own expense, so genuine, so unselfconscious, made it the most beautiful picture he'd seen.

Since having children, their relationship had changed. Their us-against-the-world bond had come to feel like a corporate partnership, each of them running autonomous divisions. He helped with the kids when he was around, but he often wasn't. If she had to put a finger on when she first felt the shift, it was shortly after James was born, the early months when love is commingled with obligation, intimacy with isolation. Within a few months Kate had decided not to return to work for the time being — the maternity leave was so short, and the long chaotic hours, very early or very late, seemed incompatible with bonding with a baby. The passionate attachment was unlike anything she'd experienced; she never thought it possible to have such strong feeling for something that could reciprocate with nothing but its presence, need, and eventually, a smile. Soon afterward they'd moved to the suburbs. The isolation was also unlike anything she'd known. Whole days would pass when her only conversations consisted of la-la-la and arguments with the cable company. She'd felt compelled to join a playgroup through the town newcomers' organization just to get out of the house and have adult conversation.

One night, Chris came home announcing a two-week trip to Bhutan with a look of apology and guilt, knowing that's what was called for. But under the look she'd seen something else. Anticipation. Excitement. Relief. Kate did believe he was sincere when he said he missed them while he traveled, but she also knew that he enjoyed his trips, loved the expansiveness he felt in a new environment just as she had when she'd traveled with him. More important, she recognized that something had changed; he could no longer admit the pleasure of being away. To mention it would have been small of her when, on the whole, he was a good husband and father, and worse, would make her appear needy. So tapping a small reservoir of restraint, she said nothing. As she was doing laundry not long after the Bhutan trip, she found in his pocket what she thought were crushed bits of tobacco. She didn't mention that, either.

In all, they'd had nine pretty solid years and were in good standing, even as they'd watched friends bicker and cheat, carp and belittle, divorce. She'd never doubted his fidelity and she didn't have any secrets herself, at least none of the magnitude of Elizabeth's trip to Joshua Tree with Michael. If Kate's thoughts were sometimes seditious, her actions only went so far as searching pockets, and even then only to make sure that, say, he hadn't left money in his pants before she tossed them in the wash. Once she found a business card, his own, with a foreign telephone number written across it and "Michelle" scrawled underneath. She'd tossed it on his bureau with the collar stays and loose coins without a second thought.

Chris returned from the ferry cafeteria line with Piper and James beside him, each holding lemonade and ice cream.

"You just don't like the word *no*, do you?" Kate said to him as they approached. "It's not that hard. It actually feels good sometimes. Try it."

Chris smiled, his face still creased from the motel sheets. He hadn't had time to shower before the ferry, but it didn't matter. He was one of those men whose looks improved as they aged, who had, though she'd never say this to him, a certain prettiness that becomes more masculine as they settled into their skin.

Her eyes fell to the shoes he was wearing, vented canvas sandals she hadn't noticed before. Had he run out during lunch for a few vacation items, or picked them up during a free moment on a trip? In the early years he would have gone shopping with her, or would have shown them to her when he'd gotten home. *What do you think of these, hon?* he would have said. *Too crunchy?*

Minutiae, she told herself. It was natural that in a busy family, small things would begin to go unsaid.

FIVE

The bungalow was down a dirt path so nondescript that it was more a pair of ruts than a road. Huckleberry, sheep laurel, and juniper grew thickly on the sides and scratched cars that listed too far left or right. About two hundred yards down, the path forked left into a small driveway. The shingled cottage was deceptively plain and shady.

Kate turned the key in the lock and gave a push, and the front door opened with the sucking sound of vacuum-packed juice. The kids raced past her into the house. Kate dropped two duffels of linens and assessed the familiar space, a single square footprint that was kitchen and family room in one. She yanked back heavy seasonal drapes the length of two walls, and the room grew spacious. Enormous windows opened onto a yard like a football field, and beyond it, the ocean.

The house was compact, with an economy of space that had never felt cramped. The interior's whitewashed timber and plain cream-painted walls managed a sense of spare luxury without a single expensive accessory, except for an antique grandfather clock that undercut its own seriousness by chiming on whim.

As Chris unloaded the car, Kate stuck her head into each of the two bedrooms off a small hallway behind the family room. The master was the same size as the other, but with its own tiny bathroom and French doors opening onto one end of the wrap-around porch. She crossed the braided rug and opened a door in the corner. Inside the closet, behind the rod that would have held hanging clothes, a short ladder had been built into the wall. In the next room the children bickered over beds. She touched the smooth wood of the ladder, ran fingers over a worn rung while she debated going in to settle their argument. Then she climbed up hand over hand, and pushed open the trapdoor at the ceiling. It banged back flat against the attic floor.

This odd hybrid of cupola and loft was not technically part of the habitable house, added by the owners in the low, peaked space that would have been an attic. The boxy addition was less than seven feet high at its tallest point and angled down to about four feet at the corners, with three walls of windows facing the harbor. Kate climbed through the opening and took in the distant water views from tight quarters, a contradictory comfort of expanse amid restraint.

Rows of built-in shelves ran the length of the walls under the windows, and were filled with an eclectic mix of books. The sole piece of furniture in the loft was an upholstered chaise, pushed against the single windowless wall with light sconces built on either side. Kate clicked them on, and the bulbs glowed, flanking the couch at shoulder height.

This was where she envisioned reading Elizabeth's journals in the evenings, possibly even this afternoon if the housecleaning went quickly.

October 21, 1979

I'd say I'm sorry that it's been so long since I've written, but it hasn't been. I HAVE been writing for the past three years. I started a new diary after we moved to Connecticut. But I made the mistake of writing too much about everything — the new school and how hard it

73

was to make friends, how much I missed Anna, how badly Mom was doing, and how she got much worse after Dad moved out.

And then four months ago Mom found my old diary and threw it away. The most personal things I've ever thought, she read. And then she destroyed it. She said that it was not my business to put details of her private life down on paper, and I was free to write again if I found something more <u>positive and empowering</u> to say. This is what I get all the time now, ever since she started shopping in the weirdo section at the bookstore.

So I am trying again. I'm not promising to write regularly, but we'll see how it goes.

November 29, 1979

Thanksgiving ~~sucked~~ was not as positive as it could have been. I was dreading it, but then Claire's family invited us to spend it with them, and surprise surprise, Mom agreed. I started to worry right away. What if Mom drank too much "soda"? What if she said something less than empowering? Anything was possible. But I didn't have to worry, because it never happened. When I woke up Thanksgiving morning Mom was asleep on the couch with evidence on the coffee table that she'd been drinking from the sneaky cup.

I went for a long run, and when I got home she was awake but sick as a dog, and there was no way we were going to Claire's. I asked to go alone but she got all angry then and crying, saying We're still a family damn it even if we're not a very big family and we should spend it together. She told me to call Claire and tell her we both caught a stomach bug and apologize. Then she started banging pans trying to make a frozen chicken into a turkey dinner, but cleaning the chicken made her sick again and her stomach bug came up all over her ratty flannel pjs. That's what you get when you drink from the sneaky cup.

December 6, 1979

Just got back from a weekend at Dad's. It's hard to find much to talk about with him, but we got along better this time. The more normal and happy I act, the more comfortable he seems. I think he's all guilty about the broken-home thing. Or maybe it's that way with everyone, and what you have to do is smile, smile, smile.

Michael looked at me in chemistry class today.

The name gave Kate a jolt.

He turned around and smiled. The first time I thought he couldn't be looking at me but then he did it again, so I smiled back. Near the end of class he turned completely around and leaned over to whisper something. "Would you pass that back?" he asked, handing me a note. And when I turned around to see what he meant, Alexis Matthews smiled and held out her hand.

I didn't even want to be in the cafeteria during lunch I was so mortified, so I went to the art studio to work on the painting I'm doing for Mom's Christmas present. I'm copying a picture of Anna when she was six, sitting on a bench eating ice cream with this really content sleepy smile. It's my favorite picture of her. I hope she'll like it. Our whole pretend-it-never-happened thing hasn't been working for us very well. Maybe having Anna around looking like her best self will make Mom happier.

I'm in Sarasota with Dad, went along on one of his off-site audits. We've been here for almost two weeks, and it's been really cool learning to windsurf and sail. But I know he's lying. There's no way this was a belated Christmas gift. I got permission from my teachers and brought my books, but he doesn't even seem to care whether or not I do the homework.

I think Mom went somewhere. When she called yesterday it was very windy like she was outside. There were people in the background and she sounded spacey and tired. The three times I've tried to call home there was no answer.

Before we left the house I saw them from the stairway when they thought I was still up in my room getting my bags. Mom was crying. Dad didn't hug her, but he put his hand on her shoulder and rubbed it. I heard him say, "I think this will do you good. Personally I don't go for those kind of things, but it can't hurt." When I asked him about it later, he said he didn't know what I was talking about.

Christmas was okay. I think she liked her picture of Anna, but I'm not sure it was a good idea after all. This was my corny idea of what would happen: She'd open it, gasp, and smile. Then she'd hug me and say, "It's beautiful, Lizzie, thank you. What a wonderful way to remember her." And then we'd start to talk about how we both missed her, and maybe end with some funny sweet memories.

Here's what really happened. When Mom opened the painting she breathed in and stared with her eyes wide like she was watching one of those natural-disaster shows on TV. She sat that way for so long I started to wonder what she would do when she breathed again. After a good full minute she smiled and slowly said, "Thank you, what a good artist you are. I will have to think about where to hang it." Then she went upstairs. When Dad came to get me for Christmas at his house I tried to wake her to say good-bye. But there was empty *soda* beside the bed and I don't think she even knew I was leaving.

June 15, 1980

Happy birthday to me. I have a good feeling about my 17th year. Mom and Dad gave me a present together: a bike tour this summer, the arts council one I've been bugging them about. For the whole month of July I'm going to be biking in Colorado, taking painting clinics and staying in hostels. Then when I get back home it's road trips to check out colleges, some with Mom, some with Dad.

Mom seems much better. Ever since I went to Florida she's almost been like a regular mother. She got a job at an advertising agency, and she hasn't been sick since Christmas. I went ahead and asked her where she went while I was in Florida, and she said she was home of course, but she got twitchy and overly nice. Maybe I was imagining it. Either way, it's just going to be one of those things we don't talk about.

She finally hung the painting of Anna. When I stand in front of it I remember that once upon a time I wasn't alone, and it's not a bad feeling.

August 26, 1980

I just got back from checking out NYU. The minute I walked around the campus I knew I was meant to be there, even though I can tell neither of them want me to. I can see myself hanging out in Greenwich Village and painting the people and the buildings. I love how out of control and rude and messy things are, the kind of place where real life happens.

The pizzeria was on the edge of town, plain and inexpensive. Heat radiated from the kitchen and bent the air in waves of haze. Industrial fans had little effect, did not even blow free the lines of dust clinging to the fan's cage. Kate pushed sweaty bangs off her forehead, and looked at Chris across the Formica table.

"I can't believe we got the house for seven whole weeks."

"You mean you can't believe I took seven weeks away from the office." He drank the last of the water from his cup, and shook the ice at the bottom.

"How many times do you think you'll have to go off-island?"

"I'm not sure. I probably won't have to fly out more than once a week."

Kate kept her eyes down on the table. She fiddled with the glass cheese shaker, tapping its edge on the gray laminate.

He gave a crooked smile. *Really?* She did not usually complain about his travel. "I'm not on vacation this whole time. You knew that."

"I know. It's fine." Tiny planes, dipping

from side to side. She held a neutral expression.

"It won't be an overnight all the time. Most of the work is out of Boston this summer, but sometimes I might have to get a room."

It was the kind of thing they'd said when they were younger about others oversexed in public. *Get a room.* She gave a wry grin.

"Kate." He'd misread her. "If I have to do anything longer, maybe your sister could come out."

Rachel still lived near their parents in Palo Alto, had married and settled there, and was now well known at Stanford and beyond for her research on the economics of minimum wage. She was always pressing for Kate to fly and meet her somewhere, "just the two of us," without seeming to appreciate that it was not easily done with children. Rachel's willingness to adjust her frenetic teaching and conference schedule to make time for her little sister, her only sibling in the world, seemed to trump any difficulty Kate might have leaving young children and a traveling husband.

Their trips, when they managed them, were conceived with the best of intentions. There was always a subtext of sisterly bonding and closing the age gap, those four years

81

that made Rachel seem so distantly ahead in every way. What was harder to bridge were the things Rachel had said in their childhood, the patronizing praise for Kate's grades that made it all too clear that different standards applied to Kate. And in rare cruel moments, things like *You just NEVER know what you're going to get with adoption*, murmured with innocent wonder. Of course, suggesting a younger sibling was secretly adopted was just the kind of thoughtless thing kids did to one another. And when Kate had needed proof it wasn't true, she'd known where to find her mother's pregnancy pictures, but still. In a family that thrived on ephemeral debate and valued intellectual vigor, Kate had been different, and Rachel's words stung.

Brilliance doesn't always come with social dexterity and Rachel wasn't the easiest party guest, not much for light conversation and not easily entertained. Sometimes Kate wondered whether her sister's choice not to have children had been a result of her intellectual intensity, or if it was the other way around. Raising children meant having an appreciation for the absurd and the mundane, Kate thought — the bad puns and potty humor and endless knock-knock jokes — or at least a tolerance for them.

And yet there was a connection between them that was undeniable and enduring. Whether it was her imitations and dry wit or the memory she evoked of lighter childhood days, Kate accessed something in Rachel that brought out a rare girlishness in her. Rachel had a mellifluous laugh that could be startlingly unrestrained, uncomplicatedly happy. When their father heard it, he would look up from his paperwork in the book-lined study, pull his glasses down his nose, and gaze at them, smiling. At those moments his joy was transparent, all his hopes and needs satisfied should his compromised heart give out tomorrow. But for Kate, it was at times a tiring tap dance knowing that was your role, the funny one to balance the smart one.

"Can I draw while we wait for the pizza?" James asked, and Kate handed him one of the notepads in her bag.

"Me too. Let's play hangman, Mom," Piper said, with the enthusiasm of someone who doesn't know what she doesn't know and doesn't care. She held the pen between fingertips dark with marker from drawing on the ferry, and under crude gallows, drew seven horizontal lines. The resulting word would likely be unknowable to anyone but Piper.

Confident, the preschool teacher said. Willing to try new things. But so sensitive to criticism. When she saw she'd done something imperfectly — coloring outside the lines, writing too many *p*'s in her name — she would put down the crayon and walk away. Kate rarely corrected her daughter's efforts; it was not in her nature to impose perfection. But where had Piper's shame come from? Had a teacher chastised her too emphatically? A babysitter? It was so hard to account for what someone else might say to the children.

The waiter arrived with the pizza, fully loaded with vegetables and pepperoni. The children each took a slice and began plucking off toppings according to their dislikes.

"You going to call Max while you're here?" Chris folded a wedge and inverted it, letting grease drip onto the paper plate.

"Yeah. He needs the help even more this year."

Chris took a bite, and half of the slice disappeared. "I thought he was going to sell."

"He got an offer. He hasn't decided. But he has to do something."

"Well, it's a shame if he does." The bell on the pizzeria door jangled as another family walked in, parents with four small children. Chris watched as they took a booth on the far side of the room, and each of the kids sat calmly and picked up menus. "Did you call back that guy about the thing?"

Kate frowned, not following his train of thought. She watched Piper pick up the cheese shaker a second time, though her slice was already coated with a white mist. Kate tapped the girl's plate, signaling her to eat, and placed the cheese shaker back beside the other condiments.

"The job guy," Chris said. "Your friend's place opening in Dupont Circle." He removed a few broccoli florets touching his pepperoni and then each small square of green pepper, and piled them to the side like seeds from watermelon.

Kate's friend Anthony from culinary school had called just before they'd left for vacation. He'd accepted a chef position at a new restaurant opening in Washington, and wanted to submit Kate's name for pastry. It was a great opportunity. The menu would have an emphasis on organic locally grown ingredients, and the decor was being done by the team credited with design awards throughout the mid-Atlantic states.

She shook her head. "I haven't gotten around to calling him back."

"Too much." He nodded.

"No. It's not that. It's just —"

"Ow, it's hot!" Piper began to wail, holding her mouth.

"What? Oh, hon, you shook the red pepper flakes on it," Kate said, cupping a napkin around the girl's mouth. "You were only supposed to shake the *cheese*."

Chris took a fresh slice for Piper and placed the cheese shaker in front of her. "It's just what?" he asked Kate. James toyed with the pepper flakes, and edged the shaker back toward his sister's plate. Kate took it from him and moved it to the adjacent table.

"Just . . . I just have trouble imagining it," she said. "How it would work with the kids."

Restaurant hours were brutal. They would have to hire a nanny who could work creative hours, and when Chris traveled, long ones. They had done it once before. When Piper was a baby Kate had worked with a start-up bistro in town. The nights were late, and when she'd come home she would still be electrified, her thoughts crackling with menu combinations and disappointing vendors, so that many nights she'd needed herb tea with a NyQuil chaser to ease herself back to the home front. One morning she came downstairs to find she had left the stovetop burner on the night before, a menace of flame licking low for hours. For two weeks she'd been haunted by what might have happened — the spark and swell, Chris away and her in an antihistamine haze — and eventually she'd given notice at the restaurant. She had not been done in by the late hours so soon after having a baby, though that was what she told everyone, even Chris. What did her in was knowing she could be so engrossed in her work as to neglect her family's well-being, and she could not stand knowing that about herself.

"I don't see how it would work either. It's so complicated," Chris agreed. "I mean, what would we do, get full-time help? Or an au pair?" He glanced at the other family across the room. The four children were sitting quietly and drawing, a portrait of discipline and good behavior — testimony, no doubt, to a household with one stay-at-home parent, or two parents with complementary schedules.

She began to say, *Au pairs are cheaper*. But she stopped herself. It might seem as if she were referencing their finances, as if she were suggesting that a second income might be a useful thing. Such suggestions had not gone over well in the past.

"Pastry is usually more early mornings," she said, as if that would make it easier.

"Not in start-ups. You get sucked into

both. How would we cover a schedule like that?"

"Oh, I don't know, Chris. We could juggle, get creative. That's what people do when they love their work, don't they? They find a way to make it all happen?" They looked at each other across the table, entry-level adversarial. The kids noticed their change in tone and looked up.

"What are you guys talking about?" James asked.

"Just debating what we should do tomorrow," Kate said.

"I want to go to the beach. And play miniature golf," said James. "One in the morning, one in the afternoon. Then swim."

"Well, you can't do it all. Sometimes" — Chris wiped his mouth and glanced at Kate — "you have to make a choice."

Driving up-island at night was like traveling in space. There were no streetlights and few visible houses on Harvest Road, under its canopy of trees. Scrub oak and pitch pine were like dark walls along the sides, opening sporadically onto llama pastures like deep empty rooms.

When they turned onto their dirt driveway, rabbits scattered in the headlights. That rabbits had been the culprit behind a tularemia outbreak a few years back still amazed her. Two landscapers had died of the bacterial infection, and it had pitched the island into a frenzy. Although tularemia was rarely lethal, East Coast newspapers ran snarling rodent caricatures ("Bugs Bunnies!") and vacationers canceled their rentals. When Kate and Chris had decided to come anyway — the hype seemed silly, the odds of infection remote — they thought about splurging for a better rental because rates were so low. But in the end they'd come back to the bungalow. They really didn't need anything larger, the location was ideal, and the nostalgia outweighed the advantages of a more luxurious space.

Bunnies, benign as fairy-tale characters. Their dried droppings caused infection when they blew into the air and were inhaled, innocent as dust. She eyed the vanishing rabbits, and rubbed the side of her neck, tingling with a prickly heat.

If tularemia had broken out this year, the hype would not seem nearly as silly to her, nor the odds as remote. Odds didn't mean a thing.

Six

Kate rarely read the newspaper anymore. It lay where Chris had left it on the patio table, headlines half obscured by breakfast dishes. Phrases of alarm stood out among the empty cereal bowls and plates of jammy crust. TERRORISM FEARS PROMPT CIVILIAN CIPRO STASHES. And down the page, ENVIRONMENTAL TOXINS LINKED TO ILLNESS. She looked over the paper and to the yard. The children were playing croquet, jumping over wickets with their faces to the sun. ATTACKS IN SUBURBS.

Against her better judgment, she pushed a plate aside to see the rest of the article.

Officials Say Suicide-Bomb Attacks in Suburbs Would Be Impossible to Deter

. . . Washington officials conceded that if a terrorist were to enter a crowded public place such as a shopping mall or pedestrian plaza, there would be no way to detect or prevent a suicide bombing. "If someone is hell-bent on entering a public place and causing destruction," said one administration official requesting anonymity, "it is almost impossible to stop them." Another intelligence official warned of terror-cell interest in small-town attacks as a way to further shake U.S. confidence.

She put the plate back on the center of the paper and leaned back from the table, watching the children with her coffee held under her chin.

Each day it was something new, some danger unthinkable just the day before. In the beginning it had seemed anything was possible, that the television might break in with an emergency broadcast announcing a reservoir in California had been poisoned with anthrax, that mad cow disease had been found in U.S. livestock, Ebola was airborne at JFK Airport. The news no longer surprised her, which was not to say she was desensitized. It was more of an amazement that yet another way had been found to make her feel as if she stood in an Escher landscape, the most basic things gone demented.

She'd always followed common precautions. A fire extinguisher in the kitchen, a burglar alarm on the house. But the nature of danger had changed in the past year. A few months ago, there'd been a scare that someone had tampered with the D.C. water supply, and not long after, a bomb threat had forced the evacuation of the Metro while she'd waited for a train. For thirty minutes she'd moved slowly upward and out through the tunnels, the pack of frightened commuters craning their necks for the scent of information.

What little could be done, she had done. If things became untenable in Washington, a friend's cabin in rural Maryland would be their retreat, and the car was stocked with bottled water and canned goods. She and Chris had decided together on the cabin — most people they knew in the District had a designated place — but she'd loaded the car supplies herself, tucking the heavy cardboard box in the corner of the trunk. When he'd seen it, he'd rolled his eyes. *You've got to be kidding me. This is Washington, D.C., Kate, not Chernobyl.* She'd laughed along, and removed it. So far, he hadn't noticed the supply in the spare-tire well.

She pushed the newspaper aside and

drank the last of her coffee, which was also the last of the coffee at the house. Kate picked up her pen and began jotting a grocery list, beginning with breakfast ingredients and ending with staples for their favorite dinners. *Rice wine vinegar, ginger, chicken breasts.* In the yard the kids had moved from playing croquet to playing dirt shower, a wash of grass and soil over each other's heads. *Laundry detergent,* she added. *Shampoo.*

But tonight she would not be cooking, at least not beyond something easy for the children. They had arranged for a sitter from a list of college students on the island, and were celebrating their anniversary at their favorite restaurant. Phlox had opened five years before as an eclectic café in the woods, and had developed a cult following for fresh seafood and its organic produce grown in back. Soon the newspapers and magazines took note, and it had expanded with a lounge, which had drawn the kind of patrons seeking the new hot thing. Reservations became harder to get, even if the quality was lost on much of the clientele, who would have eaten sea bass from tanks slicked with algae if it were printed on the menu in a trendy font.

She should have been looking forward to

dinner, great food prepared and cleared by someone else. She would style her hair and put on her pink sundress, the one too feminine for her taste but that Chris liked. They would have a glass of wine and comment upon the bar crowd, and have uninterrupted conversation that was broad and worldly, like the old days. Her edgy humor would return and he'd smile at her in the loose way that showed pleasure unrelated to his work, and when they returned to the bungalow, the sitter would be hastily paid and there would be no flossing before bed.

But that apathy was creeping in again, the sense she'd had lately that things didn't quite live up to their billing, so why bother. It was the same ambivalence and letdown she'd felt a few weeks before, out to dinner with friends. She genuinely liked the women, other mothers from Piper's preschool, but had had a sense of dislocation all evening. She couldn't get in sync with the conversation and humor, and her responses felt a quarter-beat off. Home renovations had never been her forte. But even when they'd talked about their kids' activities she would fish for a contribution and come up empty. None of it mattered; she was unable to shake the sense that none of it could be counted upon to last.

94

She had started feeling this way after Elizabeth's death, but instead of fading as the months passed, it intensified. Sometimes it was a fog, a sense that she had not a single thought in her head worth sharing; sometimes it was a growing panic that at any moment something could go very wrong. She'd always been conscious of her family's safety, but this was different. Danger was everywhere and nowhere, immediate and elusive, and no one was prepared. It was as if she alone could smell it, subtle as the metallic first moment of rain.

She hadn't said anything to Chris, unable to imagine it. But she could imagine his response. After he stopped smiling, because surely his first thought would be that she was kidding, his look would change from one of identification to one of sympathy. He would suggest that she should get out more often — join a gym and get back to swimming, perhaps join one of those women chefs networking clubs. He might even take it as evidence that she should accept this new job after all, that staying at home was making her loony. Or worse, think privately that she was too loony to handle working, and that she should find "someone to talk to," because it was quite a thing, to lose a friend, and well, maybe everything that followed had hit her especially hard too. The fact of his suggesting it would be enormous, because he was an own-bootstraps sort of man and *therapy* was not part of his lexicon. That was her fear: not professional help, which had occurred to her but which she believed wasn't necessary, but that Chris would look at her and see instability, weakness.

It had been a long time since they'd gone out to dinner together, just the two of them. She could envision a staggered silence, one line of conversation after another failing to catch hold until they finally chatted about the weather expected the next day and whether to go to the beach. There were many evenings back home when they moved around and past one another, wordless for hours at their own tasks. She was thankful for the few hours of quiet focus, but at moments, she felt the loss of quiet companionship, a like-minded silence. Their daily lives were so different; she could no longer say for sure they were of like mind.

Was it possible, she wondered, to have solitude together? She tried to imagine what he would do if after dinner she went to his study back home with her book or her laptop, and sat on the couch there instead of in the living room, as they had in the early years. He might glance over the top of his computer with a look of surprise and then a smile of welcome. *Hey there.* Or there might be a moment's hesitation. She'd sit quietly nearby, each of them feeling the weight of the other in the room and a dampening of his or her own thoughts, each looking up expectantly when the other shifted in a chair or looked off into the middle distance. She might offer a snippet of commentary about something she was reading, but it would not be easily understood out of context. After an hour or so she would stand and stretch, murmur that she thought she'd call it a night, and the following night she'd go back to the living room. It was a gift, solitude. But solitude with another person, that was an art.

She'd never thought about Elizabeth and Dave in that way. But if she had, she would have imagined them smoothly companionable. Elizabeth reading a book while Dave sat on the leather couch reviewing promotional materials for some new piece of golf equipment. When he got up for a cup of coffee or a dish of ice cream and asked in his folksy way if she wanted something, she'd smile at his thoughtfulness. Or maybe that wasn't it at all. Maybe she had wished he'd be the kind of man to walk back in with two glasses of wine, step in front of the television, and lift the book out of her hands. Maybe in truth there had been a lot of invisible wishing.

For two nights Kate had been reading the journal in the loft long after the last of the boats returned across the dark harbor, running lights trailing like phosphorescent fish. The second night she'd opened the notebook with hesitation. If she'd had to guess what her friend had been like in high school, Kate would have imagined a fresh-scrubbed yearbook editor, an all-American girl who babysat for the neighborhood. This emerging person was significantly less sunny, more independent and creative, but much lonelier. Kate found herself wishing for a photo, wondering whether she had been fashionable once, before she became the kind of mother who wore dangling pumpkin earrings at Halloween.

Last night's entries followed Elizabeth through her senior year of high school. There was a tremendous amount of writing; Elizabeth recorded details the way others whispered observations to friends. She'd passed the time waiting for college acceptance letters by painting and holding odd jobs. Like her friends, she experimented with alcohol; drinking at weekend parties made her feel indistinct, blurring the line where she ended and others began. She and Michael would sit in his car with the radio on. When he kissed her, he cupped her jaw in one hand and didn't slip his hand up under her shirt right away, which she saw as a sign of his integrity. She held out hope that soon he'd ask her to sit alone with him during lunch in the cafeteria, as the couples did.

Her art teacher recommended her to a gallery that carried the work of new artists, and she wrote giddily of the sale of two pieces for $100 each. She kept her favorite; a sketch of it in her journal showed a Warhol-style canvas of repetitive, overlapping bicycle wheels. Finally a thick envelope arrived from NYU.

She wrote in the journal all spring and summer, pages filled with longing for closer friends, a more conventional mother, a real relationship with Michael. But as the months passed and her hopes were not met, the tenor of her adolescent wishing cooled. She met Michael more often at night, but stopped dreaming he'd ask her to share a table in the cafeteria, and stopped hinting that her family used to be larger when he expressed no curiosity or concern.

The grandfather clock gonged once from the darkness downstairs, and Kate forced herself to close the book. Don't, Kate felt herself urging. Don't trust him. Though of course whatever was done, was done.

SEVEN

A breeze lifted the edge of the tablecloth as the sommelier opened the wine and poured an inch for Kate. She gave the glass a small swirl, small because she disliked wine showmanship, and nodded at the taste. He poured two glasses, and left quietly.

The outdoor patio was new, an enhancement like the lounge that had been added after positive reviews in national food publications. Around the flagstone deck, conical topiaries corralled the guests so they did not push back chairs into the organic gardens. Kate and Chris had been seated by the maître d' near the koi pond, too close. If she were to drop her knife it would enter the water like a harpoon.

Last summer, in the area where they now sat, there had been only four outdoor tables on a balcony overlooking raised flower beds and rows of mesclun. The tables had been positioned so privately that during dessert

101

Chris had slid a hand under her dress, fingers cool from his wineglass trailing condensation on her thigh.

Chris leaned back in his chair, one steel leg inches from the pond's edge, and smiled. He enjoyed it when she ordered the wine, spoke confidently of menu items and pairings. Kate could feel his pleasure in the way he watched her hand on the glass and her lips on the rim, felt his eyes on her throat as she tipped the glass upward. He pinched his fingernail in the cork and looked at her across the table. "I like that dress. You look nice tonight."

"So do you." She meant it. Summer agreed with him. In spite of his coppery coloring, the sun browned his face rather than ruddied it, and brought out the gold in hair threaded with gray. His neck was strong against the collar and his chin hadn't gone soft. Any weight he'd gained when he gave up smoking had been beaten back with diet and exercise.

She glanced down at his shoes, tan loafers. "Decided to leave the eco-sandals at home tonight?"

"You don't like them? I thought they'd be your thing." He flexed a foot alongside the table. "I picked them up on the Seattle trip last month. The hotel was threatening one of those team-building ropes courses."

"You love those."

"Right up there with trust falls and meditations around a campfire." They shared a knowing smile about forced group intimacy.

Noise from the lounge came through the doorway, the sociable sound of a party where everyone knows one another. At the back of the patio it was quieter. Fireflies blinked beyond the topiaries, and a light wind rustled the square of linen in Kate's lap. Koi rested, darted, and went still.

Chris folded his hands across his stomach and looked at her in a way that she read as expectant. She smiled in the absence of anything to say. She continued to think and smile as the seconds passed, and her mouth felt carved of wood.

"What's wrong?" he asked.

"Wrong? Nothing. Why?"

"You just seem a little quiet." He looked off across the patio, and there was another pause. It was her turn. A flush heated the side of her neck, and she rested cool fingertips against it.

"So what's going on with that Seattle project?" she tried. "Is it going to happen?"

"Probably. It's a great location. It's going to take some renovations and a lot of marketing, but it could work."

Across the patio a tray clattered, a glass broke, and a woman recoiled from the splash. There were exclamations about a dress, apologies given, soda water rushed in. Grumblings continued for several moments. Kate looked back to Chris and worked to recall the topic.

"So are you going to have to go out there much?"

"Probably a few more times. They'll be quickies." He smiled, amused; he knew she wasn't that interested in the Seattle project. "I was thinking we might be able to turn one into a vacation. We could take the kids hiking around Mount Rainier, and get a ferry over to Vancouver Island. Didn't you know someone from school who opened up a B and B over there?"

The waiter arrived with their appetizers and placed a bowl of steamed mussels in front of Chris, a beet Gorgonzola salad before her. The cubed beets bloodied the white of the blue-veined cheese.

She imagined bringing James and Piper to Seattle, going to the fish market and then to Mount Rainier, marching up mountain trails into the thin cloud cover. They'd ferry across Puget Sound to Canada and stroll past the Parliament building and moored yachts, go for high tea at the hotel that was like a castle. They might love it so much that they would want to stay. When she'd traveled in her twenties, she'd sewn a maple leaf on her backpack like most people she knew, the well-known tactic for avoiding anti-American sentiment abroad. Their children would grow up drinking pure glacial water and speaking in sentences that lifted at the end like constant questions, safe from those waging war against the more controversial neighbor to the south. She took a bite of beet, and licked red from the tines of her fork.

Chris ordered dessert and handed the menu to the waiter. She took the last sip of her wine, her second glass. The effervescence went to her eyes and scalp, her fingers and lips, all weightless and animated. The morning's concerns seemed silly. They were doing fine. She was fine. Maybe she just needed to get out of the house more often; it might be as simple as that.

He leaned back in his chair, crossed his hands over his stomach. "You were reading those journals pretty late again last night," he said.

She picked up the bottle and poured a small amount in her glass, then tipped the last into his. "It's strange, reading about the way a person thinks her life is going to go and she has no idea what's coming. When Elizabeth was young she really loved art. She wanted to be a painter in New York."

He pushed his glass back and forth, watching the wine slide and cling, and looked around the patio. "Do you know yet what she was doing with that Michael guy?"

That's what it always came down to in the end. The single greatest point of interest about a woman's thirty-eight years was not what she had done, but what she hadn't told anyone she'd done.

"No," she said. "I'm still reading about high school. It's sad. She was a pretty lonely teenager and didn't have a great relationship with her parents."

"That doesn't sound like Elizabeth."

"I know. It's like I'm reading about a stranger."

The playgroup had formed arbitrarily, eight new mothers grouped together by the town Newcomers' Club. Kate had found them a bit much in the beginning, too polished too early in the morning, and their conversations had had no edge, no spice. But over the three years she'd been part of the group, they'd settled into a camaraderie: parties for the celebrations, meals cooked for the crises. Kate had felt closest to Elizabeth; with her, she hadn't worked to fill silences when it felt as if there was nothing in particular to say. In the quiet she'd felt tacit understanding of . . . she didn't know what, exactly. The simple things, the important things. But silences, like solitude, could contain any amount of comfort or discomfort, any degree of truth.

"I still can't believe she never told me about her sister." As she said "sister," Kate was thinking *affair*.

"Maybe she just got used to keeping it to herself. Or the time was never right. It was years before our CFO told me he was a recovering alcoholic." Then Chris thought a moment. "You know Andy, our communications director?"

"Sure. The guy we had dinner with? And his wife, just before we moved."

"I just found out she's actually his second wife. His first wife, the mother of their kids, died of cancer a few years ago."

Kate tried to remember their dinner together, whether there was anything that came up that would have suggested that it was a second marriage. "He just mentioned it now? You guys travel a lot together."

"A decent amount. Like I said, I guess it just never came up."

The waiter brought their desserts, a

cheesecake with pomegranate sauce for Chris, a fondue for Kate. She speared a chain of berries and swirled it in small chocolate circles. The impression of the fruit stayed for a few seconds, then smoothed itself as if the fruit had never made a mark.

"The fifteenth was Elizabeth's birthday. She would have been thirty-nine." Kate stroked at the surface of the chocolate with the long, thin fork. "Last year on her birthday Emily was only a month old. A year ago at this time, they had no idea what was ahead of them." She wondered what had been on Elizabeth's mind as she blew out her candles. Each year Kate always thought *happy and healthy family,* but on her own thirty-eighth birthday three months before, her wish had struck her as meaningless. How happy is happy? How healthy is healthy?

"I wonder if she would have done anything differently if she could have known it was her last year."

Chris studied her, quiet a moment. "You do that a lot these days."

"Do what?"

"Look back. Analyze in hindsight. 'A year ago today.' 'At this time two months ago.' " He stretched his legs, and his knees gave a small pop, one first and then the other. "I don't understand why you find that so interesting."

He said it as though he were merely curious, but something else was there too. Patience. Or impatience. One done carefully enough was sometimes a mask for the other.

"Well, I guess it's poignant, looking back at the person who doesn't know what's about to hit her. To think that someone can be going along, naïve and content, having no idea a major event is about to shake up her world. Sometimes I wonder how we'd live if we could know in advance."

The levity she'd felt from the wine had dissipated, and now she felt only tired. She did not remember how she'd gotten into this line of conversation, but it was not where she wanted to be. She looked over her shoulder for the waiter. She needed a transition; a cup of coffee, maybe a glass of port.

"Well, whatever's going to happen is whatever's going to happen, and the person of a year ago couldn't know it," he said. "It doesn't cast any judgment on the person you were, or make you naïve."

She'd touched a nerve. "It's not a judgment." He minded the notion that a person could be accountable for what he hadn't known and had not done. "It's just a point of curiosity. If anything, it's a reality check for the way you're living today. Take that bomb scare in the Metro. . . ."

He shook his head. "You have to let that go, Kate. It was a false alarm."

So slowly, in the dim tunnel. They'd all moved up and out so slowly. She was sure she'd smelled smoke, had put her hand to her mouth anticipating the choke and burn.

The fondue fork shook in her fingers, and she placed it on the dessert plate. "I know. That's not the point."

"The point is that you're fine, the kids are fine, we're all fine. You never know what's going to happen, so just live each day with no regrets, no loose ends. Right?"

That wasn't her point at all. She frowned at the chocolate.

"I just wish you'd move past that 'one day left to live' mind-set, Kate. That flashback thinking, dwelling on the past, trying to figure out how to live differently because of what you didn't see coming. It doesn't help. It doesn't make anything turn out differently." He flicked a few crumbs from the table into the pool, and the fat koi turned toward them mechanically.

Flashback thinking. That was one way of putting it. He wasn't wrong; in the past year it had become a reflexive part of her mental toolbox, the way she measured and made sense of time. *On this day last year.* As if it were possible to wrinkle a gap in time and align two moments side by side, to let the knowledge of the later moment rub shoulders with the naïveté of the first, and soften the blow. There was the person she'd been before last autumn, when the world had gone all wrong not once but twice. And there was the person she was after.

"You know," he said, sticking his fork into the last of the cheesecake, "I read that there's a baby boom coming, all the people who reacted to the past year by hunkering down, having another kid. Investing in the future, optimism and hope, all that stuff."

He was using his nonchalant voice, or rather his trying-to-be-nonchalant voice, looking down at his dessert plate. But he glanced up to see how she was reacting to his words, flashing a crooked smile.

She laughed, incredulous. "You're serious. Even with your travel schedule, you're serious?"

"It's gotten better. You know it's better than it was." That was true. It was also true that she had become accustomed to his travel, and that there were small compensations. She cooked more simply. There were fewer sounds to wake her in the night. When he'd first begun to travel so much, she would not have thought she'd come to feel this way.

Kate shook her head. "What happened to Mr. Two and Through?"

"Well, we're doing a pretty good job of two, aren't we? Tell me these aren't two of the happiest, most well-adjusted kids around."

"Sometimes."

"Sometimes."

Kate thought of Emily Martin on her lap, curious sausage fingers reaching for the food on her plate. The smell of her baby shampoo. She would be lying if she said it hadn't crossed her mind. But not in a long while. It seemed a dangerous thing, having more children than hands.

When they arrived back at the house and paid the sitter, Chris said he wanted to walk down to the beach, get some fresh air and check out the ships in the harbor. Kate peeked into the kids' room, tucked Piper's splayed legs back under the covers and retrieved James's stuffed dinosaur from the floor, the one he claimed not to sleep with anymore. The light was already on in the master bedroom, and she stepped out of the pink dress and pulled on a black tank top. She would not be reading the notebooks tonight.

She brushed her teeth and rushed through her facial regimen, some anti-aging foolishness recommended by a dermatological spa. She'd won a free consultation in the preschool auction but that's where the free part had ended, and she still felt buyer's remorse each time she opened the two tiny bottles of serum. That's what they'd called it — serum — with the gravity of something that sprang from James Bond's briefcase, most likely to justify its cost. Still, she'd bought them. Well, what if there was something to it, the molecular sugars, the unpronounceable acids? Why was it hard to believe that things you couldn't see or understand might help, when God knows there were plenty that did harm? She turned away from the mirror and clicked off the bathroom light.

When she stepped back into the bedroom she noticed a notebook lying open on her bed. It was the same size as the rest of Elizabeth's journals but with an unfamiliar cover, apparently one from deeper in the trunk. The closet door was open. So was the trapdoor at the top of the ladder. Why would the babysitter go snooping? How would she know about the loft, or care about the notebooks?

The back door opened and closed with the soft sound of someone trying not to wake children, and Kate moved the notebook to her nightstand. Chris appeared in the doorway, hair windblown and shirt unbuttoned, and leaned against the frame looking at her in the tight threadbare tank.

In a marriage certain things become predictable, certain signals and routines, and Kate felt the women's magazines had it wrong when they wrote off predictability as a bad thing. Questions and answers are conveyed in a shorthand of touch so that no one's feelings need be hurt with mixed messages. A hand on the shoulder means one thing, a hand on the lower back, another; a glancing kiss on the cheek, good night, but a half second longer, not good night. Even an old tank top could have a translation. Not good night.

So after they'd rolled apart from one another in bed and he turned back toward her a moment later, kissed her slowly, then hesitated, she knew the shorthand. *We're okay, right?* He'd been dismissive at dinner and he knew it; it hadn't precluded intimacy, but it didn't necessarily mean all was forgotten, either. She could return the kiss, drawing it out in the same way he had, re-

114

assure him that there was no offense taken and that all was as it always had been. No matter that all wasn't, not quite. But that was not on the table at the moment, the subtle drift. Nor was the fact that the desire that used to come so naturally, the instincts, the intentions, and the effectiveness of touch, no longer came quite so naturally.

When she returned the kiss, she drew it out a moment longer than usual. *We're okay.*

As she did she tasted something under the toothpaste she hadn't noticed before, a flavor that was not Pinot Noir or cheesecake or mussels. Sharp and acrid, layered under toothpaste and mouthwash, was the bite of tobacco.

No, she thought. Oh, no. You worked so hard.

She imagined him on the beach. Looking over his shoulder to be sure the house was out of view before lighting up, face low to his cupped hand, inhaling deeply and squinting his eyes in appreciation of the pleasure, a pleasure made richer for having to enjoy it in secret.

EIGHT

The months Chris had struggled to stop smoking had not been their proudest as a couple. Shortly after they had gotten engaged, Kate urged him to quit. He knew the gloom-and-doom statistics but claimed not to believe them, blaming an overzealous medical establishment, health extremists, the media.

Then one day he announced he had quit. He did not want to dwell on his methods or his achievement — he had just wanted to do the thing quietly. Only as it turned out, he never had. During the months between his vow to stop and her discovery that he hadn't, there were times she'd found stubs in his apartment, matches in his car. Those were from the old days, he'd say with a wave of the hand, or they belonged to someone else. Once he'd looked her in the eye, forthright and calm, and told her what she smelled on him was not in fact cigarette smoke. It was as if he were telling her the earth was flat, and she faced him trying to reconcile contradictory things she knew to be true. This was how tobacco smelled. And: Chris did not lie.

He was so matter-of-fact in this and other denials that when she learned the truth, she was more than hurt by his dishonesty. She was embarrassed by her own naïveté, and with this new feeling of being found a fool, it was as if something in her definition of herself had slipped off its rails.

They had moved on, because it was just smoking after all. But two things stayed with her: his ability to conceal, and the proof that she could be blind to something so close at hand.

Long after Chris rolled over and his breathing went deep and steady, Kate was still awake. When it was clear she wouldn't be getting to sleep, she climbed the stairs into the loft with the journal she'd found open on her bed. Before she returned it to the trunk she held it a moment; the book was several years beyond the one she was currently reading. She flipped through a few of the pages, saw the phrase "my punishment," and began to read.

But as she did she felt a movement on her

shoulder, or in her shoulder. It wasn't a touch exactly, likely just the quiver of tired muscles, but the sensation was one of being touched, the way a grandmother would place a gentle reminding hand on a child's shoulder. Up the length of her arm the follicles puckered. Each pale hair rose on her tanned skin. She gave a cautious sidelong look, knowing even as she did that she would not see anything, or anyone. Then, slowly, she put the book back in the trunk.

She sat down on the chaise with the older notebook she'd been reading, the one that had begun Elizabeth's college years.

October 5, 1981 NYU

I was smart, I was careful, but not smart or careful enough. It's inconceivable. (Terrible word choice.) I have no idea what to do.

That's not true. I know.

Stupid, stupid girl. And I'll have to deal with this myself, because calling Michael is out of the question after how he acted at the end of summer. I told him about Anna and the accident, and by the time I finished I was bawling like a baby, and he acted as if I'd just signed him up for couples therapy. When I left for school I gave him my new number at the dorm, and he looked at it like he couldn't wait to throw it away.

Last night after I found out, I couldn't stand to be around anyone so I went walking. Washington Square to Union Square up Park Avenue, up to Grand Central, up to the park, past the Plaza, where a bride was fairytaling her dumb way down the steps, then back down to Gramercy and turned onto 20th, and sat in front of the fence facing the National Arts Club, where I swore just last week that I'd have an exhibit someday.

I sat there for a long time. It's just the most spectacular little building, brilliant people going in the door and appearing up in that big bay window a few minutes later holding a glass of wine, and even the way these people scratch their noses is creative and sophisticated. They look immune to everything, like nothing disastrous ever happens to derail their plans. Is it possible to take a detour like quitting college and working to raise a kid by yourself, and still end up standing in that parlor soaking up compliments on your exhibition? Not likely. I can't envision a single solitary scenario that makes any sense at all. I have no business being a mother. I'm barely responsible for myself.

My appointment is next week. It's just a tiny ball of cells, like a yogurt culture or something. This is what I tell myself.

Kate had to read the entry and the next few pages several times. It was not the disbelief that Elizabeth had had an abortion, or that she had never told Kate. It was how little Elizabeth appeared to dwell upon it, or at least not in writing. After the next page, it was no longer mentioned.

Reading about Elizabeth's college years was like fiction, it bore so little resemblance to the woman Kate had known. Elizabeth had thrown herself into the New York art scene. She joined a student artists' collective and worked on mixed-media exhibitions. Photos wedged between the pages showed unusually shaped canvases with bold patterns, some with ribbons from competitions, all signed in the lower right corner, Elizabeth D.

Her writing was alternately angry and detached, then at times coolly independent. She declared her major in psychology, and spooled theories about what makes people do the things that they do. She wrote frequently with curiosity about her mother — the privacy, the obsession with self-help literature. Mentions of her father were infrequent. He came into the city occasionally to take her to dinner and once came to one of her exhibits, but she fumed after he said her portraits reminded him of Van Gogh. (*I'm sure the only thing he could think of to say because it's the only PAINTER he could think of.*) She stayed in New York over the summer, amassing extra psych credits with an aim toward spending a junior semester abroad studying art in Florence.

In her sophomore year Elizabeth lived in an industrial walk-up on Avenue A with two women from the collective, Haviland and Rue, and their apartment became a gathering place for artists and writers. They smoked clove cigarettes and bought cases of cheap wine, and admired the works of Georgia O'Keeffe and Frida Kahlo. Toward the end of her sophomore year she mentioned dating a few men, one Vietnamese, and another Pakistani. Her writing about race and culture suggested she was either worldly in her loves, or in love with the idea of being worldly.

A photo paper-clipped to a page showed her nestled on a couch between two flamboyant women. Kate pulled the photograph from the paper clip and held it between her thumb and forefinger. Elizabeth was almost unrecognizable. Her hair was cut in an asymmetrical style, the left side reaching to her chin, the right side buzzed to a curve above her ear. She was curled affectionately toward a woman with wild dark hair and heavy kohl liner around her eyes, smoking theatrically with her chin in the air. Kate held the picture up close, as if bringing it nearer would make it more believable.

Elizabeth's parents were paying her tuition, but she worked at a café in the West Village to cover rent and supplies, earning tips that equaled *about a tube of cadmium an hour.* She loved the café, the preopening ritual of grinding the coffee du jour and frothing the perfect cappuccino foam, spooned from the tin pitcher in the consistency of stiff whipped cream. But she wrote critically about the patrons, corporate types who talked about *buying a cute place like this someday,* and mothers who strollered in with loud children, stayed too long, and left in their wake all the whining and crumbs. *Why bring kids to coffee shops? The moms aren't happy, the kids aren't happy, and the people around them sure aren't.*

Kate read, both chastised and amused. You did this, she thought. We did this, together, all of the time.

Kate had not been the exuberant babysitting type herself, yet she'd always found children entertaining — mispronunciations, boots on the wrong feets, costumes worn long after Halloween. She hadn't planned a timetable for parenthood; children would doubtless happen, her thinking had gone; at least she'd hoped they would, when the time was right.

Elizabeth's dismissiveness about children was strange. How did someone who did not enjoy the company of children, who felt them to be an irritation, come to so thoroughly embrace not just her own but all the children in their playgroup? The pictures didn't jibe.

Elizabeth didn't write about her semester in Florence so much as she drew it, page after page of art and architecture, parks with sculptural trees, Florentine bustle with commentary in the margins. She'd drawn the Duomo, reworking its bell towers from many angles. She sketched the commercial curve of the Ponte Vecchio, and the statues and fountains of the Boboli Gardens. An entire section of one notebook was dedicated to Michelangelo's *David*. To Kate's untrained eye, the drawings were the work of a gifted hand, realistic sketches on one page and offbeat departures from them on the next. She couldn't imagine being this talented at anything, then simply giving it up.

In Florence, Elizabeth lived in a small pension near the Pitti Palace with a handful of students in her program, and appeared to spend a good amount of time with the house's *patrona* and her three young children. There were domestic sketches, a square-faced woman chopping at the counter, a young boy feeding cats, curls unruly over his collar. Recipes written in the margin for carbonara and chestnut cake, the best starter for two-day bread.

When the semester ended Elizabeth decided to stay longer, and her adviser agreed to freeze her student status. Her mother visited her then, and it was clear to Elizabeth that the agenda was to convince her to return to school. *She showed her true wacky colors: It's about finishing something, she said, seeing it through. It's bad karma to leave your life out of balance.* Elizabeth stayed through the fall, took a night job at a trattoria and spent several days a week working for an art instructor in Santo Spirito, cleaning brushes and handling registrations in exchange for work space in his studio.

Kate flipped through the pages as if she

were viewing a travelogue. She'd been to exotic places with Chris and had done a few foreign locations for her cooking program, but had never been to Italy. In fact, she'd never been out of the U.S. for more than a week at a time, never long enough to participate in the culture of a place as more than a spectator. The times she'd talked with Elizabeth about how she envied Chris his trips, Elizabeth had listened with her attentive smile, but had only mentioned passingly her semester abroad.

In Florence, Elizabeth sounded happier than Kate had ever read in her journals. It was not just a matter of pleasure or confidence, though they both played a part. There was an optimism to the way she wrote about her circumstances and her future; there was no sense of longing to be anywhere other than where she was. Yet it was still not the friend she had known. Kate struggled to put her finger on the difference: It was a matter of vitality, and of candor. Not the tranquil observer she'd become.

September 17, 1984

It's unnerving how I don't have a constant take on my own work. I'll roll along for a week loving it, then walk into the studio one day and think it's crap, all derivative clichéd garbage, the light all wrong and about as original as a Hallmark card. I'll get desperate over it for hours, certain I'm wasting my time, a caricature of a kid playacting and I should go home and finish my degree. Then I'll work at the trattoria and wait a few days, and when I go back to the studio it doesn't look so bad. A new day, a new light.

November 29, 1984

Dad called last night, rang the house phone at Signora P's, which he's never done before. Made small talk, which is not his thing, asking when I was coming home. What is it, Dad, just say it.

Your mother is sick, he said. She shouldn't be living by herself anymore.

She downplayed it of course when I called, and was mad that Dad had told me. But she sounded awful and didn't fight me when I lied and said that I'd already booked my ticket home. I can't get a straight answer beyond the fact that it's not a surprise to her, she's apparently been sick for a while.

Tomorrow I'll put my paintings in a ship-

126

ping container and collect my pay at the trattoria to cover my rent to Sra P. When I told her I was leaving, she was washing dishes. I sat on the stool in the corner, the cracked wooden one that always seems just about to break, and rubbed the cat's head with my knuckles. I said I had to fly home in a few days, told her my mother was sick, or at least best I could in my limited Italian. She stopped, hands dripping above the sink, asked what it was. I didn't know the word for cancer so I patted my chest. She thought I meant heart — mal di cuore? — and I struggled for something other than what the men on the street say about women. Mammella. The cat battered his head against my legs like a baby goat and I leaned down to pretend to be interested in him, but Sra P knew better.

Cara mia, she said, and walked over and hugged me, leaving wet marks on my back.

NINE

The bike path ran along the northernmost stretch of Great Rock, a five-mile loop that extended to the lobster-boat docks, passing through conservation land and the meadow of a llama farm known for its hand-dyed wool. It was too far for Piper to ride and she had paired off with Chris, fishing. They claimed responsibility for dinner, if not by rods then by way of the fish shop by the docks.

Five miles of biking was a reasonable goal for James. Back home, Kate had taken him on a three-mile ride early one Saturday morning in the spring. A residue of sunrise had still stained the sky as they'd ridden past the monuments and around the tidal basin, cherry blossoms dusting the trees like a late-season snowstorm. They tried to see the White House, but some latest terrorist threat had scrambled security forces into defensive positions. So they peered from behind tall barricades trying to catch a glimpse of the famous white pillars. As they stood staring, the presidential helicopter had flown above and away, *chuck-chuck-chucking* in a sky trailing pink. Watching it grow small in the distance Kate had felt extraordinarily earthbound, tethered in every way.

For years, traveling as a family had been something undertaken with determination, their agility weighed by bulky gear and days defined by naps, meals, moods. It had seemed as if those years would last forever, though a small part of her wished they would. Memories of even the difficult times — children crying themselves to exhaustion in cars, planes, hotels — were beginning to take on the cast of nostalgia. She had watched them fall asleep at last, puffy mouths gone slack, with equal parts relief and heartbreak. They would never, she'd thought, be as fully hers as they were at that moment of surrender. The dawn of traveling freedom shimmered ahead. But Kate suspected this, like other things that surprised her, would come with a wistfulness for what had passed too quickly.

The paved path ran parallel to Harvest Road, wide enough for two bikers to ride abreast or to pass in opposite directions. Between the path and the road was a low split-rail fence that trellised in some sections with unkempt wild roses, in others with poison ivy. The fields to their right grew with black huckleberry and sweet fern and rolled hill upon creasing hill down to the tidal pond. Plover Neck Sanctuary was Kate's favorite place to ride. Elsewhere on the island swaths of fields and marshes were being clear-cut for development, but the sanctuary had been secured. The land was following its natural ebb and flow, the fields in slow transition to woodland. Uphill from the tidal pond, white spruce and Scotch pine grew in stealth, a silent guerrilla movement encroaching on the meadow.

A line of riders approached from the other direction, and Kate could see James teeter, rattled by the pressure of keeping his bike to the side. The greater his concentration to avoid them, the more his bike followed the magnetic pull of suggestion. Resistance stiffened his small earnest back.

"James, just keep on looking straight ahead. You're doing great," Kate called to him. The riders passed one by one, giving him wide berth. The last one, a woman about ten years older than Kate, gave her a knowing smile. *So sweet*, it said. And

Passes so fast.

After they'd gone by, he pressed the pedals backward and slowed with a small skid. "Stopping," he called back to her. "I'm stopping for a water break."

That was his pattern: press himself to do the thing, then stop immediately once he was in the clear. Angst, achievement, relax. He was tense about taking risks, always had been. But lately he'd begun trying to pretend otherwise, blasé when he was successful and feigning indifference when he was not. It was like watching a documentary on developmental psychology playing out before her eyes, the emerging skills shaped with the attributes of each parent — Chris's natural aptitudes, Kate's intense focus. Subtle, but so much change in him in such a short time. It reminded her of a sign in the hospital where she'd delivered both kids, lettered in Crayola colors and hung over the door of the nursery. "If You Look Closely Enough You Can See Us Growing!"

Of course change didn't happen in tangible bursts, but if she went back to work it would seem as if it did. She would come home one night to hear from the nanny that James's bike was missing. When she prodded, he'd admit he left it in the front bushes the day before, which she wouldn't have noticed when she drove in late at night. Press further, and she'd hear that he had been teased by older boys who could pop wheelies when he couldn't, and that he didn't want to ride his bike anymore, and wanted to take up something tough, like karate. And she wouldn't know any of it until the bike had gone missing, 80 percent of the way through the drama.

Elizabeth had been the first to know about almost everything, because almost everything had taken place at her house. She'd never worked outside the home once her children were born. There'd once been a career in advertising, some department assistant position, but it was hard to say because she rarely talked about her old career, or much of anything about her life before children. She'd treated her singlehood as if those years were uninteresting to her, details of a forgettable novel read long ago. Yet the episodes of her life in Florence reminded Kate of the rich travelogues of writers who'd lived abroad, people who had discovered themselves through their fascination with another culture and their pleasure at finding themselves embraced by it as well. Since reading the Florentine journals, Kate's sense of loss when she thought of Elizabeth had changed. It had become tinged with a bitterness of having been denied something she'd not been given, not quite, but under different circumstances might have.

Kate and James sat in the grass at the edge of the llama farm with their water bottles. She unwrapped a granola bar, split it in two, and passed him half. "You're getting good on the bike. Does it feel very different to ride a two-wheeler on a bike path?"

"Not really, just more fun."

Kate looked across the meadow at the llamas, moving with their distinctive fussy walk and leading with their lips, as if they had something they couldn't wait to tell the others.

"Once a long time ago before I met your dad, I went to a country called Peru —"

"I know about Peru, Mom," he said, impatient.

"Okay. Well, I heard about a farm where they made beautiful sweaters from the wool of their own llamas. There was a field like this full of them, and I drove around and around trying to find the farmhouse. But I got lost and the road only led to the top of a cliff, so I had to turn around and leave without ever finding the farm. It was the strangest thing, like the llamas lived all by

133

themselves on a farm in the middle of Peru, taking care of themselves."

He peeled back the paper and scrutinized the bite he was about to take, sizing up the bits of cranberry and sunflower seeds and considering whether they should be taken off, like vegetables from pizza.

"How does a mom get lost?"

"Get lost?" Kate paused, uncertain. Was he looking for truth, or reassurance that she wouldn't?

"Well, just like anybody else. I need maps and stuff, and sometimes I take a wrong turn. But I've been on this trail lots of times."

He fanned a fly trying to land on his snack bar. "That's not what I mean. How did Mrs. Martin lose her mom?"

Ah, that kind of lost. Kate stopped chewing, tried to register what he knew and how he knew it. The journal on her bed the other night. Not the sitter, but James.

As far as she knew, he'd never even been up to the loft alone before. And though she'd told the kids about the trunk of notebooks in the most cursory way, he hadn't seemed interested. It boggled the mind, thinking of her son as old enough to read someone's journals and absorb even this much. Her baby who'd slept all day and fussed all night, missing the cues for night and day, now mulling hints of adult grief. How does a mom get lost. From now on, she would keep the trunk locked.

"Did you read about that in the notebook? Did you go up into my trunk, the one from the Martins'?"

"No," he said, suddenly breezy. "It's just something I thought up in my head."

She'd spoken too quickly, and chased away whatever confidence might have been coming. "James."

"Really. I was just wondering. About people getting lost."

She paused. Getting information from a child was like feeding a skittish animal. "I'm not mad that you read it, even though you really shouldn't have. I'm just surprised that you would have wanted to."

He took another bite of his granola bar and bent to scratch a mosquito bite. She tried again.

"When I was a girl, I loved to hide away with things, just like you. Our house didn't have a cool room up high like this one does, but my grandma had a big closet with a window inside it. I used to like to sit in the closet under her dresses and look at her old photo albums."

She leaned back on her palms, and did

not look at him. She looked instead at the nearest llama, walking toward them with small lilting movements of its head, chin high.

"It's sort of like a treehouse up there," James said. "When Piper was coloring I asked the babysitter if I could bring my book up and read like you do."

Kate continued to look at the llamas. "But then you saw all these notebooks with cool covers." He nodded.

This was one of those opportunities that the school called a teachable moment, and Kate weighed which parenting path to take. The respecting-private-things route, or what-it-meant-to-lose-someone. Losing won.

"Do you know what those books are, James?"

"Yeah. They're Mrs. Martin's stories."

"Sort of. She wrote about her life, for herself, the things that made her happy and sad."

He considered it, then put it in the context of what he knew about books. Libraries, stories. Things written for other people. "Why did she write them?"

Kate had been wondering that herself. Maybe Elizabeth felt a need to synthesize things as they were happening, especially if she didn't confide in others. Or maybe it was to leave an imprint behind, a record that these things had once happened, and had mattered.

"Some people like to write down the things that happen to them and the things they think about so they can remember them later, when they're older."

"Maybe they do it so other people can remember them when they're gone."

"Maybe."

He folded the empty granola wrapper and scooped a ladybug from the grass. "Do you write books like that?" he asked.

"No." She shook her head.

The ladybug plodded along the yellow logo toward his thumb, and she wondered whether he'd drop the wrapper when it touched him or let the bug crawl up his hand. Drop it, probably.

"Well maybe you should," he said, "so we can remember you when you're gone, too."

Kate's chest constricted. In the past year there had been some questions about death — almost entirely from James, Piper was too young — but not as many as she'd expected, and she had kept the answers simple. Mrs. Martin was gone, her plane had crashed because of an accident. Sometimes terrible things like that happened, a sad accident. And sometimes bad people made bad things happen, like the other big crashes afterward, but not often at all, almost never. James seemed satisfied with this version of events, but occasionally asked for more. Whenever he cracked open that door she tried to show there was nothing too scary on the other side, or at least to make it seem that way.

"That's probably not going to happen for a very long, long time," she said. He was blowing on the ladybug. Kate had lost his interest. She put her hand on his leg and leaned forward. "It's okay to feel sad about people dying, and it's normal to sometimes think about losing the people that we love. But it really doesn't happen very often, and usually not until people are very old." *Liar*, she thought.

James continued to play with the wrapper, inverting it and watching the bug soldier on even as its world went upside down. "Is that what happened to her baby, too?"

"Whose baby?"

"Mrs. Martin's baby, how it got lost."

Kate sat a moment, confused. Lose a baby? That's not how Elizabeth had written about the abortion. Then she rubbed her temples at the realization of what was to come. Oh, Elizabeth.

"I don't know about that. But sometimes babies aren't growing healthily when they're inside their moms. Sometimes they aren't growing well even after they're born."

He looked back at his bike, and could have been trying to make sense of the rules that applied to living and dying; sometimes you're old, sometimes you're sick, and sometimes you're neither. Or he could have been thinking about the Lego robot he planned to build back at the house.

"That's sad," he said.

"Yes, it is."

They sat together facing the herd, and bits of trivia came back to Kate from her knitting days, back when the kids were babies. Llamas have no upper teeth, but adult males grow large, sharp lower canines for fighting; humming is a common manner of communication among llamas, and they do it both when they're feeling content and when they're aggressive.

How hard to be a llama, she thought, when the same sound could mean happiness or danger.

TEN

Kate sat in the chaise in the loft, lit only by dim sconces on the wall. In the journals, Elizabeth was packing to leave Florence. She visited her favorite places one last time — the leather vendors at the San Lorenzo market, the food stalls at Mercato Centrale, the wild boar statue at Mercato del Porcellino, where like everyone following the superstition, she rubbed its nose for good luck. She didn't know if she'd be returning. She did not know whether she was going home to help her mother recover, or to bear witness if she would not.

December 3, 1984

When I got in from the airport yesterday Mom was asleep on the couch. I just saw her in August but the difference was awful. Everything about her is thin and gray. The worst of it is her nose. I didn't know a bony

140

nose could change someone's face so much. She was sitting up asleep with the white afghan that Aunt Lucy made her as a wedding gift when <u>she</u> was sick with it. My whole life it's never come out of the antique trunk because Mom always said it was too special, and so was the trunk for that matter, one of the few nice things of Grandma's. And here was the afghan with a plate spilled sideways, crumbs all over it.

This place is the picture of neglect. The refrigerator is pretty much empty, and what little could get moldy already has. I scooped five dead fish out of the aquarium, but it looked like a few live ones were cowering behind the castle so I pinched a little food in. I can't believe she still has Anna's tank.

She asked how long I'm staying, but the tone told me what she's really asking is, When are you leaving? As if in this arrangement, I'm the one who cramps <u>her</u> style.

I'd be lying if I said I hadn't thought about hopping the next flight to Florence, but there is literally no one else here for her. And honestly, there's no one there for me, either.

Kate wondered if Elizabeth had ever

141

looked back, thought about the way her life might have gone if she'd remained in Italy. Though knowing Elizabeth, it wasn't something she would have admitted aloud.

All through the second week on the island, Kate read about the year Elizabeth spent caring for Amelia. There was a constant rotation of three tasks: making sure her mother took her medicine, getting her to the doctor's appointments, trying to make her eat. On better days they went driving; Elizabeth would fill a travel mug with peppermint tea and they'd pass through the historic district in town, winding among the elegantly restored Victorians. They'd always end at the beach, watching the gulls over the water, parking in the same place where Elizabeth used to park with Michael.

As the months passed, their relationship seemed to become more comfortable, though never intimate. *There are none of those emotional epiphanies that are supposed to come from so much caretaking. We are cordial to each other and sometimes there's warmth, but that's as far as it goes. I give her credit for becoming more normal these past few years, and there are some of the trappings of closeness. But I still don't feel like I know a damn thing about her.*

Yes, Kate thought. I know exactly what you mean.

In March, Amelia and Elizabeth received a call about the mortgage. Their finances were not in good shape. Around the same time, the advertising agency where Amelia had worked part-time called to see whether she intended to return soon, or if they should look into a permanent replacement. On impulse, Elizabeth asked if she could take her place temporarily, and offered referrals from the gallery where she'd worked in SoHo sophomore year. She began working at the agency three days a week, driving to Stamford in her mother's car, and within a few months transferred to administrative assistant for the design department. Elizabeth put in extra hours on the side helping with graphics, bluffing her way until she'd learned the computer programs. By the time there was an opening for an entry-level designer, no one asked about her credentials or degree.

Amelia qualified for a clinical trial at the Yale–New Haven Hospital in May, which meant she'd need a ride back and forth several days a week. At first, Elizabeth's boss, Malcolm, balked at having to accommodate her schedule, and urged her to find some other transportation for her mother. *What would I do, pay a car service? Hire some random nurse? That's not what I came home for. I might understand some strangers better than I understand her. But I didn't come home so I could pay someone else to take care of my mother.* In the end, Malcolm let Elizabeth work part-time from home for reduced pay.

For a while, Amelia was in a holding pattern. *That's what her team calls it, like she's a 747 circling LaGuardia.* But in the summer, her condition worsened.

August 12, 1985

It's spreading. She's much worse and eats almost nothing. I make shakes bulked up with organic baby food flakes and buy her silly straws from the toy store because they make her smile. But none of it makes much difference. She's irritable almost all the time, but every so often if I catch her medication just right, I get a nugget of something I've never seen before. Or maybe she always has been that way, just not out loud. Or just not with me.

This afternoon I got her to talk about her book, the ratty old thing she's carried around like a Bible for years. It was probably more her willingness and state of mind than anything I said or did, because she's never responded to my questions before. I've thumbed through it a few times while she was sleeping. There's a lot of blather about fire and soul, rechanneling anger and bad habits, truths and divinity, with some long-haired guy on the book jacket. I think he has something to do with wherever she went when I was in Florida with Dad junior year, just my gut feeling.

That's a pretty cover, I said, pointing to it. It would look great as a painting. I meant it; it has some kind of Asian strokes against a leafy pattern that must have been nice before it got so dirty and bent up. I knew I risked trivializing it, but you look for an opening where you can.

Pretty cover, she mimicked. It always comes down to aesthetics for you. I wish you had something you really believe in, Lizzie.

I took a second to swallow the irritation that comes up when she uses art as an excuse for anything she thinks I'm lacking, then tried to think of a response that sounded open, not defensive. I tried to imagine what it must be like to feel that you don't have much time left, and know you won't be able to pass along the one thing that matters to you in your life. To be a mother whose child is nothing like you are and is probably a disappointment, and a constant reminder of the one you weren't able to keep.

I do believe in lots of things, I told her.

She shook her head. You're closed, Lizzie, not receptive, not inviting to people.

I couldn't help myself then. Closed? I wonder where I learned that from, Mom. You're the queen of secretive. I looked at the book and wanted to add, Though maybe you weren't with these people. But I didn't.

She looked at me hard with shiny morphine eyes and said, Part of growing up is accepting what your failings are and instead of blaming other people, just fixing them. Sometimes people can do that themselves, and sometimes they need help. I'm not just talking about religion, she said. Faith is also about believing in yourself, and faith in what people can harness with their minds, groups of people together. With the right mind-set and the right kind of support, it's amazing what you can accomplish.

It usually makes me uncomfortable when people get all power-of-positive-thinking culty on me. Nasty little words come to mind. Like Crutch. Desperate. And, Freak. But my mother is not an unintelligent person, and whatever self-helpism took hold in her, who am I to say it hasn't helped? After she went away she stopped drinking, she seemed less angry, she started being able to talk about Anna, she got a good job, and she just plain seemed happier. I'm no authority on the way the world works. It may be round and logical and we all descended from apes and such, but there might be intelligent life on Mars, and just maybe there's intelligent life in positive-thinking long-haired-guru cults. . . .

Kate felt a click of identification. This passage reminded her of her own credo: You never know. There might be value in things you don't understand, might be an explanation for things that seem inexplicable. She and Elizabeth had had that in common. When someone else didn't have an open mind, Elizabeth used to say, *She's afraid her brain will catch cold.*

. . . She was irritable but she wasn't shutting down, so I kept going. Mom, why did you go to that place? My junior year, when I was in Florida with Dad?
I figured if she'd tell me that, maybe I

could sort out the other half myself — why someone would go somewhere else to open up to people for strength and togetherness when her own flesh and blood was right next to her looking for the same thing.

She clicked her thumb on the morphine pump and looked out the window at the hydrangea bushes by the curb, blooming three or four puffy shades of cotton candy. She knows next to nothing about gardening beyond the fact that they are perennials, but every year she seems surprised to see them return, as if Mother Nature could change her mind. Like the swallows of San Juan Capistrano might one year just say, Screw it, let's go to Long Beach. I guess if something so arbitrary can happen as an eight-year-old girl getting blown off her bike on a quiet street, why shouldn't the flowers stop blooming?

She closed her eyes but I knew she wasn't falling asleep, not yet. She might be a mystery to me, but I can tell the difference between when she's not paying attention and when she's very much paying attention but pretending not to. She has hardly ever answered my questions directly, and I guess she's not about to begin now.

Then from nowhere: There are times in

your life when it's helpful to find people who have strength in ways you do not, with the power of community in places that are especially conducive to that.

I waited to see if she'd say more, but she sank lower on her pillow and sighed. Be sweet and close the shades, could you? And that was that for confidences.

In late August, Elizabeth took a leave of absence from the agency. Malcolm tried to talk her into working from home — nights, odd hours — but Amelia's condition had deteriorated too much. *Clearly he hasn't had any experience with cancer if he thinks it differentiates between night and day.*

One afternoon after Elizabeth had been at the market buying pumpkins to decorate the porch, she came home to find a message from her old boyfriend Michael on the answering machine. He was in town for their high school's homecoming game and had heard about Mrs. Drogan's illness. Elizabeth didn't call him back at first, but gave in to curiosity. A few days later they met for a drink.

He was balding prematurely, a detail that gave Kate a start. *The sun radiates from his smooth head. . . .* Glasses gave him a studious, thoughtful look. He was inquisitive about her painting and listened well, both of which surprised Elizabeth. She resisted the temptation to tell him about the pregnancy — *I don't see a single good thing that could come of that* — and turned her cheek when he leaned in to kiss her good-bye.

Kate closed the cover and sat back in the shadowy loft. It was the last page of the notebook. She looked out the window at the ocean, watched a boat moored in the dark harbor strung with small lights along its mast and sails.

Elizabeth had not debated coming home from Florence when she found out her mother was sick. She'd just done it. Packed her artwork in shipping crates, paid her landlady, and left the life she loved to care for a woman who had barely cared for her during their difficult years. Whatever else Kate had read that did not sound like the friend she'd known, this did.

Shortly after Piper was born Kate had developed mastitis. In the course of an afternoon, her breasts went from sore to rock-hard simmering hot, and she struggled to care for James and the baby while her fever soared. Chris was traveling, so Elizabeth came over with her children and cared for all four kids while Kate lay sweating in bed, ice packs pressed to her chest. Elizabeth convinced Kate's obstetrician to give a prescription over the phone, then called another playgroup friend to collect it from the pharmacy. Dave was away too, and Elizabeth stayed at Kate's house with her kids into the night, until her fever broke and she was able to care for her own children herself. Elizabeth's competence and compassion were unlike anything Kate had experienced before, a mix of a maternity ward nurse and the best possible relative, one who understands that caretaking is more care than outsmarting the illness.

There was a small sliver of moon over the bay, dappled wide as a field of sand. Downstairs the water went on and off in their bathroom, Chris brushing his teeth for bed.

Kate could easily imagine Elizabeth caring for her mother, but could not imagine what it was like to do so without hope. Kate had never been close to someone who was seriously ill. She'd never had to watch the deterioration, knowing that all your caretaking — all your doling out of medications, spooning of broth — never led to a return to health, only to preparation and comfort, and sometimes not even that. Kate's closest experience with death had been Elizabeth, and there had been no preparation or comfort.

It was a shame, Kate thought, that Elizabeth's mother became sick before Elizabeth was married and had her husband's support. Or, it seemed, much of anyone's. In the writings after her return from Florence, Elizabeth had never written explicitly about loneliness, but it was there on every page.

Dave was the kind of person who would probably do illness well. He was more sweet talk than substance for Kate's taste, southern vowels opening and stretching like happy boll weevils in the sun. Yet it was possible that charm like his could have a palliative effect, could make uncomfortable moments bearable. Perhaps there was a place for platitudes when nothing that was true could be of comfort.

Kate removed the next notebook from the stack, a book striped in pastel chalk. The one beneath it was covered in an enlarged and laminated photograph of Elizabeth with young Jonah and Anna, the one she'd seen that night in the motel parking lot. The kids were laughing as if tickled, Anna's toddler grin tucked deeply into her chest, Jonah's head thrown back in contortions of glee. Elizabeth was smiling into her son's dark curls, her blond hair across their faces catching the light like tinsel. The photo was overexposed to neutron white and there was no hint of background. Only hair, eyes, and laughter, as Elizabeth half disappeared in the searing light. It looked like the kind of place she'd have ascended that day in August, if you believed in such things.

Kate went to replace it in the trunk but found she could not let it go. So she took this journal out as well, and propped it atop the bookshelf under the window facing her chair. She sat looking at it for several moments, an image she wanted to keep close. Then she closed and locked the trunk for the night.

Just one more entry, she told herself, and chalk from the striped cover frosted her hand.

September 25, 1985

She's much worse. Can't read anymore. Her eyes are going and she falls asleep midpage, so I read aloud to her. She's always enjoyed travel magazines, so I picked one up at the store with a cover story about Sedona.

When I was done she said, The desert's a very spiritual place, Anna. She calls me Anna now. It makes her happy, so I don't

153

correct her. Did you know, she said, some people believe that if you're quiet enough you can hear the cactus humming? She touched the photo of a tall saguaro with hands like straw. I picked up the moisturizer from the cart and squeezed a dollop in my palm, massaged the cream across the top of her bony knuckles and down each finger to the tip. She looked at me with her eyebrows raised, what's left of them, then back down at the page of the magazine. I've always wondered if that could be true, she said. The humming.

I looked at the cactus, spines growing in vertical pleats. The photo showed a tiny bird sitting in the crook of an arm, either unaffected by the needles or finding protection there from something else. Who knows, maybe the humming was some kind of resonating effect in the open space, or some metaphysical echo of sand and sun and lizard life. Or maybe a cactus can just hum, like a seashell.

I looked up from her hands and she was still watching me, waiting. I nodded, and smiled. Who knows.

"You coming to bed?" Chris called up the stairs.

Kate looked down at the book, skimmed

the next entry. *Sold the house today. Signed the papers, left my mother's keys on the counter, and pulled the door shut behind me.*

"In a minute."

She heard him stand at the foot of the ladder a moment more, as if there were something else he wanted to say. Then after a bit, the creak of bedsprings. Kate waited, reconsidered joining him. Then she turned the page.

Elizabeth moved into her own place in Stamford, a one-bedroom apartment in a subdivided Victorian house. It was not well cared for but it had a certain charm, and offered an independence she'd never had before. For the first time, her life felt centralized. *There are no pieces of me scattered anywhere else anymore. I've herded in all the sheep. Anything that had been at my father's he gave back before he moved to L.A. I brought the rest of my paintings from my mother's basement and they're squeezed here behind the television. Took her antique trunk, and am going to use it for my journals. It's probably the nicest thing I own.*

At night Elizabeth would go running, mile after mile through the streets of Stamford, and afterward, eat take-out dinners in front of the television. Her work colleagues were the only friends she mentioned, but she didn't seem to see them much outside the office. She reflected on her mother's accusation that she was neither receptive nor inviting, and suspected she was right. Even as a child she'd been told to smile, but didn't know how to begin without it appearing forced. She knew she had to make a change. *I don't join groups, I don't form bonds beyond a few people here and there, haven't belonged to anything resembling a community since the art collective. I could rot here and no one would notice.*

Kate paused at this. Elizabeth had been the heart of the playgroup, had quickly become integral to everything they planned. In all the time Kate had known her, a smile had appeared to be her resting expression. If being part of a group had not come naturally she must have had a lot of practice somewhere along the line, or had hidden it very well. Then Kate checked herself. A person did not pretend among friends.

When Elizabeth announced to her work friends that she had sold her mother's house, Jody and Peg from her department suggested they celebrate with a weekend away. They planned a four-day weekend around deadlines for a client's golf tournament, and booked a flight to a folk festival in Colorado. *Hiking and spa stuff. Girlfriendy stuff. Dancing to some band with cups of beer. I'm afraid I am going to disappoint them, not light and chatty enough about things women get light and chatty about. But I'm glad they suggested it.*

The trip went well and they talked about doing more together socially. But within the year Jody got married, and not long afterward, so did Peg.

Elizabeth spent most weekends renting movies. *This is not where I want to be in ten years. Alone in the living room with Thai takeout, taking care of Anna's old fish tank.*

February 1, 1989

First night in the new digs: I'm a New Yorker again! I may get mugged five times before I pay next month's rent, and it's a hellhole of a third-floor walk-up, but I love it here. I am so, so sick of the suburbs. I needed some fresh air, some general aerating of my life. Malcolm would be so proud, such apt use of golf terminology. If he weren't so mad about my going to work for the competition, smack on Madison Avenue.

They're calling her the Central Park Jogger, a name that fits any one of the thou-
sands of us who loop the reservoir at night
with the secret fear something like this will
happen. I was in that exact place maybe
twenty minutes before. If I'd stretched out
a little longer or had answered the phone
before I walked out the door, I would have
been right there.

How many things in life are like this, near
misses? Every day consists of these tiny
choices with 57,000 trickle-down effects.
You catch a different subway and brush
against a stranger with meningitis, or make
eye contact with someone you fall in love
with, or buy a lotto ticket in this bodega
instead of that one and totally cash in, or
miss the train that ends up derailing.
Everything is so fucking arbitrary. Every
move you make and a million ones you
don't all have ramifications that mean life
or death or love or bankruptcy or whatever.
It could paralyze you if you let it. But you
have to live your life. What's the alternative?

The temperature in the loft dropped ten
degrees. Kate wrapped her arms around

herself and curled into the chair. Elizabeth had chosen the flight that she did only because it left an hour later. That was the single reason. She'd joked about it in an e-mail: *I'm paying $50 extra to sleep in.* As arbitrary as it gets.

For most of the past year, Kate had stepped out the door of their house wondering when it would happen. Somewhere the next thing was gathering steam, some episode of destruction that would either echo what had come before or, inconceivably, top it. A suspicious backpack left on the Mall. A potent tablet tossed into the McMillan Reservoir, a whole jar of them. The chemical would wend its way through the Washington Aqueduct, trickling toxins into her family's kitchen if she turned on the tap before the poisoned water made news. There were accidents of chance, like Elizabeth's crash, and there were accidents of malice. But the end result was the same, all of it arbitrary.

ELEVEN

The house phone rang in the bungalow kitchen, tinny and old-fashioned. Kate had given the number to only a few people as an alternative to her unreliable cell phone, unreceptive one day and uncharged the next. So few calls came in on the house line that they forgot it existed, and its urgency broke the morning quiet like a siren.

She paused in the yard, garden hose in one hand over the wading pool, and listened for Chris to answer. The phone stopped midway through the third ring. She heard his murmured small talk inside the house, then silence.

My father, she thought. Something happened to my father. Working late at the university, he sometimes skipped his heart medication.

Chris walked out onto the porch and glanced at her with an expression she couldn't read.

"Is it my parents?"

"No, it's Dave." She raised her eyebrows, and he shrugged. She let the hose drop in the pool, and it writhed in the shallows like a freed snake.

She had not expected to hear from him while they were here, and in truth, would not have been surprised if he did not initiate contact again. *Take care* was all he'd said after he'd packed the trunks in her car, his tone final as a send-off.

She picked up the receiver from where it lay on the kitchen counter. "Hey, Dave, how are you?"

"Oh, we're fine — it's hotter'n hell here though. How's summer treating you island-ers out there?" His voice was light and jocular in a way she had not heard much in the past year.

"Oh, we're fine. Beach and ice cream, beach and ice cream," she said. "Though none of it keeps the kids from fighting."

"Jonah pulls the I-wish-I-had-brothers-instead-of-sisters business."

"That's when you bring out the preschool line, 'You get what you get and you don't get upset,' " she said.

"That was Elizabeth's mantra."

In the yard, James and Piper screeched as Chris turned the hose on them, thumbing the nozzle into a pelting spray. They ran, backs arched, out of the range of the water, and immediately ran back for more.

"Sounds like the kids are having fun," he said. Through the phone she could hear the thin pitch of Emily's whine, so close she could imagine the toddler needy against his shins.

"Okay, Em, you need a clean diaper," he said. "Well, Kate, I just wanted to check in and see how y'all are doing, and make sure the trunk made it out there with you in one piece."

"Absolutely. Tucked it away in a safe place. What a great little antique." She heard her own chirpy tone and was disgusted with the transparency of her nervousness.

"Elizabeth got it from her mother or aunt or something." His voice was flat. He was not interested in talking about the antique. "Well, all right. I was just wondering if it was all going fine, the caretaking thing, whatever you're doing with the notebooks. But I'm sure you've got it under control."

He was curious. The ramifications of this sizzled to life, disconcerting. She looked toward the whitewashed beams of the ceiling, thought about anything bland that could be said about the journals. "Well, reading the notebooks is a longer process than I would have thought. I'm just now getting to her after-college years."

He paused, either surprised or wanting to make her feel as if he were. "So you decided to read them?"

"I think that was the point, don't you?"

He sighed as if it were one more burden for him to bear. When he spoke the buoyancy was gone from his voice. "I thought you might just be storing them."

Kate pushed at crumbs on the kitchen counter. "If she was just looking for a storage facility, she could have gotten a safe-deposit box. She didn't need me."

"I don't rightly know. It's hard to say." His diction had become excruciatingly slow. "Sometimes folks don't know exactly what they want, and things just need time to set."

Kate twisted the coils of the phone's antiquated cord. Its rubber was grayed with decades of agitated fingers and was cowlicked in several wrong directions, tying her to the counter on a short lead. She could mention the directive in the note from the lawyer. *Start at the beginning.* But it seemed too callous a reminder that Elizabeth hadn't chosen him. Peanut butter, bread, and jelly lay spread out around her where Chris had been making sandwiches for lunch at the beach. She could excuse herself, volunteer

163

that she had to go help.

"There are a lot of books," she finally said, as if the sheer volume of them spoke somehow to the need to be read. "I guess writing was a good outlet for her when she was a kid." She let it hang there, the suggestion that Elizabeth might have been most prolific in her youth, that maybe there would not be too much sensitive information about her adult life. Ridiculous, because the most sensitive thing was already out there, Elizabeth on a blanket with a man named Michael.

"She didn't have the happiest childhood," he said.

"It seems that way."

They fell quiet again. Kate's kids ran inside in their wet swim suits, wanting something. She shook her head and turned sideways.

"She didn't talk much about the past," Dave said. "I didn't meet her until well after her mother passed, but even then, she just didn't like to bring it up."

"Cancer must be a terrible thing up close." *Morphine eyes, hands like straw.* Kate wondered how much Elizabeth had told him about her year spent taking care of her mother, if he could understand how bad it gets.

"Did you read the end of her books yet?" he asked. "About last summer." This, then, was the reason for his call. His voice was tense with the effort to sound casual.

"I didn't get that far yet." Kate wasn't prepared for this directness. "I started at the beginning, like she asked." He was silent. "In the lawyer's note," she added. He might as well know.

At the mention of the lawyer's note, he brought the conversation to a close. "Well, Lord knows from the stink of this kitchen I got myself a diaper to change. I should get to it. I'm glad you guys are having a nice time out there."

She exhaled. "You know, you all could come out any time. We don't have much in the way of sleeping space, but we're happy to double up."

"Well maybe we'll think about that." His tone was polite, but she knew he would not.

It was clear and windy at North Beach. At the entrance, where the narrow path through the dunes first opened onto the sand, it was a parking lot of towels. Kate and Chris walked a quarter mile with the kids before James found a location that satisfied him for a sand castle.

Chris got them started by digging a round

ditch that Piper said needed water, lots and lots of water, to be a proper moat. Damp sand created a corral of stanchions, and Piper carried buckets of water from the shoreline. But the moat would not hold; the rut absorbed every kelpy load poured in. Back and forth to the waterline she went, Sisyphus with ponytails, each bucketful soaked in before she returned with another that would do the same.

Children joined in from neighboring towels, and Chris was relieved of his duties. He lowered himself into a folding chair beside Kate and picked up the bottle of sunscreen, smoothing it across his nose and cheeks in an inverted V.

Sitting. Incredibly, they were sitting. "I'd take out a book, but something tells me they'd notice and it'd break the spell," she said. "I think this is the first time we've both sat down at the beach since having kids."

Out of habit, he looked to the children, now closer to the waterline. "Well, there was the Cape."

"But they weren't *with* us."

"God, no." He reached over and stroked her shin.

That anniversary year Kate and Chris had rented a house in the dunes for a long weekend away, and Rachel had offered to come stay with the children. When their mother had offered to come as well, Kate was not sure which of them was more relieved, Rachel or herself.

The overcast weekend had driven away most beachgoers. Kate and Chris had sat in the sheltered dunes below their deck, temperatures pleasant enough, reading and dozing, and playing Scrabble pulled from the shelves of the rental home. In the evening they'd brought their dinner and wine into the beach grass at sunset. She was reclining with her eyes closed when he went inside for another bottle of wine, and didn't notice until he sat casually beside her that he'd strolled out without a shred of clothing. Her braying laugh had drawn the attention of an elderly couple walking below. Back home, they'd said they were lucky not to have left with a summons, or with the beginnings of a child who'd have to be named Sandy.

Piper continued her hopeless relay. Finally, she laid herself full-length in the moat to try to stop its absorption of water, and became distracted by the sensation of wet sand, rolling and basting herself. Kate tried to remember the point at which she'd stopped enjoying covering herself in sand, at what age there was dawning awareness,

This feels itchy or *This is messy* or even *So-and-so looks nicer than I do in her bathing suit.* She was in no rush for her daughter to be there.

"I found out last night that Elizabeth's mother died of breast cancer," she told Chris, burrowing her toes in the warm sand. "She'd been studying art in Florence and came home to take care of her. Just packed up and quit school to come home and be her caretaker."

"I can see her doing that," he said. "Man, cancer. That must have been brutal."

"It sounds awful, the slow deterioration. That's got to be one of the most horrible ways to die."

"I don't know," he said. "Lou Gehrig's disease isn't a walk in the park. A shark attack would be pretty horrific. Or slow dehydration on a desert island."

"Don't joke, Chris. Cancer is so common, it's scary." Kate put on her sunglasses and squirmed her chair down lower into the sand. "I'm so glad you quit smoking."

He made an agreeable sound. She studied him for a moment out of the corner of her sunglasses, looked for a coloring, a clench of the jaw. He stared ahead, expressionless. If she said anything further it would bring them back to that old place of undermined trust, and change the tenor of their vacation.

Five kids now worked with James and Piper by the water's edge, laboring with their own pails and shovels to create a second tier for the castle walls. Chris called out to them. "It looks good, guys, but make sure the new sand isn't too wet. If it's too heavy it'll collapse your walls." He pulled his water bottle from the sand and took a long drink. "What did Dave have to say this morning? Are they gonna come out for a visit?"

So that was that, then. They would pretend about the smoking. She tried to remember which year they'd gone to Cape Cod, which anniversary that had been. Three years ago? It felt like much more.

"I don't know," she said. "I invited them again. But he had his polite voice on that says he'll never really take me up on it."

Chris nodded. "Dave's holding things together well, but there's a lot of politeness going on with him. I'm not sure I've ever seen him irritated. I get the feeling he lets you see exactly what he wants you to see."

She palmed a dollop of sunscreen and worked it in circles across her chest and neck. "This morning he asked me how far I'd gotten in the journals. I feel like he's torn between wanting to find out the truth about her and not really wanting to know."

Chris shook his head. "To have that loss, and then get that kind of information about the person you thought you knew? That's as big as it gets." He watched James straddling the castle, wanting to make himself king. "I guess you never really know people. She's the last person I would have suspected of fooling around."

"We shouldn't jump to conclusions, Chris. I mean, she was all about her family. Everything she did was for them."

Two women in bikinis strolled by at the waterline just below where the kids were repairing the castles. When the sand flying from James's shovel neared their shins, they jumped back with mincing steps, as if they'd been burned. Both had long, full hair, carefully turned with blow dryers and brushes. As they walked, their breasts bobbed in their bikini tops like buoys in the water.

Chris's eyes followed them as they passed. Kate looked at him until he noticed her watching him, and then both looked back at the kids at the sand castles.

"Just because Elizabeth was a perfect mom doesn't mean she couldn't have an affair. But if that's what it was, are you going to tell Dave? Or give him the books, or what?"

Fair and sensitive. Kate watched the women move down the shoreline. "I'll have to see what feels right. I don't know what would be more cruel — to hand Dave proof, or leave him wondering what she was doing. I guess it depends on whether the truth seems like it would benefit him in any way, or just hurt him."

Chris frowned. "Well that's a little controlling, don't you think? Deciding what kind of truth he can handle."

"I'm not 'deciding' anything. I just don't know how much is appropriate to share. Dave and the kids have their memories of her a certain way, and all that could be shot to hell. That's not what she would have wanted."

"Well maybe she should have thought of that before she started screwing around and put it in her diary. Don't you think Dave deserves to know whether his life was a sham?"

"A sham? Come on, Chris. Everyone keeps little things from their spouse. Something they think, something they do. Or a bad habit." She tried to keep her voice from becoming too pointed on the last two words, and she stared straight ahead at the water. "But even if she did have secrets, she's still entitled to her privacy. A person's wishes don't stop being real just because she's gone." Kate sat back in her chair, surprised by her own vehemence.

Chris turned to her, eyes unreadable behind dark lenses. "Dave is the one who's still here, and his life counts too, Kate." He reached for the water bottle, found it empty, and tossed it into the sand. "No offense, but maybe this project has become a little too much about you, and this idea of yourself as her protector."

She opened her mouth and leaned forward in her chair, but was interrupted by chaos at the castle. Six kids were now within what was left of its walls, including Piper, jumping up and down on the remnants of towers and turrets and screeching with destructive glee. James stood to the side, near tears.

"Don't! Don't!" he yelled at them. "I'M THE KING! THIS IS MY CASTLE! DON'T WRECK IT!" But it was too late. The walls had already crumbled.

TWELVE

Their third week of vacation had been earmarked for the children to attend farm camp, an island of structured time on the open calendar. Kate had loosely envisioned the new things she'd try solo while the kids were occupied, kayak tours and birding excursions. But each morning, after she pulled out of the driveway with the kids and their backpacks and Chris sat down to his work, there were two things she wanted to do. First, she'd swim in the ocean, rediscovering the fluidity of movement that used to come naturally. Then she would pull on a cotton tank dress over her swimsuit and go to the café to read.

In New York, Elizabeth had thrown herself into a variety of activities. She joined a professional organization of graphic designers, and took a board position with the New York Road Runners club. She became enamored with the city all over again. *My*

Saturday mornings: run in the park, then get a bagel with lox from the wild yelling deli guy, and watch the roller derby near the fountain. They set up boom boxes and enormous speakers and pylons, and all kinds of people come, kids and cross-dressers and old fogies. I love this crazy place, all these people not worrying how they look, just smiling and skating and being exactly how they are.

Elizabeth dated many people, some of them met through chance encounters at the gym or in a bar. Once it had not gone well, a man from the gym whose style went from assertive to menacing, and she vowed not to go out with strangers anymore. *New rules, the Two Points system: I have to have two points of reference, two people to vouch for the person. Get back on the horse, Sourpuss. But it's two points, no exceptions.*

Kate put the notebook down on the table and looked around the outdoor patio of the café. During culinary school and afterward, Kate had had a wide circle of friends and colleagues in New York. Experiences with total strangers, people without a single person to vouch for them, were uncommon. Except Chris. But there'd been a solidity to him, quiet and assured, reliable; he showed an astute awareness of others and a comfort with where he stood among them, and apart from them. It had seemed the greater risk not to give him her number. But Kate had had the safety net of roommates who'd known where she was and with whom. Elizabeth had lived alone. It was a chancy thing, meeting a stranger in New York.

When Kate arrived in Manhattan for culinary school, it was as if a secret had been revealed, a West Coast conspiracy exposed: in fact, New York, not California, was the greatest place on earth. People moved at her speed and shared her sense of humor. There was a mind-boggling variety of things to do any minute of the day or night. She didn't mind the noise and overlooked the grime. Kate had become so passionate about the city that her family and old friends in Palo Alto rolled their eyes when she mentioned it. In this way she learned a valuable lesson: most people outside of the city did not take kindly to New Yorkers' mental map that placed the Big Apple at the center of everything, though of course New Yorkers would never call it that. Later, when she joined the Southbrook playgroup, she found that few of the women went into the city unless it was, say, their anniversary, or they were dressing up the kids in their Christmas best for Radio City. To talk about the city like an insider, to beat the drum about the restaurants in a way that made their suburb sound like a hamlet, was like being that expat who came home and wouldn't shut up about how much better things were in Europe.

Kate rechecked the date at the top of Elizabeth's last journal entry. June 12, 1989. At that time Kate had been out of culinary school for a year, living on the Upper West Side, and had not yet met Chris. It was a shame she hadn't known Elizabeth in those days, she thought, and the thought surprised her. It would not have occurred to her to wish she'd shared those days — childless, a little wild — with Elizabeth.

She had an hour more until camp ended. Kate went back inside the café for a scone and a refill of her coffee.

Elizabeth enrolled in a painting class at an art program in the Village. The instructor had a cultlike following among young artists dazzled by his access to galleries clear to London and his status in the city's social scene, and Elizabeth studied under him for three terms with thoughts of amassing enough of a portfolio to hold a show. Classes were held in the evenings; soon she was staying after, and eventually, staying over.

It was hard to imagine Elizabeth with men before Dave. For Kate, intimacy had always been as much about the sensual buildup as the act itself: with certain colleagues there'd been a frisson in the kitchen, the heat and urgency and even the tempers simmering, until one night it was inevitable they would not be leaving alone. But there were some women for whom sexuality seemed an afterthought, a point of mere biology. Elizabeth had seemed like one of those women.

February 8, 1990

When my alarm went off this morning Ted was staring at me in an irritated way. He gets like that sometimes about the alarm, though he teaches at nine and wouldn't have been able to sleep much longer anyway. After my shower he was watching me with a provocative look while I toweled off. Not let's-get-it-on-again provocative, but I'm-gonna-push-your-buttons provocative. I stepped into a thong thinking it could go either way. He was either going to make a comment about my skinny white ass and pull me back to bed, or start in on me for something.

I don't know how you can keep going to that <u>job</u>, he said.

But he took it too far this time. He said I was pimping myself for vodka ads and golf brochures, that I was just "punching bloody computer keys."

Later I thought of a million things to say, but at the moment all I came out with was, At least I'm able to pay the rent, which is more than you seem to be able to do most of the time.

Game over. Oh well. It's been fun, all the gallery openings and dinners, and God, he did know how to light me up like a pinball game. And I loved the studio time, always lose myself in the studio, but who am I kidding? I'm never going to give up my job and be an Artiste. The truth is, I like my job. There, I said it. Designing a page that's going to end up on packaging or in a magazine or on a banner, getting the font and color just right. There's a kind of artistry and beauty to that, too. And to having money in the bank. This skinny white ass is keeping its day job, but not its boyfriend.

The journal entries through the spring and summer reflected a person contented with her life. Elizabeth's twenty-seventh birthday came and went. She socialized with members of the running club, ran a half marathon, and had a brief, disastrous relationship with her boss, Fitch. *I don't know why I felt the obligation to be loyal to him when <u>he</u> so clearly didn't. Maybe loyalty is for swans and bird-minded people too afraid or too unimaginative to see the alternatives.*

Alternatives. To loyalty. The words stood out as if they were written in red ink.

What little Elizabeth wrote for months after that was mostly related to work. She was given a supervisory role for the beverages and spirits clients, overseeing promotional materials for sporting events. She depleted her savings to buy a large computer monitor so she could work at home, and picked up freelancing graphics work on the side. As her savings grew slowly, she dreamed of someday buying a place of her own. There were a few relationships after Fitch, short and passionate, with partners referenced only by initials. Circumspect, it seemed, or coy.

Then Fitch left the agency, and there were departmental changes; someone else received a promotion Elizabeth had hoped would be hers. She'd gotten great reviews, pulled off several large campaigns. They had both been with the company the same amount of time. She concluded that either human resources had found out about her relationship with her boss, or he'd spilled her secret that she'd never received her college degree.

> . . . I've noticed that the few times it has come up in conversation with people, they respond with this patronizing sympathy. I know Fitch thought that if I had any get-up-and-go I would have gone back and finished. He's probably right.
>
> I'm a dropout, a quitter. Let's call it what it is. At the time it just seemed to happen, a series of unrelated accidents: choosing to stay in Florence, coming home to take care of my mother, starting to work and then sticking in my rut. But there are no real accidents, only decisions that feel like accidents, one after another, that take you down a certain road and take on a momentum that can't be reversed.

Kate put down the book with a bit too much force, and its cover slapped on the wood tabletop. The woman sitting at the next table glanced at her briefly, then back to her own children.

Kate had never seen this side of Elizabeth, cool and bitter. It was the opposite of fatalism, this stark recognition of the effects of choices that had not seemed much like choices at the time. So, college had been a sore point for both of them. Maybe marrying Dave and having children — three, one right after another — had been her way of breaking the pattern of accidental choices, her big decisive act. Interesting that this had never come up in conversation, whether they'd always anticipated motherhood. Kate could not even recall how Elizabeth and Dave had met.

Elizabeth's friend Peg from her old firm had taken a new job, and to celebrate, Peg wanted the three friends to make a return trip to the folk festival in Telluride. Peg and Jody left their children at home with their husbands; the three women hiked, had massages, and took an ATV tour of a mining ghost town. They danced with men in tie-dyed shirts, cups of beer sloshing on their bare feet. One of the men asked Elizabeth for her phone number but she brushed him off, and Peg accused her of not trying hard enough to meet people. Elizabeth hated blind dates, but agreed to be set up with Peg's cousin Steven back in New York just to get her to stop talking about it.

They met at a famously fashionable restaurant on the Lower East Side. When she arrived he was sitting at the bar in a Burberry coat, martini held in a manicured hand. Immediately, she planned excuses to leave early. But he surprised her; he was an animated conversationalist, and asked engaging questions. As he spoke he looked her in the eye, he smiled, and he didn't talk about anything controversial or negative. And he asked more about her than he offered about himself, which left her with the warm, if superficial, sense of being found interesting, and liked.

They kissed good-bye with off-center pecks and murmurs about getting together again, which she knew wouldn't happen. But she felt she'd been left with a valuable lesson: how to move with ease among people, make them feel as if you had something in common. Her lack of this, she now recognized, was to blame for not getting the promotion.

September 7, 1992

The golf tournament was more fun than usual this year. That guy I met at the Telluride folk festival was there. I thought he was putting us on when he said he was a professional golfer, but there he was yesterday in the corporate tent, giving a putting clinic for our client, an old friend of his. I hardly recognized him, all clean-cut in a white polo shirt and preppy plaid pants.

What's up with this? I asked, flicking his visor. Not allowed to wear tie-dye, Dan?

Well I'll be gosh-darned he said, and sounded five times more southern than he had two seconds before. If it isn't the Telluride belle who wouldn't even give me her phone number.

He was a piece of work all afternoon, jocular from one corner of the tent to the other, followed by a big black dog he apparently takes everywhere even though dogs aren't allowed. He insisted on working on my putt, even though I told him there's nothing to work on when someone has never actually golfed before. ("Played golf," he corrected me. "You play golf. Golf is its own happy noun.") Then he walked with his hand on my upper arm like we were at some cotillion. It was as if he were mocking his own cheesiness. Meta-cheese.

When Peg made a show of slipping him my number, ha ha ha wink wink, I didn't put up a fuss. He's over the top but seems harmless. Does it satisfy two points if one of the points is yourself from your own vacation?

Bye, Dan, I said with a little wave over

my shoulder, the closest I've come to normal flirting.

I'll answer to whatever you want to call me, darlin', he said. But the name's Dave.

THIRTEEN

Kate walked into the bakery and a bell jangled. The old screen door flapped shut behind her with a bang.

"Be right with you," came a voice from the back.

She looked around the small room. Flour looked the same as it had last summer, the same as the past seven years since Max had bought it, which was basically the same as the previous fifteen under the original owners. To brighten the shack in the woods he had added light green paint and homey touches like wainscot, hand-painted pottery, and fresh flowers, but little else. The creaky screen door could have been repaired easily with a single new spring, and the fact that it never had was probably not an oversight. Its folksy imperfection, some might say studied neglect, reflected the pride of the owner that the food would speak for itself. He had been wrong about some things, but that was not one of them. She would miss this place if he had to sell.

The curtain separating the front of the bakery from the kitchen was parted by thick hands, and a white apron emerged that barely covered a loud Hawaiian shirt.

When Max saw her, he smiled. "Kaaaaatie." He opened his arms and folded her into the broad hibiscus of his chest. "Jesus Mary and Joseph, I was about to resort to hiring college students."

"Not that," she said. "Let's not do anything rash."

The embrace lasted an extra moment, a recognition that they had not seen one another since his breakup. Then she pulled back and looked at him. His wavy gray hair, once so lustrous that classmates called him Vidal, had thinned since last summer, and shaded circles pooled under his eyes. He cocked his head and flashed her a theatrical smile, mocking her scrutiny. *All okay here, folks. Move along.*

"Oh, Max," she said.

His smile faded, and he rubbed the back of her shoulder with his knuckles, his form of affection. Then he walked back through the curtains. "So how many weeks you here this year? A lot longer, right?"

"Seven," she said, following him to the

kitchen. "We got a good deal, and Chris is working from here." The boxy room behind the curtain had its familiar feel of an orderly yard sale. Row upon row of shelving filled the walls with worn but well-organized appliances and containers, with cutouts for two windows. Kate took in the scuff marks on the walls, the chipped paint. Max had always been meticulous before about repainting the kitchen during the off-season.

"How's business?" she asked.

"Oh, fine. Good." He reached behind her into the glass display case of pastry, and tossed her a piece of rugelach as if it were something he was trying to be rid of. "But the investors are making all kinds of suggestions. They want to add tables and wireless. And that would bring in ALL the riffraff, the novelists and stroller moms and whatnot, kill the whole ambience and kill me with the racket. I won't do it."

"Good for you. The world doesn't need one more place to check e-mail."

"Amen, sister."

She leaned against the butcher-block island. "So what about the offer? Have you decided yet?"

"No." He picked up a sponge and wiped the counter with round, slow strokes.

"Don't you have to let them know soon?"

"I have a little time yet."

The bakery had cachet, and history. For years, long before Max bought the place, islanders had been coming to the outpost on Harvest Road for the cakey old-fashioned doughnuts first thing in the morning, a secret among locals and those in the know. Max bought it and expanded the offerings, and the crowds grew to include summer people and weekend tourists. He added quiche, folded with unusual vegetables and cheese. Rhubarb streusel muffins. Tiny berry tarts glazed with amaretto marmalade, boxed as beautifully as Fabergé eggs. She imagined him starting over, an assistant chef in some charmless storefront bakery. Sitting home nights drinking Scotch and trying to reacquaint himself with working for someone else, and with living alone.

"God, I hate this," she said, kicking the base of the wood island. "I really hate him for it." Her voice caught at the end, and he looked at her with tired eyes. They'd been through all this on the phone.

Max stepped behind her and wrapped both arms around her shoulders. She was enveloped by his warmth, the wholesome scent of yeast and soap that had always defined him. His soft gray hair brushed her cheek in a way she could never imagine her father's doing, clipped so short.

"Let's go to Italy," she said. "We'll hunt him down."

"I just wish that if he had to clean me out, he'd taken the exercise equipment while he was at it," said Max. "No more jocks for me. I hate all this big metal in the house, like hulking robots."

"Sell it. Scrap it," she said. "Program the damn things to knead bread."

He smiled. "So, when can you come in? Tell me you can work next week. I have a bunch of tarts to do for a dinner at one of the harbor houses."

The children had camp, and Chris was working but was not scheduled to travel. She went to the drying rack and picked up two muffin tins, moved to put them away in their cupboards. "I might be able to come in for a while. Let me check if Chris can watch the kids after camp."

"Bring 'em. We'll set them up with paint-brushes." He gestured to the walls. " 'Paint covers all ills.' " He was mocking himself, quoting himself.

Max had been an architect in New York before he'd retired early to attend culinary school. His amateur enthusiasm revealed real skill and he'd had his pick of the best apprenticeships, a sore point among those

189

who scoffed at second careerists and hobbyists. It bothered critics even more when he took a job with one of New York's top chefs, only to fritter away the urban opportunity, as they saw it, and leave to run a bakery-café. On an island. When he was first getting started she'd had him as a guest on her cable show several times, setting up cameras and filming from his kitchen while she was on vacation.

To say Flour had been an overnight success wouldn't be true, though some of the reviews had been written as if it were. In the years since, he had been approached about expanding his brand, but he'd declined. Pick what's going to be your masterpiece, he'd said, and do it well.

He had done it well. But then William ran off to Milan with a man much younger than Max, as well as most of the money in their bank account.

Kate watched Max wipe the butcher-block counter. His arms were thick as logs, but he moved like a person who believed himself to be fragile. He swept the crumbs into a careful pile and then into his palm, cupping the bits like broken glass. After he'd dumped them into the sink, he stood looking into the yard. The thick shrubs behind the bakery ended at a small cliff, and a stony path wound down to the Atlantic. Kate knew it well. The summer after James was born she'd been working at the bakery and strolled out back for a moment of air and kept walking, hungry for wild spaces and loud sounds. Wind rattled the beetlebung trees, and waves broke on the rocks like dishes thrown to the floor. At the bottom of the cliff she sat on a boulder and choked on heaving breaths she hadn't felt coming, overcome with the difference between the muggy quiet of her days and the humming community of the bakery — the claustrophobia of her own quiet love, against the connection to something larger.

She followed his gaze out the window. "Let's take a walk."

He dismissed the idea with a wave, a place he didn't want to go. "I was actually heading out when you came," he said. "Guess who's in town?"

Kate looked at him blankly. She hadn't talked to any of their culinary school friends in a while.

"Fiona and Charles," he said.

"Fiona. No kidding." She hadn't seen her in years, since shortly after Fiona and Charles's wedding.

"They just got in today. I was going to meet them for a drink. Come with me."

Fiona would take everything over, and Charles — well, Charles was Charles. Though maybe that's what Max wanted right now, the mindlessness of them.

Kate grinned. "Well, at least he can give you tax advice. Let me check with Chris. He's expecting me back."

"They're always expecting you back." He untied his apron and pulled it over his head. "Besides, you look like you could use a drink too. No offense, hon, but you don't look yourself. Did you get a cheap cut again?"

"Thanks a lot." She put a hand through her unkempt bob, badly in need of a trim. "No. It's outgrown, but the same."

Max hit the lights in the kitchen, then turned back and pulled aside the curtain for her to pass through.

"Lose weight?"

"Nope."

He studied her as she walked by, touched her middle back. "You're all washed out. You should put on some mascara or something."

"Yeah, the kids really care about those thick lashes."

"Don't you go letting yourself go. You can't let the turkeys get you down." Ever a product of the seventies, Max still owned a

T-shirt with the Boynton cartoon bird and its trademark blasé stare. It had worn to threads around the neck, but he called it an antique work of post-ironic expression. He called all the outmoded clothes he didn't want to part with works of post-ironic expression.

"No, indeed," he said softly, pulling the door closed behind them. "You cannot let the turkeys get you down."

The old tavern had been on the verge of falling apart for as long as Kate could remember, perched precariously on the edge of the channel. Each time she entered she had the unsettling sense that if too many people sat on the far end of the bar, the whole place would pitch forward and sink.

"Kate! Max said you might be out here on the island." Fiona waved, her watch a blinding mix of platinum and gems. She had grown her hair long, and yes, wore lipstick. Kate would not have recognized her. "You remember my husband Charles?" she asked. He sat beside her, gelled hair stiff as his button-down shirt.

In culinary school, Fiona had been so rough around the edges that she'd been nicknamed Sarge. She had worn her hair short, military short, and she'd had a freedom in her eyes that said *I couldn't care less*. A few years after school, Kate heard she'd married a reporter who covered stocks and bonds for a weekly business magazine. Friends who'd attended the wedding had been amused to no end that Sarge had not only married, but had married a business writer, a stuffed shirt who seemed to have no particular brilliance for finance save the coincidence of his name. Imagine, a finance reporter named Charles Schwab. Kate had met up with them once, in the early years. Now they had a child and lived in the Boston suburbs, and Fiona worked at the kitchen of the most uptight French restaurant in the city and painted her toenails pink. Evidence, Kate supposed, that with enough will, a person could make herself over any way she chose.

They moved through the pleasantries of updates. It was clear from Fiona's light banter that she did not know Max's situation. Kate looked away as he gave vague answers to questions about the bakery, plans for the future. During the first pause, Max raised his hand to the bartender. "Two martinis, please," and he pushed a napkin in front of Kate.

"No, Max, I'll just have a beer," Kate said.

"Since when do you drink beer? Have

some style, drink like a grown-up." Kate shrugged. It had been a long time since she'd had a real drink.

"Olive or twist?" he asked.

"Twist." Even the word felt strange in her mouth, as if it were said by someone else.

"Did I hear you moved to D.C.?" Fiona asked.

"Two years ago. Chris's company wanted him to work out of the headquarters."

She nodded. "Where are you working now?" Fiona's mind had always been a database of restaurants in virtually any city.

"Not really anywhere. A little bit here and there when people call me in, but not regularly. I've been home with the kids. For now."

Fiona smiled as if Kate had said she sold herbs from her window box. "That's great. It's a special time when they're young."

"You know, Kate, I heard about a catering company starting up in Washington," Max said. "It's small, but they're doing some good stuff. Events at the Smithsonian, the zoo, that sort of thing. A nice way to ease back in."

Kate nodded. "There are some great options out there." Catering would be one way to do part-time work. Still, restaurants were what she missed, a sense of place, the feeling of belonging to something larger than yourself. Each day had a rhythm, a coordination rising to a barely bearable chaos. There could be pandemonium across the room on the line but she rarely minded. It fed her focus. And then it came back down, it always did, and there was regrouping, and the cycle of beginning fresh the next day.

"Wait, I just remembered — did Anthony call you about the restaurant opening in Dupont Circle?" Max asked. "He really wants you."

"Yes. It sounds amazing." Kate swirled her finger in her glass, pushed the lemon rind against the rim. "They're working with Klein & Ashbaugh on design. It's going to be really nice."

"It's gonna take off is what it's gonna do." Max lifted his eyebrows at her understatement. "That would be a great place to be."

"Long hours, though."

Fiona looked at her, curious. She took a long sip of her wine.

"Fiona, how much time did you take off work after your daughter was born?" Max asked. "Like, two hours?"

Charles shook his head. "If that. I think she left the bread rising at the restaurant and got back from the hospital in time to punch it down."

Kate laughed and shifted in her chair, looking for a bowl of nuts, popcorn, something to occupy her hands. "Well, before I take on anything, we need to figure out whether we're staying in Washington. Chris travels a lot, and I actually don't think it matters much anymore where he lives. We could be going anywhere." It came out as easily as if it were true.

Max held her eye a moment, his look soft, then changed the subject. "You're right in the District, aren't you? Near the zoo?"

"The zoo's our second home. The kids talk about the pandas like they're their pets. Tian Tian this, Mei Xiang that . . ."

"Great city. I worked for a small paper in D.C. for a few years," Charles said, plucking at his cuffs. "I started up a financial newsletter on the side, a real long shot, but with my name, you know, it really took off."

He paused to take a sip of his drink and to give her the chance to express her fascination. The bar noise filled the long pause. "Well," he said finally. "Do you like it there?"

"Sure, I guess. The museums, the weather . . . everyone loves D.C." Kate leaned back in her chair with her drink. The Metro tunnels, the frightened commuters. Long slow escalators, impossibly high. "But it's a company town, no soul. I miss New York."

"You weren't *in* New York, honey," Max said gently. "You were in Connecticut."

"You were in Connecticut?" Fiona laughed. "Hoo, boy. Watch out, suburbs. I'd hate to get on the wrong side of *you* at a PTA event."

Kate laughed, but arched her brows, confused. "What do you mean?"

"You, nasty girl. Torturing Jasper Friedling during the exam."

Kate shook her head, trying to remember.

"You hid his stuff, remember? You moved the whisk and the spatula from where he'd put them and it was making him crazy, up against the clock, his utensils turning up in weird drawers or the fridge. That temper, he was turning *purple*."

Kate threw back her head and laughed loudly. Heads turned throughout the bar. God, she'd forgotten; fifteen years since culinary school, but it felt like a million. Back then she'd done so much cooking that her chapped hands never healed one day to the next. But she'd loved it; hours would pass pulling together a menu in a way time never had doing anything else.

"Evil woman," said Max. "Your poor cursed children."

Kate dipped her head, still laughing softly. "It was evil. But that guy was horrific, such a little Napoleon."

The camaraderie in school and in restaurants had seemed unique to that world too, the high emotions immediate and true, people candid with one another and saying what needed to be said. Even the pranks had been raw and honest. It seemed like no one did truly *out-there* things anymore — hilarious and blunt, calling someone out when his behavior was too much. Social checks and balances. Everything in her world now was small and subtle, little passive-aggressive digs. She preferred it the other way. At least you knew where you stood with people.

She thought of Elizabeth telling off her old boyfriend Ted when he'd criticized her job, and of their spontaneous breakup. That was the sort of thing Kate herself was known for — acting first and realizing the repercussions later, for better or for worse. There had been something honest and free about Elizabeth in her twenties, a person Kate never would have imagined. But she sensed she was on the cusp of watching it wane. How strange that it should make her sad; she'd never known Elizabeth then, and never would fully know what had been lost.

"I heard Jasper got even worse when he opened his own place," said Max.

"But did you hear what he's doing now?" asked Fiona. "He's giving ten percent of the profits to families affected by the terrorist attacks."

"Jasper *Friedling*? The man who wouldn't give anyone change for the coffee machine?" Kate said with a guttural sound of disbelief.

"The father of one of his daughter's friends worked a kiosk in the World Trade Center. The guy had five kids, and no benefits. Jasper started with them, giving the wife ten percent of a week's profits. Now he gives to a different family every week."

Kate held her drink and played with the rim. Her smile faded. She'd read so many of the profiles and could easily envision this man as well. A father at his kiosk. Maybe he'd stayed a moment too long, reluctant to leave his cart — food or flowers, maybe imitation designer handbags. Worried about how he'd pay for five pairs of sneakers if he abandoned his inventory, and so he hadn't run when he had the chance. She pushed the thought away, didn't want to add it to the collection of obituaries, the snapshots so jarring in their potent brevity. Reading them and all the other news had proven that the city she missed, the city she and Elizabeth had been shaped by, no longer existed.

"Well, I'll be. Jasper Friedling, charitable powerhouse," said Max. "Who knew?"

Fiona pushed at the edges of her napkin with a neat squared nail. Charles sighed, and reached for a bowl of nuts. No one spoke. When that day was mentioned, this was usually the way. *Did you know anyone who . . . My brother-in-law worked on the . . .*

Max lifted his glass to catch the bartender's attention, and turned to Kate. "Another?"

She checked her watch. Six o'clock. "Thanks, but no. I have to get back." She tried to leave Max money for the drink, but he waved it away.

"Remember," he said. "Next week. The tarts."

She headed out into the street and winced at the light, jarring after the dimness of the bar. As she oriented herself there was a loud roar overhead. She flinched and looked up to see a small plane flying low over the harbor, close enough to read its number on the side and see the outline of the pilot's profile. Surely a plane had never been so low, so loud. It was aimed directly for the bell tower across the street. The drilling whine of its propellers reverberated clear through her eustachian tubes, her sinuses.

She put both hands over her head, dropping her purse.

Others on the sidewalk were passing by as if nothing were amiss, barely glancing at the sky. Someone asked her if she was all right, and a second person stopped to help her retrieve her cell phone, wallet, and keys scattered on the ground.

She gathered her things with murmured thanks, then watched as the small plane flew on toward the airstrip in the middle of the island, growing smaller until its fading roar was indiscernible from the airhorn of an incoming ferry.

The house was silent, door unlocked. A note on the counter read, *Went to get manicotti from the pizza place. Back soon.*

Kate stood in the family room taking in the scattered objects her family left behind. Splayed books, a menagerie of plastic animals. A spill of Legos. Chris's open laptop, battery dying. She used to enjoy the quiet of an empty house, but now it unsteadied her. This was the way the room would look if its inhabitants were suddenly gone, the fossil of a family.

She went to the refrigerator and took out a beer, then brought it out to the patio with Elizabeth's notebook. The sun was low on the bay. In the sky, the simple black shell of a plane moved through the clouds like a cardboard cutout in a diorama.

September 15, 1992

Dave was a toned-down version of his golf-tournament self at dinner, not too jovial or overly familiar, both of which I was afraid would get old fast. Greeted me inside the restaurant with a light touch on the back, ushering toward the table, polite. Very traditional.

Things I noticed: Freckles across his nose and cheeks make him look like an overgrown six-year-old. Very strong jaw and chin, big shoulders and chest. He'd gotten a haircut but it was still all over the place. He does have one head of gorgeous dark hair. Right after we sat down and were pulling out our napkins he smiled wide and said, Thanks for coming. His smile goes all the way to his eyes, just about the warmest brown I've ever seen. I got a tightness in my throat. Be nice, Elizabeth, I thought. Smile more.

I asked him about golf, about the tour, how much he plays, and where he calls home (an apartment just outside NYC, though he's there so rarely a neighbor is in effect a co-owner of his dog). He worked in pro shops after graduating from Georgia Tech and played on some mini tours until he got his tour card, and has been scrabbling — his word — year after year to qualify. I'd remembered him as glib and chipper, but one-on-one he's more serious. He chooses his words as if each one matters and it's very important that he say exactly what he means.

He asked about my family, and I kept it simple — Vermont, Connecticut, divorced, deceased. When I said cancer, something slid shut behind his eyes. Yup, I know a thing or two about that, he said. His sister, last year. We were both quiet for a minute, and just when I started racking my mind for something else to talk about, he said, That's just not something a body should have to go through, and not something that anybody should have to watch. Neither of us wanted to say any more about it, so we didn't.

After dinner he cabbed with me to my building, and before I could ask if he wanted to come up, gave me a soft peck on the cheek and strolled off. I watched him walk away toward the corner with a rolling gait that bounces on the balls of his feet, solid and heavy like a draft horse, but light like a very contented one. He looks as if he could carry you a thousand miles if he had to.

FOURTEEN

Kate pulled up to the fence of a small farm on the northwest part of the island. Several Holsteins lifted their heads. Piper and James unbuckled their seat belts and hopped out, eager to get to the barn.

"Heyyyy . . . aren't you forgetting something? Like, good-bye?" Kate called.

They returned to the car with caught-me smiles and leaned in the window. Kate cupped James by the chin and planted a kiss on his cheek, then Piper's. "Have fun. See you at one." Freed, they sped toward their fellow campers.

Kate sat in the car and watched her children slide in easily with their peers. She could barely remember the days when they'd clung to her, toddlers with "separation anxiety," as the books called it. In a way the earliest months were easier to remember, the exhausted nights that bled into one another with a disbelief that it would ever again be otherwise.

There they were, grown campers with peers. Animated, confident, independent.

January 1, 1993

I don't think I've ever rung in the New Year with a significant kiss at the stroke of midnight before. It isn't the cliché I always thought it would be, like roses on Valentine's Day or standing under the mistletoe. It's like there's an embedded promise of agreeing to share the year to come.

When Dave turned to clink glasses with me last night at the party he didn't say a word, just gave me that slow mysterious smile, the one that says he's really happy because he's always one-quarter sad so he knows full well what happy feels like. And he slipped his arm around my waist and pulled me in tight. His kiss is slow, like he's still asking permission. When we wake up in the morning he grins like he's grateful and not taking anything for granted.

February 27, 1993

Watched the Nissan Open. He didn't make the cut. After the first and second rounds he was four and five strokes over; a ball in the water here, a putt blowing by the cup there, it adds up. Watching is nerve-racking. He rarely makes it anywhere near the top half of the leader-board. Still staking out the hinterlands, he says with only the barest hint of disappointment. But I've never heard him say a word about anything else he'd want to do, career-wise, or how low he'd go before throwing in the towel. I think he honestly feels lucky to do what he loves to do and be able to pay the rent. More or less.

March 15, 1993

Bertha's gone. So sad. Poor girl's legs gave out completely. Dave said she hasn't been able to walk herself outside for days, so we took her to the vet. He told us that she's had a long life for a dog, let alone a Newfoundland, but enough is enough and it's time to let her go. He gave us the choice of doing it now or bringing her home for one more night, and Dave said No, we need to do this. We shouldn't prolong it.

Dave stood on the threshold of the vet's office door, rocking on the balls of his feet and looking down at the ground. I wanted to give him his peace, so I walked over to poor Bertha sedated a little on the table and put my hand on her massive head. The fleshy red parts of her lower lids were even puffier and runnier than usual, over-worked it seemed from the effort of stay-ing awake. Her breathing quickened a bit as she rolled her eyes toward the doorway and stared, then looked up at me. I turned back to the doorway, and Dave was gone.

I thought he must have stepped out to the bathroom, or maybe even to his car. Maybe he needed a minute alone. I stroked Bertha's head, ran my thumb down her long, wide nose. Fifteen minutes later he still hadn't come back.

The vet came in and asked if we should proceed. When I suggested we wait for Dave, he explained that Dave had already left a credit card and signature at the front desk. His long silence then, full of some-thing besides awkwardness. Disappoint-ment. Sympathy, maybe. You can either stay or not stay, as you wish, the vet said.

I looked back down at big old Bertha, rubbed her wide black forehead, working her silky ears between the thumb and forefinger like I've seen Dave do. She continued to look toward the doorway, though whether she was watching for him or if that was just the path of least resistance for her eyes, I couldn't say. I stayed until the injection was finished and her breathing slowed to nothing. Her eyes stayed on the doorway until they lost their shine.

I went back to his apartment but he wasn't there. I waited awhile, then left, and then called later, but got no answer. When I called the next day he didn't even explain himself — why he'd left, where he'd gone.

Are you okay? I finally asked. That was such a strange way to leave.

He was quiet for a minute until I wondered if he wasn't going to talk about it at all. Then he said, I just couldn't, Liz. I don't do sickness very well.

I didn't say what I wanted to, which was, Well, hon, we're not often given the luxury to choose to "do" sickness or death. It just happens. I also didn't say the other thing that was on my mind, which was, What if I wasn't there? Would you have just left her there on the table, alone?

But instead the New Softer Liz said, I know it's hard. But we did the humane thing. Come over tonight. But he said he wanted to be alone, he'd catch up with me tomorrow before he left for Florida.

I know this should be telling me something important, something I should be noting carefully. My mother's voice is echoing in my head with something about community versus isolation and the importance of pulling strength from others when you are lacking. And my own inner voice behind that: It's about responsibility, it's about what you owe to someone you love who is in a bad way, a pact that you make when you enter into a relationship — yes, with a pet, too — to see her out of this world as she saw you through it. But the poor guy lost his dog, and it's not for me to tell him how he should have done it better. Even if it seems as if he did choke in the clutch.

The next morning Kate woke early. Pale light filtered through the filmy curtains, and the birds had already recognized the start of the day. She crawled from bed, picked up the journal she'd been reading, and carried it out to the family room.

In June 1993, Elizabeth turned thirty. Dave surprised her with a flight to Maui to join him in an off-tour pro-am tournament. One of her clients was among the sponsors, so her boss told her to bring her laptop, make a show of double-checking promotional literature, and call it a work trip. *I love this job,* she wrote. *They will need to pry me away from this place with a crowbar.*

Each time Elizabeth described her work, Kate felt as if she were reading about another person entirely. She'd written about designing logos and advertisements with the obsessiveness that Kate and her culinary school friends shared for rare ingredients; the journal was filled with details like the shape of a recurring geometric motif, the selection of fonts, choices of colors. But she'd never said such things aloud.

Although Dave had been to Maui any number of times, he behaved like a tourist with Elizabeth. They bodysurfed in Lahaina and watched the sun rise from the top of Kilauea volcano, a moonscape of brick-colored rocks backlit in orange. They trespassed in a sugarcane field and tasted some just to say they had, gnawing on stalks stringy and sweet, like a candied asparagus. Her fears of traveling together — that she'd be claustrophobic amid so much together-ness, or be lost in an orgy of golf — proved unfounded. She had time to herself. He respected her privacy. And though he was absorbed in the tournament, he was not consumed by it.

On the night of her birthday he brought her to a restaurant in a converted general store set in the middle of an old pineapple plantation. As they sipped passion-fruit margaritas, he slipped a small velvet box across the table. Her heart seized. *My first thought was Oh no, then had a parade of images — mortgage bills, poopy diapers, boredom. But when I flipped up the lid it was the most beautiful pair of diamond earrings, small perfect octagons with starry refractions from the candles and water glass. In the card he wrote, You're my rock.*

Kate heard a step behind her, then felt a hand on her shoulder. "Hey." Chris walked past the couch to the kitchen. "You're up early."

Kate rested the notebook in her lap. "The birds woke me up. They were like something out of Hitchcock."

He rubbed his head and reached for the cabinet where the cups were kept. "You make coffee yet?"

She glanced at the table beside her where a mug would be. "No." Once she'd opened the notebook and begun to read, it hadn't crossed her mind.

Chris filled the water chamber on the coffeemaker and emptied old grounds from the filter basket. Outside, the sun glowed pale on the long lawn.

"What got you up?" she asked.

"I have to write something up on Southeast Asia," he said, rubbing his face. "There's a hotel there that might be going on the market."

He opened the refrigerator and took out a cup of yogurt, and added a handful of fresh blueberries from their cardboard pint. Then he leaned against the counter lost in thought, the container brimming with berries held before him like a gift.

When Chris had asked her to marry him, it had been a surprise to her. They had been together just under a year. Kate had been working in the restaurant that night — she worked most nights — when the maître d' strode into the kitchen with one of her crème brûlées, apparently sent back by an unsatisfied customer. "Just look at this mess!" he said, gesturing disgustedly at the broken crust. She took it in her hands, brows tight. Sticking out of the middle was a diamond ring, gleaming in the caramelized sugar.

In that instant, the vision of her life rearranged itself as effortlessly as cellular division, their togetherness expanding in the crevices of her free time, his belongings reproducing in the small space of her apartment. Unlike Elizabeth, she hadn't automatically equated marriage with children or debt or suburbs, but even if she had, those things would not have been unwelcome. She hadn't thought beyond the two of them together, living together, planning and saving together — all things she trusted would happen, one step at a time.

Chris ate large spoonfuls of the yogurt and blueberries, staring unfocused across the room, his thoughts on hotels half a world away. She itched to open the notebook, but of course it would be rude.

"I thought the kids might like a jeep tour this afternoon," she said.

He looked at her like a man awoken from sleepwalking. He had no idea what she was talking about.

"Off-roading on the peninsula," she said. "They loved that last year."

He nodded. She could see him doing the math, the number of hours he'd need to get his work done in order to go, the constant tallying of how much of a time commitment was absolutely necessary and what could be reduced in small pinches. He wanted to come. But his time here was not really his own. This is the way their arrangement worked, and there were sacrifices.

"Or we can save it for another day, if another day would be better," she said. She didn't want to go without him. It was more fun when he was around, and it was also easier. That was the economics of parenting; together, each could relax his or her vigilance by half. What happened when there was only one parent? she wondered. Did Dave Martin have to operate at 100 percent all of the time? Did he ever feel entirely at rest?

"No, let's do it today. In the afternoon," Chris said, and walked back into the bedroom, where his laptop and briefcase were waiting.

January 1, 1994

Dave's coach threw a blowout bash in Hilton Head, and we flew down for it. Big golf world muckety-mucks, including a Titleist exec who thinks Dave should give up the tour and come work for them. Gear manufacturing, testing, promotions, whatever. Both of us had too much to drink and when we were by ourselves in a corner of the room, I told him it was not a bad early-retirement option. He laughed, but it was bitter. You been talking to my father?

Soon afterward he was jovial Dave again, working the room and getting a woman from Cartier to talk seriously about sponsoring him. I was on my own for a while and found a spot near the bar and talked with another player's wife. She was pretty in the typical photographed-alongside-the-putting-green way, long blond hair, but an edge — a triple ear pierce and irreverent about golf. They have a toddler, and she's pressing her husband to leave the tour because he's never home. But she doesn't want to nag because, as they say, a drag at home drags down the playing. "Game face, right?" she said. "We all have to do game face." Then she said with a sly smile, "Come on, let's go outside."

Before I could respond, I looked across the room and saw Dave watching me, wholesome Dave Martin. ELIZABETH DEEEE, he called out, like a pronouncement or a crowd introduction at a sporting event.

I knew then that it's not true anymore that my choices are open. Unless you want to breach every expectation, live life with no boundaries or limitations. There are repercussions. . . .

Choices, repercussions. Kate got up and poured herself a cup of the coffee Chris had made, stood in the kitchen, stirring. It was a strange way to think of dating — a limiting

217

of your options and lifestyle because you'd chosen one type of partner over another — though it was technically true. It was true of most decisions. The effects of your choices might not be clear at the moment they were made. But if you turned back to see where you'd come, there they'd be, the ghost of the path not taken leading to the places you would never go.

Piper wandered into the room asking for pancakes, vacant eyes suggesting she was still half in her dreams. She curled up on the couch fingering her blanket, feet curled beneath Kate's left thigh. The cold toes made Kate shiver, but she pulled her daughter's feet in closer and rubbed them to warmth. It became automatic so quickly, that impulse to do things to ensure your child's comfort, even as it sacrificed your own.

Kate stretched out alongside her, scooping her in close with an arm around her waist. Piper's hair smelled of verbena shampoo, though Kate always told her she smelled like pennies and carrots, since her hair was the same pale coppery shade as Chris's. Kate reached to lay the notebook on the floor, but before she closed it, she read the last few lines of the entry.

. . . At 11:59, Dave found his way back to me. Happy New Year, Miz Drogan, he said. There was general mayhem as the ball dropped on TV, and everyone sloshed champagne around like we'd won the Super Bowl. He kissed me long and hard, then pulled back like he was sizing me up. In a heavy mock-Georgia voice he said, I think this is gonna be a big year for the last name Drogan. It's a-goin' DOWN.

On the children's last day of farm camp, Kate came back to the house after swimming to read on the patio. She poured a glass of iced tea and put it opposite the notebook, as if she were having a drink with a friend. The pages representing the early months of 1994 flew by. Elizabeth's subtle resistance to Dave melted. The glass of iced tea warmed in the sun, forgotten.

In March, Elizabeth and Dave traveled to Georgia for his father's sixty-fifth birthday. The Martins' huge Greek Revival home was unlike any she'd seen, plantationlike on acres of oak and magnolia trees. The family's camaraderie was similarly impressive and overwhelming, Dave's brothers so exuberant that sometimes she'd slip away to the bathroom to sit quietly alone. His parents could not have been more unlike her own.

His father runs the show and has to have the last word on everything, as one Scotch turns into four. On his birthday he was giving Dave the business about failing to make the cut in Hawaii, and kept at it long after it stopped being funny. Dave's mother is the most tranquil, agreeable person I've ever seen. She seems medicated.

There were pictures of Dave's sister, Dani, everywhere in the house, beautiful, frozen in time at thirty-one. Her widower, Zack, was there with the two children, and around them, Dave was the uncle everyone wishes they had: fun, patient, indulgent. *He spoils them rotten.* Family members shared stories about Dani as naturally as if she were someone who simply happened not to be visiting that day. But not Dave. He never mentioned her, and when someone else did, he left the room.

Odd, Kate thought, that he would put up such a firewall against discussing her even with Elizabeth, who had lost a sister herself, as well as her mother.

Friday, March 18, 1994

Earlier tonight sitting alone with Dave on the porch I mentioned how nice it is that everyone keeps their memories of Dani going with so many stories, and that it's probably good for the kids, too. We were on the porch swing and Dave was rocking it back and forth a little, heel to toe. The setting sun sank a good three inches behind the azalea bushes before he said anything.

Yep, I suppose, especially for the kids.

I knew I was going out on a limb but I gave it a try anyway, and asked if being back home made him miss her more. We both stared ahead at the sky as if the sunset were the most fascinating thing in the world, and after what felt like hours he said, Nothing makes me miss her more or less. I just plain do.

I thought about saying I had a sister too, but it felt all wrong. Not just because I'd be horning in on his grief, but because I can see his look: You're telling me this now? . . .

Kate reread the last sentences once, then again. Elizabeth had never told him.

. . . I never have been able to think of the words to tell about what happened to her, can't imagine saying it out loud. When you ride ahead of someone who's barely eight, what happens behind you is still

221

your fault. Especially if you're being careless, and unforgivably if you were trying to
get ahead because you didn't feel like being followed, didn't feel like being responsible for someone else. It screams out that
such a person can't be trusted around
children.

Sunday, March 20, 1994

We're leaving tomorrow morning, and I've
enjoyed it more than I thought I would. Big
families take on a life of their own, pull
you in like a commune.

I had a curious talk with Zack last night
while we were doing the dishes. He's
quieter than the brothers, and I get the
feeling he likes to step away sometimes
too. He was asking how Dave and I met
and how long we've been together, and
when I told him about a year and a half he
said, That's good. It was odd the way he
said it. Not, That's good, as in, That's nice,
but as in, That's good for him.

I didn't know what to say to that and we
were quiet a minute. I was going to ask
about how the kids were doing when he
said, It's nice that you guys are together.
Dave seems happier than I've seen him in
a long time.

I asked about Dave and Dani when they were younger, because he doesn't seem to mind talking about her. He said they were practically like twins, that after college she spent time traveling with Dave on the mini tours. Then he said something strange — that he was glad to see Dave sticking with the tour. After a little silence he said it had started to seem like Dave wasn't sticking with anything, like he was bailing on things before they could bail on him. He said he didn't mean that as a knock on Dave, but it was like instead of making things seem more precious to him, losing Dani made things more expendable. He said, I'm glad to see that's not the case anymore.

Unfair as it is, I couldn't help thinking of Bertha.

Back in New York, their dating life was happy and uneventful for months. Elizabeth traveled to some of his tournaments, and any weekends he wasn't traveling they spent together.

One day, Elizabeth received a phone call at work following a routine visit with her gynecologist.

The results from my annual appointment were abnormal. Bad cells. Cervical dysplasia. The doctor told me to come back in on Monday and we'd discuss treatment options, though none might be needed. Sometimes it disappears on its own.

I called Dave, caught him back at his apartment after the second day of the Buick Classic just over in Westchester. He made the cut and was headed out to dinner with a few of the guys. I probably should have waited to tell him until he got in later but I was feeling shaky and didn't want to keep it to myself. He's usually good at making me feel better, pointing out the upsides to things. But when I told him he didn't say a word.

I tried to do the glass-half-full talk: it's totally treatable, sometimes it doesn't even need anything, just goes away on its own, it's probably not a big deal. But he still didn't say anything. Finally he offered me some vague reassurances and asked if he could call me later. It's been three hours, and I haven't heard back yet.

He still hasn't called. I can't think of a single excusable reason why.

FIFTEEN

Three kinds of lettuce, two kinds of tomatoes. Zucchini, cucumbers, herbs. The owners of the bungalow cultivated a garden in the side yard and, as a condition of renting the house to Kate and Chris for the summer, asked them to water and weed. Kate had never been much of a gardener but was surprised by how satisfying she found the work. Though she would not be on the island when the tomatoes matured, she enjoyed watching the tiny buds open on the Sweet 100s, and seeing the heirlooms grow bulbous and obscene until the vines bowed under the weight of their own success. While she pruned, James and Piper wandered into the neighbors' yard. Mrs. Callum usually offered something good to eat.

Before Kate met Chris in New York, she shared a tiny apartment on West Seventy-Second, the envy of her friends not just for its low rent-controlled price or its full-sized kitchen appliances, unheard of in a small walk-up, but for its fire escape. The postage-stamp-sized landing was exactly large enough for one folding chair and a coffee cup, and from the rusty iron railings she grew mesclun and herbs haphazardly in three hanging window boxes. Whatever grew made its way to her salads, and the herbs to bread.

Elizabeth had been the better gardener. The evidence had been all over her kitchen; flowers on the table, season permitting, bunches of basil tied with string in a glass on the windowsill. This domestic piece had fit naturally into the spectrum of her home-making, all of which had seemed to come so naturally.

Kate pulled one scraggly weed after another. But less and less was as it seemed with Elizabeth. Kate hadn't known that Elizabeth had had cervical dysplasia; Kate's sister, Rachel, had once had it as well. There had been several white-knuckle days until tests showed it had not progressed to cancer, several phone conversations in which Kate had struggled to strike a new note, one of authoritative comfort from a younger sister. How far had Elizabeth's dysplasia gone, Kate wondered, and how had Dave re-deemed himself after being so absent? Kate

yanked a weed with more force than necessary, and tore out an entire small stand of
lettuce.

From Mrs. Callum's yard Piper's voice
went high and squeaky with excitement.
Kate stood from the garden and squinted
into the light, shielding her eyes with a dirt-
covered hand. Both children were crouched
with Mrs. Callum by her porch, looking
tentatively at something under the shrubs.

"Careful how you touch them, dear," she
heard the older woman say. "They're just
babies."

"Look at their ears," James said. "They're
hardly even long yet."

Kate walked across the lawn telling herself
she was merely curious. Her pulse drummed
in her ears.

"Look at their tiny noses. Their tails are
sooo soft," Piper gushed, then saw her
mother approaching. "Mom! Look at the
baby bunnies!"

Kate came beside them and peered down
at a nest of five or six tiny rabbits, their sides
fluttering in the rapid panting of the small,
or the unwell. Piper and James were touching them gently, each stroking a soft gray
back with a single finger. Her thoughts
automatically went to tularemia.

"Oh, kids, that's not a great idea," she

heard herself say with a voice calm and steady as if it came from someone else. "When their mother comes back and smells that humans have been touching them, it will upset her." The kids pulled back their hands reluctantly.

"They're so cute," Piper said again. "I wish we could keep one."

"They're not pets, sweetie, they're wild animals." Disease-ridden wild animals. "This is their home."

"Well I wish their home was in *our* bushes," said James.

"You can come over here and peek at them any time you'd like. We've always had so many rabbits here," the older woman said, rising from her crouch and turning to Kate. "I guess they know a quiet place to multiply when they see one."

"Mmm." Kate forced a smile as she watched her children entranced by the baby animals. They were at a petting zoo. They were at a normal, sanitized attraction, and she was like any other mother who was smiling at her children's enthusiasm and who did not have hot welts spreading below her right ear.

"We should get a pet, Mom," Piper said. "Like a bunny. Or a kitten."

"Or a hamster," said James. "Robert in

my class has two hamsters, and they chew boxes and hold food in their cheeks."

"Maybe," said Kate vaguely. "After the summer." She stroked Piper's hair, and her fingertips exerted pressure ever so gently away from the bushes and back toward their own house. "Did you kids tell Mrs. Callum about how well you played miniature golf the other day? About your holes in one?"

"Well, now, that's not easy to do. Congratulations." The older woman smiled. Kate could feel her desire for them to stay. "I don't know if it's too late for a snack, but I have some fresh cookies in the kitchen. Maybe when we come back out, the bunnies will be awake."

"That sounds nice, but we have some early plans tonight." Kate put her hand on James's shoulder. "If we clean up and have an early dinner, we can go back and try again at minigolf tonight."

She waited until they were in the house, then said what she'd wanted to say since she joined them by the bushes.

"Come on inside and wash your hands, let's wash up really well." She went into the bathroom with the pump of antibacterial hand soap from the kitchen, and began to rub it into each of their palms. She glanced at the label — *kills 99 percent* — as she handed them towels. "I have an even better idea. Let's take our showers early."

"Showers? Now?" James wrinkled his nose. "It's still afternoon. We haven't even eaten dinner yet."

"Oh, but let's get all cleaned up so we can eat and play minigolf early, and maybe we can get in a round plus ice cream before it gets dark." She was throwing out her whole arsenal. "Come on, take off your clothes, kids." She pulled back the shower door and tugged down the towels hanging from their hooks.

Chris walked past the bathroom in the hallway. "They're taking showers now?"

"Sure, why not?" She spoke nonchalantly, fiddled with the hot and cold shower handles.

"It's barely four o'clock."

"Well, we could get a jump on an early supper, and then since they were all washed up, we were talking about going to play minigolf in the evening."

He looked at her as if she were suggesting dinner in Paris. "That makes no sense. Let's enjoy the rest of the day. I was thinking about going to the beach. Kids, you want to go to the beach for a little while before dinner?"

They looked up, eyes wide. It kept getting better.

"Chris, I really don't think . . ."

"Think what?" His tone had been merely perplexed, but now it was turning testy. "We're on vacation, Kate. Don't be rigid. And what's up with your neck?"

She glanced in the mirror and saw that her hair had become damp with sweat, slicked away and no longer a drawn curtain. There was the red flush, center stage.

"Is there poison ivy in the garden?" Chris winced.

"I think so." She touched it casually like a mild irritation. "It's getting worse. I should probably pick up something at the store to put on it."

"That came up fast." He looked on with mild concern. "Well, we'd better watch out where the kids are playing in the yard. Come on, let's go to the beach."

The kids abandoned the shower and headed out the doorway, dropping their towels on the floor. Kate looked at the ground and breathed deeply. Then she re-hung the towels and followed.

The beach was quiet in the late afternoon, peopled by walkers and kite fliers, fishermen setting their tackle and young couples napping. The kids threw down their sand toys and headed to the water's edge. Kate laid the blanket beside her beach bag, a tote filled with her regular accoutrements. Bottled water and grapes, sunscreen and wallet, a novel that probably would not be read, though she brought it every time.

Chris joined her on the blanket and watched the kids with an expression of satisfaction. "Man, I love it here."

Chris was a man easily contented. It wasn't that he was simple or easygoing, because he was not; he was irritated by people who stood in the way of his goals, and people who made things more complicated than they had to be. But he recognized small pleasures, appreciated things gone right, and basked in the moment rather than focusing on what should be or hadn't been. He possessed naturally a balance others sought in the chairs of shrinks and the arms of lovers, an innate equilibrium that kept him from the shaky highs or debilitating lows. The downside was that he had trouble sympathizing with people when their troubles derived from something intangible. He called them complicated. *They need a hobby*, he'd say, *something to look at besides their own navels*.

He pointed his chin into the breeze and

closed his eyes as if he might fall asleep upright, leaning back on the palms of his hands. This was one of his favorite places anywhere, and he'd been to beaches all over the world. Kate had accompanied him to some. But none of his travels had spoiled his ability to enjoy himself in ordinary places, even shoddy ones. Shortly before they were engaged, they'd gone to the Bahamas to check out the investment potential of an old resort just outside of Nassau. He'd been given a tip from a new source but it had been a bust, the hotel so down-at-the-heels that it was beyond rehabilitation. They had stayed for only one day and one night, and gone to dinner downtown, their cab passing faded pink Colonial-style buildings padlocked with chipped wrought-iron gates. The fences were papered with public-service posters, "Give blood, Mon!" and "Protect ya ting: Wear a rubba all de time!" They'd dined in an expat place in Parliament Square, eaten overcooked lobster tails in sour champagne sauce on a veranda near a party of Americans exuding entitlement as loud as tacky laughter. Afterward they'd sat on the beach behind their hotel in the dark, opting to sit in the sand rather than on rusted loungers, wordless under palm fronds that flapped like party streamers. And he'd had that same smile he wore now.

Where's this good mood coming from? she'd asked that night, surprised that he wasn't disappointed by the wild-goose chase of a trip.

What's not to be in a good mood about? I'm here with you. And then he'd smiled as if it were a given that that would be enough.

If she had gotten sick before they were engaged, if she had gotten a diagnosis like Elizabeth's, Chris would have dropped whatever he was doing and come to her. She leaned forward, resting her forearms on her knees, and studied the grains of sand in the russet hair of his leg. She was certain of this.

"What was going on with you?" he asked, drawing her out of her thoughts. "Back there at the house."

Kate was surprised to hear his voice. She'd thought he was nearly asleep. "What do you mean?"

"The business about the early shower. You getting all Lady Macbeth, scrubbing the kids." His tone was light, flippant.

She tried to think of a wisecrack. She always had some fallback line. But nothing came. What if for once she didn't cover her tracks, and simply told the naked truth? She

235

tried to imagine it; each day he'd be gauging her condition, watching to see evidence of paranoia winning out over logic, and his regard for her as an equal would be contaminated. Sympathy, even well intentioned, would set her apart, and he would treat her with kid gloves. She shivered in the sun.

But what if she was underestimating him? What if she started with the tularemia and kept on going? He would furrow his brows because he wouldn't understand but he would be concerned, because he did love her and what happened to her happened to him, and to all of them. All that energy and effort to conceal, released.

She took off her sunglasses and turned. "Remember tularemia?"

He shielded his eyes with his hand, watching the kids at the waterline. Piper shouldn't go in above her knees without one of them there. He turned to her and tilted his chin up, an acknowledgment of her comment, and gave a small grin.

A grin was not what she'd expected. She waited for his question or comment, the one that would open the door to all the rest, or for him to recoil as he saw that she'd become complicated. But he kept watching the kids.

Slowly, she realized she'd been misunderstood. He thought she'd made a joke, *Remember tularemia.* His grin said, *Good one.* She was that pathetic, with her paralyzing fears. She put her sunglasses back on and faced the water as well.

The kids called out to them from the shoreline, "Come play, come play with us in the waves." Chris stood slowly, stretching his arms overhead and then twisting his back with a light crack.

"You coming?" he asked, and smiled, held out a hand to help her up.

She sat for only a fraction of a second, then took his hand. "Of course," she said. She stood and tossed her book in her beach bag, followed him to the water, leaving the beach bag open in the sand.

Monday, June 13, 1994

Had my doctor's appointment this afternoon. Before we discussed treatment options she asked if there was any possibility I was pregnant. I told her it wasn't possible. But she tested anyway as a precaution, and before our eyes it became possible. In an instant I was 18 again, blood pounding in my ears, thinking, Inconceivable, and Stupid, stupid girl.

Pregnant. Pregnant and sick. Pregnant

and sick and alone. It's like a bad made-for-TV movie. I walked for hours until I noticed it was getting dark, and when I slowed down, there I was in front of the National Arts Club. Sat down on my heels with my back against the park fence. Same beautiful windows. Same beautiful people, wineglasses and air kisses, craning necks and applause.

I expected very different things of my life when I sat here 13 years ago thinking through this same decision. What they were exactly I can't even remember now. I guess I thought the decision I made would springboard my life in a certain direction — exhibits, travel, culture, the whole package. And none of it happened. I saw myself painting my way up from the bottom and achieving . . . something. Not riches, but entrée into some kind of community of artistic types who slaved away at what they loved with the vision to create something out of nothing. And none of it happened. I never even graduated.

Wasted opportunity, wasted education, and suddenly it felt so wrong that I snuffed out a life for some vague idea of accomplishment that I squandered. I was so full of self-righteousness then about my own potential and the injustice of bad luck.

My choices and motives at that time were confusing enough that it was forgivable. But I don't know if the same thing can be said now.

The lights went on next door to the club, a building filled with the evening activity of people coming home. Mealtime, homework, kids practicing their music. It's odd theater, sitting outside and being able to see it all. Next door to the arts club was a second-floor room with a child after her bath. The girl was in constant motion and chattering away while the woman worked a nightgown over her head and tried to comb out her hair. The woman would stop to laugh, then hold her by the shoulders and point her forward again, and go back to brushing. Something about them reminded me of that babysitting job I had when I was 12, the kind mother with the three-year-old girl, their happy little universe. The girl's room and the window on the party in the arts club were just a few feet apart, but seemed a million miles from each other.

Thursday, June 16, 1994

The doctor advises against doing anything about the abnormal cells, calls it a low-

grade case and said, Watch, it will probably rectify itself. She gave me the name
of an OB and said I should go as soon as
possible for a prenatal visit, and that we'd
monitor the cells closely. Sometimes
pregnancy makes them grow faster; sometimes they go away on their own. She
didn't ask what, if anything, I planned to
do about the pregnancy.

I'm thinking about leaving Dave another
message, and this time going ahead and
telling him about the baby. But not telling
him what I intend to do about it. I admit I
am tempted to hurt him this way because
it would shatter his self-image as a family
guy, and he'd know it was all because he's
a coward. Straight through my birthday,
not a word. Did not surprise me, because
how could he pop up for that when he'd
already gone this far? Part of me hopes
he'll come forward yet. I want to believe
the honorable person I've known these
past two years is not a figment of my
imagination. Though if he showed up, that
would come with its own repercussions.

Tuesday, June 21, 1994, 2 a.m.

My apartment is in shambles. Last night I
moved the sofa against the wall, threw a

drop cloth over the floor, and set up the easel and canvas. I haven't felt so consumed by something in years, lost track of time completely. I started off thinking in terms of shapes and colors and raw energy, but what started coming through was something much more restrained. A simple contrast of the two scenes in Gramercy Park, the woman combing her daughter's hair, the party at the NAC.

When I finally fell into bed I dreamed about Florence at Signora P's but my NYU friends were in the kitchen. Haviland gorgeous and haughty sitting with her cigarette and when she laughed at me, smoke curled out of her nose.

Friday, June 24, 1994

I left him a voice mail. I told him about the baby, recorded it right onto the little tape of no return. I wish I could say that I just left him the information — that I intend to do this with or without him — leaving him hanging about the diagnosis just to see what he'd do. But I'm not quite brave enough to test him that way and have to live with the outcome.

So I did the cop-out: I told him the dysplasia is mild and not a big deal, which I knew would free up his paralysis and make it easier for him. He's not a strong man, but every fiber of his being needs to believe that he's a good one. I did this pretty much knowing he'll come around, though now I'll never know whether he would have come back on his own if I'd been really sick. But I don't have that luxury. I don't want to do this by myself.

The future's like a superhighway through a big bland desert. Marriage, kids, mortgage, suburbs, little hands getting into my paint. I will not give in to the sentimentality of wondering about the other options, partners, lifestyles, the whole Road Not Taken thing. I already did that, and it brought me here. This is where I am, and he is where I am. It will be okay. But the price I'll pay for not having to do this alone will be never having the certainty that I can count on him.

Sixteen

Kate stood at the kitchen counter staring into her beach bag in disbelief. She rifled through its contents — water bottle, key chain, sunscreen, book. But no wallet. She turned the bag upside down on the kitchen table in a waterfall of pens, receipts, and snack bars. Spare change clattered onto the counter, but no trunk key, which was not a surprise. That had been zippered away, night after night. And now it was gone, stolen with the wallet at the beach.

Driver's license and credit cards, replaceable. Cash, negligible. But she was fairly sure that this was the only copy of the trunk key. She poured herself a glass of water and sat down at the kitchen table. There might be another copy somewhere at the Martins' house — it was hard to believe Elizabeth would have given her only key to the law firm. But to ask Dave would be to raise all kinds of unpleasant issues, chief among them his belief, she was sure, that his wife's journals should not have left his house.

She could call the police to see if a wallet had been found; she would check the beach, and call some island locksmiths. But for now, since no one would see, she sat at the table with her face in her hands.

She was alone. The kids were next door at the Callums' so she could work at Flour for a few hours, and Chris was en route to Cambodia. An exclusive Angkor Wat hotel was rumored to be ripe for purchase; it had been empty and in a state of disrepair for some time, and its owner, a Saudi prince, let slip that he'd just as soon sell. When the president of Chris's firm heard, it was as if he'd been given the coordinates of the Holy Grail. Finding a property of this quality so close to the famous temples was unheard of. Chris got on the next flight to Siem Reap to check it out and, if it was promising, begin negotiations. He'd likely be gone a week, ten days. When he returned, they'd have a week left of their vacation.

Kate had felt a jolt at his first mention of Southeast Asia. He'd been many times, but not in the past year. She knew what had been happening in the region lately. Anyone who followed current events did. All over the news, cities were reduced to pinpoints glowing red on maps, more terror cells and training camps discovered every day. When she'd mentioned her concern to Chris — breezily, like a parody of spousal worry — he'd assured her that those things weren't happening where he was going.

It was normal to have concerns. But she also knew she had lost perspective in the past year on the way an ordinary person might reasonably feel under certain circumstances. She saw Chris in town squares and markets, places that were targets for desperate hate-filled men and hateful acts. If he was in the wrong place at the wrong time there would be smoke, cries, and prayers; his wallet would be found, blown to the curb, his passport in pieces, photos of their children loose in the street with charred edges.

Kate got up from the kitchen table and went to the loft to examine the trunk. It sat in the middle of the floor like a squat rebuke to her carelessness. Why had she kept the key in her wallet? She crouched to scrutinize the lock, some sort of metal weathered to dull brown. A classic vintage keyhole, a small round opening above with a tiny notch at bottom.

Kate went back downstairs for anything that might be made into a tool — Piper's barrette, a paper clip, a pair of nail clippers with a fold-out file. She wriggled each in the lock without luck. All of them caught on the notch, too thick to slide the rest of the way in. She remembered the little key for their car's rooftop storage unit, and retrieved it from a dish of loose change on Chris's dresser. Just looking at it she could see it was too thick. Next to the dish Kate noticed the photograph of herself laughing over a dropped soufflé in the studio, the one he always brought with him when he traveled. She hesitated, wondering what, if anything, it meant that he had not taken it this time.

She went back up to the loft and the trunk. If an island locksmith was not helpful, she might try tracking down a trunk company that still made tiny locks and keys. But even as the thought crossed her mind, she knew she wouldn't have the time or patience. In the end she would pry it open any way she could.

She sat back on her heels and looked out the loft window. Propped on the inside of the windowsill was the notebook with Elizabeth smiling into the sun. On the chaise lay the pastel-striped notebook. Two notebooks still outside the trunk.

■ ■ ■ ■

The screen door slammed shut behind her with a hollow bang. "I'm here," she called toward the kitchen, and put her bag behind the counter.

"It's about time." Max's voice came from behind the curtain. "Do you *know* how many tarts we have to make for that dinner party?" Kate poured herself a cup of coffee and stood at the window that opened onto the side patio. At the largest table three men sat with coffee and doughnuts, their golf shoes piled on a nearby bench.

"Hollywood people," Max muttered from the kitchen. "They order two kinds of tarts in double the number they actually need, so they won't run out of either kind. Then they have the nerve to ask if they can return the extras."

One of the golfers' cell phones began to ring. He looked down, grimaced, and pressed a button to silence it without answering. "Ahhh, no, I don't think so," he said. "Not right now."

Kate watched as he pushed the phone away and leaned back in his chair. His friend laughed. She fought an urge to go out and tell him to answer his damned phone, that you never knew why someone might be calling. She turned away from the window and walked through the curtains to the kitchen.

"Sorry I'm late. I had to get a sitter for the kids. Chris went to Cambodia." She picked up an apron from the pile folded on the shelf.

"Cambodia? What's he doing there?"

"Checking out another exotic hotel."

"Exotic *hotels*. Ah, yes," he said bitterly.

She looked up, eyes narrowed. He stood half inside the refrigerator, removing ingredients. But his jaded comment, she reminded herself, was not about Chris.

"Have you heard from William?" she asked, tying the apron strings behind her back. "Anything at all? Or about him?"

He moved around the butcher-block island collecting utensils, and for a moment she thought he had not heard her.

"No," he said finally. "And I don't expect I will."

"Well there has to be something you can do. Go after him legally?"

He handed her a whisk and a rubber spatula. "It would be very hard to do." He tapped the spatula against the counter lightly, as if he'd thought it over but decided against it. "I'm not going to go that route."

248

She wanted to say that she'd never liked William much anyway, but that sort of proclamation was never useful after the fact. It hadn't stopped her from saying it the spring day Max called with the news. But the courageous thing would have been for her to have said something years ago, when she'd felt a chill from William, possessive of Max and unwelcoming to his old friends. Or certainly to have said something last summer, that night out to dinner. She'd gotten up from the table to go to the ladies' room, and as she turned the corner she'd seen William in the doorway to the kitchen talking to their waiter with too much familiarity. It was all wrong, his posture and expression. And even if she'd felt he was not right for Max long before, she'd known it with certainty that night, the way he'd turned away from the waiter with that sensual languor, a twist of hips first, head last. He even saw that she'd seen him, and brushed past her with heavy-lidded eyes like a pissed-off cat. Still, she hadn't mentioned it to Max. It was awkward. It was private. And she might be wrong.

Max handed her the cream cheese as he laid out the ingredients for the tart crust. Then he cleared his throat. "I decided to sell the house."

She looked up quickly. All those years designing, then building. The walls of bookshelves, and water views if you stood just so. "Oh, no."

He shook his head. "It's just a house."

That wasn't what he meant, though. What he meant was *The bakery means more.*

She stood looking at him, but he didn't meet her eye. She scratched at his hand with her index finger. "I'm sorry," she said. "When?"

"I'm putting it on in a few weeks. Catch the summer people while they're here."

She opened the cream cheese. "Am I allowed to say I'm glad you're keeping the bakery? It's so you. It's irreplaceable."

He paused, then dumped flour into the mixing bowl. A small cloud rose from the pile. She glanced at him sideways, and saw his eyes glistening.

"Do you have a realtor for the house yet?" she asked softly. "Need help fixing it up?"

He smiled, and coughed away the emotion. She'd amused him.

"What?" she said, feigning offense. "I've sold houses. I have an eye for style."

He dropped his eyes to her baggy T-shirt and cargo shorts. "Sure you do, honey," he said, drawing out his words patiently, as if he were speaking to a child. "You surely do."

She flicked a piece of cream cheese at him, and he lifted it off his collar with a fingernail and rubbed at the place, smiling.

On opposite sides of the wooden island in the center they moved through the automatic gestures; flour, salt, and sugar blended, shortening and butter cut into pebbles, drops of ice water scattered like seeds. As he worked the dough he looked over at her, then looked again, as if he hadn't noticed before.

"What's up with your eyes? They're all red."

"Allergies."

He raised his eyebrows. "What are you allergic to? Butter?"

She exhaled. "I'm fine. I just lost my wallet, and got bent out of shape about it this morning. I think it was stolen yesterday on the beach." She dropped the block of cream cheese into another bowl and jabbed at it with a spoon.

In the scope of things, the loss of the key was not tremendous. Still, it delayed things, and reading the journals was becoming too consuming. While she was playing with the kids, she found herself wondering what had drawn Elizabeth to stay with Dave, and what had finally pulled her away. The other night after they turned off the light, as

Chris's hand brushed the flat of her stomach above the waistband of her briefs, she'd had a jarring memory of Elizabeth's thong, her art-teacher boyfriend, and her rant against loyalty. Even without having finished reading the journals, Kate wondered how she would be able to look Dave in the eye.

"Okay, so your wallet was stolen," Max said, puzzled by her emotion. "You'll get a new license with a better picture, and you'll have to memorize a new credit card number for your online shopping. It's just a wallet."

"It's not just a wallet." Kate sprinkled a fistful of flour across the island for a kneading surface. As she told him about the journals and the lost key, she trailed her fingertips across the counter, creating long wavy lines through the flour.

"And the rest of the journals are locked inside?"

"A few. The last one or two."

Max turned the dough onto the floured island and rolled it in her direction. "Maybe the husband has another key somewhere."

Kate palmed the ball, letting the heat from her hands soften it, streaking the butter through the dough to make it flaky. Then she pushed it against the countertop. This was not something she wanted to ask Dave. "There could be another key somewhere at his house," she said, working the dough in short tight strokes. "But it's awkward. How do you think he feels about my reading these books in the first place? I don't know how he'd take hearing that my key is gone."

She could easily see Dave's response, matter-of-fact with a chilly edge. But there could also be an explosion, all that anger at the world's injustice finally let out of its box.

"So dodge the whole thing," Max said. "Stuff the trunk in your basement, and if he ever asks, just tell him it's a lot of girly angst and that his wife would have wanted them thrown away."

That might have been possible at the beginning of the summer, but now Dave wanted to be involved, and expected a resolution. Perhaps he'd always had more backbone than she'd credited him with. Or maybe the past year was still rolling out its effects, like the way Dave perceived his marriage and privacy: what had been hers, what had been his, and what of hers was now his.

She told Max about what Dave had already read of the last journal, about Elizabeth traveling to meet someone named Michael. At the suggestion of infidelity Max's expression hardened. "I don't know why this matters so much to you," he said. "Protecting her."

"I'm just trying to do this thing that she asked, Max. I'm just trying to figure out the right thing to do with these books."

His hands continued to move fluidly as he flattened another ball of dough into a disc, but he said nothing.

"If someone you cared about died and trusted you with something like this, wouldn't you take it seriously?"

He contemplated it, but didn't answer directly. "Well, losing the key isn't the biggest deal in the world. It's not as if you lost the books themselves. You can always smash the damn thing open. Surely it's not made of titanium."

Kate set the cream cheese mixture in the refrigerator. "I will if I have to. But it would be a shame to ruin it. The trunk is a family heirloom."

"Well, her family isn't seeing that trunk again anyway unless you make peace with the fact that you can't control the way she is going to be remembered. What she did is what she did."

He pushed a large bowl of kiwi toward her. She took one and began to peel, digging out the core on each end. She thought of all the marital hopscotching she'd seen in New York, the indiscretions of people she had never thought capable of cheating.

Maybe loyalty is for swans and bird-minded people. Not a sentiment she would have thought could come from Elizabeth.

This wasn't something she was going to be able to leave unfinished, or discover quietly and put aside. Dave would call again, and again. Elizabeth was not an unintelligent person, but this — leaving the journals to someone else, without specifying what should be done with them — had been a careless way of safeguarding them.

If it had been Kate, and she'd had secrets she'd wanted kept private, she would have done things differently. She would have stipulated that the books be destroyed.

SEVENTEEN

Kate sat in the loft and listened to the murmuring downstairs. The children had quieted their bedtime silliness once the lights went out, and would be asleep soon.

The remaining half of the pastel-striped journal was thicker than the other notebooks. Elizabeth had supplemented its pages with sheets torn from notepads, backs of flyers, scraps of thought scrawled on the edges of train schedules. She wrote wherever she happened to be, on whatever she happened to have.

Dave had called Elizabeth right after he received her voice mail about the baby, as she'd expected. They reconciled. His apology and remorse seemed sincere to Kate, and moving, but Elizabeth held herself at a remove. *I marched through the necessary gymnastics of it with him. The tears and apologies, the self-recrimination and gnashing of teeth, then the parade of kindness. It had to be that way, or he wouldn't be who he is.* Gradually the analytical tone disappeared, and when she wrote about the return of passion, it was without irony or reservation.

One hot night Elizabeth and Dave sweated through failed air-conditioning in his building. The fan rotated in the dark just inches from the bed, making sheets clammy then hot again wherever they lay. He got up for ice cream and walked naked to the kitchen, and Elizabeth watched the streetlights cross his body like a toga. He returned with two small granny-glass sundaes, a ring in hers where the cherry would be.

Kate read this with the odd sensation of wanting to turn to someone, like two friends watching a movie, and say, *How can she just forgive him and move on?* and *What is it with men and engagement rings in food, anyway?* But the person she wanted to turn to, she realized, was Elizabeth.

With her friends in Washington, the other mothers she'd met through her children's schools, conversations tended to skate on the surface of things. With her parents, there was the fear of saying anything that would not live up to intellectual standards, that would forfeit ground on the respect she'd earned as an adult with ambitions of her own. With Rachel . . . they were closer when

Kate was working. After she'd quit that last job, when Piper was a baby, she hadn't been able to explain her choice in a way that Rachel could understand or respect. At the next Christmas gathering, Rachel's confusion and disappointment, and the gulf that had opened between them, were palpable.

And with Chris — well. But reading Elizabeth's notebooks was one unedited mind to another, and also entirely inimitable in real life. The person in the world most likely to understand her now was a dead woman, and she felt more alone than she'd felt at the summer's beginning.

Elizabeth and Dave's wedding was a small gathering at an estate home in Georgia. Dave's brother-in-law Zack read a poem by Pablo Neruda, and Zack's children were flower girl and ring bearer. Elizabeth was fifteen weeks pregnant. Dave became choked up during the vows; Elizabeth was surprised by her own sadness that her mother could not be there. *It doesn't matter what kind of relationship we had. Losing your mother before you're married and have kids just messes with the order of things, a domino effect through the milestones of your life.*

Kate could not imagine what it would have been like if her mother had died before

James and Piper were born. She had flown in just before each of their births, and sharing the raw, carnal days of early mothering had brought them together in a way that had been lacking. They finally had something in common, she and her cerebral mother who could count on one hand the number of times she'd baked anything, who could become so distracted by the latest psychology journal that the water would boil over and the pasta grow rubbery. Babies were an inexact science. There were no sure fixes to sleeplessness and colic in rigorous study or circular debate, nothing academic about them. Only trial and error, and intuitive touch. In this, Kate and her mother were part of the same tribe, after all.

Tues., August 30, 1994

The resort is a more traditional one than I ever would have picked, but it's a practical stop-off before the Milwaukee Open. This afternoon I had the most fantastic nap by the pool. Woke up to cold drips on my belly, Dave shaking out his hair above me like a big hairy dog. Then he apologized to the baby and toweled off my belly. I'm wearing a bikini because I damn well feel like it.

259

I love my little potbelly, love it almost to the point of fetishism. I imagine that the baby can feel it when I rub it. The books say that at this point the baby can respond to light and sounds, can even suck its thumb and breathe amniotic fluid. I can't wait to feel it move, should be any day now. Can't wait to see it again at the next sonogram in a week.

The first one was amazing, a mind bender. It was the day after we got engaged, and Dave came to the appointment. The ultrasound screen was dark and grainy like looking into outer space, black and white bands like a crazy solar system snowstorm. Then there it was, a small white ball in the black hole of its own little universe. "That's the heart," the tech said, pointing to its pulsing core. A pixilated white light blinking away in spite of my initial denial and neglect. Ping ping ping. We went out to dinner afterward, and he surprised me with a little wrapped-up box, a tiny pair of baby sneakers.

It's amazing on so many levels: all those years of pills, pretty reliably but very occasionally not, amounts to this in the end. The things you come to trust and assume, little tricks of science that don't always trick nature after all. Nature always gets the last word. And then shock and fear turn into wobbly acceptance, and a family.

I won't pretend I'm not afraid, at least not in this book. When I think of that day with my sister, a little girl with a dopey grin who meant no harm tagging along, I feel like there's been a mistake and this baby is not meant to be. I have never been good with children, and have trouble envisioning life filled with diapers and nonsense songs and flung peas. But I'm assuming it's different when it's your own. I'm counting on it. I can imagine buying a small house, and painting the walls of a nursery with murals from nursery rhymes. But I might be doing a lot of the house hunting alone. The tour season is winding down, and Dave has to hit as many of the second-tier events as possible, try to get his ranking up to qualify for next year. While the better players went to Turnberry for the British Open last month, he went to Mississippi for one of the smallest-purse events of the tour. He did fine, about mid-field. Won back his expenses, plus enough for the honeymoon and two months' rent.

It is surprising to me that it's possible to make a living this way. I suppose it is the way he's used to, but we won't be living that way for long. I'm hoping with my steady salary we won't have trouble getting mortgage approval. I don't want to bring it up, don't want to be a nag. He might put his head in the sand about the emotional side of life, but his reverence for traditional family life and his idea of husband as provider are so strong it's like the stuff of a 1950s sitcom.

September 15, 1994

I went in two days ago for my routine OB appointment. The OB spread the warm goo and started to slide the wand around. She worked at different views while she tried to find what she wanted. The whole time I was watching for that little white blinking light.

Nothing appeared. The wand went up above my belly button and down, left and right. She went lower, pushed down harder. I asked a question but she squinted at the wall, quiet. Then she put down the wand.

"In situations like these we usually get a second opinion from another person in the practice," she said simply, and walked out.

In situations like these.

An older doctor came in and looked at the screen, then offered apologies. The monitor was frozen on the last image she'd gotten, a profile of a fully formed body curled above small crouched thighs, still.

Since then I've been mostly in bed, and I don't want to look in the mirror and see my own eyes. Keep wondering when exactly it happened, thinking of all my activities of the past few weeks and trying to remember anything odd. And I can't. Which for some reason makes it worse: Was I that distracted by the wedding and honeymoon that I stopped paying attention? I am obsessed with questions. Boy or girl. When, exactly — if it happened gradually, the heart slowing and eventually stopping, or if it suddenly blinked out. When they take it out tomorrow, whether it will still be whole. God, Elizabeth, Dave said to that, and turned away disgusted.

The doctor says chromosomes, almost certainly some kind of genetic defect, but it's impossible to know for sure. Unrelated to the bad cervical cells; those went away on their own. She insists it's nothing I did or didn't do.

But I know as certainly as I know anything in this world that it is. This is because of what I did 13 years ago, if not physically then morally, in direct retribution for my moral defect then, and maybe one I've always had. You cannot be cavalier about life and then years later expect life to drop back to you on demand. I didn't ask for it, but this baby felt so real and already part of our family, if we are one at all. This is my punishment, I'm sure of it.

Reading about Elizabeth's grief was difficult for Kate, but seeing Dave's reaction to the miscarriage secondhand was somehow even more raw. He moved through the house like a ghost, would make a sandwich, then leave it in another room, uneaten; he'd go into the spare room to polish his clubs, and Elizabeth would find him sitting motionless. They didn't share their pain, or much of anything. Neither knew how to handle the roles in which they found themselves, lacking the thing that brought them about.

I find him staring at me through the cutout in the kitchen wall when he's in front of the TV. He looks away, guilty, trying to pretend he wasn't. As hard as he is to read, I know he's blaming me for putting him in the position of loving and losing.

Eighteen

It was "Boston Day." They did it once each summer on the island, visiting the favorite sites from lunchtime until dinner — the Public Garden and Swan Boat, the *Make Way for Ducklings* statue and the Frog Pond. A stroll through the Commonwealth Avenue Mall ended at the firefighter memorial, where they'd touch the jacket of unyielding bronze, as lifelike as if it had been strewn on the wall by one of the men after a long day. It was a lot of ground to cover, and when they arrived home the kids would have to be carried from the car. But that's what childhood summers are about: falling asleep on the drive to the last ferry with ice cream smeared on your mouth and chin.

They held tickets for the 7:45 a.m. boat. While Kate waited for the children to get dressed, she logged on to her e-mail. News-groups and headline news analysis; she skimmed the stories with vague interest.

Economic forecasts, restaurant reviews, new terrorist camps found in Indonesia.

Chris had been gone nine days. Kate had received two voice mail messages from him, each just a few rushed sentences expressing optimism for the purchase of the Cambodian hotel and a few brief e-mail messages. Whenever Chris went to the Far East he was more or less unreachable. But she couldn't remember being this aware of the time difference before, the infrequency of updates, and the scarcity of details about where, exactly, he was.

Piper emerged in mismatched clothing holding her favorite doll, recently maimed in a scuffle with her brother. Kate had reassured the girl that the leg could be reattached at the Doll Hospital at home; they'd done it once before. Until then, Kate secretly wished she could tuck it away in a suitcase. The sight of the one-legged doll was disconcerting.

"Nice look. Very splashy," Kate said, admiring her daughter's blue plaid shorts and pink toile blouse. She pushed the girl's hair back from her face. It was a new thing, Piper choosing her own clothes.

James came and stood beside them, brushing his teeth. "Can we go to that big toy store?" he asked. "The really huge one, and buy something?"

Kate's laptop gave a ping.

Hey hon, just arrived in Manila, small change in plans. Angkor Wat is a go if we pair it with buying the prince's dog of a hotel here too, or maybe the one in Jakarta or Bali, so I'm going over there for a quick look at each then hopefully home. The place in AW is amazing, a palace ten minutes from the park temples. Tell the kids it's giving me all kinds of ideas for sand castles. Sorry again about your wallet. Did you already cancel the credit card? Remember we've got that extra cash in my bottom drawer and just use the backup card. I'm fine here using the corporate account.

See you soon, Love C

Manila. Jakarta. Bali. Kate held her coffee in midair. Was Jakarta in the Philippines or Indonesia?

"Mom? Can we get something at the big store? I'm tired of the toys here."

Where was that new trouble spot? Kate tried to remember the island groupings with the greatest concentration of red spots, and cursed her poor geography.

"Mom? I really want some Legos." James prodded her arm. "Mom?"

"Do they have a store that fixes dolls like

267

at home?" Piper asked. "I really hate her leg off like this." She thumped the doll against her hand, agitated.

The children began to argue about what kind of store they should visit. Their voices merged as a single discordant buzz.

Kate tried to go back to the Web site with the Indonesia headline but the page wouldn't reload. She called up a search of maps and news articles. Words jumped from the screen. *Jungle. Hostages. Knives. Throats.*

The children stood in front of her, their mouths opening and closing. She felt light-headed and her ears began to ring.

She closed her eyes and inhaled, then exhaled slowly, counting to ten.

When she opened them the children were staring. She closed the laptop with a decisive click. "Okay," she said softly. "Let's go to the ferry."

NINETEEN

December 17, 1994

Dave didn't get the tour card for next year, and didn't make it at qualifying school. He is talking about going on one of the mini tours to work his way back, or even the Asian Tour again, which would take him away much of next year. When he says this he's looking at me as if he's testing the idea. I can't tell if he's daring me to disagree or if he secretly wants me to argue, wishes I'd haul him back by the collar and say Enough of this, stay with me.

These past months we've been like roommates in a time-share. He's been playing and training in Florida much of the time, and when he is home, I've had to work late on a new client. When we overlap, everything is tiptoed around. Married life is a subtle turf war and quiet politeness. He can't stand the soap I buy, and the only way I knew was because he joked about it with his teeth clenched. Sometimes he actually opens the oven door when he comes home at dinnertime and looks perplexed to see nothing cooking. I could scream. We almost always got takeout before. When, pray tell, did I become the chef? We're totally out of sync and don't know what to do with each other, two people who've been handed job descriptions for work that never materialized.

We weren't together for Thanksgiving but we will be for Christmas. You can't play golf on Christmas.

January 17, 1995

I think Dave going on the pseudo pro tour is a mistake, and I decided to lay it all on the table and tell him. If we are going to make a go of this marriage we have to decide if it's for real, and not just the product of a baby that no longer exists. He never mentions it. To me, she's as real as if she were hovering like a fog in the corner of the room, the better parts of both of us that seem to have disappeared.

I made us a real dinner the other night, cracked open a bottle of wine, and forced the conversation. I asked him not to go on tour, to be willing to try with me for another baby. It was like talking to a statue. When this guy dies, his tombstone is going to read I Didn't Want to Know.

Now he's gone and I'm alone in the apartment and it's like I've shot back in time, Thai takeout in front of the TV. I'm spinning the ring on my finger, not sure if I'm still supposed to wear it.

February 28, 1995

Dave skipped two tour dates and drove home, surprised me with a romantic three days together for our six-month anniversary. He took the initiative, even laid out a marriage revival plan. Wants us to make a point of seeing each other every two weeks — either he comes home, or I fly down there. Wants us to start looking for a house again, to think about another baby. I fell asleep last night to his fingers through my hair.

I have the feeling that he's living on the edge down there. Last night I noticed furrows down the sides of his mouth, deep worry lines, and he's lost weight. He says he's playing well and I've seen the deposits in the savings account. But I know he's slept in his car more than once.

271

A magazine clipping, a circular piece ripped from the middle of a page, fell from the journal.

GOLF WEEKLY, March 3, 1995

THE BOGEYMAN
weekly commentary by columnist Chad Flax

. . . It's like the wild savanna out there this year and these guys are feral, a lot of alphas scrapping for mangy kills. Not much to be won, but much to lose. Dave Martin is digging deep and doing penance for a lame PGA year, and it's paying off. We expect good things from him if he can get back on tour next season.

May 1, 1995

Pregnant again. I'm ecstatic, scared, hopeful but not daring to believe that this is a given. I feel strong as an ox, but my body isn't something to be trusted. I'm tempted not to tell Dave until I pass the twelve-week mark, though that didn't prove to be any magic safety zone last time. I can adjust my own expectations, consider this a maybe-baby until we're out

272

of the woods. But I don't think he can.

I saw a great house today. A three-bedroom Cape that needs work, but very cute, good bones, good yard. It's in the town with the best schools where we looked a little last fall. It would be a stretch, but if we did the repainting ourselves and waited to renovate the kitchen, it could be doable. I'm up for a raise next month.

He's coming home tomorrow after three weeks away, says Let's go have a look. I'm almost out of the first trimester. I'm going to tell him.

Kate could not fathom keeping a pregnancy to herself. There were the mechanics of it — the nausea, all the upleasantness of the first trimester, hard to hide even if your husband was away most of the time. And then there was the worry, the excitement, the imaginings. For Kate and Chris it had been a game. Even before they'd crossed the relative safety of the early months they'd invented names, each coming up with nonsense and insisting it was his or her first choice. Trebuladon would be a prizewinning urban architect. Bellapagoda would

273

redefine Asian fusion cuisine. Neither admitted the truly beloved names, keeping them close to the vest until later. There was also the secret fear of naming something the size and fragility of a sea horse, spine still fusing as it slept behind unblinking eyes.

For three months Elizabeth had done all that first-trimester excitement and anxiety alone. Even if it was intended to protect her husband, her ability to conceal was breathtaking.

Downstairs Kate heard her cell phone ring. It was 9 p.m. — morning in Cambodia. He was due to check in. She imagined him sitting on the edge of the bed shirtless, rubbing his face and stretching before he picked up the phone to call. There might be an ashtray on the nightstand where the photo of her should have been, filled with stubs of some unfiltered foreign cigarettes. Then she envisioned a form mounded under the sheets beside him, a bare brown calf peeking from beneath the exotic dyed comforter. The long, lean leg of someone with a euphonious name and a sultry smile, someone who would not be critical of his vices or distracted by the writing of a lost friend.

Even as she thought it, she was horrified with herself. Where had that come from?

She caught the phone on the last ring before the voice mail would have picked up.

"Hello?"

"Hey, Kate. It's Dave."

"Dave?" Surprise supplanted manners while she tried to hide her disappointment.

"Yeah, your old pal Dave Martin. Jonah and Anna's dad." He was loose, glib. He'd forgotten to say Emily.

"Sorry. I thought you were Chris. He always calls on the cell."

"Yeah. I tried the home number but it wasn't working." She glanced at the house phone, knocked off the cradle by one of the kids.

"Where's Chris?" he asked.

"Southeast Asia. He had a project come up and had to fly to a few places, Cambodia, Jakarta, Bali."

"Well now, that's an interesting part of the world. He has to have just about the worldliest job of anyone I know." Dave was circumspect. If Southeast Asia gave him pause, he didn't let on. "But it is a shame he had to leave in the middle of your vacation."

"Well, he shouldn't be gone much longer. He flew out six days ago. He just e-mailed today that he had to make a few more stops, but he'll be back soon."

"Hmmm." He paused a half beat too long. She could almost hear him trying to scrape together something polite about the region that would sidestep current events. "I once played a small tournament in Manila. Some pretty places there, out in the countryside. Monkeys would come right out onto the fairways."

Kate had never heard Dave talk about his tour days, had always thought his nonchalance about his playing career, his ability to move on without looking back, showed a lack of passion. She now wondered how much of what she'd assumed was superficiality might have been his way of masking something he felt too much.

"You played in the Philippines?"

"I went on the Asian Tour, minor-league stuff. Man, I would have played off the top of steaming landfills if I thought it would have gotten me closer to making the tour." He was mocking himself, keeping it light, and his tone had an intimacy to it. "That was before I met Elizabeth, back when I was trying to qualify for the PGA." His voice cooled and became more precise. "Lean years," he said simply.

"I had those too. Cooking in some real dives before culinary school. I'm surprised I didn't catch something in some of those places."

He chuckled low. From the end of the dark yard came the gurgle of waves running up the beach and receding.

"Well, Kate, I hope you don't mind my calling to check in again. I just think of you sometimes, sitting out there and reading and reading. It's quite a thing you're doing."

She walked outdoors, leaving the door open as she stepped onto the patio. A breeze rustled the plantings in their window boxes and swept across her legs, bare under her nightshirt. "I know. It is."

"Going straight into someone's mind like that." She heard clinking, cubes in a glass. "I mean, really. Even in a great relationship, there are limits on how well we can ever really *know* another person."

She pressed her fingernail into the porch railing. Chipping paint buckled, and she picked up a flake. "I don't think we really can."

There was a pause, and she heard him take a drink. "So. How far along are you?"

She paused, and knew that he heard her hesitation. How she responded to him now would set an expectation going forward.

"Do we really want to do this, Dave?" she

asked. "Isn't it kind of raw?"

"Don't tell me about raw, Kate," he snapped. "At least tell me where you are in them. What year."

She pressed the paint chip between her thumb and forefinger, and it crumbled into tinier pieces. Every sentence made it that much less likely she'd be able to tuck away the journals quietly in an attic when she was done. "Just after Elizabeth went to see the Southbrook house for the first time. Before Jonah."

He made a guttural sound like the scuff of heavy furniture being moved. He might have been thinking of the miscarriage, or the fact that Elizabeth waited for weeks to tell him about the second pregnancy. Or maybe that wasn't strange to him; hard as it was to imagine, maybe he was the kind of old-world husband who hadn't expected to be let in on women's matters until the women had them under control.

She reached for something neutral. "She was excited about the house, planning to do a lot of work on it herself, even pregnant. She was tough."

He snorted. "Tough, yeah. She was strong all right."

Kate heard the sarcasm like something cracking open, wide and ugly. She reached for something that would press it closed, the first distraction that came to mind. "Dave, was there a second key to the trunk?"

"A second key? What do you mean?"

"She wouldn't have given her only key to the lawyer. Maybe you found another one in her jewelry box or nightstand or something?"

He exhaled, irritated. "What are you trying to say, Kate? Are you asking whether I had another key and read more of the books before I gave them to you?"

"No, that's not what I'm talking about." This line of conversation had been a mistake, but it was too late now. "I'm actually locked out of the trunk. I kept the key in my wallet, and it was stolen last weekend on the beach."

"You lost the key to the trunk?"

She tried to read his tone: angry, or incredulous? She spoke carefully, trying not to sound defensive. "I didn't lose it. It was stolen." She touched the sensitive spot on her neck as it began to flame.

"No. I do not have another key. Life has never really given me that kind of a safety net, Kate." His voice was as controlled as hers. What she wouldn't give for one of her children to wake now, granting her an excuse. "So what are you going to do now?" he asked.

"There are some locksmiths I've been talking to." It was partly true; she had left them messages and stopped by the shop of one, but it had been closed. "Worst-case scenario, I don't think it's that strong."

"So you'd break it."

"I could. As a last resort."

She turned toward the house, turned her back on the sound of the tackle of the smaller boats moored nearby, tinkling agitated and sleepless. She looked at the lights of the loft through the window and saw the top of the chaise against the wall. Depending on how many pages were left, the last resort could be coming soon.

"I've got to be at work early tomorrow. It's been a long day." He sounded suddenly very tired. She could imagine him rubbing his face, sighing. *This is the last thing I need.* "You take care, Kate."

He hadn't reacted to her saying that she might break the trunk. He might be un-happy, but he hadn't told her not to. Maybe he didn't even blame her, she thought. You could never tell with him.

TWENTY

September 20, 1995

Totally wiped out from wallpapering, painting, and hauling garbage from the attic left by the old owners. I like our new neighborhood, a quiet street with families. But still getting used to this town. There's a certain attitude — women in SUVs who pull into parking spaces at the mall without caring who might already be waiting for the same space. Moms who get all dolled up to go to the grocery store. Even the way they talk to their children is self-consciously perfect, as if they think everyone is listening and grading their performance.

Dave loves it here. There's a very good town course, no membership required, and the starter pencils him in for tee times even when they're fully booked. He's gearing up to try at qualifying school again, determined to get his tour card back for next season. Which begins in January, right when the baby's due.

November 3, 1995

Dave and I finally had the talk about work and child care. We've been avoiding it, or maybe I've been avoiding it, the big fat proverbial elephant in the room. He's never said it openly, but I think he feels one parent should stay at home with the kids. It's tied up with his ideas about his own upbringing, distrust of strangers, willingness for self-sacrifice, control. He's never cared much about money, at least in terms of letting it be a driving force. So the economics of a two-income home against child care costs isn't really part of the equation. It's just not the point. The truth is it's not for me, either. But for different reasons.

I told him I'd like to negotiate working part-time, that I thought the agency would go for it and I could make a decent salary with not too many hours. We were having dinner and he went quiet. I suspect he thinks my being at home full-time will make up for his being gone. When I talked about working part-time, he sat there fingering the neck of his beer bottle with the smile of someone who's gotten underwear for his birthday.

I didn't realize you really wanted to keep working, he said. You complain about the deadlines, and I thought you'd be glad to be done with it. You've been so excited about this baby.

A bolt of anger went through me, the way I used to feel when my mother made assumptions about what I did or didn't believe. It was like my enthusiasm for the baby was being used against me, and the miscarriage, too; if I was relieved enough to be carrying to term, if I loved it enough, I'd want to give myself over completely. You can't really think that, I wanted to say. You can't really think that being excited about a baby automatically means being excited to walk away from ten years of work that you love. But I knew it would come off all wrong.

It's funny — as like-minded as we are about most things, they're really just voting issues, theoreticals. This is something different altogether, and I don't think he honestly thinks men and women are the same, that my work can be as integral to who I am as his is. I think he really believes that women's love for children is automatically tied to self-sacrifice. Any time I even hint at suggesting otherwise his eyes cloud over, confused or disappointed. I haven't even become a parent yet, but this is my first taste of parental guilt.

In hindsight, Kate had been naïve when she left for her maternity leave. She hadn't thought to be wistful or protective of the parts of herself she might be leaving behind, because she did not have an inkling she wouldn't be coming back. She said goodbye to her colleagues as if she were going on sabbatical.

She and Chris loved their work and both assumed they could manage the juggling act with hard work and determination. But in the end, both were as inexperienced with the work of parenthood as they were with the possibility that their feelings about it might change. At first it did not seem plausible that a person awake every hour, roused like a victim of a sleep study, might be able to function safely the next day. Then the intervals became more regulated, and Kate came to enjoy those hours of quiet darkness with James. She'd never imagined that when the time came to return to work, she would feel so needed at home, or find it so difficult to leave.

The last weeks of Elizabeth's pregnancy progressed through late autumn and early winter. At the maternity store she met other women who were expecting, and they told her about playgroups organized through the town's Newcomers' Club. By December she outgrew even her largest clothes and could not imagine getting any larger. *Dave has started calling the baby Jonah because the rest of me is the Whale. We laugh because it's terrible, but it's sticking.*

Dave advanced through the stages of the PGA Tour Qualifying Tournament in hopes of earning back his tour card, playing white-knuckle rounds against hungry amateurs and top competitors on the Nationwide Tour. Tucked between the pages of the journal was a clipping from a golf magazine. The photograph showed Dave sinking the putt on the last hole to reclaim a place on tour. Alongside the green, just on the other side of the ropes, was a very pregnant Elizabeth.

Kate examined the photo, held it closer to the dim light of the wall sconce. Elizabeth's hair was quite long, as it was when Kate had first met her, and she wore small round John Lennon–style sunglasses. Her enormous belly bloomed under a bright floral shift and was further accentuated by the fairway ropes she leaned against, draping beneath her stomach like the belt on a friar. Her hands were pressed together in front of her open mouth as if in prayer, but her eyes were wide, newly informed. The photograph had been snapped at the moment hope turned to celebration.

January 22, 1996

Jonah William Martin arrived six days ago, nine days late. I went into labor just as Dave got on the flight home from Tucson. Which would seem like perfect timing, but it wasn't until thirty-six hours later that the baby came, barely in time to meet his dad before Dad had to go to Palm Springs. He came back yesterday, leaves again tomorrow. I can appreciate that he needs to get back in these tournaments with a vengeance, that he's clinging to his card, etc. etc. But I don't have to like it. I do, however, have to be a good sport.

The baby is fascinating, all odd instincts and raw nature. The squinty efforts to focus on me, the flailing fists and chicken legs and bony little heels. One of his ears folds over a little, as if it was pushed that way while he was growing. His lower lip disappears into an overbite while he's sleeping. I can't stop watching him.

Went to the first meeting of the newcomers' playgroup I was assigned to, eight mothers, Wednesday mornings. The idea is that the kids roll around on the floor and make little friends, and the moms throw Halloween parties and birthday bashes together. Today was at Brittain's house, massive and filled with sculptural furniture that you can tell is named after some French king instead of a category in the Pottery Barn catalog. We sat in a circle on the playroom floor with our babies on blankets in front of us like we were a postpartum Lamaze class.

Apparently there are all kinds of things I'm supposed to be doing or not doing that I've never heard of. Using cloths for wipes instead of disposable store-bought ones, because of chemicals and rough fibers. Questioning immunizations, even if the pediatrician encourages them and the state requires them. Putting your child's name in for nursery schools now, or they'll flip burgers for life. They were perfectly nice, if a bit much, but they talked about baby things the whole time. No one said a

287

thing about her own interests or jobs (from the sound of it no one is going back to work), and when I mentioned mine they were polite but really not interested.

We had coffee in hand-painted European mugs, decaf all around as if it were a given, since everyone is breast-feeding. I guess I missed the memo, because I made the faux pas of asking for regular. It turned out Brittain hadn't even brewed regular. After she made it just for me, over my protests that decaf was just fine, everyone stared as she poured. Then Petra said, "Top me off with regular too, that sounds good." God bless her.

I felt like I was the only one who's rattled by motherhood, because no one mentioned the kinds of things I can't stop thinking about, like whether they missed their old lives or looked at their baby's flaws and wondered whether they'd fade in time or grow into something truly hideous. Whether anyone else wanted to beat their husbands with a diaper pail when he slept through the baby's crying. Or if sometimes, instead of being flooded with love and wanting to spend every minute cradling this little miracle you've created, you want to step back in time just for one hour of

nobody touching you, waking you, need-
ing you.

Kate heard coughing from the children's
bedroom. James had had some bronchial irritation all day. So far it had just been a dry
cough, nothing that rumbled, and she
hoped it wouldn't develop into anything
that required a doctor's visit. She went
downstairs, propped him at an angle on the
pillow, and held a glass of water to his
mouth. He drank with only half recognition
of his mother or the glass, eyes clouded with
sleep.

When Kate had joined their playgroup,
the women had struck her as a bit precious
initially, but not as judgmental. Perhaps they
had been more wooden in the beginning,
before Kate had joined. She could imagine
Brittain, anxious in ways they had not
known until later, pulling out the best dishes
for their first meeting. It was also possible
that in Elizabeth's self-conscious first
months as a mother in the suburbs, she had
imagined herself more isolated than she
was, or needed to be. Fortunately, she'd
become at ease with the group quickly. By
the time Kate moved to Southbrook, ten
months after the group began meeting, Elizabeth had become the de facto leader.

Kate stroked James's hair until he finished drinking the water, and after he lay back on the pillow, she stayed until his breathing steadied and slowed. She waited until his eyes were closed before she stepped quietly to the doorway. When the children woke in the night, ill or flushed with bad dreams, she didn't like them to see her leave the room.

March 13, 1996

I hosted playgroup this morning, all of us wedged into the all-purpose family room of our minuscule Cape. I pulled out all the stops — picked up hand towels and a little bonsai tree for the downstairs bathroom, bought some matching coffee mugs, and plenty of decaf. Proud of our little place, all dressed up for the prom.

"What does your husband do for work?" Brittain asked, looking around the hallway like she was trying to see the rest until she realized there was no rest. When I told them he was a pro golfer (but not one they'd heard of) they acted like it was the quaintest thing, a man pursuing his hobby, like he threw pottery in the basement and sold it on the corner.

Petra was the last to leave and helped

me clean up the kitchen and playroom. She's from Italy originally and we spoke a little Italian, so I guess my year in Florence is not entirely gone without a trace. We had another cup of coffee ("caffè normale, grazie a Dio") while the babies sat in bouncy seats on the floor. I told her, I'm so tired I could fall facedown on the table. No one else in playgroup seems exhausted or unshowered, just deliriously happy.

Yeah, well, she said. Belle dal fuori. Good appearances. What are you gonna do?

I could have kissed her.

April 6, 1996, 11:30 p.m.

The fire truck just pulled away, lights still spinning. I don't know whether to laugh or cry. So I'm sitting down with a glass of merlot doing a little of both. After I put down Jonah for the night I was straightening the changing table and dropped the thermometer, the old-school kind with mercury inside. It hit the wood floor and shattered. When I picked up the pieces I couldn't see any mercury. Ah, good, I thought; it must be protected in some kind of inner chamber. No, I couldn't see it because it was ROLLING ALL OVER THE FLOOR IN LITTLE SILVER BEADS.

I'd just read something about how some states were considering banning mercury thermometers, and then it struck me: If this is so toxic, what if it could be airborne? What if I'd released it like a virus, and tiny bits of mercury were right at that moment going into Jonah's lungs? So I called 911. Don't move or touch anything, he said, especially not the baby. They were sending in a squad, and was the front door unlocked?

Not three minutes later I heard the sirens, then saw the lights blazing through the window and across the nursery wall. Three knocks on the door, then "MRS. MARTIN, WE'RE COMING IN." Heavy booted feet up the stairs, and three men in hooded yellow hazmat suits appeared in the doorway. I would have wet my pants laughing if I hadn't been so scared, because they looked like they were responding to an outbreak of the Ebola virus, in bulky space suits and knee-high boots and helmets with plastic windows.

The first one lifted me with gloved hands from where I stood barefoot, then two of them moved into the room and stood over the spill like it was a Superfund site, debating The Cleanup. The third called Poison Control on his radio, and learned mercury can't be absorbed by humans through touch, and can't become airborne unless it's at very high temperatures.

After that things settled down. Defcon #1 and Defcon #2 debated the best way to clean up, but the mercury kept splitting into tinier balls and rolling between the cracks of the wood floor. They started to sweat, took off their helmets, then stripped off their elbow-length gloves, scratched their heads. What about Scotch tape? I said, half joking.

So that's how we cleaned up the toxic spill that commanded the entire hazmat squad of Southbrook, Connecticut. With Scotch tape, like lifting lint from a suit. They were there for two hours, and Jonah slept the whole time.

Wednesday, April 10, 1996

Told playgroup this morning about the mercury thermometer incident. Mostly expecting to get a good laugh, but also hoping they'd reassure me that Jonah isn't going to grow up neurologically stunted, unable to say his own name. But after I told the story they were silent. Literally, no one said a word. Five seconds passed. Then Leslie said, "Oh my God." And Regan said, "Did you take him to the pediatrician?" (No.) Then another silence, and Petra said, "I'd never keep a mercury thermometer in the house. It's just not worth the risk." And everyone murmured yes, yes.

Without trying to seem defensive, I offered that my pediatrician had told me that mercury thermometers were the most accurate. And then Brittain started talking about how she'd chosen her pediatrician and checked out his credentials, making sure there'd never been a malpractice suit against him, etc.

Cyanide tablets in the coffee. Blow darts tipped in anthrax. These were the things I wished I had at my disposal.

I smiled, and I'm going to keep smiling. I am not going to deprive Jonah of little playmates to roll around on the floor with, dress up in baby costumes with on Halloween. But it's going to take a real effort not to give them mercury thermometers in the trick-or-treat bags.

Friday, April 12, 1996

The boss lady said the agency wouldn't

agree to part-time. I can't believe it. I really thought they would. So we're setting up a freelance contract, and I'll work part-time from home. Trust me, Victoria said. I'll make it work.

Dave finished in the upper 30 percent. He's never been so high on the leaderboard before. Saw him interviewed on ESPN, a good balance of enthusiastic and professional and modest, but the smile of a six-year-old sneaked in there too. He can't help it.

Friday, April 19, 1996

I'm interviewing part-time nannies on Monday. We finally put an ad in the paper after I talked Dave into feeling okay about three afternoons a week, especially since I'll be working right upstairs. Victoria has been great about feeding me work, as much as I can handle. It's crazy, but I'm enjoying it more than I ever have. She tossed me a client that no one else is very excited about, a Japanese sake manufacturer, and last night I absolutely lost track of time working up ideas for the label. Came up with a cutout silhouette-style concept that looks like kirigami, wispy fronds of rice blowing in a field. Finally stopped at 2:30 a.m. when Jonah woke up for a feeding. Of course I'm cursing myself today, can hardly see straight I'm so tired.

It's pathetic how much it means to me, but it feels like it's something all my own, a part of me that isn't given over to nursing or laundry or checking ESPN all the time to see how Dave's doing. It's the one tiny vestige of myself in a day where everything feels like it's about someone else. Having that time away, I enjoy the time with Jonah more. But I'm learning that sneaking an hour here or there when he's napping is beyond frustrating. Getting a rhythm, then being interrupted just when I'm thoroughly engrossed, is worse than not starting at all. I need to get a regular sitter. That will make all the difference.

Elizabeth and Dave didn't like any of the sitters they interviewed. No spark, no twinkle in the eye of a single one of them that suggested a genuine enjoyment of babies, merely bland competence. Elizabeth was discouraged, but suspected Dave was relieved. *How much work do you really have to do? he asked. It's not like we're desperate for it or anything.* "It" being money. She decided to carve out work time around the edges of Jonah's naps, plus some nights and weekends, to fulfill her freelance contract.

Kate put down the notebook and looked at the windowsill, the smiling photograph of Elizabeth framed by darkness. It was painful to imagine her friend with this intensity Kate had never seen. It was as if in addition to the woman she'd known, there had been a second lost friend, and she was hit with fresh grief.

Beside her on the chaise, her cell phone rang. Out of Area appeared in the caller ID window. She took a breath, wiped at her eyes.

"Hello?"

"Hey, hon, oh good, I finally got a connection. The cell service here is the worst."

"Chris." She breathed his name like a statement. "Where are you?"

"Jakarta. I just got to the airport and I'm getting a decent signal for just a second."

"Are you just getting to Jakarta, or leaving there?" Leaving. Let him say leaving.

"Just getting here. I think it's just a one-night thing, and then a quickie to Bali. You wouldn't believe these hotels for sale. They're crazy, all this insane luxury falling apart. Some are beyond help, but I think we can do something with at least one other. Especially if it means getting the Angkor

Wat one. It's a gem."

She struggled to put herself in the mind-set of Indonesian real estate. "So it's working out? You're going to buy them?"

"Looks that way, if we can get a decent price. This would be a total coup for us, Kate. I know this is a pain for me to be off-island for so long, but this is a once-in-a-lifetime deal." The word *coup* rang in her ears. "How are the kids?"

"Fine. Great. We're doing all the regular stuff. They miss you though."

"Good. Hey, I'm having trouble hearing what —" There was crackling alternating with silence.

"Chris, you there? How are . . . things there? Does it feel safe?" Silence. "Chris?"

Their voices overlapped, and his disappeared. A small static of background noise came and went, the sound of connections made and broken.

"Chris?"

"I'm here. I just asked how the journals were coming. Any revelations?"

"Not really."

She said it in part because it was the last thing she wanted to talk about on an international call with a poor connection, the unsettling mixture of empathy, irritation, and loss. But it wasn't the only reason.

When she and Chris had last discussed the journals that afternoon on the beach, she'd told him she was keeping an open mind about whether or not Elizabeth had been having an affair. But even as she spoke, she knew it wasn't altogether true. She now read as if she were following bread crumbs, looking for wisdom about what makes two people fall out of sync and then imperceptibly apart, perhaps without one of them even knowing.

"Kate? I can hardly hear you," he said. "I think I'm — I'll call you from — tell the kids —" Suddenly the static was gone, and so was Chris.

Kate looked at the phone, and saw a sequence of the things that might cause it to suddenly disconnect. She clicked it shut, and placed it on the counter with a shaky hand.

TWENTY-ONE

There was an entire section of pages torn out. Kate pulled the binding wide and saw there were fifteen, possibly twenty pages missing. The last entry was dated in April 1996. The next section of writing began in November 1996.

Kate ran her thumb across the ripped edges. She thought back to Elizabeth's angry writing after her mother had destroyed an early journal, her reaction to having been censored. This time, it appeared she had done it to herself.

Monday, November 18, 1996

I've turned the corner. I no longer get out of bed in the morning counting the hours until I tuck him back in. The one thing I will give myself credit for is that throughout, I've been providing Jonah with a smiling face and a stable home. I will say this for myself: every decision I've made that's led to this place, I made out of optimism. At each choice I did the gut check and decided I can do this, or that I wanted to be a person who could. Enough said. No one wants to hear a mother talk this way.

Thanksgiving is coming, and I'm hosting everyone: Dave's whole family, including Zack and the kids, even my father, his third time visiting me from L.A. Dave finished the tour season the highest he ever has, and will definitely be on tour again next year. . . .

The writing continued, a litany of plans for the holidays and Dave's progress on tour. It read like training-wheels writing, someone moving shakily to acquire a new skill, or outlook. As Kate skimmed the workmanlike entries, her thoughts drifted to what might have been in the missing pages. Postpartum depression was her guess, but she wondered if there'd been something more, if this was where the man who invited Elizabeth to Joshua Tree had made his appearance.

Gradually, Elizabeth's old voice returned. Whatever edginess that had been critical of others was now turned on herself. She became increasingly attentive to the playgroup and neighborhood.

Wednesday, December 11, 1996

There's a new woman in playgroup, Kate. She just moved here from New York. She lives a few streets over, and I remember seeing her when she moved in, saw her telling off a cable guy outside. It was hilarious. "I'll tell you what," she was saying in the driveway with a baby on her hip. "How about we make a date for ME to come to YOUR house tomorrow afternoon. And you can sit there for four hours waiting for me even though you have a million other things to do, and then I'll come two hours late and tell you, 'Oops, I don't have the right stuff, gotta come back tomorrow.' How would that work for you?"

I was walking by with the stroller and laughed out loud. She turned to me, "Am I wrong?" It'll be nice to have some fresh blood in the nabe.

Moving to Southbrook should have felt like the most natural thing in the world once Kate decided not to return to work. If you are going to stay home with a baby, she'd reasoned, at least surround yourself with others who are doing the same thing and talk to one another across their driveways.

Except that no one came into their driveways. They pulled out of them in their large SUVs, straight out of the garages and then back into them, so that for the first week Kate knew what her neighbors' bumpers looked like but not the neighbors themselves. She invented reasons to be outside several times a day — never mind that it was midwinter in Connecticut — and bundled newborn James in so many layers that only his eyes were exposed, peering from the stroller. But no matter how many times she went walking, no one stopped to talk. Until Elizabeth.

As Christmas neared, Elizabeth was consumed with juggling holiday shopping and the demands of freelance work. The playgroup had become a cohesive unit, a bona fide group of if not close friends, at least very good acquaintances, and Elizabeth felt part of a group for the first time in years. The women came together for playdates every Wednesday morning and helped in a pinch, watching one another's children for cumbersome errands and doctor's appointments.

Once when she was up against a design deadline and had no luck with sitters, Elizabeth asked Brittain to watch Jonah. *Brittain hesitated before saying yes. "Oh, for work,"* *she said kind of coolly. I don't know if it was that she forgot that I worked, or if being asked for work made her feel like a nanny, but I should have known better. The few times I've brought up my job it's been a conversation killer, and I end up feeling it's something that sets me apart.*

At the end of the month the playgroup had a gift exchange, a Yankee swap of inexpensive presents given and regifted. It was intended as a gag, but Elizabeth found the playgroup women were in earnest. *At the end, Kate was stuck with the schmaltziest gift, a cloisonné "I Love Mom" necklace Leslie brought — though Leslie probably liked it, she's that kind of precious. Kate put it on and struck a princessy pose and you could see it dawn on Leslie that she was being made fun of. And I thought Oh man here it comes, there's gonna be no way to stitch up that yawning hurt. But Kate noticed in time thank God, and said we should all get them, they'll be like the friendship bracelets of the play-group. I like Kate, but she skates a little close to the edge. She's only been here a few weeks and I wish there were some way I could give her a silent signal. Careful (ear tug), that won't fly here.*

Kate's face went hot. Elizabeth was right; she was never as aware as she should be of the way her comments were taken. She thought of the letter she'd received years ago from the viewer critical of her flippancy on the cable show. All these years, it was still jammed in the back of her top drawer at home. *Give her a few toddlers underfoot and see if she can "make it happen" then. Not everything is as simple as it seems.* Chiding and ominous, a voice from the future. There were difficulties that went unseen, and it was dangerous to make assumptions.

Jonah's first birthday came and went. Elizabeth brought him to the aquarium in the morning and Dave flew home that night just in time for cake. Jonah mashed icing in his face and hair, screaming with glee, and fell asleep in a hiccuppy tantrum of too much sugar and too much attention.

March 21, 1997

Kate watched Jonah so I could get to the dentist for a cavity. Chris is in Europe for some hotel thing and Dave doesn't get back until Monday, so she invited me to stay for dinner. She whipped up these crusty little homemade pot pies and poured us wine, and we had a civilized meal while Jonah and James screamed and pitched their bottles on the floor.

She has something to say about everything, an encyclopedia of current events. It's like she's doing a monologue, all worked up about the future of cloned animals in the food supply while she's standing at the counter prepping the little pie pans. "James and Jonah could be drinking milk from cloned cows in five years" — her hair swings under her chin while she rolls the dough — "and all that genetically screwed-up milk could send them into puberty at age eight or something." CNN was on in the background on her kitchen TV and none of it was news to her, from the terrorism in Tel Aviv to the discovery that much of the art in French museums had been stolen by Nazis. She had some choice words for the French and the international art establishment, and I drooled Pinot Noir through novocaine lips and tried to sound smart. She groused about Chris's travel, mentioned some of the cool places she'd been able to go "back in the day." Ko Samui. Goa. I've never even heard of Goa. I nodded and wasn't sure whether I was supposed to commiserate about husbands traveling or chime in about cool places we'd been. I told her that while we were dating, Dave surprised me with tickets to one of his tournaments in Hawaii. That's nice, she said, and looked at me like I'd said Gary, Indiana.

I'm between projects for the agency so I've started painting Jonah's room, a jungle theme. Moved him into our room so I can work on it at night. When I bring him in each morning to see the new animals he points with such force — this! that! — that his finger goes double-jointed.

Round two at Bay Hill today, and Dave came in just behind Payne Stewart, about two-thirds of the way up in the pack. Called a few minutes ago: "At this rate we'll be able to redo the kitchen this summer."

July 3, 1997

My kitchen renovation has become the topic of choice at playgroup. We talk about refrigerators and ranges and tile back-splashes, and I am so bored I could scream. They'd be horrified if they knew I didn't care. So would Dave, who thought it was the birthday present of the century when he presented the brochures tied in a bow. It isn't that I don't care about the kitchen. I care about having it DONE so I don't have to talk about it anymore. Oddly, the fact that Dave "gave" me a renovation — and that we're looking at luxury ranges and other appliance ridiculousness — seems to have elevated us in social status. When his golf ranking wasn't as high, his work was treated like a trade compared to the corporate husbands, as if he might be able to repair their toilets in a pinch. But the other day Brittain referred to him as a "professional athlete." I almost choked on my coffee.

Then Leslie brought up the Stamford town-house fire, which was probably the only thing worse than talking about my kitchen. Everyone who hadn't seen the news last night had to hear about the mother home alone with her kids, the baby dropped out the window who fell short of being caught, the interview with the poor husband who'd been at work, all in awful detail. I was a wreck watching it last night — pregnancy hormones make me react all out of proportion. Dave climbed into bed with me and to cheer me up put on the wedding video his golf buddies made. It used to make me too sad to watch; by the end of the night gravity was working against me in the tight dress and I couldn't quite pass as the virginal bride. Who knows when we actually lost the baby; during the honeymoon? Maybe even that night. But watching the video this time I felt sad instead for the person I was, no idea what was coming, thinking I'd gotten all my ducks in a row. Believing that such a thing was possible.

Then Brittain had to go for the coup de grâce. "Yes yes, so terrible, those poor people, the mother found curled around her two-year-old in the closet." Kate was sitting near the window and didn't seem to be listening, but when I caught a look at her face I saw that she was crying and working very hard not to show it. She scooped James up and mumbled something about Regan's cat and her damn allergies, and apologized that she had to leave, and then she was gone.

September 4, 1997

A man came to the door this afternoon wearing a black suit and white button-down shirt and blue tie. When he flashed a badge, I opened the door. He said he was with the FBI and was doing security clearance on one of my neighbors who would be doing high-level government casework, and he was asking background questions of all the neighbors. Could he come in and ask me some questions?

Jonah was in his playpen in the next room. In the city I would never have let someone in, but I'm a mom in the suburbs now. You're supposed to be trusting and easygoing out here. I wondered what Kate would do, and if he'd been to her house. I asked to see his identification again. This will only take about five minutes, he said. Is there somewhere we can sit down?

I brought him to the dining room table and he asked me about Roy Ginnis across the street, some kind of lawyer. The agent asked for a glass of water, then asked me all kinds of questions I had no idea the answer to: what are Ginnis's hobbies; does he come and go at odd hours; does he ever drink a lot at neighborhood events; has he made any visible large purchases lately, any signs of extravagance?

Jonah started crying in his playpen and I got up for a sippy cup. When I came back the guy was standing by the windows and said he was finished. He told me the Secret Service might be paying a visit as well, and left.

When I told Dave about it tonight on the phone he went berserk. He never goes berserk. You did what? You just let him in while you were home alone with the baby?

He could have been anyone, could have attacked you, could have been casing the house. Did you ever leave him alone anywhere? I didn't tell him that I had.

What the hell is wrong with me? This is not what suburban moms do. Smart moms have a family-protecting radar and don't care about the awkwardness of keeping the door closed in someone's face. They aren't letting people in off the street and practically offering them Toll House cookies on doilies.

Why is it so hard for me? I'm always tripped up by what I think is expected of me, trying to act the right way. This should not be brain surgery. Feed child, dress child, cook food, pay bills, and don't let in utter strangers when you're home alone.

On the next page, two clippings were taped inside the notebook, one from a newspaper, one from a magazine.

THE STAMFORD ADVOCATE,
September 6, 1997

SOUTHBROOK — Police are searching for two suspects who broke into a home in Southbrook late Friday night, and tied a pregnant woman to the crib of her 20-

month-old son while they robbed the house.

Earlier that day, several neighbors had called the police to report a man going door-to-door and posing as an agent of the FBI. The incidents are believed to be connected, as the victim said one of the suspects resembled a man she'd allowed into her house the previous day, after he flashed what she believed to be a federal badge. Southbrook police declined to name the victim at the request of the family.

Police described the suspect as a 30-year-old white male, about 6 feet tall, accompanied by one or two other men in the robbery. When he had been knocking on doors and posing as an agent he was described as wearing a suit and tie, but at the time of the break-in he wore jeans and a dark hooded sweatshirt, the victim reported.

Authorities were alerted shortly before 2 a.m. yesterday, when a 911 call came from the residence. Although the caller was gagged and could not speak, authorities were able to trace the call, and officers arrived at the scene to find the 34-year-old woman in her nightgown bound to her son's crib with rope and duct tape. She had maneuvered the crib to the other side of the room and kicked over a table to reach a phone and call for help. Electronics and jewelry were among the valuables stolen. The woman and her son were unharmed.

This was not a typical event, according to Southbrook Police Sergeant Edward Gagnon, in terms of the forethought that went into selecting the home and the method of entry based on what the intruders were able to discern about the home's alarm system while inside earlier in the day.

"Although the theft claimed a significant number of personal effects, the residents were very fortunate not to have been harmed," he said.

Gagnon said the house might have been targeted because a neighbor, who had also allowed the would-be agent into his home and answered questions about neighbors, said he'd told the man that the victim's husband traveled often.

GOLF WEEKLY, October 14, 1997

PALM BEACH GARDENS, FLA. — Dave Martin has announced that he is leaving the PGA Tour and retiring from professional golf, effective immediately. The last tournament he played was September's Bell Canadian Open, which he had to leave prematurely.

This was the best year of his career, which has included six seasons on the PGA Tour, two years on the Nationwide Tour, and two turns on the Asian Tour.

"Dave Martin has had a great season, and we're sorry to lose him," said PGA Tour Commissioner Tim Finchem. "He's an example of the can-do spirit coming out of the players who work their way up and then back onto the tours."

Martin has taken a job with Titleist as a consulting director of development, and will be involved in the promotion of new equipment. He takes the position next month.

One month ago, Martin's home was robbed while his wife, Elizabeth, four months pregnant with their second child, was at home with their son.

Martin says the two events are not connected.

"I had been thinking for some time about leaving the tour, because it just felt incompatible with being the dad of young kids, and this opportunity with Titleist was golden," Martin explained as he announced his retirement at the Association's headquarters on Tuesday. "I appreciate the wonderful years I've had with the PGA doing what I love to do, and the friendship and guidance of so many great players. But nothing is more important than family."

TWENTY-TWO

"Your turn, Piper. Step up to the tee box," Kate said. At the hole before her were a cavern, a bridge, and a stream, all daunting. The girl walked forward, dragging her putter like a leash without a dog.

Tee box. The words *tee box* had actually come out of Kate's mouth. She'd viewed golf as a bit of a caricature of a sport — the pretentious clothing, the affected claps — and none of it had seemed to fit with the Martins. It had been possible for Kate to forget Dave was a golfer during his tour days, because so little in the Martins' child-centered household seemed defined by golf, except the father's absence.

But the thought of someone giving up anything he felt passionately about couldn't help but soften her toward that thing, and after what she'd read for the past five weeks, it didn't seem as if Dave would give up golf without good reason. *Normalized hours,* Elizabeth and Dave had said of the Titleist job. *Predictable income.* Now Kate saw the circumstances under which Dave had left the tour, and how close it had actually been to the break-in.

Last night she'd gone to the loft intending to read further. But she was drawn back to rereading the same section repeatedly. Keywords stood out, palpable as Braille. *Catch my baby. Rope and duct tape. So many things beyond my control.* And less dramatic but no less disturbing, *She looked at me like I'd said Gary, Indiana.* Her head ached with them today like the residue of a bad dream, or a hangover.

Piper swung from the tee and missed her ball. The girl shuffled ahead with a sigh, as if the rigors of golf were too cruel for a four-year-old. Kate walked behind her aping her slouch and sigh, and James snorted with laughter. Piper turned and tried to scowl at her mother's imitation of her, then giggled.

"Come on. Try again," Kate said. Piper picked up her putter and swung sloppily, to no better effect. When she saw that she'd missed the ball again she pounded the putter into the turf, her club gripped like a weapon.

Kate had never known anyone who had

been a victim of a serious crime before Elizabeth. The morning after the break-in, the telephone had blasted the dawn tranquillity of birds still quiet and babies not yet awake. When Kate answered, Elizabeth said simply, "I have a favor to ask." Not *My house has been broken into* or *I was tied to a crib for hours*, but that she had a favor to ask. The police had left a short while before and she had to go to the hospital for fetal monitoring, then to the police station for more questions. Could Kate watch Jonah? Her calm had been chilling. When Kate arrived at the Martins' doorstep moments later, her own nerves like exposed wires, she was prepared to . . . she didn't know what. Offer comfort, make coffee, help catalog stolen items. But Elizabeth just accepted her hug with resignation and handed her Jonah. She'd be back in a few hours, she said, rope welts visible on her arms. Dave would be flying in later that morning.

Kate stepped up to the fifth hole. She stood at the tee and gave her yellow ball a middling tap. It began with barely enough gas to get over the bridge. But once it crested the middle it picked up momentum, then slowed crossing the divots of plastic grass and finally, achingly, came to rest at the lip of the cup. It sat there a moment —

then butterfly wings beat in Peru, and it dropped into the hole.

"Whoa! Did you see that?" James gushed. "It was like magic! Mom got a hole in one! Mom NEVER gets a hole in one!"

Kate put her arms in the air like a prize-fighter, and marched a slow victory lap around the tee box.

"Good shot, Mommy!" Piper said, throwing her arms around Kate's waist and squeezing hard.

The first time Kate had gotten a full look at Elizabeth's bruises beyond the hint of welts above her collar, she was struck dumb. Elizabeth had volunteered little about the attack — *so lucky, everything was replaceable* — and no one in playgroup had pressed. When they asked, Elizabeth replied emphatically that she was fine. And everyone always believed Elizabeth. Day after day Kate had done her Kate thing, rushed in with food and babysitting and other crisis fillers, but she hadn't asked much of substance. *Were you terrified? Can you sleep at night? How can we get you past this*? Kate hadn't wanted to pry, though it might be closer to the truth that she hadn't wanted to hear. That was her way, actions instead of words, and she knew it was a crutch.

But on the day she saw the welts at the

edges of Elizabeth's shirt she surprised herself by reaching out, offering the physical comfort that always seemed to come more naturally to others. They were sitting in the playroom and she put her arms around Elizabeth's shoulders, and they sat a moment in an embrace. Elizabeth seemed to tense and then soften, as if something tightly held were being released. The fan whirred on its pole. The little boys turned the pages of their books in sleepy anticipation of naps. After a moment, long enough to be an appropriate showing of sympathy, Kate pulled away.

The bungalow was quiet soon after the children fell into bed, and the waves were audible, lapping at the edge of the property. She sat in the chaise and picked up the notebook lying beside it. For the first time since they'd arrived, she wished for a blanket. She also wished, as she never had before on the island, that she weren't in an isolated house alone with her children. Kate went back downstairs and locked the door, something they never bothered to do.

After the break-in, the Martins moved. The new house was only a few streets away, still a part of the old neighborhood, but for Elizabeth it represented a clean break from the associations of the old one, her anger and fear and guilt. *Dave has not voiced regret, not even when the PGA year-end winnings were tallied and it was clear he would have had a banner year if he'd stayed with the tour. He says he loves the new job, really stays on message. I have to accept that I have no more idea of what happens in the solitary parts of his mind than he has of mine, and wonder if all couples are like this. In love and simpatico in many ways, but ultimately unknowing and unknowable.*

Elizabeth's next pregnancy progressed uneventfully. As with the last she didn't find out the gender, and by late February she was full term.

March 3, 1998

It's a girl. Eight pounds three ounces — a full pound heavier than Jonah — and a head of Dave's dark hair, coils stuck to her head and springing out if you pull and fluff them. People always talk about how tiny babies are. But I marvel not at how small they are but how something so big and vital fit so compactly inside.

I dreamed about my sister so much this pregnancy, mostly the same dream I've had for years: leaving the pet store, holding the bags of goldfish, she's riding ahead and my bags are falling, the fish flopping and dying and evaporating into the air. But she keeps pedaling away and never turns back and I can't keep up with her. I rode the wave of hormones and frustration right there in the hospital bed discussing names with Dave, and when it seemed he really wouldn't go with Anna, I fell apart.

Dave was honestly perplexed when I told him. Anna had been riding behind me on her bike, like a kid should be able to do in small-town Vermont on a tiny street with virtually no traffic. She was eight and cute and persistent. I was twelve and wanted to be left alone. I told him how I went on ahead, acting for the first time on the urge to ditch her, weaving and teasing in the street so she couldn't follow easily. He assured me that I hadn't done anything wrong. But I didn't tell him that I hid on a side street and let her ride past, or that I saw the car swerve and go by, or that after the crash I heard her call for me before I could get to her. She was gone before she could finish saying my name, so her last words were unfinished like everything about her. She was the best thing about our family, and without her we failed one another in a million small ways.

Kate choked back a sound, then put her hand to her mouth and shook quietly. It was so awful, so inconceivably awful, and Elizabeth had lived with the memory as a dark secret stain her whole life.

When I finished telling him he looked so confused. Why hadn't I ever told him this before? How could he not know his wife had had a sister?

What is there to say? It's not a logical thing but also not the most illogical, never to have found the moment or words to describe the worst thing you've ever done. He was gentle and concerned of course, but I didn't feel any relief in telling. I couldn't share the worst of it, the emptiness all the time of missing the person I imagine she would have become, the one person I might really have been able to talk to, and the shame of knowing it should have been her who had the chance to grow up and have children, and the certainty that she'd have been better at it. He would have said God, Elizabeth, in that same voice after I wondered too much about the miscarriage. In the end I go back to that same feeling I've always had about confidences. The other person rarely has anything useful to offer and usually you leave feeling no better, sometimes worse.

Anna Danielle Martin is on the bed beside me as I write, curled between my left arm and hip, a wisp of a girl and a girl in every way, long eyelashes and puffy mouth, Dave's full lips thank God instead of the thin slash of mine.

I really thought I was having another boy. I am not a giddy person but I'm light-headed with the possibilities, all the mother-daughterisms I always envied. Write this in blood right now: I swear she — they — will always feel unconditionally loved, and the house will be a normal place of happiness and comfort.

Kate put down the book and went downstairs, then walked outside and stood on the lawn. The porch lights were not turned on and she was enveloped in darkness. She looked up at the clear night sky, stars like pinlights hung low in mesh netting. She wondered if Elizabeth had looked skyward and thought of her sister. She did not even know whether Elizabeth had believed in God.

Kate sat in the grass, then lay down flat on her back the way she had as a child. She thought of the little girl eating ice cream in the painting that hung in the Martins' kitchen, and all the years she'd looked at the picture with no idea what it represented. Now it would only ever represent all Elizabeth had never confided, and the ways she imagined Kate would judge her. Kate wondered what Dave had thought hearing for the first time that his wife had had a sister. How could his mind not go to the moments she might have told him, but hadn't; the times his own sister had come up in conversation, and the times she'd deflected questions about being an only child. Perhaps he'd wondered, and maybe not for the first time, whether he really knew Elizabeth at all.

There was only one thing Kate had ever purposely withheld from Chris. Shortly after they'd married, a new chef had been hired at her restaurant, a man with whom she'd interned during culinary school and had a brief relationship. Guy Giradeaux was the most gifted chef with whom she'd ever worked, and arrogant; his inability to admit a mistake was noteworthy, as rare as anyone's ability to remember his having made one. Kate chose not to tell Chris that she'd once had a fling with the man who'd just become her new boss. It had been brief and insignificant, and the fact that she'd now be working with him daily, late into the night, would only create tension in their new, untested marriage.

One night at the restaurant Kate was last to leave the kitchen, cleaning up excess flour and struggling with a fifty-pound sack, and Guy came down from the upstairs office. He stood beside her and began helping without a word. She struggled to make small talk but he smirked and said nothing, just stood close performing a task so below the realm of his job as to be inappropriate. His silence was suggestive and ridiculous. Then he dumped too much flour too quickly, and puffs of white dust rose from the bin, frosting his eyebrows and the front of his black hair. Kate laughed and he turned toward her, sizing her up with eyes deeply, icily blue. He didn't care that she was now married. He was standing so near she could see the dark stubble fade to gray around his chin. He leaned closer. She stepped backward but tried to appear jaunty, as if getting a better angle to swat flour from his jacket; then she collected her things to leave. His faint smile twisted into a sneer as he realized she would not lean toward him, mesmerized by his eyes and his power, and he stalked back to his office shaking flour from his hair.

After that day her status in the kitchen fell. Shaking with agitation and anger, she'd finally told Chris about the episode, and about the past relationship. He looked at her as if she were saying she'd slept with Giradeaux once again, because withholding information was so unlike her. It had been several tense days before they'd had a resolution.

She decided there would be no more secrets. Nothing was worth that draft of cold air through their marriage.

Kate thought of her reaction to the baby rabbits nearly two weeks before. She thought of the cache of food and water hidden in the spare-tire well of their car back home. She had not intended this. But it had grown as a weed can, spreading into something unmanageable from dark roots choking out that which is healthy. If she felt this way about the things she left unspoken in her marriage — shame, balanced by need — she could not imagine how Elizabeth must have felt about concealing Michael.

She rose from the grass, wiped dew from her bare legs, and went back inside the house.

Two kids under two. Other people do it all the time, but Sourpuss can't seem to get the hang of it. I'm totally wiped out after a day with my own and God help me after a few hours of also watching Kate's son, too. ("No big deal" I always say when she asks, because I <u>want</u> it to be no big deal.) It doesn't seem to affect Dave in the same way, even when he is with them all day. I'd like to believe it's because he grew up in a large family, though it's probably just who he is. His skin is thicker, he's got more patience, he smiles more. The kids are lucky to have him, luckier than they are to have me. In the blackest moments it's a kind of relief, knowing that if I weren't here they would be fine.

I'm not cut out for this, like I always suspected. I get too frustrated, blown off my rails by small things. The mailman rings the bell and wakes Jonah after just a twenty-minute nap and I could cry I feel so robbed. I open my eyes every morning feeling like I've woken up in someone else's life, and I'm so tired it's like there's sand under my eyelids. Terrible thoughts of what I'd do for another hour in bed, not even asleep necessarily. Just quiet. Alone.

Yesterday I was nursing Anna while Jonah was upstairs fighting a nap, and he cried until he threw up. All over the crib and all over the floor, the only carpeted room in the house. I had to put Anna on the ground midfeeding and she was livid, purple-faced while I cleaned up Jonah, who was no happier. Okay, Dr. Spock. Which one is going to be in therapy in 20 years because of being left on the rug while you cared for the other one? Who needs you more?

Kate rested the book in her lap, and thought of that first summer of motherhood on the island, the afternoon she'd left Flour and gone down the cliff path to sit on the high rocks by the crashing waves. For a moment she'd imagined stepping off the rock, dropping into the froth and surge and letting her lungs fill with water. She loved her son, she loved her husband. But that love only added to the impulse. She'd known, after she climbed back down to the sand, that it wasn't something she could explain to anyone.

When she looked up Max was there at the bottom of the path, the bulk of him filling the opening in the brush. He took her hand and led her back up the hill to the kitchen.

What if all the women in the playgroup had felt that way? The loft receded in a moment of vertigo. What if all mothers experienced times of hopeless obliteration, and no one told?

May 11, 1998

Victoria canceled my contract, said the agency isn't doing any more freelance subcontracting. I want to throw the phone through the window, or go stand on a highway bridge and pitch rocks at trucks. It's not like I did all that much work, maybe 15 hours a week, but it wasn't about the amount of time or the money. It wasn't even about the occasional client meetings with honest-to-God adult interaction, though that was something. It was the identity, the ownership, the 1 a.m. moment behind the idea and then bringing it to fruition that had nothing to do with Dave or the kids. I can't help feeling like a door has closed on that part of my life.

May 23, 1998

Schlepped my portfolio and breast pump to TriBeCa, walked some junior VP through four different campaigns I'd done. But I could tell halfway through that he was just being polite. The truth is, not many agencies use freelancers these days, and the ones that do just subcontract to former employees. Everyone wants a known entity; there's nothing more annoying than a freelancer whose technology is old and unreliable, unless it's one whose kids are crying in the background. He said they might have a position opening up full-time and I should check back in a month, but of course I can't do full-time.

I left with a smile, handing him one of the new business cards I ordered to show that I'm a serious part-timer, not just someone winging it while the kids are napping. When I lifted my arm at the curb to hail a cab, the breeze was damp on my blouse. I looked down and saw that I was leaking. Wet spots the size of quarters, as obvious as tasseled pasties at a strip club. I could make myself insane wondering how long they might have been there. When I got to Grand Central I ran to the bathroom to pump and had to sit in a toilet stall, the machine on battery mode and wheezing so loudly I could only imagine what everyone thought I was doing in there. An electric razor? A vibrator? Before last week's interview, I had to pump squatting in a custodial closet.

After I bagged five ounces I ran out into the main terminal in danger of missing my train, and while I was looking up at the schedule boards I ran smack into someone else. Five ounces, everywhere. Then the sitter called to tell me Anna was hungry but refusing the bottle, when would I be home?

I cried on the train, face turned to the window. Who am I kidding? You can do all your gymnastics to try and fool Mother Nature, use all your fancy gadgets and pills and pumps and sitters, but biology always wins in the end.

July 20, 1998, midnight

I asked Kate to watch the kids, claimed a late-afternoon doctor's appointment, and I went to the copy shop to add some things to my portfolio and mail a few more résumés. Before I headed out the door I threw some shirts and pants in a garbage bag. What's that? she asked, and it came out easily, Dropping stuff off at Goodwill.

After the post office I got on the highway. I put the windows down, opened the sunroof, and blasted music I don't even know, horrible numbing stuff. I passed one exit, then another, and another. I hit the Bruck-ner Expressway and turned the music up until I could feel the bass in my breast-bone. Then I heard the fumf of a blown tire.

Standing there with the AAA guy I saw my life as an endless loop of the same scene. No matter how many times I imag-ined driving away or how many times I packed a bag and really did it, I would never reach the FDR.

August 27, 1998

Dave is in Texas for three days at an equipment conference, and I've decided I will paint the baby's room. Put Anna in the cradle in our bedroom, and have been spending the past few nights in a land of small animals and nursery rhymes, a cheerful task that "bridges both worlds," as Nadia suggested. . . .

Nadia? Kate struggled to think of any mutual friends in town, or anyone that had been mentioned earlier in the journals, but came up with no one.

. . . Bunnies everywhere, a cottontail orgy. I find that merlot helps me channel Beatrix

Potter and gives a pleasantly forgiving view of my day. I am getting better at this. I tell myself this and I 70 percent mean it.

We are having Anna baptized next week and I find myself offering up snippets of prayer. Not just that I can discover some inner well of the qualities I need to be a good mother, but that I can fake it until I can become one. LIVE AS IF. A phrase from my mother's playbook.

By midfall Elizabeth had fallen into a parenting rhythm, balancing activities that gave the children pleasure with things she wanted to do herself. One warm Friday afternoon in late September, the Martins hosted a margarita-and-juicebox party to christen their new swingset. As children trampled the tomato plants and fought over sandbox toys, and the husbands asked Kate's opinion about restaurants in Manhattan, Elizabeth slipped away. She walked inside her house, went upstairs, and watched from her bedroom window as the party functioned perfectly well without her. Next to the window a stack of her paintings leaned against the wall, and she flipped through them dispassionately, eyeing them as a stranger might. *The dimensions are off here. This one's saccharine schlock. This one not bad, possibly salable.* As she came back down she overheard Brittain in the living room, resting her third-trimester legs on an ottoman and talking to someone in a stage whisper about home security systems. *So useless without glass-break coverage,* she said. *I hope she learned from the experience and got a better system put in here. I still can't believe . . . Personally, I never would have . . .*

Elizabeth stood just out of view in the doorway and watched Brittain sitting with Kate, who sat quietly nursing Piper as Brittain went on. Elizabeth leaned against the wall unseen, listening to hear whether Kate would agree. A few moments later after Brittain left the room, Elizabeth joined Kate. *Calm moments like this, when she isn't on fire being entertaining, she really is a different person. Everything about her is softer with the extra weight; women always want to lose the baby weight without realizing how it makes a face kinder. I wish I could sketch her profile, thick hair curving in a dark sweep under her chin. But I don't want to ask if I can and then see that moment of discomfort, struggling to find a polite no, or more likely turning it into a joke.*

Kate was aware of everything speeding up: her breathing, her heart; her whole body suddenly at attention — mouth dry, eyes

335

staring stupidly, every follicle prickling on her arms and legs. Thirty minutes earlier she had been exhausted, ready to close the book after the long day that had begun with miniature golf and hadn't slowed. But not any longer. It was as if she were privy to a confidential review she was never meant to see. And yet it had been handed to her.

November 2, 1998

Kate started working for a restaurant start-up here in town, a bistro being launched by someone from her culinary school. It struck me that they must need some graphic design done — logo, menus, ads, whatever. Leslie's sister-in-law doesn't need her nanny in the mornings now that the kids are in preschool, and she's available a few mornings a week. It could work. I might just hint at it and see if she's receptive. Kate will probably ask to see my portfolio, so I'll need to update it. I stayed up too late last night looking at fonts online, thinking of the way she described the bistro. Bleeding Cowboys is a good font, old-school, fading at the edges, western but not too. Or Vielkala-hizo, crisp and simple.

Dave's been away for three days in

California. Life with two little kids is like a three-legged race — I can't get anywhere easily or respond quickly. Sometimes I'm seized with an irrational fear that something's going to happen and I'm destined to lose one of them. It's crazy but for those seconds it's real, my punishment for taking to motherhood too slowly.

November 18, 1998

I had a brief conversation this morning with Kate after playgroup about consulting for the restaurant. She was vague and breezy, Hmmm, I don't know what they're doing for their graphics. She talked a little bit about the bistro concept and some of the people on the team, all with great NYC credentials. But in the end she sidestepped it. Was perfectly nice of course, and professional. But I could tell she was squirming, and she was noncommittal in a way that I know means it won't come up again.

If they have someone else on board already doing their graphics I think she would have said so. Is it that she doesn't want to work with a friend? Or that she assumes I'm not very talented? She could have at least asked to see my portfolio.

It was so obvious what was going on that we both had to pretend it wasn't. She just isn't willing to put her own reputation on the line to put me in front of her people. I'm Elizabeth of the bunny murals on the bedroom wall.

When Elizabeth came to her pitching freelance design work, Kate had only the vaguest idea of what Elizabeth's past work consisted of. She knew it was with an ad agency, but thought her responsibilities had been mostly administrative, and for periods of time forgot that it existed at all. Kate dug for any recollection of Elizabeth talking about designing ads, victorious over finishing a project or clinching a new client, but she came up with nothing. There might have been an occasional reference to being overtired from working late into the night, but Kate had assumed it was the family's own bills or taxes, which Elizabeth had said she found tedious. The truth was, Kate hadn't asked. So the idea of putting Elizabeth in a room with the New York designers and chefs, a team of investors already squeamish about whether the town was sophisticated enough for their restaurant, was not one Kate had considered seriously. At the time, Kate had been consumed with managing the transition between her lives as chef and mom, two halves that would not integrate. She could barely recall the conversation. Elizabeth's request had come and gone and Kate hadn't thought of it again, it had been that inconsequential. To her.

She was hungry and nauseated, was tired yet felt as if she could run for miles. She didn't know what she felt, beyond an agitated awareness that her perceptions were off, and in some ways always had been. Kate stood abruptly and climbed down the ladder.

She paced around the main room picking up kids' books, then putting them down two feet away, adjusting pillows on the couch. She saw now that she had made a quick and inaccurate assessment of Elizabeth. She'd seen propriety and generosity and someone who always said yes, and had thought *simple*, thought *dreamless*. She'd mistaken reticence for a lack of passion, and what Kate had seen as slovenly contentment — Elizabeth slouching about in maternity clothes long after Anna's birth, hair lank and unwashed — was something far more complicated, a dark, sad place. Kate's mantra that you never knew what was going on with others had somehow not extended to Elizabeth, and she had conveyed her low expectations of her in countless small ways.

She opened and closed the refrigerator door without registering its contents, and opened it again. *She could have at least asked to see my portfolio.* There was no iced tea, no yogurt, no ice cream. Kate had failed to pick them up last time she'd gone shopping. *She just isn't willing.* Her cell phone sat on the kitchen counter, where she'd allowed its battery to run out again. She felt suddenly defined by everything she had not done.

Kate plugged the phone into the wall and it showed two messages. The first was from yet another locksmith declining to work on a tiny lock on an old trunk. So busy these days, house breaks on the increase, what with the insane cost of living . . . She erased it and advanced to the next one.

"Hey, Kate. I know we just spoke, but I have a new work development." It was Dave. His voice was slow and loose. "The company wants me to go to Boston tomorrow, and I thought maybe I'd bring the kids and we'd come out the next morning on our way home. Just a little day-trip diversion, if it's not an inconvenience for you all. I'm thinking midmorning. Call me."

Dave, coming to Great Rock. She would have thought spending the day with her was the last place he'd want to be. She pulled a beer out of the refrigerator and stood a moment in the chill of the open door, considering what it would be like to have him here while Chris was not.

He blamed her for the loss of the key. Stolen, lost, it didn't make a difference to him. Kate took a long sip. She wanted to be past that hurdle, to be able to say she had it under control.

She opened the front door of the bungalow, looked out into the clear night. She walked, feet bare on the damp grass, around the back of the house to the shed where the tools were kept. Gardening hoes and trowels, hammers, an ax. She picked up the claw-handled hammer and brought it up to the loft. The photo-covered journal was still folded open on the chaise; she was about two-thirds of the way through. She took a long draw from the beer.

She raised the hammer and brought it down on the lock, a glancing blow that skittered off to the side and left barely a scratch. She raised the hammer higher and slammed it down, and it railed against the side of the lock in a splinter of wood. She brought it down again and again, metal on metal. The old lock dented, became bent and off-kilter, but still did not spring. If it had been a boxer, it would be kneeling dizzily at an eight count and struggling back up, resisting to the bitter end. She bashed it once more and the lock gave way, the defeated lid hanging unevenly on dented hardware.

She lifted it and saw inside, on the far right stack of books, the plain tan cover of Elizabeth's last journal, the one she'd written in before she'd gone for the flight to Los Angeles.

There was a cry of alarm from downstairs, Piper calling for her, afraid of the strange sounds. Kate went down the stairs to find her daughter standing at the bottom, flushed with interrupted dreams and midnight need. It would take time, coaxing her back down.

TWENTY-THREE

Saturday morning breakfast was interrupted by feet on crushed stone, the sound of running on the driveway. Jonah and Anna appeared at the side of the house and ran up the porch. Dave Martin came along more slowly, following Emily as she walked crookedly through the grass.

Kate watched their approach and startled at the sight of Dave. His hair had grown long, curling over his ears, and he'd lost weight. The shoulder seams of his shirt drooped like a jacket from a too-small hanger, and folds of cotton sagged on his chest. He approached the porch with Emily and paused while she navigated each stair in thick-soled toddler sandals. Kate held the screen door and waited.

"Hey there," she said, squinting into the morning sun.

"Look at you, all tanned and lovely." He leaned in to kiss her cheek, cupping her right shoulder in his hand. His eyes had the dark circles of someone who'd worked the night shift. "This is quite the place you've got here."

"That's why we keep signing on every year." Kate leaned down to Emily, wobbly in the doorway. "Hello, you big walker." She held the door open as the girl toddled inside. "You guys eaten?"

"A little. Not really. Some junk on the ferry."

Kate went into the kitchen and pulled three more plates off the shelf, and since there were no longer baby toys at the house, put out some measuring cups on the floor for Emily to play with.

"Coffee?"

"No thanks. Got any Coke?"

Kate gestured to the refrigerator as she piled pancakes on the plates. He pulled out a soda and cocked the tab, then took out milk for Emily's sippy cup. He did it naturally, as if they spent time in one another's kitchens every day, the way the women in their playgroup had behaved in one another's homes. They exchanged small talk as the kids played on the other side of the room. Maybe this would be fine.

"Do you see the playgroup families much?" Kate asked.

He took a long drink from the can and rested it on the counter. "Sometimes. But as far as regular playdates go, the group had kind of dissolved already." They both understood *already* to refer to the time before Elizabeth died. "You know, with kindergarten and preschool there are plenty of other activities going on. But we just had a cookout last month with Regan and Brittain."

Brittain. Hearing the name was like a wake-up call; Kate should telephone and check in. Just before Brittain had her second child a few years before, she'd found out her husband was involved with a woman at his office. She had been miserable, swollen and ready to burst in every way, but still keeping up appearances. Kate would never have known if it hadn't been for something odd in her expression watching Elizabeth and Dave banter warmly at the margarita party, a look both envious and sad. Later in the living room, while Kate was nursing the baby and Brittain was resting her legs and making snide observations about Elizabeth's security system, Kate had asked the most basic question. *Is everything okay?* And Brittain had cracked. Her relief had been palpable, as if she were just waiting for someone to ask.

Snap. There were flashes of light from the sofa where the kids were playing, James taking pictures of Jonah and Anna.

"Careful with that, James," Kate called. "That's our good camera."

"I know how to use it," he said, and zoomed in to take a photo of Jonah's tongue.

Emily whined, and Dave pulled a spatula and measuring spoons from the drying rack and handed them to her. "You talk to Chris lately?" he asked Kate.

"A few days ago, just a quick call while he had cell connection at the airport in Jakarta."

"So he's in Jakarta."

She thought she heard relief in his voice. Kate cut a plate of pancakes into tic-tac-toe lines and glanced at him to see if he'd say more. He took a piece of pancake for Emily and crouched to offer it to her. She turned the bit in pudgy hands, considering it.

"How's your nanny working out?" Kate asked.

"You know, she's pretty great." He stood and leaned against the kitchen island. "The kids love her. She's just out of college and has tons of energy, and she comes with a whole backpack of crafts and stuff. She has dinner going when I get home, and if I have to work late she gives the kids their baths. It makes everything more or less manageable."

Kate delivered plates of pancakes to the children at the table, and put one in front of him as well. "It sounds like that agency got you a good match. I've heard that doesn't always happen with the first try."

She sipped her coffee and leaned back against the counter opposite him. What would it be like to be a young woman working for a recently widowed dad, she wondered, moving all day through a house filled with pictures of the mother of the children she cared for daily. Hugging her children, disciplining them. She imagined Dave coming home at dinnertime and stepping into the kitchen, where the kids were eating their chicken nuggets, *Hi family, I'm home*. There must be awkward moments working in the intimacy of a house, brushing against one another accidentally in the small kitchen. Oh, sorry, they'd both say politely, backing apart and busying themselves with the children. Would she think of him as just an employer, or could she not help seeing him as a single man? The fact that he was a widower might make him untouchable, or it might have the opposite effect, the potent loss so poignant, irresistible.

A bright flash snapped in Kate's face.

"Cheese!" said James.

"Okay, that's enough with the camera," Kate said. "Here. I'll pack it to bring with us today."

"Are we going to the beach?" Piper asked.

"Sure. Everyone have their suits?"

"Yes!" said Anna. "I have a pink one with a skirt."

"I have pictures of sandals and ice-cream sundaes on mine," said Piper.

"Actually, now you have real ice cream on it too," Kate said. "You dropped your cone on it yesterday and we haven't washed it yet."

"Well, now, that's no matter," Dave said, his Georgia creeping in. "It's all going in the drink one way or another."

The late-afternoon sun came through the high trees and striped the lawn like a game board. Kate sat on the porch step molding hamburger patties as she watched the children play croquet, already dressed in pajamas for the long drive. Emily followed behind them on the grass like a small fairy in a pink nightgown, pulling up wickets and trying to make off with the bright balls.

Dave lit the grill, then sat beside her on the steps. He leaned forward with his elbows on his knees watching the kids in the yard.

Sea salt dusted his forearms and clung to his dark hair. Dense freckles overlapped one upon the other, making him appear even more tanned than he was.

"That's a disaster waiting to happen."

"What's that?" Kate plopped a rounded patty on the tray.

"When the kids notice that Emily's stealing their balls and messing up the course all hell's gonna break loose."

"Maybe." She picked up another handful of meat. "Or maybe she'll get bored with it. I have some books in the house for her to read. Well, to look at."

He winced as Jonah swung his mallet and narrowly missed Anna's shin. "Reading. Man, that's something I haven't done in a while. I stopped reading the newspapers and magazines last fall because they depressed me to no end, and I never got back in the habit. I should probably pick up some biography to stretch my brain, something besides watching TV every night."

"I know. I have a whole stack of books I brought out here that I haven't even cracked open."

The moment it was out of her mouth she regretted it. The reason she hadn't read any books was that she'd been consumed with other reading.

"I forgot the rolls. Would you like a beer or something while I'm up?"

He nodded. She walked through the patio doors into the house, trying to remember whether there were, in fact, a few bottles still in the refrigerator. On her way into the kitchen she noticed her cell phone, which she'd forgotten to bring to the beach. There was a message.

"Hey, hon. I just wanted to call so you wouldn't worry. That bombing in Bali was nowhere near us. We were out by the beaches. Anyway, we're all done here. I'm connecting through Seoul tonight and should be back tomorrow night. And then I'm not gonna leave the beach for the whole last week we're there. Give the kids kisses for me."

Bombing? She reached for the edge of the counter. She hadn't turned on the TV or radio all day. Maybe that's why Dave had acted oddly when he'd asked if she'd talked to Chris lately, and was relieved when she'd said he was in Jakarta. Ten days he'd been gone, but it felt like months. She hadn't even known he'd left Jakarta for Bali.

Let it go, she told herself. It's over, he's on his way home. She took two bottles of beer from the refrigerator, popped off their lids, and put one against the side of her neck. The cool penetrated her skin like an epidural.

When she returned to the porch, Dave was on the lawn showing Piper the way to hold a croquet mallet. He stood behind her, holding her arms so that the mallet swung forward and back cleanly between her ankles. Kate picked up the camera from the patio table and focused the lens on them, a pendulum of large and small limbs. They sent the yellow ball a smooth seven feet or so to rest against the next wicket, and Piper's eyes widened in disbelief. Dave gave her a thumbs-up. Then he took a step backward and swung the mallet broadly, a pantomime of a slow-motion drive in miniature.

Kate had never seen him play golf. But she could imagine it in his stance, feet planted slightly apart as he held the mallet like a club, and in his muscular swing, free and easy as an afterthought. There was a smooth confidence in the way he moved, and she wondered whether he'd always been that graceful, or if grace came with being a professional athlete, years of practicing something tied to the performance of the body, and then years more of doing it in front of crowds and cameras. She could probably make a pie crust in her sleep, but even on her best days, there was nothing physically grand about the rolling of dough. She had never before thought of golf as elegant. But watching Dave on the lawn she could see that it was.

Farther down the playing field James knocked his ball through the wicket, a long shot hit with a confident whack.

"Yes!" Dave called out, taking three long paces toward him with his arm raised for a high five. "And Spenser comes through with the birdie shot he needs to reclaim the lead." Their palms met in midair with a clap.

Elizabeth's description of him with his niece and nephew long ago had been an apt one. He was like a camp counselor of an uncle. *His skin is thicker, he's got more patience, he smiles more.* At the time she wrote that, Elizabeth had struggled with two children; all day, here on the island, Kate had watched him fairly untroubled by three. Though perhaps by the time Elizabeth had had Emily, she had hit her stride too. She certainly had appeared to. Kate remembered meeting Elizabeth in New York a few months after Emily was born. Kate was up for a culinary affair, and they'd met in the city for some fancy kids' concert. When Jonah and Anna were horsing around, Elizabeth slid expertly between them without visible irritation. When they'd continued to be truly disruptive, she'd finally gotten up and ushered them out, one hand on the back of each of their heads, the baby across her chest in a sling carrier. She'd cast a breezy oh-well smile over her shoulder at Kate, and Kate remembered how unflappable she'd seemed. Kate had not yet reached those later years in the journals to know whether that was an accurate perception.

Dave returned to the step and took a long drink from the beer she'd placed on the stair.

"Do you miss golf?" she asked.

He hesitated a moment before answering, and she thought he'd sidestep the question with a blasé reply. *I still work in golf.*

"Yes and no. I love the game, no doubt about it. But it's like that was the life of another person. What I did before, and what I did after. Act one, act two."

He didn't qualify his *before*. Most *befores* referred to Elizabeth's death, but this could have meant prior to the break-in, before he quit the tour.

"I don't know much about golf, but you were on a pretty good roll there when you left, weren't you?"

"I was doing all right," he said lightly,

flicking at the label on his bottle with his fingernail. "Higher on the leaderboard, the money was better. But it takes over your whole world. I was never home. And when certain things happen in your life . . . I wasn't really being much of a dad. Or a husband, probably. So it was time to find something else." He stood, took the tray of patties from her, and began lining them on the grill like a dealer laying cards. "But yeah, it was hard to walk away from the tour. I worked hard to get there."

It didn't seem to bother him, talking about golf. She had expected it to be a forbidden topic. Maybe that had been true at the time. Or maybe that was just the way he and Elizabeth were with one another, locked in their disappointments. Too much vested in a certain version of the other to allow for variation, or weakness.

"It was hard for Elizabeth to stop working too," Kate asked.

Dave paused, spatula in hand. "Yeah, to some extent." He pressed down on a burger, and it sizzled. "The work had been dwindling for some time, but it was after Anna was born that she decided not to renew the contract."

"Elizabeth 'decided'?"

He looked at her sharply. Flames leaped

as the fat from the burgers dripped below. As soon as she said it she wished she could take it back.

"Things were so busy with two kids," he said. "It became more of a pressure."

He did not look back at her a second time. But she felt that even if he had, she would not be able to read in his face whether he believed it himself.

Ice cream ran down their arms, and chocolate drippings stained their pajamas. The kids were silent with joy as the sunlight faded in the yard.

"I am going to miss this lawn when we go back to D.C.," Kate said, licking her own cone. "It's the best babysitter going. Just open the door and out they go, noise and fighting cut in half immediately."

"We live in ours," Dave said. "As long as it's not pouring, we're out there. We hardly ever go anywhere else. People come to us." He pried open a plastic tub of blueberries and placed a few in front of Emily. "How many years you been coming here, this house?"

"This is our tenth. I love this place. There's a reading room at the top where the attic would be, this little nook. I'm up there all the time."

Dave toyed with one of the blueberries, hiding it beneath his palm while his daughter pried up his fingers, one by one. "Sounds like a pretty good place to read the journals."

Kate hesitated, then bit off a chunk of fudge in the ice cream. "It is. Up there at night, when no one needs me. It's nice to look out over the water in the dark, see the lights on the boats."

He held his beer bottle in front of him in both hands and rolled it between his palms. Emily pressed blueberries flat with her finger against the table, then drew in juice on her pajamas.

"Kate, I know you take it seriously, these notebooks."

A line of ice cream slid down her cone to her finger, and she licked it slowly. The chocolate felt like lard between her teeth. He paused as if he expected her to interject.

"So now you're gonna do whatever you think is the noble thing, store the trunk in your basement or set it aside for the kids, or whatever you're deciding is what she would have wanted. But she was not herself last summer and I'm not sure that's a call she would have made at another time, giving them to someone outside the family." He had been looking out over the yard as he spoke, but now he looked at her pointedly. "I have a right to know, and I'm not just talking about last summer. So you can have your read, but I think we both know where those books should be."

His eye contact was disconcerting. There was nothing about his body language that should register menace, but on some level she felt it: an implicit promise that no matter where she lived or where she went, or however long it took for her to get to the end of the journals, he would be there, waiting.

He put the bottle down on the table, which seemed to indicate that he'd had his say and would not belabor the point. He was more straightforward than she'd thought him capable of being and much more self-possessed, and the way he looked at her contradicted all she'd thought about him. Either she'd misjudged him, or he'd changed.

Under his look, she felt confidence pooling back in and filling the ruts. He wanted her to say okay, but she wouldn't. Instead she murmured, "Mm hmm."

He nodded and sat still on the step beside her. She didn't elaborate, and he didn't ask. After a moment, he stood.

"Kids, we have to leave in ten minutes,"

he called across the lawn. He picked up Emily's sippy cup and swept her crumbs into his palm, then spoke over his shoulder to Kate. "Do you mind if I take a quick shower while you watch Emily? I'd like to rinse off before the drive."

His tone was stiff but not unfriendly. There'd be no ill will when he left, because they understood one another. This was always where the situation would bring them, and there was nothing left to say.

"Of course," she said. "The outdoor shower is great. It's right around the side of the house."

"Do you mind if I go inside instead?"

That was surprising. Modesty? Luxury? She wouldn't have expected either from him.

"Use the bathroom in our bedroom. Through the kitchen and to the right. The spare towels are under the sink."

She watched him walk toward the house, and he no longer looked diminished or tired, or as if he had lost weight. His tanned shoulders were buoyant, and as he crossed the patio he came off the balls of his feet with a levity that belied the gravity of what he'd said. *I watched him walk away toward the corner with a rolling gait that bounces off the balls of his feet, heavy and solid like a draft horse, but light like a very contented one. He looks like he could carry you a thousand miles if he had to.*

TWENTY-FOUR

September 13, 1999

Jonah started preschool today. A morning program for three-year-olds, three days a week. I dressed him in a little white collared shirt and tamed his curls with a spray bottle of water, and he marched in the door clutching his Winnie the Pooh lunchbox like a little man with his briefcase, big meetings await. Brought tears to my eyes. When I picked him up he didn't want to come to me (which I guess is a good thing) as I stood in the doorway with Anna on my hip, grinning my big proud "So how was it??" dorky smile. Maybe he didn't want to come to me because I looked like such an idiot.

It all passes so fast. I know it's just preschool, but here we are in the realm of school already. All those days when I felt suffocated by being so needed, but at that moment he didn't want to come home, it's true, I wanted to be needed like that again. It really feels like just yesterday he was a newborn in the crib and I was scraping mercury off his nursery floor with the hazmat guys.

November 18, 1999

Can't believe I pulled an all-nighter for a preschool auction catalog. Sitting up at 2 a.m. designing page after page of descriptions of sports and spa packages with grinning monkey icons in the corners.

It's taking longer than it should. I keep being distracted by the small card on my desk I can't bring myself to throw away. A simple note, three lines of sympathy for the loss of my father. He read it in the newspaper. My stupid mind reads into the familiar handwriting and imagines him more emotional, more eloquent, more mature. I try to look at it and see fatter and balder. "Love, Michael." Where does he get off? What love, Michael?

March 1, 2000

Dave's birthday is tomorrow, can't wait to see the look on his face. The car is being delivered from upstate on a flatbed. It's a mess, but it's his dream: a red '63 Spider to ogle and buff and maybe, just maybe, get to run. If he can't he'll probably just sit in the driver's seat in the garage reading golf magazines and drinking beer, and that's fine too. He deserves something to excite him. Life's too short to wait for the big birthdays.

I've been trying to paint again, trying to get excited about something myself and distract me from Kate's moving. She's all fired up about the new house they found in D.C. I try to be a good friend, listen to the details about the new kitchen with some dumb European stove that can do everything but change your kid's diaper, but it hurts to see her face so animated about leaving.

So I've been painting. I set up a canvas in half of the garage, and did a few water-colors of our backyard, not much to look at in the winter, and then saw the kids' trikes and ride-on toys piled in the corner. Something about them looked like children or animals asleep in a heap. And I'm just finishing a piece I'm really happy with, a great scene from the dog run next to the playground. There was this one mutt standing in the middle of a flock of feathery golden retrievers and he was pretty hideous, half hairless and mangy, but he was wearing fussy booties in the mud and a Burberry dog jacket. Great stuff, I could see it on canvas easily.

Turns out a mom at the preschool is a dealer for work that goes to a small chain of island galleries, and she said she'd take a look at my work. Just thinking of it hanging there has me so jazzed I was singing in the kitchen making dinner tonight. I could picture which pieces would work there, could see the whole thing spooling out, contributing regularly.

I'm not stupid. I know my work is never going to set the world on fire, I'll never make it to a party at the NAC. Raising my kids is the biggest contribution I'm going to make in this world, and Nadia is helping me put it in perspective. But from time to time I slip, and wish people might see a painting of mine and it would make them stop or think or smile, and maybe even remember my name and look for another piece.

Or maybe someday on vacation Kate will see a piece hanging in a gallery, or Leslie or Brittain or Regan, and it will be like when Dave climbed the leaderboard. Suddenly there's recognition, respect.

Kate left yesterday, came to say good-bye once and for all last night after they'd finished emptying the refrigerator and packing the car. Mini good-byes all night long. They came back and forth bringing us stuff from the freezer, and the propane tank they couldn't transport and plants that wouldn't survive the trip, and I took it all with a smile. Sure, more chicken breasts. Another ratty plant, bring it on. The last load came at 10 p.m. when she showed up with two jade plants and the goldfish. Are goldfish my karma forever? I stood there on the front step under the porch light, and there wasn't any sense inviting her in because she still had to go back and sweep their shell of a house. There wasn't anything else to say, anyway. . . .

Elizabeth had looked miserable as Kate handed her the plant. She'd held it before her in both hands, quiet and serious as an altar girl. Kate had known she would miss Elizabeth. It was nearly impossible to replicate the companionship of a friend who'd known you since the first days of motherhood. She'd miss their Tuesday and Thursday afternoons on the playground, giving structure and support to the no-man's-land between naps and dinner. And if Elizabeth were to have the third child she hoped for, Kate would not live nearby to see that pregnancy swell or see that child grow, daily. The emotion of the moment suddenly felt to Kate like too much and she longed to cut it short, make light of it. But she saw with confusion that for Elizabeth it was more still. The glow of the porch lights showed the welling of her eyes. Kate had seen Elizabeth endure many things. But she'd never seen her cry.

. . . Nothing will be the same, and she'll never know. Playgroup folks will make precious statements with no one to deflate them with some hilarious jab that brings things back down to earth even if it some-times hurts someone's feelings. No more pizza dinners when the husbands are away where a glass of wine turns into two and we're totally undone by her imitations of her husband and kids. When she really pays attention to something — a kid, a pet, even a fruit tart — that thing just lights up. Everything feels boring already. She has one foot out the door, and she'll never know.

Kate put the book down and covered her face, palms cool against her cheekbones, and drew long slow breaths through the crack between her hands. She sat that way a long while, and was unaware when her dream state segued into actual dreams.

She was on a transatlantic flight. Something to do with visiting Chris, an emergency rescue. She clutched an awkward carry-on bag in her lap, tools of escape, and buzzed a flight attendant for help securing it in an overhead bin. Moments passed, and no one came. She looked toward the front galley, then peered around her seat toward the rear. But the flight attendants lounging in back against aluminum drawers were giant rabbits, noses long and leering like rats under jaunty caps. In each row fanning back, every seat was filled with rabbits, gray with limp greasy whiskers, some with red eyes, teeth protruding like stalactites from thin lips. Kate recoiled and dropped her pack, and it began to convulse. She reached inside to safeguard her tools and pulled out instead a handful of tiny baby rabbits, bald and mewling, their eyes yet unopened. *They are all your children*, came a voice over the PA system. She cupped them in her hands but they grew smaller and more difficult to hold, slipping between her fingers and falling to the floor one after another with a grotesque wooden thud.

Kate awoke to a thud, a sound from the house that had crossed over to her dreams. She sat up in the chaise, instantly awake and trained on the sound. Footfall on the patio. A scrape of wood, and the sound of chafed lifting. A window opening.

She fell over the edge of the chaise and fumbled toward the loft's trapdoor. In a rush she envisioned weapons and rope burns and monetary demands, a search for valuables that was certain to disappoint, followed by the rage of entitlement unsatisfied. The locksmith had warned her of break-ins. Her heartbeat pulsed in her ears and her children were downstairs and her progress to the ladder was endless. The stairs accordioned out below, long and lengthening.

She'd let down her guard. She'd let something slip by. For all her planning, her fire extinguishers and water coolers and supplies in the spare-tire well, she didn't have a plan for intruders. Finally, this is how it would be. Should she volunteer the fact of her sleeping children and plead for mercy, or did that make it worse? What had Elizabeth — how had Elizabeth —

She scrambled down the ladder, missing

steps, and fell down the bottom few.

"Kate, it's me," came a voice from the family room. "You locked the door. I didn't want to wake everyone."

She stopped at the bottom of the ladder and crouched, steadying her breathing. Then she stood and walked out of the bedroom, wiping the clamminess from her palms.

Chris climbed the rest of the way in through the window looking every bit the part of a transatlantic flier, dark suit slept in, tie loose and off-center. His rust-colored hair fell in clusters suggesting the last shower had happened many time zones ago. The sight of him home, the knowledge that he was no longer traipsing in and out of prime tourist locations, gave her relief as potent as desire.

He looked up and saw her in the doorway, took in the languid posture in her old black camisole. Chris left his garment bag on the other side of the window and crossed the room.

"Welcome home," she said as he kissed her on the forehead.

"It's nice to be back." He ran his hand along her waist in the sliver of bare skin, hooked his index finger under the waistband of her shorts.

"Have you eaten? There's pizza."

"Not hungry," he said. "Not that kind of hungry."

She smiled, though her heart still pounded. "Sounds like someone had one of those special first-class movie options." She pulled back in his arms and looked him in the eye searching for anything else. He met her look, tired, but direct. If there was a brown leg on his conscience, and she had no reason to think that there was, it did not show.

She unthreaded his tie from his collar, then unbuttoned his creased jacket and wrinkled button-down shirt. She let the jacket drop to the floor. He smiled, amused at the return of the wife she hadn't been for months, and she continued with the confidence of someone who had faced down poor odds. He was back. He'd gone into the land of bad headlines and tempted all that was arbitrary and possible, but none of those things had come to pass, and he was back.

She had a fleeting thought of the things that had not happened — a self-detonating martyr, Chris's burned wallet returned to her by the embassy — and wondered if things would ever be simple again, a trip just a trip, a sound on the porch just a sound. Nothing had slipped by, no visit from destiny, not this time. Whatever accident of chance or malice awaited her, she did not yet know how it would be.

She sank to the bed and rested her forehead on his bare stomach. He reached down and put his hands through her overgrown hair, pushed long bangs off her forehead as a parent might soothe a fever, or maybe just to better see her face, then climbed past her and onto the bed. She closed her eyes and inhaled the familiar smell of him. He smelled of other things, too, things she vaguely placed in streets blowing with the unfiltered emissions of cars and strong cigarettes, smells she associated with the stained red lips of betel chewers and marketplace baskets of cardamom, clove, and camphor. He had been gone. But he was back.

For a moment in the dark she saw the face of Dave Martin, thought of his year of long nights alone, then imagined him standing in the kitchen alongside his energetic young nanny. She would be wearing a tank top in the summer's heat, her bra strap slipping from beneath the ribbed shoulder of her tank, and though he'd have a fleeting impulse to push it up for her, he probably would not.

Kate put her hand to Chris's chest, traced a thumb along the muscle. He slid a camisole strap off one of her shoulders and put his lips where it had been, long and slow, as if she had been gone too.

TWENTY-FIVE

The morning sun on the porch was nearly tropical. Kate sat in a weathered Adirondack chair and rested her coffee mug on its wide splintered arm. At the patio table, the kids were at work on Asian coloring books Chris had left out for them the night before.

"I need the purple." Piper reached across the table to the pile of crayons in front of James. "For Jasmine's dress."

"She's not Jasmine. She's some other lady."

"She is Jasmine. Look at her eyes."

James sighed with the patience of someone who's traveled the whole world over. "Other people in the world have eyes like that, Piper."

Kate slipped her hoodie off her bare shoulders. She closed her eyes and let her head tilt back against the wood slats of the chair. She'd had little sleep last night, and did not mind. They'd needed this.

There was a sound behind them. "Dad!" James called. Chris came onto the porch with a tired grin and terrible hair, and the kids ran to him, speaking over and through one another vying for his attention. He put his hand on Kate's shoulder and rubbed the back of her neck with his thumb. She reached up and stroked his knuckles, then got up to refill her coffee.

As she poured, she watched them through the window. Piper was leaning forward, chin jutting with the effort of describing her first underwater swim in the ocean. Kate watched Chris follow the retelling, saw the smile lines crease his eyes when Piper described crabs on the ocean floor. If the tables were turned, if Kate were the one who'd been away so long, she knew the sense of what she'd missed would be as strong as the pleasure of hearing. They were wired differently, she and Chris.

As she poured a cup for him as well, her cell phone rang on the counter. She glanced at the caller ID window and saw an unfamiliar number with the Washington, D.C., area code. "Hello?"

"Kate, it's Anthony. You still on vacation?"

She shouldn't have picked it up. She wasn't prepared to talk about the restaurant job. "Hey there. Yes, we have about a week left."

"How's it going?"

"Great. We come out every year. We love it here."

"Good. So, have you talked to the restaurant owners?"

"No," she said. "They haven't called."

He paused. "You were supposed to call them, remember?"

Through the window she saw James pantomime a golf putt, then jump up and down with both fists in the air. Chris gave him a double high five.

"I was? I thought they were going to call me. Oops."

" 'Oops'?" Anthony sighed. "You gotta call them, Kate. In the next few weeks they're going to get serious about lining up a pastry chef and you'll lose your jump on it. We need you. We need your crème brûlée."

Need. That had to be one of the most abused words in the language. She liked Anthony. But the minute she said no — if she said no — he'd have some other colleague on the line and would need that person's chocolate soufflé.

"Has the opening date been set yet?"

"No. They're still rehabbing the space. But I think they already have the maître d' and sommelier on board."

Outside, the kids were opening a bag from Chris and pulling out long packages. Colorful membranes unfurled in Piper's hands. Chris gestured down the lawn, and the three of them headed off the porch.

"Hey, remind me," Kate said. "Is the position full-time?"

"Full-time?" Anthony asked. "What do you mean?"

"Well, how many people are they lining up for the team? Is there any room for, you know, fewer days?"

He hesitated, confused. "You mean like job sharing?"

"Sort of. Like if there were enough people hired for desserts, then maybe everyone wouldn't have to be there all the time."

"What's wrong with you?" he sputtered. "Of course it's full-time. This isn't some hot-dog stand."

She put her hand through her hair. She shouldn't have said anything. "No, I know. Calm down. I just knew someone who had a setup like that in Connecticut."

"Well that's *Connecticut*. These investors got a Beard Award for the last place they did. You don't get that with a part-fucking-time pastry chef." He sighed. Anthony was a sigher. "Katie, if you're not serious about this you gotta let me know. It would be great to work together again, but I'm not putting my neck out so you can get all mommy-track on me."

She nearly barked into the phone that of course she'd take it. It *was* a great opportunity. She could feel the smooth steel utensils in her hand, and feel that control that led to success, the ability to account for all the variables, which didn't happen enough in other areas of life. An image of Jonah with a Winnie-the-Pooh lunchbox came to mind, three-year-old Jonah with wild curls on his first day of preschool, Elizabeth picking him up with the mixed pleasure of seeing him not want to come home. *So fast. It all passes so fast.*

"No, no, I'll call him," she said. "Give me that number again." As she reached for a pen, she saw Chris helping Piper release a brightly colored kite into the air. It rose and was carried away by the unpredictable wind and her hands froze in their outstretched position, wanting to hold on as much as she wanted to let go.

Kate walked into the yard holding two cups of coffee with the camera tucked under her arm. Chris and the kids were running down the length of the lawn trying to get the kites to stay airborne. The geometric forms were diving and bobbing about twenty feet off the ground, staying up as long as the runners kept moving.

Kate put down the coffee and took the lens cap off the camera. When she tightened the focus, their animated expressions filled the lens. James, skipping backward and looking up at his kite, hopeful. *Click*. Handing Piper the reel of string with an encouraging smile, while she looked up at him like he'd hung the moon. *Click*. Chris, with eyes and hair that belonged twelve hours ahead and a face all love.

One morning while they were dating, shortly before they'd gotten engaged, he'd surprised her in the hotel restaurant. She'd looked out over the room and there he'd been at one of the tables, just in from South America when he was supposed to have gone straight to the office for an urgent project. He had been bleary-eyed and had the hair of a deranged person, as he sipped coffee contentedly waiting to see her. That was Chris. He didn't care what he looked like or where he was supposed to be when he cared about something else more. She'd felt a love then so fierce she knew she was stuck with it always. What she hadn't known was that sometimes it would take work, living with it.

They ran back up the yard, and then Chris slowed to a walk and came to the patio for his coffee.

"Thanks." He took a sip, either not noticing or not minding that it was lukewarm from sitting while she'd talked on the phone. He looked back at the kids, roughhousing with the kites. "I give it another ten seconds in the air."

"I give it another ten minutes until it's broken."

"That's a sucker bet."

Piper's kite had already fallen, but they were trying to work together to keep James's up.

"Were you on the phone inside?" Chris asked.

"Yeah. It was Anthony. About the restaurant."

He stood and sipped his coffee while he watched the kids, taking a step toward the lawn. "What did you tell him?" His body language said that this was a thirty-second conversation.

"I said I'd call the owners," she said. "I was supposed to have already, but I thought they were calling me. So I'm supposed to get on it."

He turned, surprised. "Oh." He'd expected her to say she had turned it down.

"Well, I should at least hear them out," she said.

He smiled, curious. "What do you need to hear from them that you don't already know?"

"Some of the details. The opening date. The salary. The title."

" 'The title'?" His eyes had that indulgent quizzical look he gave when he thought something was foolish.

"Well, exactly how large of a role it'd be. Maybe it could be a shared thing. A few people taking shifts doing desserts and some other stuff."

It was unrealistic, and they both knew it. "That's not really a traditional structure in restaurants, is it?"

It was a rhetorical question but he wanted to drive the point home and hear her admission. That it was too much right now, that they weren't there yet in their lives, that there'd be other restaurants in a few years when their family was better positioned for her to go back to work. This was clearly what he thought, but he didn't want to have to say it for her.

Kate knew they weren't on opposite sides of this. They were not Elizabeth and Dave. Chris would be supportive, but he preferred knowing that while he was in Bali or Boston, she was home. She herself didn't like the idea of having full-time help for the kids, and long and unusual restaurant hours would mean missed school activities, relay-race meals, interrupted weekends. But it felt like *someone* should be making a case for the other side. Lots of mothers worked full-time jobs and jobs with nontraditional hours, because they either needed to or wanted to, or some combination of the two. Somewhere in this argument-that-wasn't-an-argument there should be a third party laying out the case for finding a way to pursue what you love. But when she tried to imagine what this third party would say, it always sounded hollow. Except when it was written by Elizabeth. *It was the identity, the ownership, the 1 a.m. moment behind the idea and then bringing it to fruition that had nothing to do with Dave or the kids.*

Chris took the camera from her gently and turned back to the kids, focused the lens on James helping Piper unsnarl her line. She was watching him with a look of admiration and trust, faith in the older brother who could make things right when he wasn't tromping on her world. Kate saw the sort of big brother he would become if surrounded by people who encouraged kindness and loyalty over the fish-in-a-barrel sport of belittling younger siblings.

Click. Chris pulled back the camera to look at the digital window at what he'd gotten. Then he tapped on the backward button, scrolling back through the pictures Kate had just taken — bright kites against the sky, bright-faced kids looking upward — and sat down to continue looking at old vacation photos with his coffee. The conversation about the restaurant was over.

Kate turned from him and went inside for something to eat. The phone number for the restaurant owner lay on the counter. It could probably be handled quickly in a voice mail, at least for now. *Hello, this is Kate Spenser, Anthony Devilliers's friend. I'm looking forward to talking to you about the position.* Or, *Hello, I'm Kate Spenser. I wanted to let you know I have to decline putting my name in.* She peeled back the foil lid on a container of yogurt, and took a spoon from the drawer. When she walked back out on the patio Chris was looking intently at the camera. She leaned in over his shoulder; she'd taken some good shots of the beach and the carousel. But he was looking at photos of croquet, of Piper, tiny between Dave Martin's long arms as he coached her in the swing of the mallet. Dave standing in their yard not long ago, sandy and shirtless, so at home in the tableaux of kids in the yard that he might have been there for days.

Chris looked up at her. "When was Dave Martin here?"

She realized she hadn't yet mentioned it. Even as she opened her mouth she knew what she should have been saying was, *Yeah, can you believe he came? It slipped my mind last night*, and put an arm around his neck to remind him of why she'd been distracted. But what she did was laugh uncomfortably and say, "Oh yeah, I haven't had a chance to tell you."

He scrolled back to the previous shot and saw the kids scampering on the lawn in their pajamas, then one more, Dave in the kitchen eating pancakes.

"Did he stay over?"

"No. They came over early in the morning. It was just a day trip. They had burgers and left that night."

"Oh."

He held her eye a moment longer, his expression unreadable. Then he looked back down at the camera, where Dave Martin was leaning against their kitchen counter, rumpled, loose. At home.

TWENTY-SIX

A few hours past sunset, and a large sailboat was still hosting a party offshore. Its outline was lit with a string of bulbs, the mast and sails illuminated like a nautical Christmas tree. Music and laughter came in through the open windows of the loft.

There were only a few entries left to read in the journal covered with the photograph of Elizabeth, Jonah, and Anna. The trunk sat beside the chaise on the floor, its broken lid listing on its hinges. Tonight Kate would start the next and last journal, the one that would take her through the rest of Elizabeth's last year — the birth of Emily, Elizabeth's thirty-eighth birthday, and whatever events had steered her toward Michael. To her surprise, the thought of having come to the end was not a relief. Reading the journals had felt like a conversation, one that had never been held, and she did not want it to end. There was nothing, no one, to take her place.

Kate settled into the chair, a glass of iced tea beside her, and opened the last pages of the notebook.

In late fall of 2000, the tenor of Elizabeth's writing had changed. Entries were more cheerful and revolved around humorous and frustrating things the children had done, the minutiae of their well-being, plans for the holidays. *The kids are in the living room playing with the Nativity set, pretending that Mary and Joseph and the angel are a golf threesome. I think the angel just called "Fore!" They're really getting into it this year, and after all those years of dreading Christmas I'm really getting into it too. Which Nadia says is as good a barometer of happiness as any.*

Again Kate tried to place anyone named Nadia, but could not.

In these months there were no longer signs of discontent; there were a few mentions of painting, and of exchanging tentative plans with the island gallery. She wrote about Dave more frequently than she had in years, and more warmly.

Dave got the Spider to run the other day and is on cloud nine. All the windows down in the middle of December, his hair windblown and showing the small thinning spot he doesn't acknowledge and I certainly don't let on I do. He came back with a million yards of garland and I wrapped it up the banister while Anna was napping. When she woke up she stood at the top of the stairs with her eyes bugging out. "Mommy! BUSHES GREW ON THE STAIRS!" Incredible to think that at this time next year, we'll have a third.

It sounded more like the Elizabeth Kate had known, a mother charmed by the idiosyncrasies of family life. There was enthusiasm for the pregnancy, every detail recorded, each ultrasound as if it were her first. *The wand zooms down a spinal column like a staircase, then up close on a face. The baby had one hand over its eyes like it was already tired of all of us and our constant peeping: ah, the paparazzi again.*

Right after Emily was born, Kate had traveled up from Washington and made it to the hospital before Elizabeth was discharged. She sat beside her on the bed looking down into the infant's opaque eyes, unreadable and still as those of a large fish. They commented over the imperfections a mother is not supposed to see: an ear bent double, just like Jonah's, which you hope will unfold; a whorl of hair between the shoulder blades — half angel, half gnome — you pray will molt.

Elizabeth could not hide her relief that it was another girl. *I'm so glad they'll have each other.*

Kate had given a vague smile, thinking of the mixed bag that was her relationship with her sister, Rachel. But even as she thought it, she checked herself. A relationship was a constantly evolving thing; so long as both parties lived, there was the possibility of change. Instead she'd said to Elizabeth, *Well, sometimes the friendships you make can be just as good as a sister.*

At the time, Kate had thought it was true for each of them, for different reasons. To Kate's mind, Elizabeth probably felt Kate could not imagine what it was like to be an only child, no peer to balance the eagerness of parents who loved you too much. No matter that Elizabeth had not in fact been an only child, and that there'd never been that smothering love. And Elizabeth, Kate had thought, would never understand what it was to feel second best. How little Kate had known.

There had been a long silence that was somehow both content and melancholy, and Kate had pulled out her camera and taken the photograph that had been on the Martins' refrigerator ever since. Elizabeth, pale in her maternity gown, the baby a sliver of

386

pink at her breast.

Kate lifted the lid from its broken lock and reached for the next book in the stack, but found only the plain one she'd already read after she left the Martins' house in June. Underneath that notebook were the others she'd already read, and at the bottom of those, the faded striped lining of the old trunk. She rifled through the stack in the middle and those on the far left, but there was nothing new. Her breathing sped up.

Kate tipped the trunk on its side and pulled the books toward her like a dealer raking in chips. The Hallmark-stickered composition book. The college cover painted in geometrics, and the pastel-chalked one, and many others she'd already read. She spread the pile looking for anything she might have missed but there was nothing unfamiliar. The one she'd just finished, wrapped in the photograph of a smiling Elizabeth, beamed from the top of the pile like a challenge to all she'd expected to find: first tedious details of a predictable life, then illicit ones revealing how Elizabeth had veered off and away, neither one true.

Kate tried to remember when — and if — she'd seen this missing journal but couldn't remember what it had looked like, couldn't in fact be certain she'd seen a journal for that time period at all. She thought she had flipped one open that night in the motel parking lot and seen a starting date around Emily's birth, but she was not sure. Yet there had to be; several months of significant events unaccounted for in the life of an avid diarist.

She thought of James, but since his snooping episode, he hadn't shown any interest in the journals. He wasn't even a very good sneak; before, he'd left the book sitting out on her bed. It couldn't be Piper. Not only could she not read, but she hated the stairs leading to the loft, even hated climbing steep steps at the playground.

Kate went down into the children's bedroom. James's breath snagged in rhythmic sawing. In the glow of the nightlight his profile was slack-jawed on the pillow. She looked under his bed but saw nothing but his stuffed dinosaur. Pulled open his dresser drawers and opened his closet, nudging his books with her toe. All small paperbacks, no spiral notebooks.

Kate headed back into her bedroom and paused outside the bathroom, where Chris was showering. He was out of the question. He'd lost interest in the journals almost immediately, caring more about the way they were distracting Kate than about their contents. Just yesterday, as they'd sat at the beach with the kids, she'd begun to talk about Elizabeth's mixed feelings about motherhood. He'd stared at her as patiently as a therapist, then turned to watch the kids at the waterline.

"Chris? Did you hear what I said?"

"Yes," he'd said. "Did *you* hear what you said?"

"What's that supposed to mean?"

"It means that's the most you've talked about anything since we've been out here." He said it with a smile, pouring a fistful of sand over her shin. "I know you miss her. But doesn't it strike you as a little odd to be dwelling on this so much? These are our last few days. Let it go." He swatted at a fly buzzing near her leg.

She had been irritated, but hadn't argued. Their intimacy since his return had been sweet and genuine, and she didn't want to ruin it with defensiveness. So she bumped against him shoulder to shoulder, an agreeable gesture, and smiled sadly.

But now she froze in their bedroom listening as he showered. Would he have? Just to get it out of their way for the remainder of their vacation? Inside the bathroom there was the bump of falling soap. She eased open his top drawer and ran fingers through his socks and underwear, careful to put them back in the neat lines he favored. Then she felt around in the second drawer under his stack of polo shirts. In the closet was his suitcase, empty but for a few biographies and a travel magazine he'd never unpacked.

A squeaky crank, and the sound of water stopped. She ran her hand quickly under the mattress on his side of the bed, even knowing while she did that she wouldn't find anything. It would be so unlike him, taking something of hers.

Taking things.

Kate paused, her hand between the box spring and mattress. She thought of Dave sauntering into the house to take a shower after he'd said he wanted her to return the journals. She knew her response had been unsatisfying to him, and recalled his request to use the inside shower instead of the one on the side of the house, usually an island treat to their visitors. Then she thought about his breezy, almost self-satisfied departure that evening. He hadn't seemed angry; he hadn't seemed resigned, either. Just pragmatic, perhaps like a man who had taken matters into his own hands.

As she stood in the bedroom, the idea that he might have taken the missing journal advanced from possibility to inevitability. She saw him planning the trip out to the island after he'd realized she was such an unreliable caretaker that she'd lost the trunk key. She imagined him walking through the house and into the bedroom closet, pushing aside her basket of dirty laundry, and climbing the ladder. Sitting on the chaise in the loft, looking at the broken-lidded trunk.

She grabbed her cell phone in the kitchen and walked out onto the porch. As she flipped open the phone she registered the hour but did not hesitate.

Dave answered on the third ring with a hook of anxiety in his voice. It was the hello of someone who knew a call at after 10 p.m. must be worth answering, because he had answered unwelcome calls.

"You took it. You just couldn't stand it so you took it, didn't you?"

"Kate." No confusion or denial, only a flat greeting.

"You didn't have the right to just take it, Dave. It's wrong."

"You want to tell me what you're talking about?" He had his southern voice on. He wasn't outraged or defensive. He sounded amused.

"You know what I'm talking about. You went up to the loft and you took that

391

notebook." He was silent on the other end. "You took it when you were in showering."

He took his time answering, and his voice was very slow. "Let me get this straight. So you're missing a book and you don't know how. And you automatically think me, and you're calling to tell me that I have no right to my wife's things. Even though you can't seem to value them enough to keep track of them. First the key, now one of the books. I'd say that's grounds for being fired as a trustee, dahhlin'."

She felt the flush in her cheeks, the tips of her ears, the sensitive place on her neck. "So you're riding in and taking over. What I want to know is, did you come out here planning all along to steal it, or did you just think of it over dinner?" She spoke in a rush, relieved finally to speak openly. "Was your whole little speech about how I should share it with you just a show, because you already knew you'd take it if I didn't agree? Or did you get pissed off and that's when you decided to take it?"

The southern charm disappeared entirely. "I'm not gonna dignify that with a response because I don't trust what I might say to you, Kate. I know you were a special friend of Elizabeth's but you're a real piece of work if you actually think I have *no right* to them

— if you think you have some entitlement that goes above mine."

" 'Entitlement'? Who said anything about entitlement? Jesus, I didn't ask for this responsibility, and all this time you've been acting like I've wronged you somehow when all I've done is what *your* wife asked me to do. And it's giving me hives and keeping me from sleeping, trying to figure out what I'm supposed to do with —"

"*I'm not finished.*" His voice was controlled and explosive at the same time. "If you're throwing around accusations about stealing when what you really did is lose one, then letting you have Elizabeth's books was even worse than I thought in the first place."

"Letting me *have* them?!" The words came like buckshot. "As if I came knocking at your door *asking*? As if I even wanted this?"

"But whatever you do, Kate, don't try to tell me what's *my right* and what isn't. I don't have to justify anything to you. If I wanted to take one of those books, God-damn it, it's my right —"

"— and if you have a problem with it, then your problem is with your wife," she said, over and through him. "Because this is not what she wanted, to have you go digging around in her books yourself."

Chris came onto the porch, shaking wet hair with one hand. When he heard her, he stopped and raised his eyebrows.

"Don't you dare talk to me about what my wife wanted," Dave thundered in her ear. "You knew her about as well as a cardboard cutout. You used her for whatever you needed. You think I couldn't see that? Elizabeth might not have, but I sure did. It made you feel so clever and important to have her look up to you, and you treated her like a sidekick, or a babysitting service!"

Kate gripped the porch railing and sent out the dogs. "You don't know what you're talking about! We helped *each other* out — it was a two-way street. You weren't even *around* most of the time!" Her momentum was unstoppable. "If you knew your wife so well and saw things so clearly, how is it she was going off to California with some other guy? Go ahead — *you* figure out what she was doing in Joshua Tree. Because I've had it. I've had it with both of you, putting me in the middle. I'm done with the whole thing." She disconnected the call and pitched the phone into the grass.

Chris looked at her, wide-eyed. "What the hell's wrong with you?"

Kate walked a few steps down the patio trying to slow her breath and pulse, all out of sync, then leaned back hard against a railing post. "Dave took one of Elizabeth's notebooks while he was here, the one that explains why she was flying to L.A. He just went in and took it right out of our loft."

Chris put his hand behind his neck, and looked down at the floorboards in a *Lord-give-me-strength* way. When he looked back up at her it was with wonder.

"It was *his* wife's journal, for Christ's sake. If I were you I'd say good riddance and let him deal with where his wife was going. It's been making you crazy all summer."

"Don't you get it? It was up to me to figure out what to do with them." She stomped her bare foot on the floorboards. "She trusted me — this is all she wanted. And I didn't do it." Emotion clenched her throat and she didn't trust herself to speak. She looked at him as if he were missing a most basic point of logic.

"Why do you care so much about protecting them from each other?" He craned forward for eye contact, and she looked away, eyes filling. He stepped closer and took her gently by the shoulders. "Give him the rest of the notebooks and be done with it. Why are you so fixated on making this your problem?"

Of course it was her problem. How could

he not see that it was? Elizabeth had asked this of her and she owed her at least that, to make amends.

Amends.

Kate stopped thumping her heel and went still with the surprise of having her motivations so unexpectedly clear. The air was suffocating, even outdoors, and pressed in on her like a cloud of gnats. She leaned forward from the railing and began to walk down the porch. The lawn stretched toward the ocean in dark relief.

"I'm going to walk for a while."

"Kate," he said. "Come on. Let it go. Enough already."

The grass under her bare feet was thick and damp as seaweed. She waited until she passed beyond the range of the porch lights and walked faster.

"Kate!"

Once she was past the pool of porch light she began to run. Darkness closed in as she put behind her Dave's words — *cutout, sidekick* — and the trunk that in the end told her nothing except that Elizabeth was not as placid as she'd seemed, but might have acted that way because Kate had treated her as if she were. The soft cold grass grew coarse near the beach, but she didn't slow as she hit the sand. She turned and kept running along the water, even as the stones dug at her insteps and dried eelgrass scraped her ankles.

The side of her foot struck a rock, stopping her short. The stabbing sensation shot from her little toe up her ankle. She inhaled sharply and doubled over, crouched with hands on her knees until the sparks of pain dulled. The water was a few yards away, dark as blanketing earth. She stayed bent until her breath returned. *Sidekick*. Then she pulled her sweatshirt over her head, stepped out of her pants, and walked step by step into the sea. The cold water numbed her toe and she went in without flinching. Gooseflesh rose above the place where the water met her shins, then her knees, then thighs. The hair stood along her legs and arms and across her scalp, electrifying. Stronger than the emptiness, more tangible than anxiety.

Kate dove in and when she surfaced fell into the rhythm of the swimmer she hadn't been for years. She swam straight out from shore, turning for air every fourth stroke, toe throbbing with each kick until she ceased to notice. She swam with her eyes open but the stinging wash of salt did not flush the vision of Elizabeth's face with its most common expression, one of bland

397

inscrutable goodwill, watching and listening but offering little of herself. In the look there had been an unnerving collage of admiration, envy, and resentment, but underneath it all, need. *Stay*, it had said. *Let me have more of you.*

She swam with no sense of time, thinking only briefly of the harmful things that might be under and around her — rusted debris, infectious bacteria, sharks. There were few sounds. Wind over water. The clang of a ship's rigging. Then music and laughter. She paused, lifting her head from the water, suspended.

The party boat she'd heard earlier was up ahead, close enough to hear the music clearly and to see the people standing on deck with their drinks. A woman in a black halter dress, a man whose shirt was open to his navel. She touched his arm in response to something he'd said, and threw back her head in showy laughter.

The scene felt a million miles from shore, from Kate's bungalow and children and the daily grind to keep them happy and grounded and safe, and another million from where Dave was likely pacing his yard and cursing her. Kate thought then of the painting in the Martins' kitchen, the two brownstones. A woman drinking wine with her head thrown back in manic laughter, while next door, a woman combed her daughter's long wet hair.

Kate continued to tread water, imagining what Dave was doing at this moment. Swinging his driver in the darkness of his yard, or sitting in his Spider and drinking a beer with the radio on. Or he might be at this moment reading Elizabeth's second-to-last journal, learning about her fascination with a man whose ability to accept her for who she was had roused her from a domestic coma. As Dave read her impressions of this man and her decision to travel with him, he might look up and across the garage beyond his car to the far wall, where her easel was folded and gathering dust. He might put a hand through his hair, thick but for the spot Elizabeth had pretended not to see, and wonder where things had gone wrong, what had happened to bring them from a ring on an ice-cream sundae to *Three days until I leave. Never anticipated anything so much or expected this much.*

Kate began to tire, treading water. Her toe became inured to the cold and began to throb. She turned toward the bungalow, a few windows glowing at the end of the lawn. It was a cool night, good sleeping weather, and she would pull up the hand-knitted afghan that belonged to the homeowners — designed, no doubt, by someone with some story behind why it was made and for whom. Everything had a story. Every word, it seemed, every small gesture, was the result of something that had moved someone, or moved her to pretend as if it hadn't.

Kate turned away from the boat and began slow strokes toward shore. Chris would be waiting for her back at the house, a little worried but not too much. He wasn't the worrying type, but he would be on a night he'd seen his wife so unhinged. Maybe they would stay up and talk, and he would be understanding of her guilt and obligation even if he didn't really understand.

Or maybe she would just return, and that would be good enough, and when he crawled under the covers she would go too. There was no longer anything left for her to stay up and read.

TWENTY-SEVEN

In their last week they went to four of their favorite beaches, built entire cities in the sand. Kate taped up her toe and limped through the agricultural fair, flew down high sackcloth slides and clomped through the barns with 4-H exhibits, and watched enough log-chopping and frying-pan-throwing competitions to occupy a frontier town for a lifetime. They grilled a surf-and-turf dinner for the neighbors, and she made the kids cupcakes with animals piped in bright icing that stained their lips blue. She was the best mother in the world, the very best.

As much as she had sworn to Chris after her swim that she was putting the whole business behind her, she couldn't. It was there at the beach, there when they played their last rounds of miniature golf, and when they walked around town with over-sized waffle cones of ice cream. She hadn't finished. There was supposed to have been a trajectory; she would read all summer and decide what to do with the books when everything became clear. But it never had.

Kate didn't doubt that there had been another journal, but she was no longer certain of whether Dave had taken it. She replayed his visit and departure — how long he'd been inside showering, whether he'd been carrying a bag that could have concealed a notebook. Of one thing she was certain: When he'd said good-bye in the driveway, his defeated bearing was gone. He walked away with an ease that seemed to her evidence he'd seized an opportunity.

Yet as days passed, her doubt grew. Three days after she'd called him, while she was going through the early tasks of closing up the house, she recalled a passage from the final journal, a phrase she'd breezed over at the beginning of the summer. She'd stopped cleaning the refrigerator and gone up to the loft.

The air was stale with the windows closed, and the notebooks were still scattered on the floor. It was there in the last journal, the one she'd read after leaving the Martins' house. *Now I have to get myself together and say good-bye to the kids and remember to make a fuss over packing the painting sup-*

plies they bought, jam them in somehow with all that awful writing. It was possible Elizabeth had taken this missing journal with her on the plane. Kate couldn't imagine why she'd bring that older one, instead of the new book she'd begun before her trip, but if she had, then the angry exchange with Dave had been unjustified. And even worse, Kate realized with a drop in her stomach, she would never understand what had drawn Elizabeth to Joshua Tree.

Memories of what she'd read were like a hangover that faded and returned. Kate would be cooking dinner and remember an episode from her Southbrook years, then find herself recasting it with this new version of Elizabeth. When the playgroup women had overstayed at her house, evenings they'd been invited for pizza and left the family room in shambles, Elizabeth had always told them not to bother straightening up. She had her own way of organizing things; it would only take a minute for her to do later. Now Kate could imagine Elizabeth sighing with relief when they left, then working on design projects that would keep her up until 2 a.m. because she loved the work even if this was the only way she could manage it. And never telling them, as if the desperation for something of her own would undercut her credentials as a dedicated mother, and set her off from her friends. Kate tried to recall the number of times she'd asked Elizabeth to babysit while she worked intermittently in restaurant consulting. She had always thought she had reciprocated as often as she'd asked. But maybe she'd just wanted to think she had.

Had they taken advantage of Elizabeth? Like most things in life, it was more complicated than that. Elizabeth hadn't volunteered much, and Kate hadn't asked. How much could a person be expected to see when someone else showed so little? Elizabeth had felt herself to be alone, but she had also felt herself to be unique, that her experience was both unusual and unshareable, when in truth it was not.

But she had opened herself to Michael.

How did you recognize that potential understanding in a person, Kate wondered; how did you recognize whether it existed in your own spouse, untested? If she could find this Michael, she felt she would know.

There had been three high schools in Elizabeth's town, each with graduating classes of over a thousand. Three days before they were to leave the island, Kate spent the evening on Internet searches. She clicked through town board-of-education sites and people-finder databases, the alumni sites posted in banner advertisements.

The next day she called school administrators, and though they turned her down, citing alumni privacy, class lists were traced online easily enough. In Elizabeth's class there had been seven Michaels. But there had been only one Claire. With a few keystrokes she emerged, Elizabeth's closest high school friend, married and living in New Jersey.

Claire answered on the third ring. After exchanging pleasantries and then sympathy, Kate came to the reason for her call. *I'm trying to find the guy she dated in high school*, she said. *Michael.*

There was a confused silence. A small child cried in the background.

Elizabeth never really dated anyone, Claire said as she tried to soothe the agitated child. Then she reconsidered. *Well, she could have without telling anyone. Elizabeth was funny that way.*

The screen door opened on resistant hinges and Kate entered the bakery. The front was empty, no customers, no Max. The pastry case was filled with what remained of the morning offerings. From the back there was singing.

"You fill up my se-e-e-nses . . ."

She looked through the curtains. Max was cleaning pans with his back to her. The music played faintly from the stereo in the corner, but it was his voice, an octave above its natural range, that filled the room.

She set her large cardboard box on the pastry case and stepped through the curtains, crooning back. "Coooome let me looooove you . . . you adorable maaan-chiiild."

Max shook a soapy whisk over his shoulder in her direction and continued singing softly.

"John *Denver*?" she said, brushing suds from her T-shirt. "This is what you sing when you're alone? You're a closet John Denver fan?"

"There is not one closeted thing about me and you know it," he said. "I can only imagine what you sing in the shower. *Someone — left the cake out — in the rain . . .*"

"Donna Summer is a very underappreciated artist."

"Mmm, yes. Years before her time." He fished a knife too quickly from the sudsy water and winced. "I thought we weren't meeting the realtor until two," he said, considering the pad of his thumb.

"I thought I'd come a little early. I wanted

to bring you these." She went back through the curtains to the front of the bakery and carried in the cardboard flat with three potted plants. "Something to help your house show better. Not that it needs it."

"Well aren't you sweet." He touched the wide, flat petals of the white phalaenopsis as gently as one would the cheek of a newborn. "Love orchids. So much better than cut bouquets."

She took a piece of rugelach from the case. "So this realtor. Is she going to be your buyer's broker on a new place too?"

"Not sure. I might rent. I'll get the full picture of what I'm dealing with in the fall."

His house was not extravagant, but it had been designed to his tastes — heavy on kitchen, dining room, and library, light on space appropriate for large-screen televisions or bulky children's toys, the types of rooms most sought after in real estate these days. It would not be easily dispensed with, or replaced.

"The full picture of what you're dealing with from investigators, or from your accountant?"

He waved his hand, a summary gesture that included the all of it. "The fall, the fall," he repeated, with the rhythm of a poet wrapping up a reading. "Everything will be clearer in the fall."

She dropped into the worn wooden chair beside the butcher-block island and watched him wash dishes at the sink. So ugly, the whole business. William had been flaky, certainly, but she'd never imagined anything on the scale of this. Max rarely wanted to talk about it, and she was never certain how much to press. She leaned low over her legs, releasing the tension in her hamstrings.

"I won't mind having fall come, myself. School, fresh starts, and all that."

He stacked baking pans in the drying rack. "Already? All year long, you're counting the days to summer."

She shrugged her shoulders.

"You still reading your friend's books?"

"More or less." She dropped a sandal and rested her bare foot on a rung of the stool. "There are a lot of them. I can't imagine putting yourself out there like that on paper."

Max pulled a spatula from the water and scrutinized its edge. "It's not the most uncommon thing in the world. I keep a journal, you know."

Kate looked up. "You do? I never knew that."

"For years and years."

He moved another stack of muffin tins to

the sink. She watched as he cleaned one, scraping crust from its edges.

"Why? If you don't mind my asking," she said. He paused in his scrubbing. "I mean, are you going to do anything with them? Do you love writing?"

He looked over his shoulder at her. "It's not a matter of loving writing. It's something I need to do. It helps me vent and figure things out. I don't have to think about anyone else's feelings or judgments. It's the one place I really get to have my say."

"Why not just call a friend?"

He gave her a wry smile that suggested she'd missed the point in some important way. " 'The unexamined life' and all that, m'dear." They sat in silence while he drained the sink. "Besides. Who wants to hear all that? Really."

She watched as he picked up the utensils in the drying rack and began to put them away.

It occurred to her that there could be in most relationships two distinct tracks of conversation taking place at any given time: what people actually discussed about their lives, and what people did not discuss but was very much on their minds. *In the end I come back to that same feeling I've always had about confidences. They rarely give*

409

anything back, you rarely leave feeling any better, and you can get more out of just writing to yourself.

Max's conclusion could have as easily come from Elizabeth. *Who wants to hear all that?* he'd said.

She was not certain she had ever conveyed that she would be available to him in that way. But never before had it occurred to her that she should; if people wanted to talk, she figured, they'd talk. There was a fine line between expressing concern and violating privacy. But another thought pricked. Perhaps laziness was a point on that spectrum too. She had not extended herself as she ought to have with a friend. She walked over to the sink to help put away the dishes.

"So these journals of your friend's," he said. "Explain to me again how you came to have them?"

"She put a line in her will. If anything happened to her she wanted me to decide what should be done with them."

"So she designated a trustee. Interesting." He reached to a high cabinet and put away a stack of bowls. "Did you ever break into that trunk?"

"Yes." She shifted in her chair, pictured the lid hanging brokenly on its hinges.

"And?" he said. "Did the perfect mother

410

make a cuckold of her loyal husband?" His mouth curved in an unpleasant way.

Kate frowned. "Don't be flip, Max. It's a big deal. Some of what she wrote could really shake up her family and change what they think of her."

He was quiet while he puzzled together the pieces of the industrial-sized mixer, slid the bowl onto its fitting. Neither of them spoke for a moment.

"You know, I don't want to sound insensitive, but that's life, Kate," Max said, wiping the side of the appliance. "If it roughs up what they think of her and they have to do some mental adjusting about what their family was all about — well, that's life." He banged the mixer bowl back into place a little too forcefully. "You don't really want to get in the middle of that, do you? Choosing what gets known, what doesn't. Why would you?"

It was a fair question. Elizabeth's story where it intersected with Dave's was his as well. If it made him a little more bitter, a little less trusting — well, that is what his story consisted of. But the thing that continued to give her pause was what Elizabeth's story would consist of, going forward.

"It's a powerful thing, Max, reading through the way someone has felt all her

411

life. She started off like one kind of person, and ended up making herself into this almost overkill mother that she thought she should be. And whether or not we agree with the gymnastics of it all, I can't help feeling that she won't get credit for it. She'll be judged for some of the things she thought and did, and the great mom she really was will get lost."

"How's that really different from any of us?" Max turned to her and leaned against the sink. "You're a great mother too, but I'll bet you didn't start off that way. Everybody changes. You grow into what you have to do. Don't you think her husband knows her well enough to be able to see that?"

Did he? She honestly had no idea. "I don't know. I hope so."

"Well, maybe you could help him see that." He lifted the last mixing bowl from the drying rack, and gave her a long look down his nose. "Hmmm? You're pretty good at giving people the benefit of the doubt, all your 'you never know' business. Maybe that's why your friend left the books to *you*."

He picked up a broom and began sweeping around the island, making a small pile of flour and dried bits of dough. It made sense, the idea that Elizabeth had wanted to have her say. She wouldn't have wanted the

412

books destroyed or hidden. She would have wanted them understood.

The easiest thing would be to give the writing back to Dave, or nearly all of it. With the rip of a few pages, the Elizabeth looking for an exit strategy — clothes in a garbage bag, her mind on the open road — would never have existed. Omit a few more pages, and after the jagged thread of paper had been pulled from the metal spirals, there would be no mother with unmotherly feelings. But to edit her books would be just another way of not accepting Elizabeth for who she was, and of falling back on old stereotypes of what was motherly and unmotherly.

Kate stretched her legs long in front of her. "How'd you get to be so wise, Max?"

"I spend a lot of time alone with bread." He swept near her feet and noticed the bandage. "What happened to your toe?"

"Stubbed it on a rock."

He grimaced. The phone rang and he glanced at it to see who was calling before letting it go to the answering machine.

"Oh, that reminds me," he said. "Did Anthony call you? You really have to hear more about this place he's launching."

"Yes, I talked to him. I know all about it."

"And?"

She shrugged. "I'm going to talk to the owners. There's no harm in talking."

He nodded. "You don't really want it." It was more statement than question.

"No, I do." She could see herself working there. She could imagine all the aesthetics of a brand-new kitchen: the gleaming surfaces, the stainless-steel ranges and the stretch of metro rack shelving. She could see the spread of ingredients mounded in matching bowls, the crimson of berries in pooled sauces, and her plated finished product, crust peeling in flakes like mica. She could feel the bustle of the kitchen, the brisk efficiency of some of the best professionals in the world humming along and occasionally losing control. And when there was yelling and running and burning, she'd be settled in her space making beautiful things. Even the unpredictability was predictable. She missed that control in the eye of the storm.

But eventually, the storm would move to encompass her home as well. She would find herself forgetting show-and-tell days and unaware that James's bike had been abandoned, not stolen, because of the damned wheelies he couldn't do. And the control would be gone. She would resent the job at times and her family at others, but above all resent herself for whatever failing made her unable to split herself between the two.

"You don't have to tell me you want the job," Max said. "I'm not Anthony."

"I do want it. It's a great opportunity." She picked at the grain of the wood on her chair. "It's just not the best time."

He sighed and shook his head. "It's okay to say that, you know. It's a great thing, staying home with your kids." Kate looked from the corner of her eye for a sign of sarcasm or of a punch line to come, but there wasn't. "You're good at it."

"If I were better at it I could handle both."

"That's not true, and you know it." Max had little patience for self-flagellation. "It's just what your tolerance is for letting stuff slide. Because something's always gonna slide." She raised her eyebrows but didn't argue.

"There will be another restaurant when you're ready," he said.

"That's kind of what I'm thinking." She slid her thumb along the worn edge of the wooden island. "But that catering gig, that part-time thing in D.C. you mentioned a few weeks ago. Maybe you could give me the number if you still have it."

"I think I could find it." He leaned forward

to rub a smudge of flour off the shoulder of her T-shirt. That was his way, small plucking touches. "You know, it's not like by taking a few years off you'll miss out on the latest research in pie-crust technology or something." He turned to put the last of the utensils into their drawers. "Though *I* certainly wouldn't hire you then if I were a top restaurant. You clearly are going to get soft on technique, and you'll have to spend a lot of summer hours practicing here with me."

That evening on the Internet she located contact information for five of the seven Michaels. She dialed each in succession. Three had never heard of Elizabeth. One thought she might have sat beside him in algebra, but didn't remember anything else. The fifth expressed surprise that she'd married and had children, since he'd heard she dyked out in college.

Kate hung up the phone and stared at the glowing screen of the people-finder Web site. The loft was quiet and so was the shoreline; downstairs, there was only the faint hum of the television. She looked at the cursor, still blinking in the box asking for First Name. Again she typed Michael. But this time she left the Last Name box empty, and in the space for the city, she entered Joshua Tree.

Revise your search, the screen prompted. *The boxes marked with asterisks are required.*

Her eyes stung, and she pressed her fingers into the sockets.

Somewhere there was a man who had known all of Elizabeth, been so accepting and understanding that she had driven away, but this time kept going. What would draw her to confide in him, what would signal that it was safe?

He would be inquisitive, Kate thought; he would be fascinated, each new fact conveying acceptance of the one before, and it would feel as if he would not give up until he knew all there was to know about her. That raw beginning with a stranger, the infatuation and excitement of rolling out the map for the first time — it was an easier place to begin than redrawing the landscape with someone who knew you best, yet didn't see it all. She thought of Chris and his impatience when she balked at taking the Metro after the bomb scare. There was a force of momentum at work with a spouse, a vested interest in things as they were, and always had been. She was the mother of his children. She was the one who held things together. It was important that she be constant, competent, and strong.

She tried a fresh search, this time with only the letter *M* for first name, and then the state, California. She was being foolish, throwing a dart at a globe.

Where the cursor had been, a colored pinwheel began to spin and continued with no sign of stopping, giddy at the irrationality of the request.

TWENTY-EIGHT

Kate stared at the bedroom wall. Moonlight through sheer curtains created crosshatch designs on the whitewashed wood, a flat origami of tree limbs. Hours passed. Finally, she flung back the sheets and walked gingerly to the family room, feeling her broken toe with each step.

It had been a long time since she'd watched middle-of-the-night television. On one shopping channel jewelry shimmered, diamond chokers from the choicest South African mines, hers for absurdly low prices. Another station offered a vegetable juicer, providing vitamins and minerals guaranteed to improve her family's mental acuity a thousandfold. The next channel extolled the value of educational recordings, miraculously raising the IQ through osmosis even as one slept.

Kate slouched in a daze as each spokesperson reached new heights in promises made.

Late-night television preyed upon the desperate, those out of sync with the sleeping world at an hour that played tricks on the mind and made a person susceptible to a gleaming product, a beautiful face, an authoritative vow. The subtext was clear. *If you buy this you will look better, you will feel better, you will be better*. She clicked the channel one more time.

A man stood beside a mansion on a beach, waves crashing to his left beyond an enormous wraparound porch. This was not a house, he was saying; this was the physical manifestation of positive thinking, the great success and material wealth it could bring from the generous universe. "This is *truth*," he said. "This is *knowledge*."

Kate hobbled to the kitchen and took two ibuprofen tablets from the bottle on the counter. The man's monologue continued. "Truth and knowledge are not only attainable, but *unavoidable*, if you make a commitment to *dig* for your greatest potential."

As she filled a glass with water, she glanced at the papers piled by the sink. Chris had left his travel magazine open on the counter. A tall cactus stretched across the double-page spread, branching across the headline, "California Mysticism Blooms Anew." The words were printed in a tall, narrow typeface that faded in a wash at the tops of the letters. Bleeding Cowboys, Kate thought. Vielkalahizo.

The voice of the man on the infomercial continued.

"When you think you've got nothing left, when answers continue to elude you, you must *dig* to the bottom," he said, "then dig again."

The trunk sat in the loft where she'd left it, repacked and ready to return home with them. Kate lifted out the first stack of journals, then the second, and the third. She fanned out the books in front of her looking for anything she might have missed, but they all looked familiar. She separated the journals from one another with a small shake, one at a time.

A piece of paper fell from between the covers of two notebooks. It was a letter folded in thirds addressed to Elizabeth's daughter. *Happy third birthday, Anna Danielle!* Kate skimmed the page, which seemed intended for a baby book, or part of a collection of letters. *I love your spirit, roping everyone into conversation in the grocery checkout line. The world embraces friendly, confident people. You can do anything you want to do!*

This was the Elizabeth Kate had known. The optimism, the cheerleading. Kate refolded the note and tucked it into the back cover of the last notebook.

The bottom of the trunk was covered in thick striped paper like the rest of the interior, but torn in places. There were a few scraps of paper loose on the bottom. She lifted out one ripped sheet, a shopping checklist for Christmas 1998. There was a Post-it note, a list of gifts received from a baby shower. Along the left side of the trunk a photograph was stuck in the seam. She pulled it out and saw a young girl eating ice cream, long brown ponytails curling over her collarbones. The picture had been cut in half; a sliver of a red shoulder remained of whoever had been sitting beside her, someone only slightly larger, with long blond hair over the edge of the red shirt.

Elizabeth might have cut herself out in anger, fueled by thoughts of fault and blame. Or maybe she'd cut it that way because it would be easier to perch on the side of the canvas while she painted. There was no way to know what Elizabeth had thought, not anymore.

The child was seated on a bench in front of a red barn, her eyes half closed and sleepy, or deeply content. She doesn't exist any longer, Kate thought; she was real and she was loved and now she is gone, along with everyone else in her family. She could have been an aunt. She could have been a confidante. Instead she was a void, and an absence that would not allow for forgiveness.

Kate itched to put the photo in her pocket, but it was not hers to keep. She put it back in the side of the trunk. Then she wondered how difficult it would be to find the cemetery, to walk among the headstones unnoticed with a bag of tulip bulbs.

She was about to close the trunk when she saw that at the bottom, caught in the folds of ripped lining, was a small business card. Kate pulled it out, turned it over. The Aura Institute, it read, in letters the color of sand. One Saguaro Way, Joshua Tree, California 92252.

The Web page for the Aura Institute was muted and simple, as if it were designed with people in mind for whom too much clutter might be disturbing. At first glance it appeared to be a spa. There were photographs of people meditating, doing yoga, dining at a communal table. One showed a woman sculpting, and another, drawing. Kate clicked from image to image in the gallery looking for a thumbnail of people painting, hoping to find a mention of visiting artists, seminars, retreats. It might yet be true about the workshop with Jesús.

A box in the center of the page had an arrow designating a video clip. *Join Us*, the caption read. Kate clicked.

The film appeared at first to be an interview. A woman in her thirties sat on a couch holding two small children on her lap. The camera zoomed tightly on her face, faint smile lines wrinkling the corners of her eyes as she talked about the energy level required to care for her children. As she wiped at her eyes, the children's heads bobbed under her chin, animated and oblivious. Then she pulled off her hair.

Treatments, she said, had left her exhausted and losing the will to fight, dispirited about the future she would never share with her family. Until she discovered Aura.

The scene abruptly changed from the woman's chintz couch to a sweeping desert vista — sand and sky and swooping hawks set against a soaring instrumental sound track. The video quality was extraordinary, the stuff of nature documentaries; Kate could see this even on her old laptop, its screen covered in smudged fingerprints.

In the distance, a tall man stepped from behind a cactus. He wore khakis that melted into the desert, and a blue shirt the same hue as the cloudless sky.

"What is your burden?"

He stood at a distance from the camera, but the words came through the computer speakers like a soft wind.

"Are you in pain? Are you suffering an illness? Are you depressed?" His voice was the voice of radio, sonorous and soothing. "Have you been told by doctors that your path back to health will be very difficult, or even impossible? That the journey to healing will require a regimen that will nearly kill you, and you are afraid you are not strong enough? And does a small voice inside you say *It isn't true* — that there must be something you can do to be strong enough to combat this sickness in your body or your mind?"

The camera moved off the man and rose up the side of a mesa striated in red and brown. The visual drama and musical crescendo conveyed a surmounting of obstacles, the achieving of great heights.

"There is."

The camera left the mesa and returned to a close shot of the man, his face and shoulders tight against the robin's-egg sky. His eyes were arresting, contrasting bands of hazel and gray, made even more distinctive by his large, smooth head. Tanned and powerful, it seemed to radiate sun from within.

"My name is Michael, and I'd like to help you meet your challenge. Come to Joshua Tree."

TWENTY-NINE

Chris spooned sugar into his coffee. "You were quite the restless sleeper last night."

Kate leaned against the kitchen counter and flipped the pages of the travel magazine. Next to it was the scrap of paper with the number she'd written down for the Aura Institute.

"My toe hurt. I got up to take a pill, and watched TV for a while."

She knew better than to tell him what she'd found. There'd be the look. *The notebooks, again?*

"We should go fishing. We've hardly done any fishing." Across the room, James was trying to bring his sister around to his version of the day, the very best way to spend their last full day on the island. She wanted to swim at the biggest beach.

"You're just afraid of hooks, and fish mouths," he taunted, mimicking the gaping lips and wide eyes.

"Don't fight," Chris said. "We could do both." He inclined his chin toward Kate. "We could drive out on the peninsula and catch something for dinner. Give the kids pizza early, and we'll have a last dinner on the porch after they go to bed. Pick up some steamers too."

They could afford a leisurely night. The house had been straightened, and they were mostly packed. The ferry was tomorrow at noon, and they had until late morning to strip the beds and load the car before the cleaning crew arrived. She nodded. "Sounds good."

While the children went with Chris to the bait shop, Kate stayed behind to get dressed and finish her coffee. The forecast was hot even for early August, and she went out to water the pansies in their patio troughs. The cut-glass pitcher caught the sun as she moved down the line deadheading shriveled blooms. Violet and yellow, fuchsia and white. Some mottled with a dark core, centered as an unblinking eye. She went into the house to refill the pitcher, and as she held it under the faucet, she glanced at the slip of paper on the counter.

The phone rang three times before she was connected to an answering machine.

"Namaste. It's a beautiful day in Joshua

Tree. Thank you for calling the Aura Institute." The woman's voice had an unplaceable accent, mellifluous as a chant. "We are very interested in your inner strength and well-being, but are unable to take your call at the moment. Please leave a message and we will call you back as soon as possible to begin your journey of healing."

Kate clicked her phone shut abruptly and slipped it into her pocket. It was just shy of nine o'clock, too early for a receptionist to be picking up calls on the West Coast. Then again, the toll-free number didn't have to be operated in Joshua Tree. It could be ringing anywhere: a glassy headquarters office in Manhattan, a strip mall in New Jersey, a call center in Bangalore. Michael himself could be sitting in front of a rotary phone in a trailer park, playing solitaire and buffing his head. He might be nothing more than a cheap freelance actor who spent off-hours slinging eggs in a diner between tryouts for summer stock.

Kate clicked on one of the television morning programs as she changed into fishing clothes, choosing cargo shorts with pockets large enough for a few of Piper's dolls.

How her choices had changed. In her twenties, maintaining professionalism —

right down to the uniform and accessories — had seemed so critical; self-esteem was tied to building on her achievements and the respect she'd worked so hard to earn, and brought true joy. Each imperfect plating felt like an indictment of the best that she could do, and anything that got in the way of her work seemed irresponsible, a misplaced priority. Now those words had new meaning — *responsibility* and *priority, esteem* and *joy* — and their significance was all the deeper because she appreciated them from both sides of the work-family divide. Hopefully, that was how Elizabeth had come to feel too by the time she'd made bushes grow on the banister.

The morning show went to its top-of-the-hour news roundup. Kate hadn't watched much television news for weeks, but paused in front of the screen now. The world was a mess. There was footage of burning streets in Kabul, and desert sand hills steaming from missile strikes. Airport security lines were stretched out the doors, and municipal water facilities couldn't conduct contamination tests fast enough to keep up with the threats. U.S. cities were spinning their terror-alert status so frequently, yellow to orange to red and back, that it seemed television stations should spin color wheels.

This morning's news anchor appeared grave as she delivered an update on the vial of nerve gas missing from a government facility out west; an unsubstantiated report claimed it had been found in one of Washington's Metro stations.

The Metro, which Kate rode almost daily with the kids. To Chris's office, to the museums. Which she'd take to reach Anthony's new restaurant, if she accepted the job. She turned off the television.

Kate went to her laptop sitting open on the kitchen counter and typed in a brief search. There were things she could do to protect her family. The stash of food in the spare-tire well and the fire extinguisher weren't enough anymore. Web sites sold protective air hoods for civilian use, protection that could be kept under the bed, even portable ones designed to fit in a purse. And the drinking water; there was a water-cooler delivery service she'd meant to call before they'd left on vacation. What a relief to have fresh bottled water from some remote mountain spring, someplace safe, flowing right into her kitchen. That would help. Every bit would help, until they could leave the District.

She'd suspected it would come to this. It was idiotic, living right in the capital of the country. It was as if there were a giant bull's-eye over Washington; she sensed it, actually felt at times the crawling of her scalp, as if she were being watched through crosshairs. Maybe Chris's company would agree to let him work somewhere other than the headquarters. Vermont, Maine. Maybe they could even live here on the island, year-round. Kate sat on the edge of the couch, laptop balanced on her knees, and scratched absently at the spot growing warm on her neck.

How would Elizabeth have responded to how crazed the world had become? A mother today had to have her antennae going in all directions, always. The people with whom your children came in contact; the people to whom you opened the door. The pesticides and growth hormones, the contaminated-food recalls, the chemicals and toxins in everyday objects. Kate did not believe in fate, though she often wished she did. How much easier to give a karmic shrug and believe an outcome was meant to be, trust that what we clung to or resisted so desperately was the edge of some grand unknowable plan. The constant vigilance was exhausting. Think about it too much, and it could paralyze you.

Paralyze you. She'd heard that phrase

somewhere before.

Kate put the laptop aside and went up to the loft. She skimmed the notebooks containing Elizabeth's years in Florence, then the time she spent caring for her mother. She found the passage in the Manhattan years, the night after the attack on the Central Park Jogger.

How many things in life are like this, near misses? Every day consists of these tiny choices with 57,000 trickle-down effects. You catch a different subway and brush against a stranger with meningitis, or make eye contact with someone you fall in love with, or buy a lotto ticket in this bodega instead of that one and totally cash in, or miss the train that ends up derailing. Everything is so fucking arbitrary. Every move you make and a million ones you don't all have ramifications that mean life or death or love or bankruptcy or whatever. It could paralyze you if you let it. But you have to live your life. What's the alternative?

Elizabeth had been more resilient than she. That, at its core, was the truth. Here was Kate, unhinged by vague threats — bombs that may or may not menace her city, disease spreading among cattle an ocean away — while Elizabeth had moved beyond setbacks and fear with methodical attention to what was required of her. Kate might be the brassy one on the outside, but Elizabeth was tougher. Whatever happened, somehow she'd moved forward.

Back in the kitchen, Kate closed the laptop on the photos of parents and children in escape hoods and picked up her cell phone. On the second ring, a receptionist answered.

"Aura Institute. It's a beautiful day in Joshua Tree. How may we help you?"

Kate hesitated, surprised to hear a live person. She was silent a moment wondering how, exactly, she did expect them to help.

"Is Michael in, please?"

"May I ask who is calling?"

"My name is Kate Spenser. Michael knew a friend of mine, Elizabeth Martin, who was supposed to have come to Joshua Tree last year. I have to talk to him about her."

There was no harm in assuming. If she was wrong, the worst they could do was not return her call.

"I see. I'm sorry, but we have a policy of not discussing clients."

"Actually, she was . . . she is deceased, and I'm working with the family" — here

Kate paused, having no idea where to go with this line of inquiry — "to settle her affairs."

"I do see and I do appreciate that. And I am sorry for your loss," the woman said again. Kate could imagine the employee mantra. *Acknowledge the situation. Hear the conflict. Affirm the sadness.* "But he is not available. May I have one of our spiritual coaches return your call?"

Kate left her name and number, knowing she wouldn't hear from anyone. Cult freaks, she thought, and hung up the phone.

Rarely were beach conditions just right at the height of the season. Crowds were usually too heavy or the music was too loud, too many greenhead flies were biting or conversations were too close, someone was too vocal about how a screenplay had been optioned. But on this last day fishing conditions were ideal, and there was solitude on the peninsula. Chris had chosen this location for surf casting, hoping for striped bass, bonito, false albacore. They drove out past the sunbathers and ballplayers to the tip of the peninsula, the car prepared with an oversand permit and half-deflated tires, where they had almost complete privacy.

After the first half hour the kids became

bored with their rods, and after an hour of clamming in the low tidal pools their rakes and trowels had been lost, broken, or abandoned. But the dunes were empty and the wind was mild. The car had already been packed with necessities for the day, so they set camp, convincing Piper that this was as fine a place to swim as her favorite beach.

Chris had pored over tidal charts for the various parts of the island, and when conditions were optimal, he stood and waited with the determination of Ahab. The waterline inched upward; beach plums appeared to grow full and ripen in the hours that passed. Still there were no bites. He offered examples of past successes, the time he'd caught a forty-pound striper in just this spot by casting with live eel, same as he was today. Still nothing, right up until their departure. But Chris being Chris, he shrugged it off.

"I thought I'd get one today," he said lightly as he steered the car off the sand where it reached the turnoff from the peninsula. "I felt the fishing karma."

"Fishing karma rarely comes to those who are accompanied by loud six- and four-year-olds," she said. Bayberry bushes and wind-twisted juniper lined the access road, and she inhaled the scents of summer as the car brushed by.

"You never believed I'd get one anyway." He said it as if he were wounded. He was sunburned and crusted in salt, and his left elbow hung out the window casually. He smiled, sad and flirtatious. "No faith."

Kate grinned. "You, my dear, are the one who suggested lobster and steamers. You're the one with no faith I'd come along unless you bribed me with a clambake." She thrummed her fingers on the sill of the car door, sun warm on her arm.

Life on the island was incompatible with concern over nerve-gas vials and water contamination. As she thought this, she came close to believing it. There was no contrary voice whispering imagined warnings — sinking ferries, toxic rabbits, tainted clouds wafting from Boston. That was the fallout of an overactive mind, a mind accustomed to being in control. And — here was the surprise, an unexpected gift of logic — perhaps life back in Washington, or anywhere, could be incompatible with such fears as well.

Chris reached the end of the long sandy access road and waited to merge into traffic. At the corner was a farmstand, a wooden lean-to with a few tables of produce and flowers. As Chris idled, Kate watched the woman at the farmstand, knitting. A small boy beside her drove toy cars around cardboard pints of mixed berries.

"So how did Max's place appraise? Is he really going to sell that house?" Chris asked.

"I haven't heard from him yet. But it sounds like he is."

For sale among the woman's vegetables lay handmade children's sweaters and hats, and even from the car ten yards away Kate could appreciate the skill. Baby blankets spread across the table showed elaborate basket-weave patterns. A cabled cardigan was draped around the larger vegetables, an armhole slung over summer squash in a chummy embrace.

"You know, I was thinking about coming back out here in the fall, helping Max get ready to move," Kate said. She could be of help packing boxes, running the bakery. He might appreciate the company, someone to talk to, or even just to keep a companionable silence. "Would you mind staying with the kids some weekend so I could come back out?"

Chris shrugged. "Sure, as long as I'm not traveling."

The boy knocked over a cardboard pint and the woman put down her knitting to right it, fat blackberries and raspberries, small blueberries rolling every which way.

Kate needed to call Anthony. He deserved to know that she would not be putting her name in for the job. It had been tempting to imagine herself made whole by the things that used to provide such satisfaction, and to hope she might be capable of compartmentalizing now in a way she hadn't then. It might well have been managed. That had been her automatic retort to Chris, though he really hadn't offered provocation. Mostly she had been arguing with herself.

After Elizabeth died, the sound bites about her went like this: great mother, great wife, great friend. The moment a person is gone it becomes critical to define her, making a life into a thing memorialized. The complex and contradictory person she had been was slowly being reduced to its essence: she was dedicated, naturally maternal; she was all heart, the true center of her home; a devoted member of the community of moms, a galvanizer, a workhorse. To what extent these things were true was beside the point. In a reduction some attributes are exaggerated, and some evaporate.

As far as Kate knew, no one had ever said, *Elizabeth was a very creative person, a painter who produced interesting work that was sold here and there*, even though a few of her paintings might yet be hanging in someone's home, picked up cheaply years ago in a little gallery on Avenue A, or in that island gallery, if that connection ever materialized. It was never said of her, *Her graphics appeared in this or that magazine advertisement,* or *She worked hard to carve out a fulfilling working life in the late-night hours on the side of raising her family.* These weren't her sound bites and were never to be her legacy. Maybe Elizabeth hadn't trusted that others would understand the nuances of what she loved. Perhaps she thought that eventually she'd miss work and painting less. Or maybe it was simply that she had come to believe that at the end of the day, what matters is who you are, not what you do.

But sometimes, Kate thought, what you do is integral to who you are. And what Elizabeth might not have appreciated was that there were ways of putting elements of your life together wherever they fit, patiently, at different points in time — ways short of giving them up or denying they exist. She might have come to appreciate it if she'd had more time. Maybe she'd begun to.

Chris dropped her off at the house for a

shower and went on with the kids to the fish market. She walked inside the bungalow, unlocked always, as was the island way, and thought how odd it would be to be back in the District in their alarmed, double-bolted house. And yet it wouldn't. She knew they would slip back into their lifestyle as easily as they'd shrugged it off, as matter-of-factly as the child wore his gas-mask hood. People were resilient, people adjusted to all kinds of things. What was the alternative?

Kate turned on the shower and had pulled her tank top over her head when her cell phone rang in the kitchen. It would be Chris, asking if she wanted littlenecks or cherrystones, chicken lobsters or larger ones. She reached it just before the fourth ring.

"Hey," she said, untying her bikini top. She could taste the clams already, small and meaty, slicked in butter. Littlenecks or small steamers, if they had them. That should be the last night's send-off.

"Is this Kate Spenser?" A man's voice, unfamiliar.

"Yes. And this is?"

"This is Michael from the Aura Institute."

Kate stood rooted in the kitchen as her bikini loosed and fell. "Yes. Hello."

"I understand you were inquiring after Elizabeth Martin." His voice was so close and so personal, she wanted to draw back the phone and keep him at arm's length. She wrapped her arms across her chest as she walked to the bathroom for a towel and turned off the shower.

"Yes. She was my friend."

He sighed. "Normally we don't discuss our guests, but I wanted to let you know I am sorry for your loss. That was a terrible shock. We knew she was on that plane. I hope the family received our condolences."

Ordinarily, his professional sympathy would have made her roll her eyes, the soothing voice slipped on like Mr. Rogers's sweater to deal with such circumstances. *Grieving friend.* But her humor, her cynicism, her wariness, all stalled after he said "our guests." He'd known Elizabeth. This was Michael.

He cleared his throat to draw her back into conversation. "We sent flowers to the house following the memorial," he said. "I hadn't wanted to bother the family with a phone call. But we were so shocked and sad. I had been looking forward to working with Elizabeth."

Working with. Kate digested the phrase. "Yes. Everyone was shocked."

"I imagine it has been a very difficult year for them."

"It has been," she said vaguely, buying herself time while she tried to make sense of what she was hearing. "But Elizabeth's husband is holding things together."

There was a pause while each waited to hear the other's agenda.

"I understand you're working with her estate," he prompted. "As I said, normally we don't talk about our guests. I hope you understand, but it's part of our confidentiality charter. I wish I could be of help in some way."

"Yes. I do see, and I do appreciate that," Kate said, adopting the receptionist's syntax. She strained to think of a line of conversation to keep him talking, making an effort not to say, for once, the most direct thing. *So why was she coming out to visit you people?*

"It has been a tough time, and there have been many details . . ." She paused, grasping for nouns that might be appropriate to the situation. "Debts and credits, accounting sorts of things that the family should not have to deal with alone. I'm serving as a trustee." This wasn't untrue. Here she found her foothold. "And there were certain sums paid in advance."

"Ah," he said. "And your interest is in the fact that she paid in full even though she never participated in her stay."

His cautious diction reminded her of Dave, or at least the way he'd begun to sound this summer. But the telegenic warmth was still there, and Michael's intimate tone that spoke knowledge, as if he knew her mind, and understood.

That's what he does, she reminded herself. He wins confidence, eases minds.

"Yes. I am looking into these kinds of matters on the family's behalf."

"Well, Ms. . . . Spenser? At the risk of sounding businesslike and lacking in empathy, I have to remind you of her contract. I'm sure you're aware from the paperwork she left behind that her visit is considered nonrefundable. Arrangements are made in advance, rooms reserved, and she did receive our pretrip counseling."

"I see," Kate said.

"This is a difficult thing, I know. We are sensitive people. But the nature of our business is the business of life, and life is so arbitrary." That word again. "With the nature of our retreat, some of the people who seek us out are quite ill and . . . well, there are no guarantees."

She paused, her own heartbeat drumming

in her ears. "And she wasn't doing well." She made her voice flat and factual, a statement rather than a question. As she heard herself say the words, it became less difficult to believe.

"That's not entirely true. And at any rate, our role is not to assess physical conditions, or replace traditional medical therapies. This is no Place of Last Hope."

"Mmm," Kate answered. But her mind was already withdrawing from the conversation, imagining a sickly Elizabeth painting in the desert, trying to transform depression and rage into renewed health.

"I hope you understand," Michael said. "Some would call it a tragic random happening, but in our institute we don't believe in the tragic or the random, or in the notion of waste. Elizabeth was on her path, and this was part of it. She had in fact already gotten a great deal from her short time preparing, and I believe her writing probably reflects that. She had plans for working things through, and sketches she'd made in her notebook after her diagnosis."

The word echoed ugly on the line. Kate thought of the missing notebook, and how much more must have been included in those few months following Emily's birth. *All that awful writing.* "And so she was bringing some of her writing with her." She was careful not to raise her voice in a question.

"Working with one's own writing was part of the process for some, and we encourage that, especially in people who are as prolific as she was, working with both words and painting. But we don't really talk about the process with nonguests. I hope you understand."

When Kate did not reply, he continued. "She was more at peace already by the time she left for California, less angry. Shedding that resentment toward the curse of genetics, toward a lot of things. Well, you were her friend. You know."

She didn't. But she did know there was a strong genetic link to the disease that had taken down Elizabeth's mother and aunt. And she knew there was a decent chance that a woman burned once by a partner who had not stood by her during a medical crisis would not allow herself to trust again, or might again handle things in her own quiet way, as her mother had.

A rustling of papers and something in his tone suggested a summary, and she knew the conversation had neared its end. "I hope the family will take comfort in that, at least."

Kate hesitated. "I think they are beginning to."

THIRTY

The traffic was always heaviest Sundays in August. Traffic was part of summer travel, as inevitable as the thin musty pillows in rentals. Since they'd left the ferry they had moved along roads dense with the migrating herd, crossing the Massachusetts line and traveling south along the Connecticut coast, passing and passed by the same cars all afternoon. The kids had fallen asleep, but although Kate had reclined her seat and closed her eyes, she could not. She pushed back her hair and pointed the air vent toward her face.

"What time did you tell Dave you were coming?" Chris asked, voice cool.

"I didn't call."

He glanced over, then away. "What if he's not there?"

"He will be." She looked out the window.

The truth was that she hadn't wanted to give Dave notice that she was coming. She had no idea what she would have said on the phone, something sure to sound irritatingly cryptic. *I have to talk to you about something*, or more blunt, *I know why Elizabeth was flying to Los Angeles.* He might have become angry if she hadn't wanted to discuss it then, or felt he had no need for her if he had actually taken the journal. *Don't bother*, and that would be that. She didn't know any more about his inclination to hold a grudge than about his capacity to forgive. But if their rapport had been derailed by her accusation that he'd taken a journal, it wasn't going to be put back on track over the phone.

"How long are you planning to stay?" His casual tone was belied by the precise way he held the steering wheel, hands at ten and two o'clock, the way tense teens were taught in driver's ed. No more elbow out the window, one hand at the top of the wheel, captain of his own ship.

"I don't know," she said. "Probably a few hours."

He kept his eyes on the road.

The night before, after the kids had gone to bed, they'd had a late dinner on the porch. They sat at the round table with a citronella candle in the middle — the arrival of dense night insects always signaled the end of summer — and she wondered, not for the first time, why they didn't do this at home. It wasn't as if they didn't have a grill, or that Washington didn't have great seafood. Saving cookouts for their time on the island was what made vacation special, she told herself, and that was part of it, but not all. The truth was that they became too caught up in daily obligations to welcome the interruption.

She steamed the clams in a broth of wine and shallots, and halved fingerling potatoes into aluminum bags to roast with oil and sea salt. He boiled lobster on a burner attachment to the grill. Then they sat at the patio table alone together facing the yard, the water, the orange-tinged sky.

She took a breath. "I found out something about Elizabeth today."

He looked across the lawn an extra moment, then turned with a smile of endurance. *Can't we just have one nice, final night?*

"Oh?"

He didn't ask what she'd learned or how, when she couldn't locate the only journal she hadn't read. He picked up his fork and started eating.

She watched his nonchalance and tried not to let him see how it bothered her. She needed to find a way to make him care; if

449

not to help her make sense of it, at least enough to support what she wanted to do. She recounted the late-night television, the jewelry and juicers and the business card in the trunk.

He was quiet a moment longer than she would have been under the circumstances, then took another bite of food. "So Elizabeth was flying to Joshua Tree to buy a juicer?"

Her mouth fell open stupidly. He was rarely caustic, and never with her. She felt herself receding from the table like a camera trick, a fast panning-out shot pulling away.

She would keep the conversation short and businesslike. He would not be subjected to more talk of Elizabeth, which would also signal that she wasn't going to confide in him. That's what marriage could be after nine years: such a subtly tuned tool that the simple act of declining to discuss something could be both a gift and a jab.

"I think she had cancer and didn't tell anyone," she said.

He visibly startled. Ordinarily, this would have launched a conversation not just on Elizabeth but on honesty and deception as a whole — the aspects of ourselves that we show one another in marriage and friend-ship, and what we conceal. Even as she said it so bluntly, she knew it was all wrong. But she couldn't stand the thought of warbling in earnest while he sat beside her this way.

"Cancer. Well." He took a large bite of corn, then added more butter. "What makes you think so?"

She watched as he continued to eat. "I found the number for the treatment place she was going. It was on a business card. The guy there knew her. He offered condolences, knew things about the family."

This gave him pause. "When?"

"When did he know her?"

"No, when did you call?"

"I left him a message this morning. He returned my call while you were out picking up dinner with the kids."

He paused, holding his fork. She saw him register that this had happened last night and she'd spoken to Michael that afternoon, and that she hadn't mentioned it all day. Normally she'd have shared those things immediately. This was the greater issue. He toyed with his hold on the fork, then continued eating.

She had misjudged. By not bringing it up earlier, she had drawn more attention to it than if she'd just mentioned it in passing. He might have been dismissive, even testy, but at least he would have been included.

451

She forced herself to cut a small bite of lobster tail and dip it in butter.

"So what are you going to do now?" he asked.

"I'd like to stop at the Martins' on the way home and give him the trunk, talk to him a little while."

He nodded. He wouldn't have relished a whole conversation about whether or not she would, but it chafed, hearing she'd made the decision without mentioning it. It helped that she'd said *I'd like to*, rather than made a declaration. But not much.

"On a Sunday, in the summer?" he said. "We'd get home insanely late."

"Well, I thought maybe you'd head home with the kids, and I would take the train home from there a little later. I don't want to talk about it in fragments around all the kids."

This was not what he'd expected. It wasn't just the inconvenience — the Martins were an easy stop off the highway — though there was a small inconvenience. He would have to make pleasantries for a few moments and then either let the kids play briefly, or break the news to them that they would not be staying to play. Then he would have to continue home, unload at least the basics from the car, get them to bed. Solo parenting — it was nothing she hadn't done a million times while he was traveling. But it was more than that. She'd be spending the evening alone with Dave Martin. All this crossed his face.

"Well then, I guess that's that," he said, and stood to take his plate into the kitchen.

She sat at the table alone, watching the cloud of gnats beyond the citronella candle as her steamer broth cooled and her lobster grew rubbery. He came back out of the house and stepped off the porch into the dark and insects, and headed to the beach.

Eventually she'd washed the dishes and gone to bed. By the time she fell asleep, pushing back thoughts of Elizabeth handling cancer treatments alone, Chris still had not returned.

Chris pulled off the highway, and the change in momentum woke Piper and James.

"Are we home?" Piper asked.

"This isn't our home," James said, looking around. "It's the old home. Hey, this is the way to the Martins'."

Chris didn't say anything. Kate took his silence as a cue that he would not take responsibility for telling the kids that they would not be staying to play.

"We're stopping off at the Martins' house because I have to give them something," she said. "I'm going to stay and talk to Mr. Martin. But you guys are going on home with Daddy, and I'm going to take a train a little while behind you."

"Can I stay and take the train?" asked James.

"I want to take the train too!" said Piper.

"No one else is taking the train," Chris said. "Mom's going to be getting home too late."

They turned the corner onto the Martins' street. Dave was in the front yard, mowing the lawn. Jonah and Anna played in the driveway drawing with chalk and Emily was set up beside them in a playpen. This was his system for juggling three children and yard work.

In the beginning there'd been a rush to charity, everyone wanting to take the kids, a thinly veiled assumption that it was too much for a father to care for his three children alone. He'd told Kate that if he was seen in the grocery store struggling through shopping with the kids, there would be babysitting offers and lasagna on his doorstep by dusk. No matter that Elizabeth had done this, all the time. Once, a few months after Elizabeth's death, Brittain had called Kate in Washington to say that she'd seen Dave doing yard work with the kids in the driveway, and that maybe the playgroup could pull together a fund-raiser for a contract with a landscaping service? It had been offered and declined, offered and declined, until he finally asked Kate to tell them no thanks, *really*. What they would never understand was that all he wanted was to mow his own damn lawn with no one watching, or offering to do it for him, or bringing a meal over afterward as a condolence for his having to mow a lawn without a wife to watch the kids.

As they pulled up alongside the curb, Dave killed the motor of the mower and turned to their car, squinting. Kate stepped out and kept her hand on the car door handle. He didn't call out or walk down to greet her with his arms outstretched. He just stood as she walked across the lawn, his arms spattered with bits of grass, waiting.

She stood just out of hug range to spare them both the awkwardness, though it didn't make a difference. "I have something for you. Can I come over for a while?"

He glanced at the car, took in the fact that Chris and the kids were still sitting inside, and looked back at her.

"Well, I was gonna finish the grass and

take a shower. We're having spaghetti."

It wasn't much of an answer. It merely showed that they had no particular plans and that she could join in or not, but that she was neither a special guest nor an especially welcome one. Chris opened the car door and got out. As he walked toward the curb, Jonah and Anna realized their friends had come. They dropped their chalk and ran over to the Spensers' car to hang on the half-open windows.

"Hey, man," Chris said as he reached Kate and Dave, and the men shook hands.

"Tail end of the trip," Dave said.

Chris was a quick study, attuned to the subtleties of international investors with whom nonverbal cues were telling. Kate watched him size up the factors. He took in the lack of pleasantries and Dave's cool tone, his wife's discomfort. The contents of the trunk might be physically leaving their world today, but nothing in the dynamics on the lawn suggested they'd be truly gone.

"Vacation's all over. Can't stay on island time forever," he said. "But we had a good go of it, so I can't complain."

The kids squealed from the car; the Martin kids opened the door just as James and Piper were freeing themselves from their booster seats.

"Let's go play in the backyard!" Piper yelled, and the four streaked away from the car like cartoon characters in a dust cloud. Emily, realizing she'd been left behind, began to cry.

Kate watched the kids run. Piper's toes hung over the front of her sandals, and James's shorts were a bit high on the thigh. They'd grown, incredibly, in just two months. That's how change went; time moved suddenly when you took your eyes off the action, and sometimes appeared to happen all at once, the clock moving past an outgrown moment with a visible click.

"Hey, kids, I'm afraid we can't stay. We're just dropping off Mom," said Chris, moving to intercept the children before they reached the gate to the backyard. He put a hand on the shoulders of his two, turning them back toward the car. He called to Kate over his shoulder. "What train do you think you'll be taking?"

"I'm not sure." She glanced at Dave. He hadn't yet acknowledged that she was welcome to stay. Chris noted the way she looked at Dave, her small deferral, and he continued toward the car.

"I have a train schedule in the kitchen," Dave said. "Amtrak goes through Stamford pretty regularly."

Kate walked back to Chris and helped direct the grumbling children into the car. "I'll call you after I have a look at the timetable. Will you help me get the trunk out?"

Dave stood nearby looking at the ground. If hearing this was his first realization that Kate had come to give him back his wife's journals, he didn't show it. He kept his eyes on the grass. Then he restarted the mower's engine.

Chris lifted the car's rear hatch while Kate put the kids back in their car seats. Once they were buckled she joined him behind the car, and they shimmied the trunk from where it was wedged. Then she pulled one last journal out of her tote bag. When she'd gone back into the island house that morning for a final walk-through, the photo-covered journal had still been on the loft's window ledge, nearly forgotten. She'd thought briefly of bringing it home and keeping it. Whenever she opened her top drawer there it would be, along with the note from the woman critical of Kate on the television show: Elizabeth smiling into the sun, overexposed and underestimated.

Chris looked at her, waiting. Kate lifted the lid and placed this book in the trunk with the rest. Then he pulled the trunk out of the car.

"Thank you for doing this," she said.

"Doing what?"

"Taking the kids the rest of the way home. Letting me finish this."

He stood with the trunk in both hands in front of him, leaning backward a bit to compensate for its weight. "So finish it, then," he said, and walked past her toward the house.

As she leaned through the back window to say good-bye to the children, she watched Chris open the Martins' front door and put the trunk inside the hall. He placed it on the floor in front of the sidelights, and through the small vertical panes she saw him remain crouched. His head was bowed, and after a moment he rested his hand on the trunk like a mourner at a wake, then stood. Watching him, her chest clenched for both of them, and she had to turn and face the car to regain her breath.

She heard the front door open and close again, and Chris descended the steps slowly and walked toward Dave. There was no backslapping, no see-ya-soon pleasantries often traded by the playgroup husbands. Just a few words, vague good wishes for the rest of the summer. Chris looked away, and

459

Kate saw both the sympathy and resentment.

Maybe there would be no seeing ya soon. Maybe that would be the way it would end, the two families going their separate ways. And maybe that was what Elizabeth had foreseen when she left the journals to Kate, choosing a reader who was empathetic and close but who could disappear from Dave's life regardless of what she had chosen to do with the books. Maybe Elizabeth had even foreseen the tension it would cause in several different ways — between Kate and Dave, between Kate and Chris — and decided that that too was not such a bad thing, the empathy of being misunderstood, a small dose of alone.

Or maybe it was simpler than all that. Maybe Elizabeth had just needed the peace of mind after her diagnosis of knowing her journals would be safe. And even simpler still. Kate had been the best she had.

Chris stood in front of her, rolling the keys in his palm. "Call me when you know the train." He looked at her directly, which he'd hardly done at all since dinner the night before.

She had tried moving through the past year mechanically, acting as if she were as resilient as she believed she should be. But in hindsight her system hadn't worked well. This would not be irreparable, but it would take time, and a good deal more vulnerability than she was comfortable with. She would have to lay it all out there, naked talk about danger and fear, the arbitrariness of loss, and her shaky sense that nothing could be counted upon to last. He would see a needier person than the one he'd married, possibly someone unstable, and she'd lose the validity of her opinions. Then she would see the extent of his dedication toward a partner who made things, as he'd see it, more complicated than they had to be. He would feel that he needed kid gloves.

She felt a nausea as if she'd eaten bad food. But there wasn't any other choice. Elizabeth had been wrong about one thing: keeping your own confidence does not protect you. It only makes you sicker.

"Thanks again," she said. "You're a good sport." Whether or not she felt this to be true, she felt she had to say it.

Chris shook his head, a small incredulous gesture that said he didn't believe she thought he was a good sport, and that she had some nerve chalking it up to sportsmanship. He got in the car. The children craned their necks backward waving to her, but Chris did not look back.

As Kate watched them drive off it occurred to her that her whole world was pulling away, all the very best of it, everything she was that was nonnegotiable, and she knew in a maudlin moment that if anything happened to them she'd wish it had happened to her as well. She stood at the curb until the car turned the corner and, window by window, wheel to bumper, disappeared behind the fence.

In the middle of the yard Dave idled the mower, watching her. Then he gave a push and started walking, arms outstretched and braced against the work ahead.

The Martin children grew bored in the driveway and jumped on their sidewalk chalk, reducing it to colored ash. They wanted to go inside to play.

She glanced at Dave to see if he'd give her any guidance — how long he planned to mow, what he'd like her to do with the kids, when he wanted to have dinner. But he did not look up.

She went up the walkway with Emily on one hip, and Jonah and Anna followed. And Dave maintained his pace to keep up the home front, one row at a time.

THIRTY-ONE

Kate put Emily down on the floor and stood in the middle of the kitchen. It always took her a moment to adjust to the room as it looked now, counters piled with mail, cookbook shelves cluttered with poorly stacked Tupperware. The pictures held with magnets to the refrigerator door were unchanged from last summer.

Jonah and Anna looked at her expectantly, then sat at the kitchen table littered with the remnants of painting projects. She could start dinner, but she was a guest here now. To act the way she'd always acted, opening cabinets and searching the refrigerator, felt presumptuous. She thought of ducking her head out the door, trying to catch his eye. *Would you like me to . . .* No. He had mentioned spaghetti.

Kate opened a cabinet, then two, looking for cans of stewed tomatoes. Jonah and Anna asked for cups of water for their brushes and to finish their watercolor swirls. Emily looked up at her from her seated position on the floor, blue eyes large over her spouted cup. She held it tightly in two hands, ten Cheerios peeping around the green plastic handles.

As Kate heated olive oil with crushed garlic in a saucepan, her stomach clenched at the smell. Her appetite rarely reacted to stress; she'd cooked under nearly every kind of circumstance, working beside abusive chefs and hovering brides and, once, a co-worker who'd cleaved a finger neatly off, lying like another carrot stick on the chopping board. But it had been a long time since she had been this at odds with Chris. The thought of what he might be thinking at this moment, and the conversation awaiting her at home, cramped her abdomen.

She put a pot of water on to boil and heard the lawn mower engine cut off, then the sound of dragging metal as Dave returned the mower to the garage. A moment later, he walked into the kitchen and saw the sauce half made and a salad in the works. The hair over his forehead dripped sweat, and mechanical grease smeared his shins.

"Well, all right then," he said, with just a hint of a twang. "I'm gonna go shower."

She wondered what his system was for a shower after mowing. Television, maybe, with the play yard moved to the bedroom. Or maybe he would have just motored on through dinner without one, leaving sweat droplets on the dish towel and grass clippings on the floor, and taken a long hot shower after the children were asleep.

"I'll wait to put the pasta in until I hear the shower turn off," she said. "It'll be ready ten minutes after that."

He nodded and, seeing the kids were content in their activities, went upstairs. Kate turned back to the stove and stirred the sauce, breaking up the larger pieces of stewed tomato with the wooden spoon. She scanned the paintings hanging on the kitchen walls. There was the same portrait of a young girl eating ice cream that had always hung there, an inexperienced work with asymmetrical eyes but certainly good for a teenager, and, now, recognizable as the same girl in the photograph in the trunk. The painting that may or may not have sent Amelia Drogan over the edge that Christmas Day, and driven her to attend the retreat that would recalibrate her ability to deal with alcohol, with single parenthood, grief. The painting had sprung from emotions Elizabeth was too young to understand

465

— the desire to bring some semblance of wholeness back to their home, a yearning to right things — following a loss for which she would never stop blaming herself. Beneath the portrait, Anna sat contentedly under her namesake painting rainbows.

Above the chair where Jonah sat was the oil painting of two Manhattan brownstones. One brightly lit window depicted a mother combing out her daughter's long hair, the pair bathed in nostalgic lighting, while in the adjacent window a party was in full tilt. In the festive window a dark-haired woman threw back her head in strong laughter. Her glass of wine was ready to spill, and the crimson at the rim matched her lips and the gems at her neck. On the other side of the kitchen was a painting that hadn't been there before. In a rainy dog park, a mutt stood amid a pack of silken golden retrievers, bowlegged in a Burberry jacket and radiating mange. His face was so expressive Kate could caption it. *Wanna make something of it?*

So this is what you made of it, Kate thought. Good for you.

Beside it was another new painting; Dave must have decided to hang more of Elizabeth's work. Kate imagined the stack Elizabeth had flipped through that evening she'd

stood above the margarita party continuing without her. This painting depicted a pile of tricycles parked in a heap. But as Kate stared at the indistinct wash of spokes and bars, features emerged like shapes from clouds. The front wheels became children's faces; the handlebars, long harelike ears. The compact arc of each frame ended in tiny tires curled like feet, and the effect was mystical, small bodies curled in sleep.

She looked down at the sauce. To not recognize in someone close to you the things that make her who she is, even if you did not understand such things, was a kind of negation; Kate knew what it meant to be thought of as less than what you are. There had been small signs, but she'd chosen not to see them. It had been easier to accept the simple, useful version of Elizabeth. But there was also this: Elizabeth had gone to great lengths to create that version. At the end of the day, a person had to take responsibility for what she showed the world and what she didn't.

"Nooo! I'm using the red! You can't have it!" Anna screeched from the table.

"But you're mushing it all up and ruining it with the white!"

Jonah leaned across the table and snatched the tainted red canister, spilling his cup of

dirty paint water. Brown spread across the table and both of their pictures, then trickled over the edge onto the floor. As her picture went muddy, Anna began to cry.

"Okay, okay, it's all right," Kate said, walking over with a roll of paper towels, trying to dab the excess water off their pictures. She mopped up the paint water from the table and tried to reestablish calm before Dave came down. They'd have dinner, she supposed, then talk after the kids went to bed. She had no idea how to begin. *I don't think Elizabeth was having . . . You were right that Elizabeth was not going. Elizabeth was not well.* Everything was too declarative, as if the facts of her belonged to Kate. Nothing belonged to her. The proprietary anger that had made her reach for the phone and accuse him of taking the journal was now an embarrassment.

Emily toddled over and raked her cup through the brown paint water on the floor, spout side down.

"Oh yuck, Em, not your cup. Why don't you play over here." Kate moved her to play on the floor with cooking utensils. When she took away the cup to clean it, Emily started to wail.

Dave appeared in a clean T-shirt and shorts. "What happened to our kumbaya? It

was so quiet a minute ago."

He filled the doorway like the prototype of a man from a soap commercial, scrubbed clean and scented of pine. She never remembered him as such a presence back in the days when she lived around the corner, or even the times she'd seen him in the past year. When Elizabeth was alive, he'd been a cardboard cutout of a father slipping in and out of the room, tossing a one-liner as he went, or working the grill in the background. Now when he entered a room, the room knew it.

He took the sippy cup from Kate and wiped the dirtied spout on his shirt. In his casualness she felt the possibility of normalcy, and the ball of her stomach began to loosen. She shook the box of penne into the pot of boiling water with a scratchy tumble.

Just before seven o'clock, Dave went up to bathe the kids while she washed the dishes. On his way out of the kitchen, Emily on one hip and the other two clambering up the stairs, he opened the telephone drawer and tossed her the train schedule. She knew she should call Chris, but was not looking forward to the terse conversation or to his voice as it would sound, curt. She wiped the counters and straightened stacks of Tupperware. When there was nothing left to clean in the kitchen, she dug her cell phone out of her bag and dialed.

There was no answer. She told his voice mail that she would be on the 8:56, and home shortly after one. She spoke to the receiver with as much warmth as she could, tried to infuse the words with optimism.

Kate walked into the living room, stood in the doorway absorbing the difference between the way it had been and how it was now. Elizabeth had always kept it distinct from the playroom, with small adult knick-knacks and better lamps. Dave had no such distinctions, and the living room and kitchen were now scattered with puzzles, games, and books left wherever they had been used last. Kate collected a handful of dolls and carried them to the bin in the next room where they'd always been stored. Back in the family room she dealt with the miscegenation of puzzle pieces, reconstructing wooden boards of farm animals, dinosaurs, house pets.

She glanced up at the bookshelves, crammed with paperback novels and hardcover art volumes. Framed photos of the kids were scattered in front of the books, overlapping images so dense that Kate had always noticed something new each time she'd looked. Then, at the far right end of the top shelf was an unfamiliar framed sketch — pencil or charcoal, something dark and smudged. There were vague sweeping lines outward and down. A waterfall, a weeping willow. Whatever it was, it was unfinished, the rough strokes of a work in progress. As she looked closer she saw it take the shape of a woman's face, a subtle profile that gave her a shiver of recognition. A negligible nose, a curve of a chin above a slim neck, and straight-cut bangs. A swing of dark hair that curved bluntly under the chin, as it did only when properly cut and cared for, which was not often enough. And below the tilted head, the whorled tendrils drawn on an infant's head in nursing position. Piper's head.

She heard Dave enter the kitchen and open the refrigerator, and then he walked into the family room. He hesitated with a beer in his hand as he saw her nearly done straightening his children's toys. His look was like a shrug, and he walked on through the room and pulled open the sliding doors to the patio, then lowered himself into a lounge chair with an exhale. The message was the same as it had been to her on the front lawn: Come or not, as you'd like. She took her time finishing, slid the completed

471

wooden puzzles back in the racks like sleeping berths. Then she went into the kitchen and took a beer as well.

The yard was dim with what little was left of the daylight, and the empty lawn and swingset had the deserted feel of a schoolyard in summer. Through the thin woods behind the Martins' came the sound of children not yet ushered in to bed, and in the yard to the right, Kate could hear the neighbors talking on their porch. Murmured conversation came through the trees, tired parents catching up at the end of a long day. To anyone else's eyes, she and Dave might appear the same way. Their bottles rested close on the small side table between them.

He leaned toward her, reaching for the baby monitor under the table. As he adjusted its volume, the warbling voice of Emily joined them on the porch, rhythmic syllables strung together like notes. *Ma-ma-ma-ma-ma ma*, up and down her own tuneless scale. Both of Kate's own kids had said *Mama* before *Dada* too, and she wondered whether all babies had that word among their first, an ingrained verbal progression whether or not they had a mama in the house.

Dave pulled something out of his pocket and placed it next to her on the table, a photograph. She put down her beer and pinched her fingers on her shirt to dry the condensation, then picked it up. It was a picture of Elizabeth reading a story to Anna in the playroom. Elizabeth looked pale and tired beside her tanned, smiling daughter. "When was this taken?"

"Last August, a few days before she left for her trip. She looks bad, doesn't she."

Kate held the photo but didn't say anything. Elizabeth's face was puffy, her hair was limp, and there were dark circles under her eyes. In truth, she didn't look all that much different than she had in the months after Anna was born, but then Kate had misread her appearance. Even so, it was disconcerting to see how much Elizabeth had changed in the month since Kate had visited while passing through town last summer. They'd spoken on the phone several times in July and August — discussing preschools, kindergarten, and, as Kate recalled, her own rattling-on irritation over a new pediatrician. On and on, minutiae. Of course she'd had no idea. She looked away from the photo.

"She was sick," he said. "That's what you came over to tell me." He wasn't challenging her, or looking for confirmation. He already knew, and wanted her to know that he knew.

"I think so."

He seemed surprised. "So she didn't tell you, either."

"No."

He nodded, and turned back to the swing-set. He stared at it as if he were waiting for it to do something, and she turned toward it too, just for something to look at other than him. She half expected the swings to start swaying from the force of their combined silent attention.

"I thought for sure you knew all along. I thought that was why she left you the books."

"No." Though it occurred to Kate that it might have been easier for him to think it: that Elizabeth was reluctant to show the truth about one thing in particular, rather than everything in general.

"How long have you known?" she asked. She was almost certain he hadn't taken the missing journal, but she had to ask.

He stared into the yard. "Once I started paying attention, it wasn't hard to find. She handled the bills and insurance paperwork, so that was all filed away. She put the on-cologist stuff with the OB bills."

The word *oncologist* didn't seem to trip him up as it did her, the specificity of the title evoking appointments and treatments, and making real the notion that a person might handle that by herself. It was the very best of a person, or the very worst.

Dave was still fixed on the swingset as if it were holding him in place. Kate drew up her knees to her chest. "I can't imagine keeping that kind of secret. The energy it would take."

"Who could? Who would want to?" He took a drink, and put the bottle down on the table too forcefully. Suds rose up the neck and threatened to overflow. "I've known — I knew —" Dave worked to find the right tense. "Elizabeth and I were together a long time. I have an idea why she did it. But she should have known better after all these years."

It hung there, the suggestion that Elizabeth should have forgiven him for mistakes made so many years ago. He wanted her to agree, and Kate knew she should say something like, *Yes, you would think.* But maybe in a situation like that it wouldn't matter how many years had passed. It was no small thing to walk away from someone when she was sick, to convey to her, *No thanks, I didn't sign on for that.* Maybe that was, in fact, the sort of thing someone could never get over.

"Well," Kate said, "she just seemed not to

want to talk about things. I think the privacy piece kind of outweighed everything." It was a noncommittal observation, but she didn't know whether he wanted her insights. *Don't you dare talk to me about what my wife wanted.* "It seems like a habit with her, being so private. She had this way of presenting herself, a particular way she wanted to appear. I don't think her secrecy was necessarily a reflection on how much she trusted the other person."

This wasn't altogether true. If Kate had been honest she would have said, *She only gives you one chance to let her down.* But she didn't want to remind him of ways he'd lost his wife's trust early on. He had the trunk now. He'd see for himself soon enough.

"Secrecy, well, that's a strong way of putting it," he said. "There was a lot of stuff she downplayed, I knew that. Like acting as if she didn't care much about her work. If she wanted to play Mommy Pollyanna because it made her feel like a better person, that's fine. I just wanted her to be happy. But keeping actual secrets? I don't know about that. Not until this." He gestured with his beer toward the photo. "This is a whole different ball game. No trust."

So he knew how she'd felt about work.

Kate put her head back against the lounger and wondered how much else he knew. Maybe Elizabeth's journals wouldn't be as surprising to him as she'd thought; maybe it wasn't so much a matter of her keeping secrets as it was of calculated presentation, day after day. What to tell, how to do it and when; what to downplay or not tell at all. Not so different from what Kate had been doing herself.

"A trust issue, sure," Kate said. "But mostly, it's kind of a lack of trust in herself."

"That's an interesting spin."

"Well, that's what's going on when a person doesn't show what they're all about, isn't it? They're not trusting that people will approve of the decisions they make, or like them as they are. And maybe they don't so much either."

He made a derisive *pffft* and looked off into the yard. It was a different kind of hurt, being on the short end of trust. Knowing that your partner doubted whether your love was broad enough to accommodate the reality of her and, even if fleetingly, whether you might not stay. He shook his head.

"Well," Kate said, "at least you know she wasn't involved with someone else."

He looked at her blankly. She knew then that he did not know. All he knew was that

Michael was a man who'd drawn his wife away. No matter what he'd said at the bungalow about expecting her to share what she knew, his face told her that he never wanted to have this conversation, to learn about his wife from someone else.

"Was it in the journals?"

"Not spelled out."

"Tell me."

The neighborhood children had gone inside by the time she finished. She wanted to belittle the Aura Institute. Small word choices or a lift of the eyebrow would do it, put her and Dave in the same camp, a cynical response to the place Elizabeth had chosen over both of them. But as she explained, she resisted.

He didn't respond immediately. There was the chittering of insects and the murmuring of neighbors, content on their patio, but little other sound.

"You're telling me she was going to California to some crazy-ass healing retreat."

"I guess so. I talked to him myself, and he actually didn't sound all that crazy. He knew all about her, and about your family —"

"He doesn't know a damn thing about my family."

She could have agreed with him. But if

she had, there would have been no one to lay out the case for the truth about Joshua Tree. That was the fact of it. Elizabeth had paid money, had withdrawn funds slowly from the ATM, and intended to go.

Dave took a long drink from his beer. The light was growing dim and the only thing visible through the brush was the twinkle of a candle. From next door came a light feminine laugh. He tapped the bottle twice on the table, rocked it from side to side on its base, then got up and walked inside.

Two minutes passed, then five. It grew darker. A small animal rustled in the ruins of the rosebushes neglected below the porch. Kate began to wonder uncomfortably what she would do if Dave didn't come back outside. Should she go in to him? They had both loved her, after all. Or should she respect his privacy, collect her bag, and let herself out the front door? The neighbors blew out the candle and went indoors, and the yard fell silent.

If after ten minutes he hadn't returned, she'd call herself a cab. She would close the door quietly behind her, head back to Chris and the children and the city bearing an invisible bull's-eye with which she would make her peace, and the last she'd see of the Martins would be the trunk in the hall.

These thoughts had become a contingency plan when Dave walked back outside holding two fresh beer bottles. He sat in the lounge chair and rested his on his thigh, cupped in his hand.

"Her mother went someplace like that when Elizabeth was in high school, some New Agey thing in the desert." His voice was thick, and he cleared his throat. "Liz never knew exactly what it was and she made considerable fun of it, but I think she gives it credit for getting her mother on the wagon."

Kate noted his use of the past and the present tense both, and realized that's just how love was, something that would always exist between the tenses.

In the distance a siren rose and a dog bayed, then went quiet. The crickets started up, tremulous above the mundane insects that had failed to camouflage their awkward silence earlier, and to Kate at that moment it was the most peaceful sound in the world. It was partly having the indecision and responsibility of the trunk lifted, and partly the relief of being able to talk about its contents. Probably partly the beer, too. A sandal dropped from one of her feet and she let the other drop as well, then flexed her ankles.

She saw Dave look over at her feet. Presentable, nothing manicured but not too neglected, an island of chipped polish in the middle of each nail. They were the feet of a mother who kept herself up passingly well, the feet a Southbrook man would see daily on his wife padding around the house, if he had a wife.

"So how much did you hate me for having the journals?" She said it lightly, but there was discomfort in the question, even if the question was about a different kind of resentment. *Sidekick. Babysitting service.* Things blurted out under those circumstances were always the truth.

"Nah, maybe just a little in the beginning. And then at the end." His tone was light with teasing, hints of the old charm. She glanced up to see if his expression had softened but his face was still haggard, cheekbones sharper and hollowed beneath. She wondered if this was just the way he would look now, if grief and disillusionment could change the geometry of a face.

"This isn't something I wanted, you know. It was making me sick all summer."

"You just got a little carried away."

She bristled, but knew it was partly true. "I'm sorry I accused you of taking a notebook."

He looked over and frowned. "So you did lose it."

"No. I'm pretty sure she had it with her on the plane."

At the mention of the plane, he turned his face in the other direction. He didn't want to take the conversation this way. Frankly, neither did she.

"When did you start to want to know?" she asked.

"Hmmm?"

"When did you start to want the books? At the beginning of the summer it seemed like you didn't even want them. You could have read them when you had the chance before you gave them to me. There had to be a spare key somewhere, or you could have bashed the trunk open."

He paused to take a drink, and put his head back against the lounger while he swallowed. "Some mornings I wake up, and I think she's in the shower or waking the kids. It takes me a few minutes to remember she's not here. When someone is still so real it feels downright evil to do something you know they wouldn't want you to do. But honestly, I didn't really want to know, either." Small Emily sounds came through the monitor and he turned it up a notch. Soft groans threatened to become cries, but then faded. "After I read enough to know something else was going on and then gave them to you, something changed. Of course they're hers, but she's gone, and at some point it stopped being about keeping everything frozen. I might sound like a cold sonofabitch and don't get me wrong, I miss her like anything. She was the soul of this house."

She noted that his language had switched to past tense. Back and forth, closer and further from his wife.

"But she had her own agenda and a lot of the time it didn't have a hell of a lot to do with me," he said. "Nothing's any good until I figure out where all that came from, because I don't want to have that kind of happy horseshit going on with my kids. I want them to feel like they can really talk to me."

"You mean being up front about what they're thinking."

Of course there was irony in this, but she hadn't intended it. He looked at her sharply. "You don't know the all of it, Kate."

"I didn't mean it like that. I'm agreeing with you. It's important to be able to talk openly with your kids. You never know what they're picking up on but just feel like they shouldn't say." Kate picked at the fiber of the chair. "That was definitely true about Elizabeth as a kid."

She thought of Elizabeth's last journal. *I don't want any chance of this affecting the kids. It's worked so far and warped as this sounds, it's one of my proudest accomplishments.* Well, maybe. You never really knew what effect you had, what version of yourself they saw and were left with. At what age, she wondered, do kids develop a barometer for truth and lies, and for that murky area where grown-ups act one way while feeling entirely another? Probably a lot earlier than most adults think they do.

Dave stretched out his legs, and put his hands up behind his head. Then he let out a long sigh. "She always did like talking to you, Kate. She saw a realness in you that she didn't get from a lot of people around here. That's what she said when you guys came back from your beach walk last summer. 'Kate gets it.' "

Kate turned her head to the side so he couldn't see how it affected her. She swallowed and reached up to push at her bangs, wiping at her cheek as part of the gesture.

"You know, I think she would have told us both if she'd had more time," he said. Kate was surprised by how calm he sounded. "But in the end it's all just speculation,

484

none of it makes a difference. It all came down to the wrong, wrong time to get on an airplane."

At the word *time* she looked at her watch. It was 8:47. Her train would leave Stamford in nine minutes, too tight even if she were already in a cab.

"Oh no," she said. "I missed it. The train."

Dave looked over without lifting his head from his chair. He didn't glance at his own watch or appear too concerned about when and if there was another train, about how her husband would be putting the kids to bed, then waiting, and wondering.

"You could stay here. I could take you to the first train in the morning on my way to work." He was watching her with eyes tired and simple, not realizing or not caring that anything might be complicated or miscon-strued. He was a man for whom things were no longer complicated and who didn't especially care if they were misconstrued. If he knew this might create awkwardness with Chris, it didn't trouble him. This was no longer the Dave that Elizabeth had known, a man who avoided things that might be awkward or cause pain or worried about his actions and their repercussions, because he'd already been through the worst and survived. Nothing else mattered much.

Things simply were what they were at the moment, and at the moment they were fine. "Stay, hang out," he said. "Have another beer."

Part of her did want to delay what awaited her at home. She and Dave would sit as the sky darkened from dusky purple to deep night, and they would talk about what it meant for a person to conceal her illness. Whether it was possible Elizabeth honestly thought she was protecting her family and whether it was the bravest thing to do, allowing them to continue with the impression that their daily lives were untouched by anything that could spoil their world, muddied water across all they'd made. Perhaps she'd believed she could handle it alone, get herself well quietly and not have to see the worry on their faces each time she returned from treatments. And maybe her deception hadn't been about distrust, and she knew that his track record of dealing poorly with illness was something he had outgrown with years of marriage and caretaking. Dave and Kate would listen to the crickets and talk like old friends about the difference between what was noble and what was selfish: whether the act of making the decision for someone else, and not letting him have the chance to help you and, if necessary, even prepare to say good-bye, was the most or least generous thing a person could do. And when the bats darted out of the trees, one of them would notice the time and say, We should probably call it a night. They would head upstairs, her fingers trailing along a banister that had once grown bushes, and she would turn toward the guest room, adjacent to his. After undressing quietly so as not to awaken the kids, she would lie down and through the wall hear the bedsprings and breathing of yet another of his solitary nights. And in the morning, when the nanny arrived and found Kate clearing cereal bowls with hair and clothes that had already seen a full day, she might wonder the same things Kate had wondered about her, and wonder about the extent of a man's loneliness.

"I think I remember a local train from Stamford to New York, and then a late one to D.C.," Kate said. "I should check it out. Chris will be worried."

He nodded, unsmiling. "I'll call you a cab," he said, and went inside. If it mattered to him one way or another, it was only momentary. Because he was on to the next moment, and this was fine too.

THIRTY-TWO

Stamford's train station at night was neither the best nor the worst place to be, well lit but without the criminal urgency to warrant constant police patrol. Drunks loitered unsteadily by the concessions. In a corner, a young man and woman were groping, fighting, or a little of both.

Kate bought a newspaper and stood near the departures and arrivals board. She had not read any national newspapers in months, and although she had not missed them on the island, she now pored over the sections like letters from distant friends. Even the news — alarming as it was — was oddly reassuring. A terror cell broken up in Detroit. The source of the anthrax letters, close to being discovered. Canada's first fatality from mad cow disease had been tracked to Britain, which meant North American stock was not the source of contamination, not yet. There were answers in the air, precautions you could take. Most things were preventable, and if not, someone was working to ensure that they would be.

Kate flipped to the second page of the National section and paused at an article about the science of coincidence — the likelihood, say, that eleven of the world's leading experts on bioterrorism had died recently, one after the other, simply by chance. Conspiracy theorists had it wrong, the article insisted. Statistically speaking, the suspicious timing of their deaths was within the realm of mere coincidence.

Mere coincidence. Kate had come to hate that phrase. She lowered the newspaper and looked down the hall at the couple, whose affections were becoming agitated. The young woman did not want to go with him, she said, she hated him when he was like this, get *off*; his arms around her looked more like a wrestler's pose than an embrace. Kate tensed and glanced around for security.

There was nothing mere about co-incidence. Every day millions of people were done in by arbitrary events, random events, and freak occurrences of nature through no fault of their own. Fault was better: bike accident with no helmet, lung cancer in a smoker, some kind of cause-and-effect pattern to hold back the chaos. There was aggressive risk, like walking across the lobby to interrupt that couple, and there was calculated risk, like renting a bungalow during a tularemia outbreak, and perhaps even like her choice to ride this train that would get her home after 2 a.m. And then there was what people called mere coincidence. Elizabeth, who rarely traveled, being on that flight — with bad wind, a faulty rudder, and an inexperienced pilot. A little girl speeding on her bike after her older sister, whose moment of teasing coincided with the arrival of a reckless driver.

The months after Elizabeth died had been a shock to Kate, the realization that the world was a truly unpredictable place, and that life didn't follow a benign trajectory just because you ate organic fruits and vegetables and flossed daily. She knew her shock was naïve even as it left her alternately terrified and numb, and kept it to herself. At Elizabeth's memorial service she had been somber like everyone else, and if in the months afterward she became quieter — well, by then, the whole country was reeling. No one noticed that she spent more time alone, and wondering, with growing fixation, which of her kids' schools she would race toward first if Washington was targeted.

But Kate couldn't access the shock any longer, and the shock itself now seemed sophomoric. You could become paralyzed with worry about what might happen to your family, or if you hadn't yet had children you could decide not to, as a sort of proactive damage control. Either way, you would be derailing your life voluntarily out of fear that it might become ruined by chance. Or you could pick up and move on. Those were the only choices.

Back in her cable-show days she'd believed most things could be made to happen or not happen by sheer force of will. But she saw that now as vanity. Most things in life, the best and the worst of things, were not controllable. Those who understood that simply marched ahead; that was the thinking of a survivor, someone who resurfaced. The irony was not lost on her that she was beginning to learn this from someone who had not.

The arguing pair were speaking in hushed tones; the girlfriend stood against the wall and he leaned over her, palms against the wall on either side of her head. They were next to the concession window, and Kate walked by casually, as if she were not assessing the woman's safety. Their voices were now tender; the young man sounded as if he might cry.

"Large coffee," she said to the clerk.

As he filled her cup from an industrial urn, Kate looked around the counter area. There were coin jars for tips and for various childhood diseases. Taped to one side by the condiments and milk thermoses, a poster advertised an art exhibition at NYU.

She hadn't known Elizabeth went to NYU until their walk on the beach last summer, or maybe she'd known but hadn't remembered. When Elizabeth told Kate about the painting trip to Joshua Tree, she'd seen her surprise. *I studied art in college*, Elizabeth explained.

Kate knew too little about art, and usually hid her ignorance with stock references to Degas ballerinas or Pollock splotches. *I never really was liberal arts material*, she admitted, poking a stick in the sand. She imagined Elizabeth thinking of the things lacking in her cultural education because she'd gone to culinary school.

I never did finish college, Elizabeth said.

Well how about that, Kate had thought. She nearly made a joke, but noticed the tension in Elizabeth's voice.

Yeah, well, she said. *Finishing things the regular way is overrated.* And Elizabeth had looked up and smiled.

Kate took a window seat on the left side of the train, the side that afforded better views if you were traveling in daylight and able to appreciate the passing shore. She did not know whether Chris would have gone to bed or would be waiting up for her. He was a night person, but even he had limits. He was angry and disappointed and something else, something that might make him more likely to end the long day, his back turned to her side of the bed. It wasn't envy, because he wasn't someone who envied others, but it was close. What he hadn't had today or recently was a strong connection with his wife, or an understanding of what had distracted her all summer. And Dave did.

When Kate had stood in the Martins' front hall two hours before, her cab idling at the curb, she'd hesitated before saying good-bye. Dave leaned against the door frame in the dark, one shoulder against the edge of the open door and the other arm slack at his side. She could smell the soap he'd used in the shower, musky, because this was not a man who had to share soap with a woman any longer. The faded Valentine hearts were still taped to the door, hopelessly out of season.

The trunk sat on the floor beside the door. "So there they are," she said.

"Back home where they belong."

She could not think of an appropriate reply. Certainly not *Enjoy them*, or *Call me if you want to talk about them*, because they weren't hers to offer in that way. The trunk's lid was as improperly aligned as a bite in need of orthodonture.

"Sorry about the lock."

He shrugged. "I never did come across a spare key anyway."

She could have walked through the door then with a peck to his cheek and a light touch on the shoulder as she passed, and moved down the lawn back toward her own misaligned life. But there was one more thing.

"You know, her journals, in the earlier years . . . The way she talks about marriage and children. She was a different person back then." In the dark she could not see his expression. "I think she worked very hard to become the mother she was, and maybe she dealt with some depression. But just because she didn't start off that way doesn't make it any less real. I think it shows how committed she was to getting there."

Dave looked down and shook his head.

"Well, now," he said, in the honeyed voice of a parent soothing down an emotional child.

He might have had no idea what she was talking about or he might have known exactly what she meant, but it was not for her to know. Outside, the cabbie turned on his inside dome light and looked toward the house. Dave put his hand on the door handle. There wouldn't be any further talk of who Elizabeth had been.

She crossed in front of him and leaned in for a quick embrace, and he rested his hand on her lower back. They stood that way a moment, then she pulled away. He pushed open the screen door.

"I was thinking of bringing the kids down to D.C. this fall," he said. "Doing sort of a museumy thing. The zoo, the Mall, and stuff."

"They'd love it. So would James and Piper." She stepped through the door. "It stays warm into November. You should come."

"Well, maybe we will." The door flapped closed as he let go. He leaned against the interior frame, arms crossed.

She walked across the lawn toward the cab feeling his eyes still on her, and climbed into the back. The vinyl seat was cracked and sharp under her legs, and she readjusted her position closer to the door, where it was smoother. She looked up and saw the Martins' front door closing, and then the light on the porch, where she'd saddled Elizabeth with her old plants and fish, blink out. But as the taxi pulled from the curb, in the long hall window the shadow of a man remained, a figure above a broken box filled with the nearest thing he had to his wife's remains.

The train glided through New Jersey. Dim industrial forms dominated the landscape, skeletal power plants and construction equipment rendered hazy and less unattractive by dark and distance. The engine decelerated over a railroad trestle, and the staccato of its passage reverberated in the vast untenable space between water and sky. The cry was mournful, but a lull for those unafraid of what they cannot control, or on their way to becoming so.

THIRTY-THREE

The cab left Kate at the curb and she stood for a moment in her driveway. The house was dark except for a dim light in the family room. She reached in her tote bag for keys. Wallet. Phone. Pen. Then a piece of paper, unfamiliar. She pulled it out and held it under the streetlight. It was a white slip, a sheet from a prescription pad with Elizabeth's name on the patient line. It must have fallen from the last journal, which Kate had read again in the car, then replaced in the trunk outside the Martins' house. The scrip called for some unreadable milligrams of something starting with a *P* and with an *x* near the middle, prescribed by some doctor whose first name began with an *N*. Natalie . . . Nadine . . . Nadia.

It might have been a prescription for anything. Something related to her illness. Something to help her sleep. Or it might be a rabbit hole into somewhere else entirely.

Kate held it, considering the places Elizabeth had and had not gone to speak openly. Then she crumpled it in her fist and dropped it back in the bag.

She entered the house quietly and put down her tote, then walked down the hall to the family room to find Chris, likely asleep over his laptop. But the room was empty. She slipped off her shoes and climbed the stairs to check on the children, walking first into Piper's room. The girl was curled horizontally across the top of the pillow, catlike, and her purr of a snore quieted as Kate pivoted her back under the covers. Then Kate walked into James's room. His arm was crooked as if to be filled, and she retrieved the stuffed dinosaur from the floor and tucked it inside his elbow. He didn't stir. His slack cheeks and lips were as full as a toddler's, though his skinny legs, scissored on top of the sheets and covered with vacation scrapes, were startlingly long.

Kate went into the master bedroom before even locking up downstairs or getting undressed, intending to lie down beside Chris. She would curl against his back and tuck her chin in the space between his neck and shoulder, and if he woke up she would tell him she loved him. You could not take a single day or night for granted. Within every hour, every plane ride, or every routine doctor's appointment was the spark of possibility, the thing that would become your undoing. And how you left things just before the final moment — that was how they would remain. She hoped he would wake so she could say at least, I love you. That would be enough until tomorrow.

But Chris wasn't in the bedroom. The quilt was still smooth, the pillows plumped in their shams. She walked back downstairs, curious, and then concerned. The lights were off in the den, but she looked into the small room expecting to see him asleep upright in the leather chair, eerie as a stranger in the dark of his thoughts. But that room was empty too.

The kitchen hallway near the garage door was piled with suitcases and linens he'd unpacked from the car. Beside them was the box of food and emergency supplies she'd kept hidden in the car's spare-tire well. It was just as well that it had been unloaded. It all needed to come out.

At the end of the hallway the heavy back door was open. She stood inside the screen door and glanced across the yard, past the flagstone patio and grill not used often enough, beyond the soccer nets and the shed. At the end of the yard near the tall arborvitae there was a glowing pinprick of orange. It rose and descended as slowly as an aged firefly.

She opened the screen and walked outside. In the back of the yard Chris was sitting on their stone bench. He was bent over forward, elbows and forearms on his thighs, a cigarette dangling from his fingers. He watched as she approached, but didn't move. It was as if he had been sitting there motionless for years, waiting for her to come back and discover him.

She pushed both hands into her front pockets. Fireflies blinked above the laurel bushes by the house, and night sounds took the place of what would have been an enormity of silence. An evening animal scratched under the evergreens. The mechanical rattle of an automatic door opener came from a neighboring house, followed by the scraping of a barrel over asphalt. They looked for a long time at one another and there was nothing awkward in the look, nothing combative or self-protective. It was a naked look and it was all right there: the waiting and the worry, the dwindling communication and the secrecy and the deception, if it could be called deception, of understatement and omission. The anxiety, and the longing for guarantees — against calamity, against misunderstanding — when there were none to be had. The slow drift that becomes otherness after enough time has passed. They were two people who had begun to wander apart, whose paths had forked, and each had stepped off and found the route absorbing, and then had become a bit too accustomed to going it alone.

She wished she could hand him a journal, a guide to the person she'd become in the past year that would make it all clear, just place it beside him on the bench and walk away. When morning arrived he would have laid on her nightstand a book of his own, and when they came together again there would be clarity. No fear of saying something incorrectly or leaving something out, of being stopped short by a furrowed brow or an interruption at the wrong moment that makes one swallow whatever confidence had begun.

It was all so exhausting, trying to be understood. She'd once read a quote — from some high school required reading? or the lyric of a song? — that had stuck with her: *If you knew all there was to know about a man, you could forgive him anything.* There was something reflexive in the forgiveness, *but of course*, once you knew what made a person into a collection of oddities and defenses. The work to reach the knowing was exhausting, not the forgiving. That seemed to happen on its own.

Kate sighed and sat down on the bench slowly, like an older person giving rest to weary joints. She sat so close to Chris that her leg touched his along the length of their thighs, the curve of his jeans warm and familiar in the cool of night, tangible as a conversation that did not have to end. They sat looking at the back of their home touching casually but not accidentally, like newly-weds wanting the constant comfort of physical togetherness, the reassurance that they shared the same view of an unbroken future stretching across the chasm, at least as much of it as they could control.

ACKNOWLEDGMENTS

Two extraordinary women were in my mind as I wrote this book, neither of whom lived to see their children grow to adulthood. No words are adequate for such loss, but this fictional account of a lost mother was my catharsis, and tribute.

Writing a book is a solitary endeavor, but every other part of bringing it to fruition requires a community. I am endlessly thankful to have landed in the care of my wise agent, Julie Barer, whose extensive knowledge and keen judgment direct my decisions. I have much admiration for my brilliant editors at Crown, Kate Kennedy — who first believed in the book and helped shape it — and then Lindsay Sagnette, who deftly led it, and me, through the labyrinth to publication. My deep appreciation to all those at Random House who supported it along the way. And to Tom Wallace and Rick Levine, whose early support at Condé Nast led to much growth and opportunity.

Early readers offered me valuable feedback, and I am honored by the reading time and insights of Chris Abouzeid, Juliette Fay, Henriette Power, Javed Jahangir, Dan D'Allaird, Elena Rover Strothenke, and Ann Allen Hall, as well as Wayland Stallard and others at The Writing Center in Bethesda, Maryland, where this novel was born. After moving to Boston I found in Grub Street a wonderful community of writers, and I credit this organization with connecting me to the talented people who would become my friends and colleagues at the literary blog *Beyond the Margins*.

For sharing their knowledge and areas of expertise my thanks to Susan Reed, Annie B. Copps, Killian Higgins, and Lisa Bonchek Adams; to the Professional Golf Association for its elaborate archives; and to Shergul Arshad for his improvements on my Italian phrases. To M. A. Tarver Gallerani and Tracy Birkhahn Spicer for making it logistically possible for me to slip away when I needed a bit of intensive revision time, and to Priscila Moraes for her loving care of my children while I wrote. To Ken and Patricia Berkov for use of the island cottage that was the inspiration for the one in the book (you might consider adding that loft?). The novel's bakery pays homage to the original Humphreys Bakery in the woods of West Tisbury, Martha's Vineyard, and its name, Flour, is a salute to the great bakeries of Joanne Chang in Boston. It is worth noting that the flight on which Elizabeth Martin perished bears resemblance to the crash of American Airlines Flight 587, but that accident occurred three months later; likewise, the fictitious Summer Bali explosion is similar to the event of October 2002.

A toast to Carolyn Casey, Lauren Chacon, and Jackie Hendrix, whose critical listening over a long dinner helped me put heart in my reading voice. I am always mindful of the friendship of my first parenting playgroup (Alyson Hussey, Denise St. Mary, Cheryl Pinarchick, Betsy Casey, and Catherine Raynes), whose members continue to teach me the enduring fellowship of women who come of age as mothers together.

I cannot imagine the writing life without the companionship of fellow authors, and I am indebted to Jenna Blum, Amy MacKinnon, Robin Black, and Susan Coll for pushing me up the learning curve with sage advice at key moments. My endless gratitude to Kathy Crowley and Randy Susan

Meyers; every writer needs a home team to offer support, direction, and tough love, and they are mine.

To my parents, Ron and Sandra Bernier, for teaching me that we never really know what is happening in the lives and hearts of others; this compassion leads to imagination and empathy, which are both critical in writing fiction. To my siblings, Carrie, Suzanne, and Matt, and to the Ahern clan, all of whose enthusiasm buoyed me through the years of writing, including my beloved mother-in-law, Maureen, who did not live to see the book in print but did hear some of it on her last night.

To my children, two of whom were born during the writing of this novel. They teach me daily the breathtaking complex love that is motherhood. But above all, deep gratitude and love to my husband, Tom Ahern, whose unwavering support — including the gift of time to pursue a dream — is testament to his kindness, and understanding.

ABOUT THE AUTHOR

Nichole Bernier is a writer for magazines including *Elle, Self, Health, Men's Journal*, and *Boston* magazine, and a longtime contributing editor with *Condé Nast Traveler*, where she was previously on staff as a columnist and the golf and ski editor. She is a founder of the literary website Beyondthe Margins.com and lives outside of Boston with her husband and five children.

The employees of Thorndike Press hope you have enjoyed this Large Print book. All our Thorndike, Wheeler, and Kennebec Large Print titles are designed for easy reading, and all our books are made to last. Other Thorndike Press Large Print books are available at your library, through selected bookstores, or directly from us.

For information about titles, please call:
(800) 223-1244

or visit our Web site at:
http://gale.cengage.com/thorndike

To share your comments, please write:
Publisher
Thorndike Press
10 Water St., Suite 310
Waterville, ME 04901